The Great War with Germany, 1890–1914

Liverpool Science Fiction Texts and Studies
General Editor DAVID SEED
Series Advisers
I. F. CLARKE   EDWARD JAMES
PATRICK PARRINDER and BRIAN STABLEFORD

The Great War with Germany, 1890–1914

*Fictions and Fantasies of
the War-to-come*

EDITED BY

I. F. CLARKE

LIVERPOOL UNIVERSITY PRESS

First published 1997 by
LIVERPOOL UNIVERSITY PRESS
Senate House, Abercromby Square,
Liverpool, L69 3BX
United Kingdom

British Library Cataloguing-in-Publication Data
A British Library CIP Record is available
ISBN 0-85323-632-1 *cased*
0-85323-642-9 *paper*

Text set in 10^1/$_2$/12^1/$_2$ Meridien
by Action Typesetting Limited, Gloucester

Printed and bound in the European Community
by Bell & Bain Ltd, Glasgow

For
Christopher

Contents

Chapter Four: Views, Reviews, and Downright Ridicule

Chapter Five: The Victors and the Vanquished

Epilogue: Meanwhile, Across the Atlantic

Preface

This anthology, *The Great War with Germany, 1890–1914*, is the second in what will be the five-volume series of *Future-War Fiction, 1763–2001*. It follows on *The Tale of the Next Great War, 1871–1914*, which was published in 1995. That selection of short stories showed how, following the extraordinary success of Chesney's *Battle of Dorking* in 1871, the tale of the war-to-come became the most popular means of looking into, and of projecting, all the possible conditions—political and technological—that might conceivably affect the conduct of a future war.

The present anthology offers a selection of extracts from the most representative British stories about 'the Next Great War' and from the German accounts of the *Zukunftskrieg* (future-war fiction). Together they compose a shadow play of the interactions between two very different sets of expectations, as the British and the Germans moved forward from one international crisis after another to the fateful August of 1914.

All the extracts are taken from the first editions of British publications, from the few contemporary translations of the original German books and pamphlets, or from my own translations of the French and German originals. I hasten to add that I would never have undertaken the necessary translation, had I not been able to rely on the knowledge and advice of truly expert linguists. I am happy to acknowledge the careful guidance I have received from Paul Rees of Jesus College, Oxford, who supervised most of the work. I thank him for his unfailing patience, good humour, and professional rigour; and I thank Irene Mackintosh of the Modern Languages Department, University of Strathclyde, who took over at short notice when Paul Rees departed for Indonesia. The solitary French entry gained greatly in vigour and clarity from the observations of Mrs Penny Bath, to whom I am much indebted.

There was one problem in the translations from the German. The word *Englisch*, and especially the mention of *die Englische Flotte*, caused this Sassenach editor to think long and hard about meanings. Long before 1707, when the formal adoption of the name of Great

Britain signalled the union of the English and Scottish parliaments, *Englisch* meant what it said—English. As late as 1900, however, many German writers were still keeping to the traditional usage, although they sometimes acknowledged the reality of *die Britische Flotte*. For this reason, and mindful of many happy years in Glasgow, I have made the appropriate corrections to the German texts.

At times, this return journey to a time of growing differences between Germany and Great Britain has been a melancholy experience. As a member of the European Community, I have been conscious of my obligations to tell the tale of past differences between our two nations as candidly and as objectively as possible. At all times I have sought to present a representative and faithful cross-section of views and attitudes—at their best and at their worst. I believe I am free from any desire for *Rachsucht*; and I assure my German readers that I feel most strongly that past differences between our two countries belong to the past.

This anthology owes much to the help and advice of many friends and correspondents. I thank Dr Malcolm Pender, University of Strathclyde, for the remarkable competence he showed in surfing the Net on my behalf. Invaluable information and xerox copies of German pamphlets came from the Universitäts-und Stadtsbibliothek, Cologne. My grateful thanks to them, and to the Staatsbibliothek zu Berlin (Preussischer Kulturbesitz) and the Deutsche Bibliothek (Frankfurt) for the abundant bibliographical information they supplied. I am particularly indebted to Dr Paulheinz Steinmüller, Sekretariat für Zukunftsforschung, Gelsenkirchen, who spent much time in gathering information about long-forgotten German writers. Again, I thank A. P. Watt Ltd for obtaining the permission of the Trustees of the Wodehouse Estate to include an extract from *The Swoop* by P. G. Wodehouse in the anthology.

The final state of this anthology owes much to the labours and expert advice of the copy-editor, Sue Hughes; and I now thank her for the great care she took with the many entries. Finally, and most of all, I thank my wife for her unfailing help: an expert proof-reader, a most perceptive critic, and kindest of collaborators. My grateful thanks, Margaret.

I. F. Clarke
Milton under Wychwood

List of Illustrations

"One Who Knows."

Punch imagined that the appointment of the German Emperor as Field Marshal in the British Army, 13 February 1901, might lead him to 'wonder if I might venture to give them a hint or two on "re-organisation"? And I MIGHT suggest that their officers should always be in uniform—as MINE are'

Introduction: 'Horribly Stuffed with Epithets of War'

The theme of this anthology is war—with a difference. There is nothing here about past wars: no looking back at old alliances and battles long ago. Although the accounts of naval engagements, land campaigns, and invasions presented in this selection belong to time past, all their authors began by looking into the future. The result was a series of prophetic tales about the conflict-to-come between the British and the Germans which had immense influence in the quarter-century before the First World War.[1] The projected order-of-battle in these stories assigned a place and a role to Everyman and to *Jedermann* on The Day when 'the Great War' between the United Kingdom and the German Reich would commence in their fiction. Despite the decided animosities that once separated the authors of these tales of the not-yet, one common aim made them all pen-fellows of a kind. They accepted without question that it was their duty to anticipate and describe the causes and the consequences of 'the Next Great War' or of *der nächste Krieg*. This, they were convinced, would break out, sooner or later, between the major European powers.

British and German writers learnt rapidly how to set their nations against each other in the tales of the war-to-come during the late 1890s, when the Reichstag passed the first Navy Law and work started on the construction of a great German navy. By the beginning of the twentieth century these antebellum narratives were appearing by the dozen every year—evidently a novelty that found a ready market. Together they composed a paradigm of military possibilities that ranged through all the then conceivable forms of warfare—on land, at sea, and sometimes in the air. These stories followed out of, and usually mirrored in the most striking ways, a momentous transformation in the relationships between the major European nations, marked especially by the Entente between the British and the French in 1904. That change, brought on by the aggressive policies and the uncompromising self-interest of the German Reich, signalled the first stages in the countdown to August 1914. The earliest manifestations of this realignment appear at the end of the first chapter of this anthology. In 1900, as the evidence of this prophetic fiction demonstrates, British readers had their first warning about German intentions in T.W. Offin's account of *How the Germans took London*; and two German writers began their war against the British. Karl Eisenhart called the British to account in *Die Abrechnung mit England* ('The Reckoning with Britain') and Gustav Adolf Erdmann demonstrated the need for a great navy in *Wehrlos zur See* ('Defenceless at Sea').

The year 1900 marks the first major divide and the end of the first phase in these tales of future warfare. As the first book in this series, *The Tale of the Next Great War,* has shown, the extraordinary success of Chesney's *Battle of Dorking* in 1871 had taught the propagandists how to use fiction in order to put the case for conscription or for a greater fleet to the readers of the middle-class journals and magazines. For two decades the short story continued to be the dominant form in this fiction; and then, during the 1890s, the tale of the war-to-come went through a rapid two-fold evolution. Full-length serial stories replaced the short story in the popular press and in the new illus-trated magazines; and British publishers, in particular, began to seek out authors to write books about 'the Next Great War'. These popular tales were the elementary, and often naïve, products of the growing urban societies of Europe: they were the first fruits of universal liter-acy, of the mass press, and of mass publishing. Above all they were a sign that the citizens and their votes mattered in an age of democracy and parliamentary government; and so, selective evolution worked swiftly and most successfully to create a new corps of all the talents. Journalists, admirals, generals, politicians—all with a message in mind, added their contributions to the new, purposive literature of the war-to-come. For instance, in 1891 those eminent Victorians, Admiral Colomb and his distinguished associates, had no hesitation in accepting the invitation of the editor of *Black and White* to set down their ideas about the future in *The Great War of 189–*; and in 1906 Field-Marshal Lord Roberts, late Commander-in-Chief, was happy to collaborate with William Le Queux in planning the order of battle for the *Daily Mail* serial story of *The Invasion of 1910*.

From 1900 onwards, the possibility—for many, the probability— of a war between Great Britain and Imperial Germany provided both sufficient reason and abundant material for an unprecedented outpouring of these tales of the great European conflict. As the record shows, all these projections were episodes in the dream warfare that once obsessed British and German readers. In the whole course of this literature, there is only one story (*The Great War of 189–)* that was a straightforward attempt to forecast the most likely course of a war in Europe. These chroniclers of the conflict-to-come dealt in the stuff of fantasy. The requirements of their propaganda decided the shapes of their imagined future. So, they offered their readers exciting tales of consequences; and, to ensure that there could be no doubts about their meaning, they often opened with a statement of aims and intentions. The time had come, they explained, to write about the needs of the Royal Navy, or to put the case for conscription; and in like manner their German counterparts used fiction to describe future naval victories, or to advocate a sudden German foray against the British fleet. For example, in 1903, when Germany had replaced France as the expected enemy in tomorrow's warfare, Erskine Childers produced the classic tale of the German preparations for the invasion of England. In his preface to the popular edition of *The Riddle of the Sands,* he ventured 'to express the hope that nobody will read into this story of adventure any intention of provoking feelings of hostility to Germany':[2]

> It is true that the fundamental purpose is to stimulate interest in a matter of vital national importance to Great Britain; but the naval progress and naval aspirations of Germany—perhaps the most interesting phenomena in the evolution of modern Europe—receive sincere and unstinted admiration. The high problems of national defence may be studied without a particle of racial animus. They are so studied, as a matter of mere routine, by the experts; they should be so studied, to the best of his ability, by every thoughtful citizen. That is the only way of exterminating the scaremonger, who trades on public ignorance.

The Erskine narrative style—mild in manner and defensive in attitude—was characteristic of most British future-war stories of that time; for their constant theme was the need to guard against the grave threat from overseas. The style of the German writers was very different. They were more frequently on the offensive in their future wars, and often more belligerent in manner, writing like drill-sergeants eager to prepare readers for the descent on England. Contrast the Erskine preface with the very different opening to August Niemann's popular account of the German victories in *Der Weltkrieg—Deutsche Traüme* ('World War—German Dreams') of 1904. The language of the German colonial movement and of their Navy League comes through loud and clear in his vision 'of the duties and aims of our German nation':[3]

Father Neptune. "Bust my Bulkheads and shiver my Compartments, have I got
to learn German at my time of life!"

Father Neptune considers the new German Navy Laws

My dreams, the dreams of a German, show me the war that is
to be, and the victory of the three great allied nations—
Germany, France, and Russia—and a new division of the

possessions of the earth as the final aim and object of this gigantic universal war ...

In my mind's eye I see the armies and the fleets of Germany, France, and Russia moving together against the common enemy, who with his polypus arms enfolds the globe. The iron onslaught of the three allied Powers will free the whole of Europe from England's tight embrace. The great war lies in the lap of the future.

These future-war stories first began to exert their formidable power in Britain, France, and Germany during the last thirty years of the nineteenth century. They owed their origin to the following factors: first, there were the usual questions about the intentions of the French (later, the Germans); second, in intimate association with that constant trawling through matters of political interest, there was the fact of the arms race and the strength of the Royal Navy; third, and most important of all, the citizens of the first great technological nations had contained and codified their experience of incessant change within the new practice of future-watching. This was a non-stop training in anticipation. The tales of the war-to-come were part of, and had their special roles in, the great forward movement of the imagination that began about 1870; and, from Chesney's *Battle of Dorking* in 1871 to Sir John Hackett's *Third World War* in 1978, they have ever since followed wherever the feasible seemed to lead. Space travel stories, utopias, dystopias, imaginary wars—these diverse modes of looking at the potential and the possible have served for more than a century as specific responses to the universal experience of incessant social and technological change.

Before the authors of these stories begin to speak for themselves, however, it is perhaps advisable to note that, although almost all their projections proved to be right about the great European conflict, they failed lamentably to foresee how that war would be fought. This is not surprising. Most of the authors had little interest in, and usually little aptitude for, anticipating the probable course of another European war. They were, in fact, entrapped in a dilemma of cause and effect. Had they been troubled by any perception of the coming transformation of warfare, they would have found it impossible to write their conventional death-or-glory tales. The one exception was the man who wrote the most remarkable future-war stories in the history of the genre. In his first and finest tale of the war-to-come, *The War of the Worlds*, H. G. Wells produced the super-invasion. That had its origins far away from the here-and-now of the invasion stories of the 1890s—some 63 million miles distant from human space and out of all terrestrial time-frames. Although the Martian invaders arrive with the most lethal weapons imaginable, there is no call to suspend disbelief. The parable tells the tale of a great war so far beyond the capacity of European technology in 1898 that it charmed rather than alarmed.

True to the intimations of a scientific education, Wells always isolated the subjects in his tales of tomorrow. In his wars-to-come he contrived to view technological possibilities from a distance by placing the action in a mythic future. The Wellsian future-war stories—*The War of the Worlds*, *The War in the Air*, *The World Set Free*—stand apart in glorious isolation from all the other contemporary tales of invasions and decisive naval battles. The logic of his imagination caused Wells to look to universal consequences, whereas almost all of the rest addressed themselves for the best of reasons to the local and particular. Wells took care to remove himself far enough from the chauvinist preoccupations and the political considerations of his day to have the space in which he could match his imagined new weapons with their anticipated effects. His scale is superhuman. Atomic bombs and great air fleets subject all states and all living things to the inhuman control of the ultimate fighting machine. With prophetic insight he foresaw that all humankind would be the victim. Mechanism would change the world.

In the human and national scale of British and German future-war fiction, however, the post of honour went to the heroic individual, and the power and the glory to the nation state. So, the propagandists laboured to devise situations that would demonstrate the points they wished to make about conscription, the intentions of the enemy, the needs of the Royal Navy or of the *Hochseeflotte*. More important, however, was their condition of happy ignorance which made it far too easy for them to contemplate a great European war. How could any of them have had any understanding of the scale, the cost, and the casualties of the war they were certain would come one day? All the evidence told them that the future was a simple linear progression: one thing after another in a supposedly benign evolutionary advance. 'The word *war* conjured up pictures of the Battle of Waterloo, of Florence Nightingale, or perhaps of South Africa.' That was a frequent recollection from the days before 1914. 'We could most of us remember that last war, but it seemed to have been a very hole-in-the-corner affair, affecting our daily lives very little.'[4]

We know now what was beyond all foreseeing in August 1914. All of them, planners and prophets, had drawn the wrong conclusions

By the 1890s the new illustrated magazines responded to the general interest in technological innovations, for example this artist's impression of *Street Lighting, Anno Domini 2000*

from the unprecedented advances of their time. The progress of the age was, for instance, central to the thinking of that eminent scientist, Alfred Russel Wallace, whose name is for ever linked with Charles Darwin in the book of Victorian revelations and achievements. In his account of *The Wonderful Century* (1898), Wallace summed up the achievements of the world's greatest age as 'a marvellous and altogether unprecedented progress in knowledge of the universe and of its complex forces'.[5] They had the tide with them.

And so, whenever the subject of 'War' appeared in the many surveys of the age, which began during the last decade of the nineteenth century, it was assumed that future wars would not have any catastrophic effect on society. A sturdy confidence in the certain progress of humankind encouraged the belief that the ever-increasing effectiveness of technological weaponry would make wars shorter in duration and, therefore, less destructive than ever before. In 1901, at the end of a chapter on 'Changes in Military Science', a senior American officer, an instructor at West Point, wrote with total confidence that 'wars between civilized nations, when carried on by the regularly organized forces, will be short'. He was certain that 'the great and increasing complexity of modern life, involving international contacts at an ever-increasing number of points, will combine with the military conditions herein before outlined to reduce the duration of war to the utmost'.[6]

That was the view of H. G. Wells when he presented his ideas about coming things in *Anticipations* (1902). In the chapter on 'War' he fell into line with the forecasts of his contemporaries and set down their agreed schedule of the changes all anticipated: an increase in the speed of movement, improvements in small-arms and artillery, trench-digging machines, observation balloons by the thousand, ramming at sea, no dreadnoughts but light, swift naval vessels, and—here Wells differed from many forecasters—not a submarine in sight. The author of the *The War of the Worlds* made no mention of secret weapons and did not foresee any possibility of great disasters. The campaigns of the future would be swift-moving affairs:[7]

> Warfare in the future, on sea or land alike, will be much more one-sided than it has ever been in the past, much more of a foregone conclusion. Save for national lunacy, it will be brought about by the side that will win, and because that side knows that it will win. More and more it will have the quality

of surprise, of pitiless revelation. Instead of the see-saw, the bickering interchange of battles of the old time, will come swiftly and amazingly blow and blow, and blow, no pause, no time for recovery, disasters cumulative and irreparable.

They were ready for the wrong war. As one of the ablest historians of the First World War has written:[8]

The Nations entered upon the conflict with the conventional outlook and system of the eighteenth century merely modified by the events of the nineteenth century ...

Politically they conceived it to be a struggle between rival coalitions based on the traditional system of diplomatic alliances, and militarily a contest between professional armies—swollen, it is true, by the continental system of conscription, yet essentially fought by soldiers while the mass of the people watched, from seats in the amphitheatre, the efforts of their champions.

That judgement applies with even greater truth to those tales of future warfare that appeared before 1914. Most authors followed the national line for most of the time. There was nothing in their experience to make them change their narrative methods from past practice in the histories of the Napoleonic or Crimean Wars. They concentrated on decisive battles that lasted little more than a day, and the more popular stories always found a special place for acts of individual heroism that had a conspicuous effect on the outcome of a battle. The one great difference, however, was the sudden change in attitudes and political expectations. In 1891 the French and Russians were the designated enemies in *The Great War of 189–*, and the Germans had been good friends and loyal allies of the British. By 1900 the 'War Against Germany' had started, when a British writer opened fire on the invaders in his account of *How the Germans took London*. There, for the first time in this fiction, the phrase 'doubling the German Navy' appears as code for the new menace from a great continental power. Again, *der Tag*, the signal for future hostilities in the German tales of the *Zukunftskrieg*, makes an early appearance in the great naval war with the United Kingdom described in the tale of the reckoning-to-come, *Die Abrechnung mit England* (1900). As battle begins the author changes to the future-historic mode and reports that: 'The entire Navy had long yearned for the Day when they could take on the hated English; for they had brought down on themselves immense hatred and an animosity like that which the

French had experienced in 1813.'[9] It was the beginning of the *Zukunftskrieg* with Great Britain; and from here onwards this survey of future-war fiction has to plot a double course between the many anticipations of the coming Anglo-German war and the major events that led to that conflict in August 1914. Out of the politics came the projections.

During the opening years of the new century the British began to take the first precautionary measures against the perceived threat of the new Germany navy. In 1903, when Erskine Childers had given his early warning of German intentions in *The Riddle of the Sands*, the Balfour government announced on 10 March the establishment of a new battleship base at Rosyth in Scotland; on May Day the President of the French Republic gave a warm welcome to King Edward VII when he began a famous visit to Paris which greatly improved relations between the British and the French; and on 14 October the growing accord between the two countries was confirmed in the signing of the Anglo-French Arbitration Treaty. That settled the numerous differences between the two countries, and it led on to the conclusion of the *Entente Cordiale* on 8 April 1904. *The Times* called it, quite rightly, 'a landmark in the policy of the two countries ...'[10]

> ... because it represents for the first time a serious attempt to see their worldwide relationships steadily, and see them whole.... But transcending its significance in this respect is the value it must possess and the weight it must carry as a substantial pledge of the essential unity of our interests and desires. That value as a great factor in the peace of nations we believe it will retain, because it gives expression to the general, and heartfelt wishes of the two great democracies whom it concerns.

From that time onward, as the relationship between Britain and Germany deteriorated year by year, the production of future-war stories expanded in phase with the increasing seriousness of the international incidents that were largely engineered by, or provoked by, Germany. The Moroccan crisis of 1905 began with the Kaiser's visit to Tangier, where he announced that Germany had 'great and growing interests in Morocco'—a direct challenge to the new Anglo-French *Entente*. In the following year the output of British and German future-war stories came close to doubling, and the *Daily Mail* ran the notorious serial story of *The Invasion of 1910* by William Le Queux. The German press immediately seized on that absurd tale as proof positive of British ill-will. 'Never before has this rabble-rousing propaganda against Germany had so widespread and so unsettling an effect on the country.'[11] That was the observation of one German writer in a serious and restrained report on the British and their future-war stories.

And yet, while the war-to-come raged on in fiction, there were determined efforts to promote better relations between Great Britain and Germany. In 1905 a group of British representatives—mayors and county councillors—visited Germany; and in the May of the following year the chief burgomasters of Berlin, Aachen, Dresden, Cologne, and Charlottenburg came to London. They were welcomed by King Edward VII; and at a banquet in the Guildhall the Lord Mayor of London spoke of the friendship between British and Germans. On that occasion the young Winston Churchill denounced 'the attempts of alarmist journalists to set up strife between the nations'; and the *Annual Register* for 1906 noted that the visit had proved 'an important step towards dissipating the fears of an eventual Anglo-German conflict which was fostered, both in Germany and in Great Britain by a section of the "patriotic" press'.[12]

Another Moroccan crisis followed in 1911, when the Germans sent the gunboat *Panther* to seize the port of Agadir; and, once again, in 1912 there was another great surge in the production of these stories. The general view was that war had been avoided—but for how long? In the May number of *The London Magazine* for 1912 Hilaire Belloc's article, 'In the Case of War', described what the probable course of the conflict might be. He began:[13]

> In the course of last summer, and particularly in the first days of September, there was grave danger of war between France and Germany. Had war broken out, Great Britain would have dispatched an army amounting, it is believed, to 150 000 men, and in any case well over 100 000, to act in alliance with France and operate against the German forces. All was ready for conveying this great force across the Channel ... I propose to show that that army would have come into action in the neighbourhood of the town of Liège in Belgium, and further to show by practical example the absolute necessity of securing sea communications if Great Britain is to take any part in European matters.

From the start of these projected hostilities in 1900, there were instructive similarities and significant differences between the British and the German tales of their future war. Most of the authors shared a common professionalism: the majority on both sides were

Future flying machines in action over an enemy city

journalists who also wrote fiction; a few were senior officers who wrote in the interests of the army or navy; and there were occasional contributions from the politicians. Thereafter, there was a sharp division in attitudes; and this was, as the Germans say, first and last a matter of *Weltanschauung*. British writers saw their relationship with an increasingly hostile Germany as an exercise in practical politics: their task was to argue for a greater navy or for a conscript army. The Germans, on the other hand, tended to present their tales of the *Zukunftskrieg* as a matter of historical necessity. Written into their narratives was a programme that spoke of German destiny and of Germany's place in the world. For instance, at the very start of these stories in 1900, in the opening pages of *Die Abrechnung mit England*, the narrator appears in his approved role as the German patriot. He boasts that he was never 'one of those true-blue liberals ...'[14]

> ... those cosmopolitans who think first about the welfare of other nations, and afterwards remember that they are Germans and that theirs is a restricted fatherland. I was first and foremost a German; I was German through and through. So long as I could think of the Austrians as Germans who

> fought against the Italians and defended themselves from the
> Magyars, then I was for them. Never for a minute did I ask
> myself whether they had right —moral or legal—on their side.

These views, with variations on the dominant theme of war and conquest, were repeated year after year by other writers in such stories as *Der Schlag gegen Deutschland, Mit Deutschen Waffen über Paris nach London, Die 'Offensiv-Invasion' gegen England, Deutschlands Flotte im Kampf*, and *Ave Caesar! Deutsche Luftschiffe im Kampf um Marokko*. Their authors complained of unjust treatment, or that Germany had not found her rightful place in the sun, or that others had more than their fair share of world trade. In a sense they were right. In the Darwinian universe of the unending struggle for survival, there was no law that said: No admittance to late-comers! Possession is for ever! 'There is no standing still in the world's history,' so Friedrich von Bernhardi wrote in his scandalous analysis of means and ends in *Deutschland und der Nächste Krieg* (1912)—one of the many responses to the Agadir incident of 1911. Bernhardi went on to say, in a notorious chapter on 'World Power or Downfall', that there is 'no being satisfied for us, but only progress or retrogression, and that it is tantamount to retrogression when we are contented with our present place among the nations of Europe, while all our rivals are straining with desperate energy, even at the cost of our rights, to extend their power'.[15]

Bernhardi was quite clear about the programme for the advancement of Greater Germany. First, finish off the French: 'France must be so completely crushed that she can never again come across our path.' Second, take every possible step to obtain colonies: 'If necessary they must be obtained as the result of a successful European war.' Third, prepare for the inevitable war with the United Kingdom, or else—'If we do not today stake everything on strengthening our fleet, to insure at least the possibility of a successful war, and if we once more allow our probable opponent to gain a start which it will be scarcely possible to make up in the future, we must renounce for many years to come any place among the world powers.' If the Germans wanted the Reich to expand, then let them prepare for the conflict ahead:

> We have fought in the last two great wars for our national
> union and our position among the Powers of *Europe*; we must
> now decide whether we wish to develop into and maintain a
> *World Empire*, and procure for German spirit and German ideas
> that fit recognition which has been hitherto withheld from us.

Have we the energy to aspire to that great goal? Are we prepared to make the sacrifices which such an effort will
doubtless cost us? Or are we willing to recoil before the
hostile forces, and sink step by step lower in our economic,
political, and national importance? That is what is involved in
our decision.

The British reaction to belligerent views of this kind was to add them
to the long list of imprudent statements, threats, and international
incidents that were regularly reported in the daily newspapers, especially in the *Daily Mail* (founded by Northcliffe in 1896) and *The
Times* (acquired by Northcliffe in 1908). As early as 1900 Northcliffe
had talked about the possibility of a war with Germany, and in 1909
he appointed Robert Blatchford as a 'Germany watcher' for the *Daily
Mail*. Blatchford wrote with knowledge and authority: he was a
veteran socialist; and in 1891 he had founded the *Clarion*, which
gave powerful support to the new Independent Labour Party. On 20
December Blatchford summed up the aims of his articles in the *Daily
Mail*:[16]

'I have tried to show

1. That Germany aims at European domination.
2. That to attain her ends she must break the power of Britain.
3. That all attempts at conciliation and compromise are fore-
   doomed to failure; nothing will deter Germany but a
   demonstration of power.
4. That if France falls we shall be unable to hold our own.
5. That France is not generally regarded as a match for
   Germany.
6. That we are not in a position to help France.
7. That unless the British people make greater sacrifices than
   they are at present prepared to make, we shall lose our
   Empire and our independence.

These points were canonical doctrine in the tales of the war-with-
Germany. In fact, by the time these articles appeared in the *Daily
Mail* in 1909, some thirty variations on the Blatchford theme had
established the myth of a German invasion and the subsequent
victory, or defeat, of the enemy forces. The authors designed their
stories in keeping with one or other of the accepted modes of
presenting the coming peril. First, there was the preposterous notion
of 'the enemy within'. This was the subject of Louis Tracy's *The
Invaders*, which made an early start in 1901 with the old story of the

enemy in hiding. Twenty years before it had been the French in Dover who waited for the day when they could break cover and hurry away to seize the Channel Tunnel. In 1901 it was the Germans in Liverpool who came out of hiding to march boldly up Ranelagh Street and past Mount Pleasant. 'They were clothed in khaki, but not of British cut. They were quite as unmistakeably foreigners, trained soldiers ...'

Others followed and added to the tale of the secret enemy, also known as 'The Secret Army in Waiting' and as 'The Alien Army'. There was, for example, the 'Committee of Secret Preparations' in *The Enemy in our Midst* (1906): 'Their purpose was simple and definite—to make England ready for invasion and capture.' These secret preparations were directed by a mastermind, usually a German officer in disguise with the tell-tale duelling scar on his cheek. Those troops in waiting were a warning to patriots that they had to deal with a perfidious and cunning enemy. They had their secret orders. They knew the appointed day and the places where they were to assemble secretly in their thousands, exactly as it was foretold in *Great Was the Fall* (1912). Only the most credulous and simple-minded reader could have believed that, contrary to every principle

Albert Robida, the most imaginative of graphic artists, looked into the future in *Le Vingtième Siècle* (1883), and foresaw daily news programmes on television

of warfare, forty thousand German residents from all parts of the United Kingdom would suddenly arrive in Hull. They are apparently going on holiday; but that is a simple cover story; their real objective is to join forces with the sixty thousand troops who have evaded the North Sea Fleet and landed safely on the coast.

Sometimes Kaiser Wilhelm II appeared in his role as the supreme commander of the armed forces. And here there was at least some correspondence with reality, since the Emperor had long been established in British estimation as a prime mover in his own right. He had the gift of the gaffe that allowed critical observers to compile their own history of German intentions. One of them wrote that 'the growth of the German fleet cannot be separated from the declarations of policy made to explain that growth ...'[17]

> The German Emperor has himself told us what his object was and is. In the first phase it was merely to found 'a greater Germany beyond the seas'. That was at the commencement of his reign, and might have been harmless. Soon his ambition and views became larger. His next assertions were to the effect that 'Germany's future is on the water', that 'the trident must be in our hands', and then came the vaunting declaration that 'no decision can now be taken in distant lands or beyond the ocean without the participation and permission of Germany and the German Emperor.' Finally, there was the memorable and extraordinary telegram to the Tsar at Reval from Emperor William styling himself 'Admiral of the Atlantic!'

Whenever the Emperor appeared in British future-war fiction, he played his part as the supreme manifestation of the German will-to-power. He made an early and most telling entrance in *The Riddle of the Sands*, at that moment when Carruthers realized that he 'was assisting at an experimental rehearsal of a great scene'—the departure of the invasion force. The publishers of the cheap edition of 1910 evidently thought it important enough to make a major point of the occasion. The solitary illustration showed the Emperor as he assists Carruthers to lower the boat when the tug grounds in the Buse Tief. The caption repeated Carruthers' exclamation: 'It was one who, in Germany, has a better right to insist than anyone else.'

The ingenuity and sustained excellence of Erskine Childers' story point to a striking difference in quality between the British and the German tales of the war-to-come. Although almost all these stories—British and German—are without any literary merit, the few that stand out from the ruck come from British writers. Erskine

Childers is still remembered as the author of a most exciting adventure story. Charles Doughty, author of the classic *Travels in Arabia Deserta* (1888), deserves attention for his singular achievement as the only poet in European history who has written two long verse dramas—*The Cliffs* in 1909 and *The Clouds* in 1912—on the theme of invasion and conquest; and it is still well worth reading the elegiac recollections of the halcyon days beyond recall in *When William Came* (1913) where 'Saki' (H. H. Munro) reflects on the theme of invasion and conquest.

On the German side, the response to these tales of the coming invasion was equal and uniform: the British press was to blame for the bad feeling between the two nations. For instance, on 15 November 1904 the German chancellor, Count von Bülow, talked at length on the subject of 'Great Britain and Germany' in an interview with a British correspondent. It seemed to him, he said, 'as if a certain school of your publicists looks upon a paper-war against Germany as the main object of its life'.[18] A year later a German writer, long resident in the United Kingdom, took up that point in an article on 'Germany and English War Scares'. Karl Blind believed that British hostility had begun with the German victory in the War of 1870; for after that 'there followed very soon a series of alarmist outcries against an alleged German invasion danger. Pamphlets and articles appeared in the *Battle of Dorking* style.' The fault lay with Chesney: 'He gave the watchword and the signal for a display of enmity against Germany, the echo of which has reverberated ever since.' Thirty-five years after the Chesney story, Blind found that, whenever he discussed 'this matter of invasion scares' with his English friends, they generally repeated 'what they had read in the writings of those mysterious political Mahatmas who, under all kinds of fictitious names, sow enmity among Englishmen against Germany'.[19]

German apologists noted with some justification that the *Daily Mail* serialization of William Le Queux's *Invasion of 1910* was not the best of oil for troubled waters, although they never added that the translation—without the last chapters on the final defeat of the invaders—had proved to be a great success with German readers. Nevertheless, they could point with even more justification to the total drama of a most popular and now long-forgotten play. *An Englishman's Home* was the theatrical sensation of 1909. The author was Guy du Maurier, then second-in-command 3rd Battalion the Royal Fusiliers; and the producer was his brother Gerald du Maurier, the celebrated actor and joint-manager of Wyndham's Theatre in

London. When the play opened in that theatre on 27 January, it was an instant success. There were long, laudatory accounts from the critics and full-page artists' impressions of principal incidents in the major illustrated magazines. For most of the year it played to packed houses, and at the end of 1909 the *Annual Register* considered the subject and the success of *An Englishman's Home* important enough to be recorded for posterity:[20]

> ... a sensational, though short-lived success, was achieved by 'a play with a purpose'—*An Englishman's Home*—dealing with no less a matter than the invasion of England by a foreign power, whose identity was, to say the least, thinly veiled. The author, who appeared on the play-bill simply as 'A Patriot', was in reality a British officer, Captain Guy du Maurier, and the piece was a forcible and cleverly-written argument in favour of universal military training. From a strictly technical and dramatic point of view, it must be admitted that *An Englishman's Home* failed signally in construction; its effectiveness—which was undeniable—depended mainly on the ingenious realism of every scenic detail and the very close and skilful reproduction of certain unattractive types of English men and women.

Although there were immediate attempts to parody the play, the censor would not permit any mockery of so serious a topic. In consequence, the would-be deriders of *An Englishman's Home* had to wait for several months before they could renew their counter-offensive against the ill-will and the absurdities of so many future-war stories. This had been going on for several years. The lead in the campaign for common sense and general good humour had come from *Punch* in 1906, when it began to carry occasional comic articles (many of them from A. A. Milne) that made fun of the contemporary anxieties about German spies and the dangers of invasion. On 15 July 1908, for example, *Punch* had an ironic account of Question Time in the House of Commons for 6 July, when Colonel Lockwood and others asked the Secretary of State for War a series of fatuous questions about 'German spies charged with the mission of securing photographs of Epping Forest' (pp. 276–78).

This, however, was small-arms fire in comparison to the rolling barrage that thundered on without ceasing throughout the 122 pages of the most amusing invasion story in the history of the genre. More than that, the author of *The Swoop! or, How Clarence Saved England* went on to become the most accomplished and undoubtedly the most

entertaining humorous writer in twentieth-century English literature. In 1909, however, the incomparable P. G. Wodehouse was still a
writer in search of his true subject and of his proper form. He had
begun in the early 1900s with 'By the Way' articles in the *Globe* and
with a series of school stories; and then the sheer extravagance of the
yarns about 'England's Peril' and the success of *An Englishman's Home*
in 1909 gave him an ideal opportunity to make serious fun of the
'German invasion' myth. His most ingenious narrative mocked 'this
dashed Swoop of the Vulture business', as he called it, with a most
hilarious account of the defeat and discomfiture of the enemy. There
are, of course, the German invaders: 'Not only had the Germans
effected a landing in Essex, but, in addition no fewer than eight other
hostile armies had, by some remarkable coincidence, hit on that
identical moment for launching their long-prepared blow.' Chinese,
Russians, Swiss, Moroccan brigands, Young Turks, plus contingents
from the Mad Mullah and the army of Monaco—all of them come
ashore at points along the British coastline from Auchtermuchty to
Brighton and Margate. The Chinese, however, 'lost their way near
Llanfairpwlgwnngogogoch in darkest Wales, because they had been
unable to understand the directions given them by the shepherds
they encountered'.

That brilliant comic writer, Evelyn Waugh, has said of Wodehouse
that: 'half-way through *Mike*, written in 1910 ... Psmith appears and
the light was kindled which has burned with growing brilliance for
half a century'.[21] There are, however, good reasons for thinking that
the skills of the later master are already apparent in the way
Wodehouse tells his 'Tale of the Great Invasion'. He transforms the
established pattern by reversing all expectations. The nation is saved
by the totally uncovenanted and the absolutely unknown:
'Everyone has seen the Chugwater Column in Aldwych, the equestrian statue in Chugwater Road (formerly Piccadilly), and the
picture-postcards in the stationers' windows.' It is the Boy of
Destiny and the Saviour of his Country, Clarence McAndrew
Chugwater, 'one of General Baden-Powell's Boy Scouts'. He assem-
bles his followers in 'that vast tract of unreclaimed prairie known to
Londoners as the Aldwych Site'; and there the reader meets him as
he inspects the sentry posts:[22]

> The whistle of a Striped Iguanodon sounded softly in the
> darkness. The sentry, who was pacing to and fro before the
> camp-fire, halted, and peered into the night. As he peered, he
> uttered the plaintive note of a zebra calling to its mate.

A voice from the darkness said, 'Eeen gonyâmagony.'
'Invooboo,' replied the sentry argumentatively. 'Yah bô! Invooboo.'
An indistinct figure moved forward.
'Who goes there?'
'A friend.'
'Advance friend, and give the countersign.'
'Remember Mafeking, and death to the Injuns.'

The plan for the great counter-offensive depends on brain power, and not on fire power. Clarence Chugwater encourages the invading generals to compete for attention by performing in the music halls. The Russians and the Germans fall out. Their troops take up their battle positions, and in the struggle to secure the Hampstead Heights the two sides lose two-thirds of their effectives. The penultimate episode takes place in the tent of Prince Otto of Saxe-Pfennig. Enter Clarence Chugwater: 'Resistance is useless' he says. 'An hour ago your camp was silently surrounded by a patrol of Boy Scouts, armed with catapults and hockey sticks. One rush and the battle is over. Your entire army, like yourself, are prisoners.' Exeunt all invading troops in all directions.

Many Germans might have been persuaded that the British were not so hostile to Germany as Count von Bülow had suggested, if they had discovered that, in the September of 1909, the enterprising editor of the *The Sketch* had decided to employ a secret weapon in the great war against the myth-makers and the alarmists. He commissioned a series of eleven drawings from Heath Robinson, the most amusing and inventive comic artist of his day. These appeared week by week under the heading of:

AM TAG! DIE DEUTSCHEN KOMMEN!

INCIDENTS OF THE COMING GERMAN INVASION OF ENGLAND: BY HEATH ROBINSON

From the first cartoon on 20 April 1910—'German Spies in Epping Forest'—Heath Robinson made a mockery of episodes in the received version of the German invasion stories. These ran from 'German Officers Endeavouring to Enter an Englishman's Home' to a hilarious image of 'German Troops, Disguised as British Excursionists, Crossing the North Sea'. The laughter failed, unfortunately, to halt the unending production of future-war stories. British and German writers continued steadfastly and to the end.

A cover-page spread for the news of the year in 1902: 'The First Airship Journey
Over London'

By 1910, then, it is evident that a succession of writers—journalists and propagandists, most of them—a poet, a dramatist, and one remarkable artist had made the imagined war-to-come with Germany familiar matter for most British citizens. Even the young readers of *Chums*, *Boy's Own*, and *Union Jack* were ready for the war the juvenile magazines told them would come sooner rather than later. At about the age of eight, the boy who became one of the finest of twentieth-century writers, Evelyn Waugh, formed the Pistol Group. His group of friends prepared to fight the German invaders by walking in bare feet through nettles, drilling in the field opposite the Waugh home, and building a fortress to resist the Germans. One of their rules set down their standard practice for engaging the enemy: 'Never be polite to Germans. If you meet one, and feel capable of knocking him down, knock him down. If not, turn around and walk in the opposite direction.'[23] Thus, the projections of the future-war stories—spies, landing craft, and a sudden raid by the German navy—had served to fashion a new national legend. It was a war that both sides fought to a finish in the fiction of their own choosing.

The British and the Germans began with quite separate sets of assumptions, and they consequently arrived at very different conclusions about the war that could one day unite them in mortal combat. These differences were evident at the start in the contrast between Eisenhart's *Die Abrechnung mit England*—especially the intensely nationalistic episodes and the endlessly triumphant language—and in the respect shown for the great achievements and the aspirations of the German people in Erskine Childers' *Riddle of the Sands*. The two writers had started from different bases. The time frame for Eisenhart, and indeed for most of his fellows, was the recent past—the War of 1870 and the foundation of the Reich; for Childers it was a longer perspective that reached back through the history of an island people. Although he was both courteous and careful in his presentation of the German Emperor, Childers undoubtedly intended a clear contrast between Carruthers as the would-be saviour of his people and the Kaiser as a figure of menace and destructiveness. That archetypal situation renewed in popular fiction what had been repeated again and again in myth and in history. It is, therefore, not surprising that *The Riddle of the Sands* is still in print after ninety-three years. There are resonances in the Erskine Childers story that give it something of an epic quality. It is a tale of the sea, told by an accomplished sailor who has set out on a dangerous quest. He finds that a mortal peril is about to befall an island people—unless. In 1903 the reader knew that the German Emperor, like the King of Spain and Bonaparte, represented the most recent threat to the security of Shakespeare's 'fortress built by nature for herself'. The danger of invasion was bedded deep in the experience of the British people; it could not fail to arouse traditional responses long established in folk memory and in the national history—Drake and the Armada, Nelson dying at Trafalgar. The power of these icons added a significant tension to the roles acted out in the high drama of the future-war stories. Their titles often projected shadows from the past upon the future: *A New Trafalgar, The Meteor Flag of England, Seaward For the Foe, When England Slept.*

There was nothing, however, in the whole body of British future-war fiction to compare with the will-to-victory displayed in *Die 'Offensiv-Invasion' gegen England*: 'Could we not seize a favourable opportunity,' Karl Bleibtreu asked, ' to take the British naval bases by surprise, and range far and wide destroying their maritime commerce in a two-day raid?' Again, there was nothing like the ample vision of the future Germany, dominant in the world of 2021, as Max Heinrichka was so pleased to demonstrate in his *100 Jahre deutsche Zukunft* (1913). In that happy time-to-come Greater Germany stretches from the North Sea to the Adriatic. Overseas there are flourishing German colonies in Africa, the East Indies, and America. The lion's teeth have been drawn. The Royal Navy has been defeated. 'Germany now ruled the waves after the defeat of her rival ...[24]

> However, in laying down the peace terms, Germany refrained from obstructing or hampering Britain in the future conduct of her world trade. But Britain had been so weakened that she had to let Germany take the share in world trade and in world dominion that Germany claimed. Since Germany maintained a considerable number of troops in the United Kingdom for a whole decade, she gained great influence in all the naval and military matters of the island kingdom. In this way it was possible to prevent any competition in armaments or the building of more large ships than were necessary for national requirements. Moreover, Germany could expect that during the ten years of German military control the British would become accustomed to the exercise of German power. Indeed, Germany could expect that by the end of the decade the British might perhaps become so accustomed to German control that they would be ready for an alliance with Germany.

PUNCH, OR THE LONDON CHARIVARI.—September 6, 1911.

MISUNDERSTOOD.

Germany. "NOBODY LOVES ME—AND THEY ALL WANT TO TRAMPLE ON ME!"

Germany sheds crocodile tears. A comment on the Agadir crisis of 1911

As Heinrichka's utopian vision went the rounds in Germany, time was running out for the events foreseen in so many tales of the war-to-come. In June 1914 the Bosnian Serb students, Princip and

Gabrinović, visited Belgrade and there they obtained revolvers and hand grenades from the Serb Komitadjis, Majors Tankosić and Ciganović. On 28 June the town of Sarajevo entered world history, when the conspirators assassinated the Archduke Franz Ferdinand and his wife. And then the real war came in August 1914, when the elaborate system of European alliances followed old agreements and the armies mobilized according to long-established plans, as everyone had said they would. 'They went with songs to battle,' an English poet wrote long after his generation discovered that they had been committed to a form of warfare no one had ever foretold. Let the record show that last entries in the book of the Great War-to-come with Germany ran true to established form. In 1914 two writers responded to the earliest engagements of the First World War. For the author of *Hindenburgs Einmarsch in London*, the German invaders realize the ambitions of the *Zukunftskrieg* when they begin the assault on Dover:[25]

> For eight days the new giant Krupp guns had felt their way over to Dover and Folkestone, and had destroyed everything living on the south coast of England, reducing all the work of human hands to nothing. Under the sustained fire of the monsters of Essen and Pilsen the great fortification works were hammered into dust. While landings of troops were simulated between Yarmouth and the mouth of the Thames, the three waterways from Zeebrugge, Dunkirk, and Calais to England had been secured east and west by a steel wall of torpedo boats and mines and submarines.

Internal evidence suggests that Paul Georg Münch was engaged on the opening chapters of his triumphant vision during the first weeks of the war, at the time when von Kluck and the German 1st Army were making their fatal extension to the right and von Bülow was following Blücher's old line of advance towards Waterloo. On 23 August in the area of Mons, the 3rd Division of the British 2nd Corps made first contact with the German forces. In the following days, as the British Expeditionary Force retreated towards the Marne, there were rumours of a heavenly host that fought beside the British troops. (Were guardian angels entered on the muster rolls of the British regiments?) There were no reports of angelic sightings on the German side, however, as the rumours of this marvel spread throughout the British Expeditionary Force and on through the British press. The writer Arthur Machen took the legend of 'The Angels of Mons' and turned it into a famous short

PUNCH, OR THE LONDON CHARIVARI.—April 22, 1914.

ENTENTE
CORDIALE
APRIL 1904
APRIL 1914.

Bernard Partridge

AFTER TEN YEARS.

Reasons for congratulation in 1914: the tenth anniversary of the *Entente Cordiale*

story, *The Bowmen*, which appeared in the *Evening Standard* on 29 September 1914. As the barrages commence in the opening battles of the First World War, the tale of the war-to-come closes with the

British soldier in Machen's story, who 'saw before him, beyond the trench, a long line of shapes, with a shining about them. They were like men who drew the bow, and with another shout, their cloud of arrows flew singing and tingling through the air towards the German hosts.'

THE ONLY ALTERNATIVE.

John Bull. "RECRUITS COMING IN NICELY, SERGEANT?"

Recruiting Sergeant Punch. "NO, SIR. THE FACT IS, MR. BULL, IF YOU CAN'T MAKE IT BETTER WORTH THEIR WHILE TO ENLIST,—YOU'LL HAVE TO SHOULDER A RIFLE YOURSELF!!!"

Chapter One
'A Full, Vivid and Interesting Picture of the Great War of the Future'

The Great War of 189–

During the 1890s the editors of the illustrated magazines and the new mass newspapers discovered that the tale of 'the Next Great War' allowed them to combine patriotism with profit. A new publishing industry began in January 1891, when the editor of the illustrated weekly Black and White *introduced his readers to* The Great War of 189–, *the first full-length, illustrated account of the war they all expected in the near future. His formula for success was eminent writers and maximum realism.*

The narrative is an action replay of contemporary assumptions and expectations. Admiral Colomb and his distinguished collaborators kept closely to the contour lines of political geography in the 1890s; and the editor saw to it that the narrative kept to the old press style—telegrams, reports from the field, editorial comments, and very little sub-editing.[1] This was a major innovation in presenting the tale of tomorrow's war: it narrowed the gap between fact and fiction, between the prophetic and the predicted; and it brought future-war fiction out of the narrow embrace of the monthly journals into the more ample world of the illustrated magazines. The other highly effective innovation was the use of many first-class illustrations, which told their own tale of coming things in a new imagery of warfare.

Although The Great War of 189– *was by no means the most exciting and influential of the future-war stories that appeared before 1914, it stands apart from all of them in important ways. It is not a piece of propaganda: it is the considered, collective opinion of men, familiar with War Office and Admiralty thinking, who aimed to present as objective a forecast as lay in their powers. Even more important, the writers seek, for the first time, to place a future war in the total context of international politics, treaties and alliances, new tactics, and new equipment.*

The war begins in the Balkans—no surprise there for readers in 1891. The immediate cause is a remarkable anticipation of later events—the attempted assassination of Prince Ferdinand of Bulgaria. The ultimate cause, again a preview of 1914, is the apparently inevitable chain-effect of the Triple Alliance between Germany, Austria-Hungary, and Italy. First, the abominable Serbs, as predatory as ever, seize their opportunity to move against Bulgaria. Their sudden action starts off the drama of the expected: the Austrians occupy Belgrade as a precautionary measure against 'the wanton aggression of Servia'; and in response the Russians occupy Bourgas and Varna, the two principal Bulgarian ports on the Black Sea. The countdown to war begins: Germany fulfils her treaty obligations to Austria-Hungary by mobilizing against Russia, and the French support Russia by declaring war on Germany. The United Kingdom keeps to the old policy of 'glorious isolation' and at first continues to maintain friendly relations with the three powers of the Triple Alliance. (Had Admiral Colomb known of the secret British pact of 1887 with Italy and Austria-Hungary?) However, the British decision to support the Turks by landing troops at Trebizonde automatically causes France and Russia to declare war on the United Kingdom.

Three factors shape the course of this projected war: all the major operations are in Europe; the actions are quick-moving affairs; and the war is over by Christmas.

The editor introduced The Great War of 189– *in the following way.*[2]

The air is full of rumours of War. The European nations stand fully armed and prepared for instant mobilization. Authorities are agreed that a GREAT WAR must break out in the immediate future, and that this War will be fought under novel and surprising conditions. All facts seem to indicate that the coming conflict will be the bloodiest in history, and must involve the most momentous consequences to the whole world. At any time the incident may occur which will precipitate the disaster.

The Editor of *Black and White*, considering that a forecast of the probable course of such a gigantic struggle will be of the highest interest, has sought the aid of the chief living authorities in international politics, in strategy, and in war; and in the present number appears the first instalment of the suppositious records of this future War. In the construction of this imaginary but possible history, Admiral Sir Philip Colomb, Mr. Charles Lowe, Mr. D. Christie Murray, Mr. F. Scudamore, and other experts in military campaigns have taken part. From week to week the course of events will be narrated as though an actual war were in progress, and the Proprietors have obtained the assistance of Mr. F. Villiers, their own War Artist, M. C. W. Wyllie, Mr. J. Finniemore, Mr. W. F. Calderon and other artists, for the purpose of illustrating the scenes and episodes incident to the War. The various campaigns and political crises involved in the scheme will be treated by writers and artists who have a particular knowledge of their subject, and the whole narrative will, it is hoped, present a full, vivid and interesting picture of the GREAT WAR of the Future—as it may be.

The story began as the collaborators meant to go on—with reports that gave the latest news from capital cities and command headquarters ...

ATTEMPTED ASSASSINATION OF PRINCE FERDINAND OF BULGARIA

FULL ACCOUNT OF THE MURDEROUS ASSAULT; CRITICAL CONDITION OF THE WOUNDED PRINCE

(By Telegraph from our Own Correspondent, Mr. Francis Scudamore)

CONSTANTINOPLE, *Sunday, April 3* (via *Varna*)
(Noon)

A report has been circulating here since a late hour this evening to the effect that an attempt has been made to assassinate Prince Ferdinand of Bulgaria, at a mining town named Samakoff, about forty miles south of Sofia. It is said that the Prince, who had been shooting in the Balabancha Balkans, was driving into Samakoff towards evening yesterday, when his carriage was stopped, and he was attacked by a number of men armed with knives and pistols. The Prince's attendants succeeded in saving their master's life and in beating off some and capturing others of his assailants, but not before His Highness had been severely wounded.

Prince Ferdinand was carried into the house of an American missionary resident in Samakoff, where he now lies. His Highness's condition is serious, and is rendered the more critical from the fact that there is no very adequate surgical aid obtainable in Samakoff, and it was necessary to telegraph for doctors to Sofia and Phillippopolis.

The greatest excitement reigns in Constantinople since the receipt of this intelligence, and very grave anxiety is expressed in diplomatic circles as to the possible consequences of this terrible misfortune.

EDITORIAL COMMENTS

It is impossible to overrate the grave significance of this attempted assassination at Samakoff, which in the light of our Correspondent's

'The Prince, when he saw the pistol levelled at him, had leapt to his feet, with the
evident intention of throwing himself upon his murderer'

telegrams would seem to be the prelude to very serious complications in the East. It is, of course, too early to estimate its influence
upon general European politics, but we are quite within reason in
saying that the dramatic incident may prove to have endangered the
peace of Europe. We have long familiarised ourselves with the
thought that the Great War of which the world has been in constant
dread for some years back, and which is to re-adjust the balance of
the Continent, is much more likely to break out in the region of the
Danube than on the banks of the Rhine, and the incident at
Samakoff may well precipitate the catastrophe. The situation is most
perilous, and it is to be hoped that strenuous endeavours will be
made by the Powers to chain up the 'dogs of war', and spare this
dying century, at least, the spectacle of their release. Since the Treaty
of Berlin patched up the last serious disturbance in Europe, there
has been peace; peace, it is, true; but a peace subject to perpetual
menace, and weighty matter for the consideration of statesmen.
Europe has lived, as it were, in armed camps, neutral and watchful;
and all the time the nations have prepared against war as though
war were at their doors. The dastardly outrage at Samakoff comes at
a sorry time.

For we repeat our firm conviction, based on long and close attention to the political motives at work among the nations, that it is on the Danube and not on the Rhine that the torch of war will first be kindled. To a pessimist, indeed, if not to an unbiased observer, we may well seem of late to have been drawing nearer and nearer to a general war. The world has never been afflicted with more persistent rumours of war. No single day has passed without bringing us its perturbing crop of tremors and apprehensions about the stability of the European peace.

The prospects for Europe are not good: the chain-effect of the Triple Alliance will lead to a general European war.

Where is the wisdom of highly-placed men like the German Emperor and his new Chancellor assuring the world, in addresses from the throne and after-dinner speeches, that the peace of Europe was never more assured than at present, and that the political horizon is without a cloud even of the size of Elijah's ominous and initial speck of vapour? What is the truth or the wisdom of such assurances, when the thorn of Alsace-Lorraine is still sticking in the flesh of the unforgiving and revengeful French; when Italy still has some territory 'unredeemed'; when Denmark still harbours a deep grudge against her truculent despoiler; when even the peaceful Swedes, who are still animated by the spirit of the Great Gustavus, long to free their former subjects, the Finns, from the tyrannical mastery of the Russians; when the Spaniards would gladly profit by a European complication—even if they shrank from the thought of an audacious *coup de main*—to repossess themselves of Gibraltar; when the Portuguese, following suit, would never hesitate to kick their British rival in Africa, if they deemed him to be down; when the Cretans, egged on by the Greeks, are firmly resolved to throw off the galling yoke of the Turks; when ex-ministers like M. Tricoupis stump about the Balkan Peninsula, openly preaching Pan-Hellenism and Balkan Federation against the advocates of disunited nationalities; when the Servians secretly vow to settle up old scores with their Bulgarian vanquishers, and when these Bulgarian victors themselves, with their Prime Minister more than their Prince at their head, are sternly determined to be free and independent alike of Sultan and of Czar; when Austria continues to cast longing eyes in the direction of Salonica; and when, above all things, the Colossus of the North, with his head pillowed on snow, and his feet swathed in flowers of the sunny South, has sworn by the soul of his assassinated and sainted father that he will ever remain true to the

Summary justice for the would-be assassins

intention of his sire in exacting a solid equivalent of power, prestige, and territorial foothold on the Balkan Peninsula for all the blood and treasure spent by Russia in the task of 'liberating' the Bulgarians;

when all these things, all these slumbering passions and meditated schemes of aggression and revenge are duly considered, how is it possible for anyone, be he sovereign or subject, to lull the world asleep by false assurances of peace which is sooner or later doomed to be broken?

The Triple Alliance will no more succeed in terrorising the souls of all these secret plotters and designers, and in giving them pause, than three interlocked mountain oaks or firs could stay the downward course of an extended series of separate avalanches, which rend away with them pines, and oaks, and all, in their resistless rush. But has the avalanche, which we thus dread, really and truly at last begun to move? We sincerely trust not, but for the present, at least, the omens in the East have an exceedingly ugly and alarming look, and we shall await the arrival of further telegrams with the greatest anxiety. The Triple Alliance is not an embankment that can bar the advancing flood of war, but rather a detached fortress which must itself soon incur the danger of being surrounded and even submerged by the rushing, whirling waters of European strife. Though the parties to this three-cornered pact have agreed to place their fire-engines, so to speak, at each other's disposal in the event of external danger from fire to their respective domiciles, it is beyond the reach of these Powers to prevent the outbreak of a conflagration, from accident or arson, among the rickety, wind-swept and thatch-roofed mansions of their neighbours; nor is there any fact better established in connection with fires than that they are used by thieves and anarchists for the purpose of sudden plunder and disorder, at once upon the persons and property of the victims and beholders of such catastrophes.

ATTEMPTED ASSASSINATION OF PRINCE FERDINAND

The snows which have held Samakoff isolated from the rest of the world throughout the past four months are now just melted, and thus it chanced that Prince Ferdinand, who for a week past had been shooting in the hills around Philippopolis, decided to pay his first visit of the year to the missionaries of Samakoff, and had, unfortunately as it turns out, announced his intention of so doing.

The Prince, with this purpose in view, left Philippopolis on Friday evening, passing the night in his sleeping-car, and yesterday morning started in a *calèche* from Ichtiman-i-Vakarel, formerly the boundary between Bulgaria and the province of Eastern Roumelia, to drive to the little township in the mountains.

His Highness has usually been accompanied on these visits by one or other of the ministers, but on this occasion, owing partly, no doubt, to his hurriedly-formed plans, he had with him only one of the aides-de-camp who had been of the shooting-party. The Prince's carriage was preceded by half-a-dozen mounted guards, and followed by a like number, as an escort. This is a precaution which Prince Ferdinand's advisers have prevailed with him, much against his will, to adopt of late, in view of the renewed activity of Russian agents and sedition-mongers throughout the Principality and the neighbouring States, where, indeed, a great anti-Bulgarian and anti-Turkish propaganda has been actively carried on for the past year; and in view also of the growing apprehension of his advisers that the recent success in this city of assassins in Russian pay, coupled with the immunity from punishment which the Czar's representatives have shown their ability and readiness to secure for them, would prompt the conspirators, soon or late, to fly at higher game than either M. Stambuloff or the late Dr. Vulkovitch. That his Highness's advisers were in the right has been proved by the attempt of yesterday. The event, however, may be said to offer encouragement at once to would-be regicides and to their intended victims, inasmuch as it has been shown yet once again to the former, how useless as a protection against assassins is the presence of an armed escort, and to the latter, how apt is a well-matured plot to be frustrated by a commonplace accident.

The Prince's carriage was expected to reach Samakoff about noon, and shortly before that hour a considerable number of persons had collected in the main street, while small crowds had gathered round the gates of the Prefecture and about the door of the American Mission-house, which is situated in a side street leading off the high road, and where the usual modest preparations had been made for the princely visit. His Highness, on arrival, after halting for a moment or two at the gate of the Prefecture where he did not alight, drove on through the town towards the Mission-house. At the moment when the carriage turned the corner into the narrower street, a man wearing the long black gown and brimless stovepipe hat of a priest of the orthodox church stood forward from the crowd, in which were several other persons dressed as he was, and, raising a revolver, took deliberate aim at his Highness. And then occurred the accident to which, in all probability, Prince Ferdinand owes his life. The cartridge did not explode. The sham priest lowered his weapon slightly, raised it once more, and again pulled the trigger; but as he did so the pistol barrel was struck up—the ball burying itself in the wall of a house across the street—and the assassin was seized and firmly held by many willing hands.

The whole occurrence had taken but a moment. The Prince, when he saw the pistol levelled at him, had leapt to his feet, with the evident intention of throwing himself upon his murderer. As it was, his Highness's intervention seemed very necessary on behalf of the baffled assassin, who stood in no small danger of being lynched incontinently by his furious captors.

The carriage had stopped; the escort was hastily dismounting, and the Prince, shouting orders to the people to spare their prisoner's life, had alighted and, turning, was in the act of throwing his heavy pelisse to his companion, when sudden as thought a second ruffian sprang from amid the vociferating mob, hurled himself upon the Prince, and, thrusting a great, broad-bladed Circassian *khanga* into his bosom, was away and out of sight almost before any of the by-standers had recovered from this second shock of horror and surprise.

His Highness, who had sunk to the ground under the blow, though he did not lose consciousness, was at once carried into the Mission-house, distant a few yards only, and very speedily all the best medical advice obtainable in Samakoff was at hand, while telegrams for further assistance were at once despatched to Sofia and to Philippopolis, the latter place being perhaps more rapidly accessible than the capital. The first examination of the wound showed that the broad knife had turned on the point of a rib—very fortunately—and had therefore missed by a hair's-breadth the envelope of the heart. It was not till to-day that a persistent recurrence of internal hæmorrhage aroused the gravest fears of the Prince's surgeons, and prompted them to appeal to Constantinople for further advice.

The pretended priest, when searched, was found to be costumed beneath his robes in the ordinary dress of the petty trader of the towns here. His long flowing locks proved a wig, and his thick unkempt beard was also false. Upon him, among other papers said to be of great importance, but as to which I know nothing, was found a passport issued by the Russian Consulate at Odessa no less recently than last month, and bearing the visé of the Russian Chancellor at Sofia.

Chapter One

WE ARE NOW AT WAR

SOFIA, *April 10*

We are now at war, and fighting is going forward even as I write. This morning rifle-shots were exchanged between Servian and Bulgarian patrolling parties on the frontier, near Trn, without result on either side. A body of some 300 Servians then crossed the frontier and advanced about a mile, seeking to cut off a party of fifty Bulgarians, who, however, retreated and escaped. Later on heavy fighting was reported in the neighbourhood of Vlassina. How it originated is immaterial. The Bulgarians lost 17 men killed and 54 wounded. This set fire to the torch all along the frontier line. Some time before the official declaration of war, which, though it announced that hostilities would begin at noon to-day, did not reach the Minister for Foreign Affairs here until nine o'clock this evening, reports had been posted up in the cafés announcing fighting in the vicinity of Planinitza, Beuskedol, Miloslawtzi, Zelene, and Gard, in the Trn district. The Servian Minister, who had twice telegraphed to his Government for instructions during the afternoon, demanded a special train as soon as he had presented the declaration of war, and left half an hour later, under escort, for the frontier.

A solemn *Te Deum* was sung this evening in the Cathedral, M. Stambuloff and the Ministers being present. The streets are crowded—no one shows any intention of going to bed; the popular enthusiasm and confidence are immense, and there is apparently a general sensation of relief at the relaxation of the strain of the past few days, and a feeling of satisfaction that the dastardly attack on the Prince will be promptly avenged. I am, by the way, authorised to state that, by order of Prince Ferdinand's physicians, all news of these exciting events is rigidly withheld from his Highness.

Fresh troops are hourly leaving Sofia and Philippopolis for the front. At the moment of closing this despatch, news comes of an important action near Dragoman, with reported defeat of the Servians with heavy losses.

SOFIA, *April 11*

There is to be no more fighting. The brilliant and most sanguinary engagement at Dragoman, which I reported in progress last night, in the course of which the Bulgarians, who were completely success-ful, drove the enemy back from all their positions on the heights

PUNCH, OR THE LONDON CHARIVARI.—October 2, 1912.

THE BOILING POINT.

The cartoon is an apt comment on the mobilization of the Christian states of the Balkans
(Bulgaria, Greece, Montenegro and Serbia) against Turkey on 30 September 1912

above the pass; an incessant artillery duel, maintained ever since the
commencement of hostilities between the heavy Servian batteries

before Negotin and the Bulgarian forces garrisoning Widelin; and a very successful unopposed advance along the Vranja road as far as the Morava river by a Bulgarian force, composed of three brigades from Sofia, from Trn, and from Radomir, make up all there is to report of the campaign. For when hostilities were about to be opened this morning near Kumareno, which was evidently held by a large Servian force, an officer bearing a white towel, with a pink fringe, tied to a hedge stake, as a flag of truce, rode out from the Servian lines and demanded a *pourparler*. It then transpired that the Servians found themselves in a terrible quandary, and were at their wits' end what to do.

Late last night a large Austrian force had, without warning, crossed the Save into Belgrade, which city they had taken so completely by surprise that it was not until the morning that the populace was made aware of the presence of the strangers in their midst by the sight of the troops bivouacking in the squares, and the officers quietly breakfasting outside the principal cafés. An Austrian force, said the parlementaire, had also crossed the Danube to Semendria, and there were rumours that another force had crossed the same river at Orsova. In these circumstances, with their capital cut off from them, and their young king and government in a manner locked up, the Servian generals considered they had no alternative but to demand a suspension of hostilities, at least for forty-eight hours. An armistice was therefore granted, much to the Bulgarian leaders' annoyance and disgust.

We learn that Austria has notified the Powers that she has occupied Semendria and Belgrade as a precautionary measure, in view of the wanton aggression of Servia.

It is here considered unlikely that Bulgaria will have any more trouble from this quarter. On the other hand, however, grave rumours reach us from Constantinople, where apparently there is very great anxiety as to certain mysterious and as yet undefined threats by Russia. The Turkish capital is, as matters stand at present, likely to be the chief centre of interest for some time to come, and I shall therefore return there to-morrow morning.

All through the day long trains of Bulgarian and Servian wounded have crept one after another into Sofia. It is noteworthy that a considerable percentage of the sufferers are bright and lively and make light of their injuries. These are men who have been struck by the small nickel bullets of the new rifle, which has been used in pretty equal proportions on both sides.

RUSSIAN MOVEMENT UPON THE AUSTRIAN FRONTIER

MOBILISATION OF GERMAN ARMY CORPS—
WILD EXCITEMENT IN BERLIN

(By Telegraph from our Special Correspondent, Mr. Charles Lowe)

BERLIN, *April 21* (8.50 p.m.)

NEVER since the fateful days of July 1870 has so much excitement been caused here as by the news—which now seems to be beyond all doubt—that Russia, having received an evasive, or, as other telegrams put it, a flatly negative reply to her peremptory demand for the immediate evacuation of Belgrade by the Austrians, has already begun to move down immense masses of troops towards her south-western frontier; and it is even rumoured that a division of cavalry has suddenly made its appearance near the border, on the Warsaw–Cracow road, at a place called Xiaswielki. This is a grave situation, indeed, as alarming as it is sudden. The Unter den Linden, which is a perfect Babel with the bawling voices of the newsvendors, is rapidly filling with crowds rushing hither, as to the main channel of intelligence, from all parts of the city, and the Foreign Office in the Wilhelm-Strasse is besieged by a huge throng clamouring to hear the truth.

For on this depends the issue of peace or war for Germany. Let but Russia lay one single finger of aggression on Austria, and Germany must at once unsheathe her sword and spring to her ally's aid. Pray let there be no mistake as to the terms of the Austro-Germany Treaty of 1879, which was published a year or two ago, for it has often been misinterpreted. Under this instrument a *casus fœderis* does not arise for Germany in all and any circumstances of a war between Russia and Austria, but only in the event of the former being the aggressor; and it looks very much as though Russia were now seriously bent on taking the offensive. Does she really mean to do this? is the question on everyone's lips here, and the excitement of people is equal to their suspense. It is known that an active correspondence by wire is proceeding between here and Vienna, but the authorities are very reticent, and only beg the crowds to keep calm and hope for the best.

(9 p.m.)

I have just returned from the Schloss, whither the multitude, which was unable to gratify its curiosity at the Foreign Office, had surged along to pursue its eager inquiries, but only to find that the Emperor was closeted with his Chancellor, General Count von Caprivi, and

his Chief of the Staff, Count von Schlieffen.[3] It was remarked that
when both these magnates emerged from their interview with His
Majesty, and drove off at a rapid rate, they looked very serious and
preoccupied, paying but little heed to the cheering which greeted
their appearance. This only tended to deepen the apprehension of
the vast crowd in front of the Schloss, whose fears were further
augmented by a rumour (a true one, as I found on tracing it to its
source), which spread like lightning, that the Emperor had
telegraphed for the King of Saxony, the Prince Albrecht of Prussia,
the Prince-Regent of Brunswick—both Field-Marshals—as also for
Count Waldersee, Commander of the Ninth Army Corps in
Schleswig-Holstein, whom the Emperor, it may be remembered,
when parting with this distinguished officer, as Chief of the General
Staff, publicly designated as the Commander of a whole army in the
event of war.

(10 p.m.)

After despatching my last message, which I had the utmost difficulty
in doing owing to the frantic mass of newspaper correspondents of
all nationalities struggling desperately into and out of the Telegraph
Office, I had the good fortune to meet Baron von Marschall, the
amiable and accomplished Foreign Secretary, who favoured me with
a brief conversation on the momentous subject of the hour. Yes, he
said, it was unfortunately quite true that the Russians were rapidly
concentrating their forces towards the Austro-German frontier, and
that a sotnia of prying Cossacks, coming from Tarnogrod, had even
pushed forward on the Austrian side of the border towards Jaroslav,
an important railway junction point in Galicia. He had just received
intelligence to this effect from Prince Reuss, the German
Ambassador in Vienna, who added that things indeed looked their
very worst. 'But this', I remarked, 'is an act of invasion on the part
of Russia, is it not, and means war?' The Baron shook his head
ominously, and, with a kindly 'come and see me again to-morrow
morning', squeezed my hand and hurried off to see Count
Syéchényi at the Austrian Embassy, which stands over against the
former home of M. Benedetti, with all its associations connected
with the beginning of Germany's last great war.

On my way back to the Telegraph Office, where I write this, I
encountered, just at the entrance to the Russian Embassy, Unter
den Linden, its genial and honest occupant, Count Schouvaloff,
who was good enough to return my greeting by motioning me to
stop, and telling me that he had just been to see Count Caprivi,

and assure him, on the part of his Imperial master, that all these warlike preparations in Western Poland implied no menace whatever to Germany, with whom Russia had not the least cause of quarrel, but that, nevertheless, so long as Austria threatened to derange the balance of power in the Balkan Peninsula for her own selfish ends, Russia would be incriminating herself in the eyes of history if she stood by with folded hands and sought not to safeguard her most vital interests by all the means at her disposal. And, as Pitt had created a new world to redress the balance of the old, so Russia was now compelled to re-establish equilibrium in one part of the Eastern Continent of Europe by giving the would-be disturber of this equilibrium work enough to engross all his attention in another. 'These were not, of course, the very words', added the Count, 'which I used to the Chancellor, but they express the exact sense of my communication.'

(Midnight)

Berlin, which has poured all its teeming million-and-a-half into the streets, is at this hour a scene of the wildest excitement, owing to a rumour (and a friend of mine in the General Staff, whom I chanced to meet, confirmed the truth of the rumour), that the awful and electrifying words 'Krieg, mobil!' had (as in 1870) been already flashed again to no fewer than seven of the twenty Army Corps constituting the Imperial host—viz., to the 1st, or East Prussian; the 17th, West Prussian; the 3d, Brandenburg; the 4th, Province of Prussian Saxony; the 5th, Posen; the 6th, Silesian; and the 12th, Kingdom of Saxony.

Loud and long was the cheering in front of the Schloss—which is thronged by an ever-increasing and excited multitude—when this intelligence oozed out, and with one accord (for your Germans are a most wonderful people of trained choral-singers) the whole mighty assemblage burst forth with a battle-ballad in which some deft patriotic poet had been quick to embody the fears and determinations of the last few days under the title of 'Die Weichsel-Wacht', or the 'Watch on the Vistula'—a war-song which promises to fill as large and luminous a page among the lyric gems of the Fatherland as Schneckenburger's immortal 'Wacht am Rhein'. When the frantic cheering which followed the chanting of this stirring battle-anthem had subsided, the Emperor (who has now completely recovered from the accident to his knee) came out to bow his acknowledgements from the front balcony of the castle; and on his arm was the Empress holding the hand of the pretty little flaxen-haired Crown

Prince, who had been routed out of his warm bed at this late and chilly hour to add one crowning touch of spectacular effect to the *tableau* which, amid another frenzied outburst of 'hochs' and 'hurrahs', thus closed the drama of a most exciting and momentous day.

WARLIKE EXCITEMENT IN PARIS

(By Telegraph from our Special Correspondent, Mr. D. Christie Murray)

PARIS, *April 30*

Paris to-night is in a state of the maddest ferment. For some days past the public have followed with breathless interest the rapid development of events on the Russo-German frontier, and the news of the first skirmish at Alexandrovo, which was printed in *Le Soir* this evening, has roused the wildest enthusiasm. Long and anxious consultations of Ministers have been held daily, and the Press, with hardly an exception, have been urging on the Government an immediate declaration of war. Many of the better-class Germans have been hurrying from Paris—a precaution which, in the issue, has been shown to be judicious. When to-day's news became known, every trade and artifice was instantly abandoned, and the streets since three o'clock till now have been thronged by vast crowds, pulsating to a more and more impassioned excitement. By four o'clock there were literally fifty thousand people standing in the street with newspapers in their hands, and every reader was the centre of an excited throng. I was standing opposite the Vaudeville when a man, bearing a prodigious bundle of newspapers wet from the press, came staggering swiftly towards the kiosque. The mob fell upon him, despoiled him of his burden, and tore open his parcel. There was such a wild hurry to learn the news, and everybody was so eager to be first with it, that scores of the journals were torn to ribbons, and hundreds more were trampled into the mud of the pavement. The proprietress of the kiosque wrung her hands and wept over the spectacle, and a gentleman who, by pressure of the crowd, was forced half-way through one of the windows, vociferously demanded to know the value of the lost journals. The woman instantly became business-like, and appraised them roughly at a hundred francs. The gentleman produced a pocket-book and paid her twice over, shouting noisily, 'I present this glorious news to Paris! *Vive la Russie! À bas la Prusse!*' That was the first signal I heard, and in one minute the whole boulevard rang with frenzied roar on roar. Omnibuses, public carriages, and vehicles of every description were wedged immovably in the crowd which thronged the horse-road. The drivers rose from their seats, the passengers and occupants of the carriages stood up in their places and roared and gesticulated with the rest. Hundreds of people at once strove to make speeches, and the combined result was such a *charivari* as can scarcely have been heard since the great day of the Confusion of Tongues.

I, myself, had occasion to be thankful for that unconquerable English accent which has always disfigured my French. A blond beard and spectacles have always helped me to something of a German look, and to-day has given the few Germans who happen to be left in Paris such a scare as the bravest of them is not likely to forget. At one moment I was surrounded by a wild section of the mob, whose yells of 'Down with Prussia!' were far too obviously intended to be personal to me. There was nothing for it but to join in the shouting, and I cried *'Vive la France!'* and *'À bas la Prusse!'* as lustily as any of them. There was an instantaneous laugh at the English accent, and I was left alone; but I could not help thinking what would have happened had I chanced to learn my French mainly in Berlin rather than in London. One unfortunate German is reported fatally injured by the violence of a mob at the Gare du Nord. He had booked for London, and is said to have carried with him only a small handbag, and to have left all the rest of his belong-ings at the hotel, in his hurry to catch the train for Calais. The director of the Opera came near to paying with his life for his artis-tic allegiance to Wagner. Happily for him, he was able to take refuge in the house of a friend, and the mob contented itself by keeping up a ceaseless boo-hooing for an hour or more.

EXTRAORDINARY SCENE IN THE
PLACE DE LA CONCORDE

The wildest manifestation of the afternoon was in the Place de la Concorde, where an immense mob fell to dancing about the statue of Strasburg. Everybody knows the sullen threat with which that statue has been placarded for so many years. It runs 'L.D.P. (the initials standing for "Ligue de Patriotes") Qui Vive? La France. 1870–18--'. When the prodigious noise created by the mob seemed at its highest, it was cloven, as it were, by a din still greater, and a solid phalanx of men forced a way into the already crowded square. In the centre of this phalanx twenty or thirty men marched, bearing a long ladder, the heads of many of them being thrust between the

'Extraordinary scene in the Place de la Concorde. The mob tearing down emblems from
the statue of Strasburg'

rungs. In the middle of the ladder was seated a working painter in a
blue blouse. The man was literally wild with excitement, and was
roaring 'Quatre vingt douze' to a sort of mad, improvised tune, in
which the packed marchers about him joined with the full stress of

their lungs. In one hand the man flourished aloft a pot of red paint, with the contents of which he occasionally bedewed his unheeding companions, some of whom had playfully bedaubed their own and others' features, so that they looked as if they had just come fresh from some scene of massacre. In the other hand the man held aloft a sheaf of brushes, and in an instant the vast crowd seized the motive of his presence there, and the meaning of the rhythmic repetition of *'Quatre vingt douze!'*

A way was cleared for the advancing cohort as if by magic. The ladder, still supporting the painter, was drawn up lengthwise before the statue, and the workman knelt to his task. At first it was impossible for him to work, for the bearers of the ladder were jigging to the tune they sang; but by and by they were persuaded to be quiet, and a very striking and impressive silence fell upon the crowd. The man, with great deliberation, and with a much firmer hand than he might have been supposed to own at a time of such excitement, drew the outline of the figures 9 and 2 in white chalk, at as great a size as the space of the placard admitted. His movements were watched with an actually breathless interest, and when, after the completion of his drawing, he rose and clasped the knees of the statue in his arms with a joyful and affectionate cry, two or three people in my neighbourhood sobbed aloud. The man knelt down again and filled in with red paint the outline he had drawn. One grim personage, with a squint and a pock-marked face, who held a short, well-blacked clay between his teeth, shouldered me at this moment, and said, 'C'est le sang de la France, ça.' He thought so well of this that he moved away among the crowd repeating it, nudging his neighbours to call attention to the saying, and pointing a dirty forefinger at the red paint of the figures to indicate its meaning. I was waiting for an outburst of enthusiasm when the figures were completed, but to my amazement the mob accepted the proclamation they conveyed with a grave silence, as if it had been in some way authentic and official, and as if for the first time they recognised the terrible significance of the hour. Their quiet did not endure long, for one of their number, having contrived to scramble on to the ladder, clambered up the statue, and amid great cheers tore from it the ragged emblems of mourning which have so long disfigured it.

Then came an episode, the like of which would be possible nowhere but in Paris. The whole thing might have been arranged for scenic effect, and the distinguished artist who made the *coup* had never, brilliant as his triumphs have been, arrived on the stage at so opportune a moment, or encountered so overwhelming a reception.

The newcomer was no other than M. Jean de Reszke, who was on his way to dine with a friend before appearing as Faust in Gounod's masterpiece this evening.[4] His coachman was slowly making way along the crowded road when the great singer was recognised. He was greeted with a roar of applause, and a dozen members of the crowd threw open the closed landau he sat in, while a thousand voices clamoured for the *Marseillaise*. The statue had, at that instant, been denuded of its last rag of mourning, and M. de Reszke, who had risen bareheaded in the carriage, was whipped out of it in a trice, and borne, *nolens volens*, to the figure, and placed aloft on the pedestal. His companion, a lady attired with much distinction, was at first evidently alarmed, but soon gathered the peaceful intention of the crowd, and, seizing the meaning of the moment, she stripped from her own shoulders a handsome scarlet cloak, and threw it towards M. de Reszke. It was immediately passed on to him, and he, with considerable difficulty, and at the risk of a tumble on the heads of the people below him, succeeded in casting the cloak over the shoulders of the statue. At this, all the previous noises which cleft the air of Paris this afternoon seemed as nothing. The cheering was simply deafening and maddening, and lasted for full three minutes. At length perfect silence was restored, and M. de Reszke began to sing the *Marseillaise*. He was pale at first, and obviously unstrung at the spectacle of this prodigious audience, and for the first few notes his voice was broken and ineffective. He gathered confidence, however, before he had completed the singing of the first line, and gave the rest of the song with an inspiring vigour and *élan*.

By 30 April Germany is at war with France and Russia. The neutrality of Belgium is the most urgent question for the United Kingdom.

PUBLIC FEELING IN ENGLAND

DEBATE IN THE HOUSE

LONDON, *May 3*

WHILE, thus armed and fortified, France and Germany stand watching each other across the Rhine, we in England remain in a suspense profounder than we have experienced any time this side of the Napoleonic wars. The political excitement during the last few days has been intense, and, at the prospect now imminent of the violation of the neutrality of Belgium, has set the country by the ears. The people, the Press, and the politicians of England are deeply stirred, and the crowded public meeting, called at a few hours' notice, which was held yesterday in London is a proof, if proof were needed, that the Government will be compelled by popular feeling to strain every nerve to avert from 'gallant little Belgium' the violation of that neutrality, to the maintenance of which Britain stands pledged. The opposition press, ablaze with zeal for the honour of England now that there seems an opening for the charge of supineness against the Government, shrieks in scathing leaders that the voice of the nation should enforce on the *fainéant* Ministry its imperative duty of addressing vehement remonstrances to the Great Teuton power. The journals favourable to the Government cannot refrain from addressing strong representations to the Cabinet regarding the uncertain future of Antwerp if Belgium is again to become the cockpit of Europe, and the standing menace to Britain which that great fortress will become if it pass into other hands than those of the Belgians. The House, too, appears equally moved, and not a day has passed but at the question hour a rattle of shrewish interpellations has been shot across the House at the target of the Treasury Bench. The inexplicable composure of Her Majesty's Ministers has, however, at length, broken down before the insistence of the Opposition.

On Tuesday, when the German mobilisation over against the eastern frontier of Belgium was well forward, and when there remained no longer any doubt that the army gathering there would traverse that State, Sir William Harcourt rose in his place, every eye in the House centred on him, and with portentous earnestness of aspect and manner, demanded that the Leader of the House should name an early day for a debate on 'the grave international questions and eventualities connected with the imminent violation of the neutrality of Belgium, and the attitude of the ministry in relation to those questions and eventualities'. Sir William reseated himself with, indeed, a brow of care and gravity, as beseemed a statesman dealing with a momentous crisis; but the lower section of his expressive visage mantled with a conscious complacency which seemed to indicate a conviction that he had propounded something in the nature of a 'settler' for this apparently inertest of Governments. 'Take to-morrow, if you like,' drawled the Leader of the House without rising, and then he actually and visibly yawned. The smirk faded out of Sir William's face at the roar of laughter, irrepressible on the part of the Liberals and Conservatives alike, which followed Mr. Balfour's drawl and yawn.[5]

The Opposition papers have vied in vituperation of Mr. Balfour's *insouciance*, which they described as 'insolence', 'impertinence', and 'insult'. One provincial journal congratulates Sir William Harcourt on his self-restraint in having refrained from pulling Mr. Balfour's nose, and another, with startling novelty, compares the latter to Nero fiddling while Rome was burning. But yesterday's scene in the House has shown, at least, that the Government, though composed, has not been indifferent. It must have been galling to many of the hot-brained to have observed that, when in the afternoon Mr. Balfour lounged into the crowded House, he showed no symptoms of being crushed, or even perturbed, by this avalanche of invective. In opening the debate, the ordinarily bland and gentle Sir William Harcourt displayed a truculent aggressiveness which startled all listeners, so foreign was it to his previously disclosed nature. When he had finished, and the dust had settled a little, Mr. Balfour slowly rose. He spoke as follows:

> Her Majesty's Government were confidentially informed a year ago, both by Germany and Belgium, that those two States had concluded a secret convention, in terms of which, in case of war between Germany and France, Belgium was to permit German troops to pass through her territory and to utilise her railways. It no doubt is a question whether Belgium has any right thus to permit the violation of her neutrality guaranteed by the Great Powers, but the question in the circumstances is an abstract one. Who is to intervene to hinder her? Not Germany, who has made a bargain with her for the right of violation. Not France, who violated Belgian neutrality with impunity in 1870, and who, if she now is ready in time, will, in her anxiety to fight the Germans outside the French frontier, assuredly violate it again—if, indeed, the act can be termed violation when the neutrality is virtually dead already by Belgium's own act. In eastern Europe there is other business on hand just now, than solicitude for the protection of Belgian neutrality. Does the right hon. baronet propose that England should undertake this task single-handed, and, *inter alia*, force Belgium against her will to co-operate with us in retrieving the neutrality she has already surrendered? We should, and in hostility to Belgium, stand alone, in an attempt to make good the guarantee we entered into conjointly with other Powers; and I say frankly that this is not a Quixotic Government.
>
> But when we were informed, in strict confidence, of this convention, we took measures for the interest and protection of Great Britain. Those measures may give umbrage in certain quarters; that we cannot help. We claimed and obtained from Belgium the right to occupy and garrison the great fortress of

Antwerp if the convention alluded to should become operative, and to hold that fortress pending the solution of the momentous events now clearly impending on the Continent of Europe. We recognised the impossibility of enduring in Antwerp a possibly hostile neighbour so close to our own street-door, and we resolved and have secured the right to be our own neighbour over the way in the troublous times approaching. During the past week we have been quietly and unostentatiously making some needful preparations. These are now so forward that I may inform the House that a complete division of British infantry and artillerymen 15,000 strong will be embarked at sundry of our ports on the day after to-morrow, and will land at Antwerp on the following morning, being conveyed swiftly in steam transports under the convoy of the Channel Squadron. The division will sail fully equipped with an adequate supply of stores. Its commander will be a soldier whose name and fame are familiar to us all; I refer to that distinguished officer, Sir Evelyn Wood. The Belgians hand us over Antwerp as it stands, with fortress, artillery, ammunition, and all appliances for defensive operations which we fervently pray and trust that there shall be no occasion to engage in.

The cheering throughout Mr. Balfour's short but pregnant speech had been frequent and hearty; when he sat down it swelled in volume and force that seemed to shake the roof. Sir William Harcourt, with the best grace he could assume, professed himself satisfied, and the debate collapsed.

Late last night it was reported that the Government asked and received powers to enlist 20,000 men, and to call out for duty a large number of militia battalions.

The narrative turns to forecasting the most likely form of land warfare.

NIGHT ATTACK BY THE RUSSIANS
FIGHTING BY THE ELECTRIC LIGHT—ROUT OF
GENERAL GOURKO—RETREAT UPON WARSAW

(*By Telegraph from our Special Correspondent, Mr. Charles Lowe*)

ALEXANDROVO, *May* 7
(5 a.m.)

The German Army of the Vistula has just inflicted on the Russians another Plevna, and they are now in full retreat towards Warsaw.

Such, in brief, is the result of the sanguinary night battle of which I have just been a witness. The Russians were the first to practise night attacks as a means of obviating the dreadful losses certain to result from magazine-rifle fire during the day, but they will long have cause to remember their first serious application of the nocturnal principle of modern warfare.

By seven o'clock last night the 3d and 4th German Corps had completed their concentration at and near this place, and, after extending the lines of entrenchment begun by the 6th Division on capturing Alexandrovo, had gone into fireless bivouac on both sides of the railway line, their tents extending for about a couple of miles in either direction. Several reconnaissances executed by us during the day had elicited that the Russians were marshalling in great force at a place called Waganiek, and were receiving reinforcements from the right bank of the Vistula, by means of a pontoon bridge which had been thrown across the stream a little higher up, at Dobrowniki; but, owing to the dense masses of cavalry which hovered on their front, concealing their movements as a stage curtain hides from view the shifting of the scenes in a theatre, it was impossible for our scouts to bring back more definite information. One item, however, of their intelligence, gathered from a captured Cossack, had a special interest for us, to wit, that the Russian forces immediately in front of us consisted mainly of the 5th and 6th Corps, with part of the 4th (including the relics of Grodnovodsky's brigade), and were under the personal command of General Gourko, the hero of the Balkans.[6] On the strength of this information it was decided to attack Gourko before he got his preparations complete, and for this purpose to break bivouac, and start in quest of him at the dawn of day, as Prince Frederick Charles had done with Benedek at Sadowa.

I had spent the evening with a particular friend of mine, Captain von Jagdkönig, of Stülpnagel's Brandenburg Infantry Regiment, and was just on the point of setting out with him on a visit of inspection among the foreposts, when a Uhlan dashed up with the intelligence that there were signs of a mysterious commotion in front, and that something was audible in the otherwise noiseless night like the distant rumbling of waggon and cannon wheels. Anon other messengers from the front came spurring in with similar news, and as the general purport of all these 'Meldungen' could no longer be doubted, the bugles were at once set to work, and presently all the silent bivouacs, taking up the shrilling war-note one after the other, like the multiplication of a distant echo, were resonant with the thrilling call to arms; and thanks to the severe training in the discipline of 'alarms' which the German army has been put through by the present Emperor since his accession to the throne, the army of the Vistula had all started from its sleep and was standing in perfect battle array, with its face to the suspected foe, within ten minutes of the first trumpet summons.

The night was intensely dark, the moon having just gone down behind an impenetrable bank of pitchy clouds, and all fighting seemed to be utterly out of the question. Presently, however, the inky darkness all around us was pierced, one may almost say scattered, by a sudden blaze of light, which, appearing to possess all the illuminating power of the mid-day sun, flashed lightning-like upon us its blinding beams from the murky forehead of the midnight sky. 'The electric light!' ran from mouth to mouth, after a moment's bewildered pause, while every one instinctively shaded his eyes from the glare of this all-irradiating and all-penetrating lamp which modern science had thus hung up to facilitate the work of slaughter, as if the very sun refused to look any longer upon human carnage. For some moments the more than mile-long rays of this blinding ball of light, this detective bull's-eye of modern science, swept round the horizon in front of it, as if uncertain where to fix its focus—now shooting beyond, now falling short of us, and anon settling on us and suffusing us with a sea of dazzling light. Presently another, and yet another such luminary burst forth from elevations of pretty equal distances in front of us, and the process of their groping about for our lines revealed to us dense masses of grey and dark-green coated battalions picking their cautious way down the distant slopes in front of us. For the electric light has this disadvantage, that in flinging its beams about to discover the locality of foes, it frequently at the same time unveils the whereabouts of friends. This was the case here, but our gunners were on the alert, and next time the focus of the light, in its jerky search-movement, fell on the Russian troops in the course of their stealthy advance towards us, we opened the concert with a screaming chorus of shells, accompanied by a rattling orchestration of small-arms.

Nor had we long to wait for the antiphon; for next time the search light managed to flood us with its blinding effulgence, the Russian batteries, which had been planted on the same elevations, gave lusty voice, and bellowed away at us in most leonine fashion, though their projectiles, being aimed at much too long a range, flew high over our heads and left us scatheless. Not so, however, the rifle-rain of our enemies, which, first in intermittent showers, and then in a steady downpour, began to fall among our ranks with deadly effect; and the word was passed from flank to flank for all the infantry to lie down and court the shelter of our field intrenchments, which crested the ridge of our line of battle.

Between us and the Russian infantry there intervened a depression in the ground, a little deeper than that which separates Mont St. Jean from Belle Alliance; but what enhanced the value of this ground to our foes was the fact that their batteries in the rear, planted as they were on the electric light elevations overlooking the terrain, could fire over the heads of their infantry till the latter was pretty well within storming distance of our position, much in the same way as the guns of the 6th Division had been able to do the other day on the occasion of our first engagement, which resulted in the capture of Alexandrovo.

The Russians advanced against us with a steady, stolid courage worthy of the men who had essayed to capture the Sand Bag Battery and storm the redoubts of Plevna; and as the fitful flashes of the electric light revealed to us, for a few moments at a time, their dense battalions advancing and deploying into the fighting-lines demanded by modern tactics and the rules of fire-discipline, I could not help thinking of that cold and dark November morning when, without the aid of the electric light, they crowded to their doom, with the same dreadnought and devoted bravery, up the slippery slopes of Inkerman.

It was not long before the roar of the cannon on both sides became outvoiced almost by the reverberating rattle of musketry, which was all the more bewildering, as only the very faintest flashes of flame from the smokeless powder of both sides served to indicate the exact position of the opposing lines of infantry fire; and it was only when a new turn of the electric light (which, by-the-bye, might have changed the course of Egyptian history, had Arabi enjoyed the advantage of it at Tel-el-Kebir) registered the progress of the Russian advance, that we could make out the development of a battle in which unity of command was simply impossible, and each captain had to be his own general officer.

The development of a modern battle is a very slow process, and this one was doubly so from the fact, due to the utter darkness in which each side was occasionally enveloped, that there was much random and ineffective firing on both parts. But there came a point of time in the Russian advance when the manipulators of their electric lights found it impossible to illumine our lines without also including the Russians within the Asmodean sweep of their rays, and then it was that our men, seizing their opportunity, plied their magazine rifles with infernal industry and effect.

But this opportunity did not last long, for suddenly the four midnight suns of Science, of far more dazzling splendour than the tourist orbs of the North Cape, which had been rendering possible the work of slaughter, disappeared from our firmament as completely as if they had been blazing torches plunged into a pool of ink; and their disappearance was followed by a brief period of almost painful silence which overspread the broad and lengthy field of battle.

We never doubted that this pall of pitchy darkness had thus been suddenly thrown around the battle-field to enable our foes to make another rush towards us, unimpeded by the accurate aim of shell and bullet; and a curious thrill, half of pleasure, half of undefined dread, went shooting through our veins when, as we were listening intently, peering into the impenetrable darkness beyond, our ears were struck by a faint peculiar tinkling as if of jangled metal rods, and the meaning thereof at once became clear to us. The Russians were fixing bayonets, preparatory to a charge on our position; and the sound was quickly answered by the loud and stern command: '*Aufpflanzen!*' which ran all along our lines, and was likewise followed by a repetition, on our side, of the clinking and sharp clicking above alluded to.

Scarcely had silence in the ranks been again restored when another order: 'Load for magazine-fire!' rang out in stentorian tones, and at the same time, almost, the electric lights were again flashed full upon us, converting darkness into open day, and showing us the Russians striding swiftly towards us in successive irregular waves of ever-increasing volume, the nearest to us being hardly more than a hundred and fifty yards off. On they came firing all the way, equally regardless of the awful volcanoes of shrapnel which our batteries belched forth against them and of the terrific torrent of our small-bore bullets, aimed from behind the comparative shelter of field-trench parapets, which incessantly tore through their stolid ranks, mowing them down and massacring them by thousands. It was impossible for them to preserve anything like their proper formation under these trying circumstances, and disorder was spreading rapidly among their irregular ranks; but the swaying, struggling masses of the grey and green-coated soldiery of the Czar still came surging stubbornly up the slope, ever lessening the distance between them and our entrenchments, till the moment at last seemed come when they should hurl themselves upon us and try conclusions with the cold steel. And then, as if by instinct more than pre-concert, the whole surging masses raised a tremendous shout, and rushed full upon us with the bayonet.

But when only about twenty paces in front of us, their onward career was suddenly stopped short by some invisible barrier, which made them crowd upon each other like penned cattle, passive targets for the bullets of our repeating rifles that rained upon them thick and fast as hail, knocking them over like so many rabbits in a ride. This barrier, which thus strangely stemmed the rush of their storming tide, was composed of fencing wire of several coils, strongly stretched and impaled, which had been run along all the front of our entrenched lines as an additional measure of defence against the contingency of such an attack, and formed one of the most recent innovations in the field warfare of the Germans—an innovation which had commended itself to the Emperor, who himself put it to a practical and approved test at the autumn manoeuvres of last year.

A yell of savage fury rose from the storming columns of the Russians, who had thus been stopped in their career and baulked of their objective in this most bloody and calamitous manner; and though the impact of succeeding waves of assailants soon levelled all the wire fencing with the ground, still the mass momentum of their charge had been diminished, their dogged courage had also been shaken by the busy doings of Death among their huddled ranks during their temporary check; but worst of all, before the Russians could recover the force of their forward rush, the Germans were out of their entrenchments and upon them with the bayonet.

A few moments of grim and ghastly hand-to-hand fighting then ensued—and let it never after this be said that the bayonet has been entirely supplanted by the bullet; but I had only time to observe that Gourko's brave—I was almost going to say indomitable—troops were beginning to waver, to go down, to yield before the forceful push of the Teutonic pike, when suddenly again the electric lights of the Russians were turned off, and the dark curtain of night, in mercy to the vanquished, fell upon the bloody drama.

Pursuit by the Germans in such circumstances was quite impossible, but, recovering their ranks with singular precision, they sent salvo after salvo of artillery and musketry in the direction of the retreating foe, until the 'Cease firing' was sounded all along our victorious line as the faint and startled dawn began to blush—as if for very shame at such infernal work; and the bugle-sounds were supplemented by the shrill whistles of the company commanders, reminding me of the days when I loved to listen to the clean piping of the darting water-ousel among the rocky streams of the Grampians, amid scenes unsullied by the bloody hand of war.

When the day broke the results of the nocturnal battle revealed themselves in all their ghastly horrors; but, beyond saying that about 10,000 dead and wounded Russians lay in front of our extended lines, and nearly a third of that number of Germans in and about our own entrenchments, I will not disgust your readers with a realistic description of the ghastliness of the battle-field—the first of its kind, and one which has resulted from an endeavour to neutralise, or at least minimise, the destructive effects of the murderous magazine-rifle.

On 14 May British troops land at Trebizonde to support the Turks against the Russians. This action causes Russia and France to declare war on Great Britain. A naval engagement soon follows in the Mediterranean. An account of the action comes 'From an Officer in Sir George Tryon's Fleet'.

THE RAMMING OF THE 'AMIRAL BAUDIN'

It was just after daylight on the morning of the fourth day that a sort of cheering cry of 'The enemy are at sea!' ran all through the ships. Up went the simple signal 'Weigh', and there was really a horrible contrast between our anxiety and eagerness and the unmoved grind and crunch as link by link the cables came slowly in. But this was soon over, and we were at sea, forming at once in two lines ahead, as before arranged. The report was that the French had left Toulon twelve hours before, steering about S.E., but it had not been possible to count their numbers owing to the darkness. We steamed due east at half-speed; but it was plain to us all that if the French passed through the Straits of Bonifacio we might easily miss them, even though our cruisers were well spread out both ahead and astern. While we were in the middle of debate, down there rolled upon us as dense a fog as ever I saw in the Mediterranean. The Admiral had provided for this as for everything else, and we knew that we must preserve order with the steam syrens only, without the aid of guns; but as it was no use keeping speed, we slowed down. We were like this all day and all night, and at daylight it seemed as thick as ever. The ships had of course been all cleared for action, and we were ready to open fire in a minute, though one naturally prayed that the fog would lift before the enemy appeared. At 8 a.m. it began to clear, and at 9 we distinctly counted twenty-one steam-ships to the south of us. The flag-ship immediately made the signal for eight knots, and gradually altered course towards the strange fleet. We were soon able to make them out as sixteen French battle-ships, in the indented line abreast, steering south, with five cruisers in front of them. They were smoking up a good deal, but at ten or twelve miles distance we could not tell whether they were going at speed.

We soon found they were not, for we began to gain on them, and the signal was made for ten knots. We could tell by the position of the steam cones that every ship had steam to spare, and I suppose it was the desire of making sure of a compact fleet which kept us at comparatively low speed. Even at ten knots we continued to gain considerably. We were quite two miles off when the French began to open fire from their stern guns, and I am bound to say we were all very much surprised at the bad shots. They fell short and over, right and left, but after quite an hour few ships apparently had been badly hit.

We were still in two lines ahead and were making no reply at all to the French fire. We could not understand, when we had got within 3,000 yards, why the Admiral did not put us in line abreast and open fire. But in the middle of our wonder we suddenly saw the French ships open out to right and left, and before we knew where we were the whole mass of the battle-ships were coming right down upon us. We saw at once that it was in anticipation of some such manoeuvre that we had not quitted our first formation.

But the wisdom of our Admirals was at once shown. Orders were given to train the guns abeam and to let the enemy have it at the closest range, abstaining from fire till then. The French, on the other hand, never ceased to fire; but the smoke they made so surrounded them that it was plain they were wasting their ammunition, and did not see so well where they were going. But the rapidity of approach was tremendous, and I could note it as I had no guns to look after and could see nearly all round from the sheltered spot I had chosen.

My ship was near the middle of the port line, and I soon saw the great jet of smoke from the *Trafalgar*, followed by the roar which denoted the simultaneous discharge of a whole broadside. In less than half a minute there was the puff and the roar of the second ship, the *Collingwood*, and almost immediately I saw that the *Nile*, at the head of the other line, had fired. But then I directly saw what I had not been prepared for. I saw the *Nile* turning round sharp to port, and, looking to the head of my own line, I saw the *Trafalgar* steaming along our line on the opposite course to ours. It flashed through my mind like a shot, that every ship was turning round after she had fired her broadside, and that consequently the heads of the French lines or groups, after running the gauntlet of our lines, would be met by the ships that had first fired on them, and that as the battle had begun by the ships passing in opposite directions, it would be continued by all the ships with their heads in the same direction.

I do not pretend to say that I knew what all this meant at the moment; indeed, I did not know anything in another minute, for the roar and shake of the whole of our guns, trained on the port beam, knocked the power of thinking out of me. Recovering myself in a cloud of choking smoke, I was first aware that there must have been very little reply to our fire, but two signalmen were stretched on the deck beside me, both quite still; one with his shoulder torn entirely away, and the other bleeding profusely from a wound in his head. There were also, as if through the ship, new sorts of voices which, in hurried and confused utterance, warned me that there were death and wounds elsewhere.

But there was no time to think of it. We were wheeling round after our next ahead; and out of the dense smoke which we were leaving issued stray missiles tearing past, and sometimes striking

Damaged and sinking vessels after the engagement between British and French forces in the Battle of Sardinia

davits or stanchions, or shattering the planking of a boat. There was nothing, in fact, now but a roar of guns all round us, and we were covered with a canopy of smoke. The sole design perceptible was that we were only firing into the smoke to starboard, and no missiles were coming from the port side, while every now and then we got a glimpse of our next ahead and next astern.

As we steamed on, messages went from the captain to the lieutenants not to fire any more till they could see the enemy; and it was becoming clear that the French fire was ceasing, though whereabouts they were could hardly be ascertained. Presently, however, we found ourselves quite clear of smoke and could see then that the French ships must, most of them, have stopped, for our vessels—as well as could be seen—were nearly in their old formations, while the French were well astern, still somewhat entangled by the smoke, and evidently in some confusion.

Out of this smoke there quickly emerged a ship, which we made out to be the flag-ship *Formidable* with a considerable heel to port and steering to the N.W.

With the general signal flying that the Division was to continue its course, the *Trafalgar* suddenly put on steam and went after the *Formidable* full speed. The two ships were now in close action and enveloped in smoke, so that we could only make out their positions occasionally, the *Trafalgar* apparently hanging on the starboard quarter of the *Formidable*. The firing did not last more than ten minutes or a quarter of an hour, when, the smoke clearing away, it was seen that the *Formidable*'s colours were down.

What had happened we only knew afterwards. The *Formidable* had been badly torpedoed in passing, and was steaming as she hoped out of action when we saw her. As the *Trafalgar* approached, she made a short gallant defence with her guns, and fired two torpedoes at her; but the water was rising in the stoke-holds, and it was impossible to keep steam. Admiral Markham, seeing plainly what the case was, passed close under the *Formidable*'s stern, and hailed to claim surrender in the interests of humanity, or he would ram and sink her. It was the chance of war, and there was nothing but surrender before our gallant opponent.

Meantime it was plain to be seen how well Sir George Tryon's orders had worked. Some of our ships were frightfully knocked about, and the *Benbow* was almost in a sinking state from a number of shot-holes between wind and water; while the *Edinburgh* was all down by the head, having caught a torpedo near the stem, but the whole of the ships were in two lines as they entered into action, and they now re-formed and headed towards the French, leaving the *Benbow, Edinburgh,* and the prize French flag-ship together, attended by two or three of the cruisers.

But the most frightful incident of the battle took place in the other line, and I was not an eye-witness of it. I have not mentioned the *Polyphemus* before, but she was with us and sailed with us. It seems Sir George Tryon's orders to her were simply to keep out of the way in the first instance, and to strike home should any opportunity offer. Captain Brooke, it appears, running out to starboard of the Admiral's column, saw his chance in the smoke, and ran straight at the nearest French ship, whose attention was taken up by the fire of our ships on her other side. The shock was horrible, and she scarce had time to extricate herself, when the *Amiral Baudin* reeled and sank.[7]

Two German army corps cross the Meuse and advance towards Paris. The French fail to halt them at Machault in a drill-book engagement: infantry advancing in close order, horse artillery at the gallop, cavalry regiments charging in squadrons, trumpets and rolling drums, and all over in two hours.

THE BATTLE OF MACHAULT

GREAT GERMAN VICTORY

(*From our Special Correspondent with the Germans*)

DRICOURT, *May 11*

The gunners were moving long before daylight, and I went with them. Dawn was just breaking when we reached the summit of the rolling ridge which marks our front, and we could still see signs of bivouac fires burnt low on another and almost parallel wave some 2,000 to 3,000 yards to our front. The bottom of the hollow is steeper and we cannot see into it, but they tell me our Infantry are down there.

Our position faces N.N.W. by S.S.E., so again we shall have the sun at our backs. Some of our guns are entrenched, and I notice the intervals between them are wider than usual, probably, as before, to ward against the melinite shells.

Of our strategic position, all I know is that we have a Corps on either flank, and two within supporting distance—what the 2d Army is doing I don't know.

I was obliged to break off my dispatch abruptly, owing to the sudden development of events. I had just written the last line when the first gun went off about ten minutes before sunrise, and for an hour an incessant roar of artillery raged. The French shot well, but the sun in their eyes gave them never a chance.

I had now time and daylight enough to look round. Our troops were all carefully under cover at least 2,000 yards to the rear, mostly in rendezvous formations, waiting. Of the enemy I could only see his guns, and when the sun rose high enough, one could distinctly make out the line of an entrenchment just at the break of the long slope into the hollow. Even then I might not have noticed it but for the indiscretion of its occupants, who would keep moving about. It may have been about six o'clock when I saw, out of the hollows away to the rear, three great columns rise up, which proved to be six batteries of Artillery each. They trotted forward, forming line to the front, and then I realised that I was at length about to see a real Napoleonic battle, the blow to pierce the centre or fail.

Nearing the outer edge of the zone, where the splinters of bursting shells meant for us began to be dangerous, the gallop was sounded, and the whole eighteen batteries dashed forward in superb form. Our guns increased their fire to the utmost extremity, shrouding the enemy's front in the smoke of their shells, and then ceased for a few moments as the new arrivals passed through the intervals, resuming it again as soon as they were clear, and maintaining it at this extreme rate till it was seen that the others had unlimbered and were ready to take their part in the action at a range of about 1,500 yards. This move brought them, however, to within 1,000 yards of the enemy's advanced Infantry, and we saw many drop; but our own advanced posts had been reinforced by small driblets, too insignificant to attract the enemy's artillery fire, and these with the aid of a few guns that could now be spared soon took the edge off the French Infantry fire.

In fifteen minutes or less, the effect of these eighteen fresh batteries was plainly apparent; to stay where they were meant for the French gunners' annihilation, and that was not their business, and presently we saw their teams come up by alternate batteries. In the crowd of men and horses thus assembled our shells made terrible havoc, and probably not one-third of the guns were successfully withdrawn. Then the whole power of our sixty batteries was turned on the Infantry, and we had the 'defender's dilemma' before us. He could not retire his Infantry up the slope, for that meant beginning the action with a retreat; and he could not leave them there unsupported, for that would mean annihilation; his only chance was to move troops down the slope to reinforce them—and presently we saw them coming. Then a repetition of yesterday's slaughter began.

Had we known for certain what was going on out of our sight, we might have been content to let the foe bleed himself to death in these fruitless efforts; but we did not, we could only guess that he would be moving forward his reinforcements of all arms with all haste, and our game was to crush what was before us as quickly as might be.

Our Infantry were now rapidly coming up, the two divisions side by side, the brigades of each in the same order, with their regiments each one behind the other. The leading regiment had two battalions in first line and one in support, and the foremost battalions, each two companies in front and two behind, in company column. As the troops approached our guns they formed line and came forward, their drums beating, with the strictest possible discipline, for the bullets were flying in showers overhead, and men were constantly dropping.

The lines went down the slope with about 500 paces between them, and as the leading one reached the advanced posts, the latter rose, and, with a cheer, dashed down into the hollow, where they found shelter for a moment in the dead angle at the foot of the slope. Our gunners now turned their fire on the Infantry trench for a few moments with high explosive shells, and then the whole crowd of men in the hollow rose and rushed it at the point of the bayonet, clearing it in a moment and pursuing beyond. Then came the turn of the French, and gallantly they availed themselves of it. Our rapid advance had masked our guns, the French falling back before it had been taken up by their supports, and, now having only Infantry to deal with, the whole of them turned and came on again.

It did not come to cold steel, however, for again both sides stopped and blazed into each other with magazine fire and astounding inaccuracy. The air above our heads seemed alive with bullets—but our reserves were coming up under cover, and those of the French moving down hill caught many of the missiles that flew too high. Soon, perhaps in five minutes, the whole body, both assailants and defenders, began to move slowly up the hill, the movement never ceasing till our Infantry reached the top. Our Horse Artillery, followed by our Divisional Cavalry, galloped forward in support. What happened for the next few minutes I am unable to state from observation, for I, too, was moving across the valley, and looking for a reasonably secure spot from which to see further. I found one at the junction between two French Corps, where a copse came right up to the edge of their line—both Corps being hotly engaged in front had wheeled inwards a little towards the centre, and there was a gap of some 500 yards, and not a soul on the look-out. From here I could take in the whole situation. To the south-eastward guns flashing and heavy masses of troops showed the battle extended for miles beyond the left of our corps, and south-west of us I saw at least thirty French batteries in line along a low crest that ran about parallel to the ridge we had now reached, whilst up the slope towards us, but from our left front, a whole French Division of Infantry was moving towards their comrades on the hill already hardly pressed, from whom they were yet about 1,000 yards distant.

Their guns were still silent, for their Infantry masked their view, and it was fortunate for our battalions that they were so, for the fight for the moment was stationary, and we were only just holding our own.

For some moments it continued so, and the effect to the spectator was very curious. The air was so filled with the roar of musketry that it seemed to come from nowhere in particular. There was nothing, in the absence of all smoke, to connect it with these two long lines of men, whose rifles spasmodically rose and fell. Along the front of the French, owing, I suppose, to the angle at which I saw them, a row of little blue sparks scintillated like the spark discharge from an electric brush, and over both there lay a blue, grey mist which gave a curious mirage effect to the whole. The shooting must have been vile on both sides, for, according to practice-ground results, thirty seconds should have sufficed for mutual extermination; but, though men fell fast, the net result appeared wonderfully small.

This may have lasted some three minutes, but it was impossible to keep the run of the time, and then above the roll of the musketry I caught the beat of the drums, and a reinforcing line, closed and in perfect order, came over the brow to our assistance. The sight of these closed lines was enough for both sides; the French gave way, and our fighting line dashed forward. But only for some 300 yards or so, for again French reinforcements brought the movement to a check. And now the French Artillery opened fire on our following lines, and we had a taste of what it means to come down hill in the sweep of shrapnel.

Our gunners were, however, quickly on the spot. They had been waiting behind till room was made for them, but till they picked up the range our losses were terrible, and I think that that following line must have lost a larger percentage than any other troops this day.

The French fighting line was now sagging to the rear, and their last reinforcement—a still intact division—was yet some 500 yards away from them, when I noticed a couple of cavalry officers pass close to where I stood in the copse, take in the whole scene at a glance, and gallop away.

I knew then what was coming; it would be the death stroke if given in time, before the fresh French Infantry had actually joined the fighting line. These were now not 300 yards away from their comrades when the first squadron passed me galloping straight down the hill in columns of troops. The first squadron no sooner had its last troop clear of our Infantry front, than it wheeled into line, and went right at the flank of the French, who attempted to fall back to meet it, but gave way at the last moment and ran right back on the reinforcements, and pell-mell fugitives and pursuers crashed right into the angle of these fresh troops. The second squadron followed, then a third and fourth. The confusion became indescribable, and now by the same track an endless succession of squadrons began to emerge, for the first arrivals had been only the Divisional regiment, and two whole fresh Cavalry Divisions were now to follow. On the French side, too, a Cavalry Division appeared, coming out through the line of guns in line of squadron columns, and a cavalry duel was now imminent.

There was not much time on our side to prepare for it. The first regiment of the leading Division joined in the charge on the Infantry, but that blow sufficed, and the whole mass began to break up and fall to the rear with increasing velocity. The remaining squadrons, as they arrived, formed line to the front, and awaited the arrival of their fellows.

As soon as the 1st Division had completed its formation, it trotted forward to meet the enemy, who were now only some 800 yards distant. Both sides were suffering from Artillery fire, and there was no room for manoeuvre. The gallop and charge were sounded simultaneously, and the shock took place all along the front; but the German files were not closed as well as on former occasions, and the two lines fairly threaded each other, then wheeled about by troops, and went for one another again. Then a closed, locked, *mêlée* arose, and the fight became stationary. But our 2d Division was now rapidly arriving, and its leading brigade delivered a shock which set the mass in motion towards the French guns. Then another brigade was sent in, and this fairly started it on the run, and in a few seconds the whole confused mob of over 6,000 horsemen was flying in wild confusion right down on and over the gunners, who again tried to limber up, but were again too late.

German troops dealing with looters during their entry into Rheims

The battle was over, the French line pierced, their last closed reserves broken, and we had a brigade of Cavalry and masses of Infantry, who had not yet pulled a trigger, in hand.

I looked at my watch; it was just 8 a.m., and I turned and rode for the nearest wire. Crossing the ground over which we had come, I was able to notice that our two divisions had both still a regiment in hand, and of the following Corps only the Corps Artillery had been engaged, so we were in ample strength for the pursuit.

By 29 June the German forces are outside Paris; a French night-attack drives them back. The French reserve army moves out from positions at Langres, Épinal, and Belfort in a nine-day march (200,000 troops and 700 guns). Their intention is to attack the Germans in the Moselle area. A decisive one-day battle follows near Chaumont.

GREAT VICTORY OF THE FRENCH

Full Description of the Battle

The curtain is not long in drawing up for the second act, and on our side at least the actors are ready for their cue. From the crest of the ridge which we have now reached a brilliant scene is visible. A broad expanse of verdant pasture stretches away to the placid river which runs between the willows, past the white houses of the little town. Here and there is a patch of woodland, a few stately poplars, and here and there a vineyard. The white high road, with its leafy avenue of spreading trees, now turned into telegraph poles, runs direct to the bridge. On either side, in squares and oblongs, bright with blue and crimson, with flashing bayonet and brazen helmet, rests an enormous army, and still the never-ending columns of men and guns and waggons are forming up for battle for miles away on every side. On the ridge which hides this huge array from the advancing enemy are three batteries, filling the air with uproar, and attracting volley after volley of Prussian shells. One can hear the shrill whizz of the shrapnel, and turning again to the front, we see that on the slopes below us the cavalry skirmishers, kneeling amongst the climbing vines, are in action all along the line. The Chasseurs have scattered along the crest, but there are no other infantry visible. I cannot believe De Galliffet is napping. Above the town rises a great yellow globe, swaying gracefully with every breath of air, and I know that the General has a penchant for observing his enemy from the vantage-point of the balloon. If he is really poised up there, in the bright morning air, he must see those long sombre lines of skirmishers moving slowly across the plain; those heavier masses doubling rapidly over the opposite crest and moving down the slopes. He must know that there are at least six batteries in action against us, and that there are men bleeding to death beneath the tendrils of the vines.

Still not a sign. A couple of Staff officers stand near those three poplars on the hill; one of our batteries falls back, leaving a gun behind. The cavalry begin to creep further up the hill, but not an infantryman moves. The enemy has halted more than 1,200 yards away. They are lying in long rows athwart the valley, and the incessant movement of the rifles, even more than the deafening rattle, tell us that they are pouring in a heavy fusillade. Another battery to the rear, and yet another; horses falling wounded in the traces: and then, as if at a given signal, the long German lines press forward.

Their heaviest masses are away over yonder on our left, where that thick wood, with scarped, quarried slopes below, terminates the ridge whereon we stand; and over to the right, where a marshy brook, its stunted willows still shrouded in mist, breaks through the ridge to join the river, we can see shadowy columns moving in the far distance.

Another ten minutes, perhaps five, if the Chasseurs give way, and the enemy will overlook the valley, the town, and the bridges—the bridges, the most important of all. But even as apprehension gathers it is dispelled. Turn your back for a moment and look to the south. The earth is in motion. Long lines of guns are dashing forward at a gallop, breasting the gentle slope, and driving the dust behind them in swirling clouds.

Long lines of Infantry are already near the crest, and heavy columns are rapidly moving up in rear. The unsuspecting Germans are little more than a thousand paces distant when all along the brow, bare and solitary just now, two hundred field-pieces come into action almost at the same moment.

In a moment more the air is literally shaken by the rush and scream of a hurtling storm of heavy metal; and, lying down in the intervals between the groups of guns, the infantry sweeps the plain with volley after volley. The cavalry has retired behind the hill; the vineyards are no longer tenanted, and the vine leaves, cut by the sheet of bullets, fly in the air as if blown upwards by the wind.

The Prussians stagger beneath the shock. Lines shake and waver; here give back, and there lie still and motionless; columns, though far away, break and dissolve under the shrapnel, and then deploy in haste and confusion; and, above all, the bright sun shines down without a wreath of smoke to sully his radiance, or to hide his target from the rifleman. Vainly the supporting lines of the Prussians are hurried to the front. Impotently the cavalry ride forward. Their guns are already silenced. The squadrons are checked by an inextricable tangle of falling men and horses. The long line of infantry is no longer intact. Men are hastening to the rear, not singly, but in groups. Officers stand out in front for a moment, and then are seen no more save in shapeless huddled forms on the dewy grass. The volleys of the French became more regular and machine-like every moment. A mounted group reaches the hill. It is the General, his Staff beside him, his *fanion* at his side. They are too far off to hear, but I can see De Galliffet pointing to the front, and the infantry are already moving forward, swooping down upon their prey. He must be an enemy of more

than mortal courage who, decimated and out-numbered, can withstand the swift yet steady onset of these trim, regular lines of blue
and red. And look behind—there, in the interval! A long array of
tossing heads and nodding plumes. The Cuirassiers of France! Let
the infantry shake them; brave horsemen, your time is coming!
'N'oubliez pas Reichshoffen!' yells a wounded corporal by my side,
and the mighty mass breaks into a trot, and across the plain they
dash, the horse artillery racing in their wake, whilst *viva* after *viva*
speeds their onset. The German cavalry, what is left of it, comes
gallantly forward to meet their antagonists, and, if possible, to save
their infantry. But it is too late. In a few moments the plain is
covered with a broken crowd of soldiers. Groups rallying round
their officers are swept away by flying horsemen or serried
squadrons; thousands are now struggling for the ridge; in the
centre the Cuirassiers are bearing all before them in the frenzy of
the charge, and on the flanks the infantry, with rattling volleys,
sweep away the *débris* of the battle as leaves before the gale.

Before the French reached the ridge beyond, long after the
cavalry had retired to re-form, it appears that they met fresh
masses of infantry hurrying forward to the assistance of their
comrades; but the impetus of victory was too great to be with-
stood. The fresh troops became involved in the disaster of their
advanced guard, and long ere mid-day De Galliffet was in secure
possession of the second ridge, across which at daybreak I had seen
the Germans advance.

About the noontide hour both armies seemed, as it were by
consent, to allow a breathing space. It was as if some invisible
Marshal of the Lists had thrown down his baton. So here, behind the
ridge, whilst the blazing sun passed over the meridian, lay the
columns of the French. Over against them, in the rolling and open
valley, but out of range, were the faint, blue, wavy lines which
marked their enemy's position.

It was not till after two o'clock that I saw General de Galliffet—
who had been standing alone, looking intently towards the enemy
and impatiently beating his foot upon the ground—make a gesture
of relief, and turning sharp to his orderly dragoon bid him bring
up his horse. At the same moment the German infantry began to
move. The artillery had been for some time in action. A perfect
hail of shells tore up the level surface of the ridge, and our batteries were one by one retiring. Our present line of infantry is several
hundred yards behind the hill, down in the valley, cooking their
soup undisturbed by the shrapnel, and only a few are called up

now to assist the guns against hostile skirmishers. On come the
Prussians, but it is soon evident that the main attack is not against
our centre. Away to the left there, where General Jamont, the
trusted Commander of the 5th Corps d'Armée, holds watch and
ward, the sky is red with dust, and the thunder of the guns and
the rattle of musketry is threefold heavier than with us. I can see
our troops moving in the valley below, from centre to left, lines-
men and guns, hurrying to the point of contact. I am on the point
of riding in the same direction, when one of M. de Galliffet's aides-
de-camp suggests that I have already a place in the stalls. 'Down
below,' he says, pointing to the valley, 'will be played the last
agony of Prussia.'

The suspense is terrible. The volleys rise and fall, the roar of the
cannon swells and dies away. The minutes drag by on leaden wings.
The troops in our front are not advancing; even the Artillery seems
lazy this afternoon, and there, even there, where the red dust-
clouds hang over a hell of slaughter, the fate of a nation is being
decided. It is in vain I endeavour to imitate the imperturbability of
the General, our 'lance of iron', as the soldiers have learned to call
him. A messenger or two rides up, and is dismissed. There is not a
sign on that impassive countenance. Here is another, galloping at
speed, grey with dust, and horse foaming with haste. At last! The
General straightens himself up. He raises his hand to his *kèpi* with
the golden leaves, as if he were saluting a superior. Is it France or
Fortune?

The Staff, throwing away their cigarettes, are all animation now.
Officers and orderlies gallop recklessly down the hill at break-neck
speed. There is a stir amongst those sleeping columns below. Men
spring to their arms. I can hear the harsh words of command, and
note the tricolours with their golden fringes given to the breeze. The
long lines ascend the hill. What has happened? The enemy in front
is moving to the attack: we shall hold the second ridge as we held
the first. But no, it is more than this. This time, as our guns come
into action all along the crest, our infantry do not halt beside them.
There is no pause now. Straight down the slopes they go, the shells
screaming overhead, and the little groups of tirailleurs halting alternately to deliver their biting volleys.

Here, sheltered by a friendly poplar, I can look down upon the
scene. 'What worthy enemies!' cries a little surgeon who has joined
me. 'What a struggle of heroes!' And so it was—while life lasts I shall
never forget De Galliffet's charge. Sixty thousand men, line after
line, were hurled against the German centre. And how bravely those

Germans fought! And now, looking back in cold blood, how need-lessly were they butchered! Exactly opposite where I stood, their infantry moved forward with even more than the precision of a parade; in little squads, but shoulder to shoulder, with all the rigid-ity of a birthday review. I could even see the officers halting and actually correcting the alignment. Needless to say, these living targets were riddled through and through in the very moment of their pedantic folly. In the rear, too, came lines of men, gallantly moving forward to beat of drum, with that extraordinary, high-step-ping pace which excites the ridicule of the Transatlantic visitor in Berlin. How the veterans of our Civil War would have scoffed at this slave-driver's discipline! But even the veterans of the Wilderness and Gettysburg would have admired the bravery of those devoted Teutons. At 400 yards from each other the two lines came to a stand-still. Very irregular is the front; here the French are giving back, and here the German officers are driving up their stragglers; all are standing, there is no cover on that open plain; the French volleys have dissolved into fierce individual fire, and the masses sway back-wards and forwards in that infernal din.

Of a sudden, behind me, sounds the blare of trumpets and the roll of many a score of drums. De Galliffet's reserve is coming up to decide the conflict, and as the serried lines crowned the ridge, the Germans, battling fiercely in the valley below, began to break. And then, whilst the setting sun, pouring his red rays athwart the oppos-ing hosts and striking radiance from the golden eagles of the tricolours, sank slowly on that awful Aceldama, the French army moved onward to its triumph. Wild and exulting were the shouts that rent the air; far above the roar of battle and the clang of drum and trumpet pealed the maddening cry for vengeance, and like a tornado—with irresistible strength and order—the young soldiers of the Republic swept down to obliterate the sorrow and the shame of 1870.

Not for a moment was the issue in doubt. With all the hereditary courage of their caste, the German officers died in their tracks, disdaining to give back a single foot; but the Cuirassiers were once more let loose, the General himself directing their onslaught, and before darkness fell not a single sound man in the German army but was far upon the road to Metz. Our victory is complete; as I write, the cavalry is still pushing the pursuit.

The Final War

Two years after the publication of The Great War in England *in 189–, the tales of future warfare became a regular feature in the popular press. As the old-style short stories expanded to book-length narratives, there was a marked decline in the quality of the writing and a sharp rise in the authors' ignorance of military matters. The calm tone, the balanced judgements, the usually competent and well-informed narratives of the service writers—these changed to the aggressive accents, the chauvinistic language, and the hectic adventures described by journalists and authors new to the field.*

This new demotic fiction began in 1893 with the serialization of George Griffith's The Angel of the Revolution *in* Pearson's Weekly *which operated on the formula: 'To Interest, To Elevate, To Amuse'. Nine months later William Le Queux followed with* The Poisoned Bullet *in Alfred Harmsworth's new weekly,* Answers; *and the success of that lurid account of a Franco-Russian invasion of the United Kingdom sent many of the new journalists into the business of writing future-war stories. Robert Cromie, George Griffith, F. T. Jane, William Le Queux, Louis Tracy, and William Holt-White led the field by using some major anxiety of the day—spies, anarchists, demon scientists, sudden raids by German troops—as the starting point for fast-moving tales of adventure and romance. They were all sensation-seekers: they thrilled their readers with accounts of decision-making at the highest levels.*

The most eminent persons—kings, princes, statesmen, admirals, and generals—have their assigned roles in the high drama of these future wars. Strict hierarchical principles limit any proletarian parts to the occasional appearance of a loyal ex-soldier or a brave sailor. The heroes are officers and gentlemen; the heroines are courageous, high-, well-born damsels. Again, a strict nationalistic morality shows the British to great advantage, whereas the enemy—French, German, or Russian—are invariably perfidious, often incompetent, and usually eager to surrender at the end.

A good example of the new fiction comes from The Final War *by Louis Tracy. He opens with 'The Ball at the Embassy'.*

THE BALL AT THE EMBASSY

The month of May in Paris, if the elements be reasonably propitious, is a perfectly delightful period, and May Day of 1898 heralded in the promise of a gracious summer. The French capital was more than ordinarily full of visitors, and life in the world of fashion was like the changeful scenes of a *ballet divertissement*. Americans were there 'from Chicago and New York, spending millions made in packing pork', Russian notabilities abounded, and Germans, the male element vastly predominating, were in such numbers that the wonted supply of lager beer fell short in the *cafés*. A mad whirl of gaiety and light-heartedness filled the waking hours of every class of society. This social abandonment was, if possible, accentuated by a species of political electricity that permeated the air, and of which all men were dimly conscious.

The new Ministry in France had taken up and developed the policy of colonial expansion given effect to by their predecessors, and a singular *rapprochement* with Germany was vaguely supposed to have contributed in a very remarkable way to the furtherance of French ambition. Both countries had been working amicably together for nearly a year, and already the result made itself felt in the most vulnerable portions of the British Empire.

It is true that England had long ago secured all the best markets for her produce, that her ships carried five-sixths of the commerce of the world, and that her surplus population had the pick of many continents wherein to live and prosper. But a determined attempt was now being made by her great commercial rivals to take from her some, at least, of the advantages gained by centuries of enterprise backed up by daring perseverance.

The Rhine dwindled into a stream of no political significance. Men openly said on the Boulevards and in the *brasseries* of Paris and the beer gardens of Berlin that the star of England was beginning to wane. As a witty Frenchman put it: 'The bones of Englishmen whiten the by-ways of the world: they make most excellent sign-posts for our future progress.'

But at the British Embassy, Lord and Lady Eskdale and their beautiful daughter, Irene, felt that, come what might in the future, it was their present duty to maintain in regal style the hospitable traditions of the Rue du Faubourg St. Honoré, and thus it came to pass that the first night in May was chosen for an official dinner, to be followed by a grand ball.

Strange and disquieting rumours were afloat. Scarce formed into words, they hinted at a fatal blow to be struck at some predominant power. To Capt. Edward Harington—who not only filled the position of junior Military Attaché at the Embassy, but was also the accepted lover of Lady Irene Vyne—the home Government owed the first suspicion of a secret and hostile combination. He had pieced together some curious observations made in his presence by certain high officials in France, and his conclusions seemed no less accurate than alarming.

Inquiries made amongst the London bankers, with whom nearly every foreign house had large dealings, showed that there had been a steady and continual withdrawal, for no accountable reason, of the securities they held. This was enough to put the Government on the alert. Harington's timely service was of considerable value, and he reaped the benefit, for the kindly interest of an exalted personage means much. In fact, a staff appointment at Aldershot, when the next vacancy occurred, was promised to him.

His sister, Ethel, a charming girl of Irene's age, was in Paris on a visit to the Eskdales, and it was one of those coincidences suggestive of arrangement that Lieut. Frank Rodney, of *H.M.S Magnificent*, should have chosen gay Lutetia as the scene of a short leave of ten days. Harington and he were fast friends, and it was not unlikely that the ties of friendship might be strengthened, if the guardsman had not judged amiss the tendency of the pleasant-mannered sailor's thoughts. It was his ardent wish that Rodney might marry his sister, and Ethel had even stronger views on the question than her brother, so for once the course of true love appeared to be running smoothly.

The gathering in Lady Eskdale's reception room, before dinner was announced, was very select indeed. The French President and his wife, the Russian Ambassador and the Grand Duchess, the German Ambassador, the French Ministers of War and Marine, the Governor of Paris, and quite a number of other great people, made the brilliant *salon* glitter with the magnificence of their diamond stars and ornaments, whilst the lovely dresses of the women toned down the gorgeous uniforms by their softer hues.

The British Ambassador, of course, took in Madame la Présidente to dinner. His interested and urbane manner gave no indication of the troubled state of his thoughts, though in very truth there had that afternoon been much cause for perplexity. A cypher telegram, despatched at midday to London, was unaccountably interfered with *en route*, and a call from the Foreign Office for a repetition resulted in even greater confusion. In the endeavour to put matters right, he also discovered that the telephonic communication between the two countries had completely broken down.

Meanwhile, as the signs of danger multiplied at the British Embassy, 'a strange scene was being enacted at Versailles ... '

A COUNCIL OF THE POWERS

On leaving the British Embassy, Lord Eskdale's principal guests entered their carriages. Quiet directions were given to their coachmen, and the vehicles turned into the magnificent avenue of the Champs Elysées, already radiant with the freshness of early spring. They sped swiftly along past the Arc de Triomphe, and entered the Bois de Boulogne. It was scarcely ten o'clock when they passed Longchamps, on which the white tents of the soldiers, who had that day been reviewed, shone beneath the moon. Soon Passy was left behind, and the hoofs of the horses clattered along the deserted streets of the village of Versailles. The carriages drove through the great gates of the Court of Honour, and pulled up before a narrow doorway, where their occupants got out.

In a tapestried room above, a small group of men awaited them. Here, in the pleasure palace built by the great Louis, where he feasted with his mistresses and learnt the fatal news from Blenheim that shattered his ambitions—where Napoleon, too, met his Ministers after his brilliant campaign in Italy, and rested before making his last dash to Waterloo—a grim and unexampled Council was being held.

There were scarcely twenty persons present, but each was a figure of commanding importance in European politics. The military and diplomatic strength of a whole continent might be said to be represented here at its best. It was a strange alliance, hereditary foes meeting in a friendly union, and Ministers who had for years schemed against each other with all the artifices of cunning at last linked together in a common purpose.

No small issue could have achieved this miracle. Before these men was set the hardest and most momentous task that ever perplexed the strength and wisdom of the world. The President of the French Republic took the chair at the head of the table. Opposite him was General Caprivi, the Chancellor of Germany. To right and left were M. Hanotaux and Count Holbach, the French and German Foreign Ministers, and several of the chief diplomats of both countries. Near the President sat a tall and distinguished-looking man, with hair of iron grey, and a grave impenetrable countenance, who seldom spoke, but at whom, from time to time, those around him glanced uneasily. It was General Gourko, the trusted emissary of the Tsar of Russia. Other faces, too, known in every Court in Europe, and feared in many, might be seen. Each one was grave and anxious. It might have been thought that some guilty bond held them in artificial union. Distrust seemed to peer from their eyes, as a chance remark called up the lurking fires of hereditary hate. Yet there was a respectful silence when the President opened the conference.

'Gentlemen,' he said, 'I have just paid the last official visit of a President of France to the representative of the Court of England. The armies of Germany and France are on the point of success. To-morrow before noon, we shall be at war with England!'

He turned, with a true French love of dramatic effect, to mark the effect of these words. The only response was a grave bow from Count Caprivi.

'The details, we, of course, all know. It is enough for me to say that they have been efficiently carried out. England is secure and confident. Her ambassador is occupied in the dance. Her navy is distributed over the globe. Her army is in India. And yet at Brest and Bremerhaven, there are the invincible navies of the two allied powers, together with transports that will carry to the shores of England a mighty army. To-morrow we shall land upon those shores. Within a week we shall be at the gates of London. There is nothing that can withstand us. It may be, that the instinctive courage of the English race may lead to a defence of London. We may not be able to occupy the city for three weeks. But I believe you are with me, when I express the conviction that within a month, the British Empire will be shattered, and that the flags of the chief united powers of Europe will float from the dome of the Mansion House!'

He paused and requested M. Hanotaux to detail the exact position of their preparations. Reading from an official document, the Foreign Minister showed how absolutely complete were the plans of the two allies, and how unsuspicious the English Government. An army large enough to win a continent, and a navy that might sweep a dozen oceans, were ready to pounce upon the little island they all so deeply feared.

A murmur of approval followed the recital, and then Count Caprivi interrupted:

'Time is precious, and we have much to settle. The destruction of Great Britain is a matter of simple generalship. We need not waste time in estimating the number of days or the details of military occu-pation. We may regard the British Empire as already struck off the map. But I must remind you that several points remain yet to be settled in our joint treaty. How is Great Britain to be dismembered, and how are we to share her dependencies?'

Here M. Hanotaux rose, and walked behind the chair occupied by the President. Touching a cord that hung down from a roller upon the wall, he liberated a large map of the world which covered the whole space. It had many curious lines upon it, and strange colours. Across the British Islands were written the words: 'Under joint government'.

It was the map of the world as it was intended to be after the collapse of England. The strange colours were the emblems of the foreign powers that had bidden for her colonies. The lines were marks to show how, in the greed of cruel appetite, the confederates had arranged to share some fair possession and split up a fertile country into fragments.

'Here', said the President, 'is a *précis* of what we have already arranged. You will see', pointing to the map, 'that Canada falls to France, East Africa to Germany. Australia, New Zealand, and South Africa are governed by a joint board for the profit of the allies. Malta and Aden are dismantled. Dover is held by a joint garrison. England herself', he concluded, 'will be governed by a military council in the interests of France and Germany for a time, at least. We are not inclined to be merciless, and if she behaves herself, we may be induced later on to grant a limited form of home rule, which will necessitate a sanction for all legislative measures from a combined Board of Administrators, meeting alternately at Berlin and Paris. We shall also occupy Ireland, to watch movements in England, and stamp out any signs of rebellion. Turkey and the Egyptian question can be settled satisfactorily at a later date.'

'There yet remain', said the German War Minister, 'Gibraltar, India, West Africa, the West Indies, the Chinese possessions, and a number of smaller but yet difficult points.' An eager discussion now arose, in which no one seemed prepared to come to a point. And at times there passed looks of malice and anger, ill-suppressed, as some slight word lit up hideous depths of selfishness or jealousy.

At last M. Hanotaux observed: 'We might begin with India. It is a large and splendid territory. France at least—'At this point General Gourko's impassive face relaxed. Turning to the President, he said: 'There is no need to discuss that point; India is claimed by Russia.'

M. Hanotaux started—and turned red. 'A huge plum!' he exclaimed. 'Do you want the lion's share, sir, without doing the lion's part?'

'M. le President,' said Gourko calmly, paying no heed, 'there can be no discussion on this head. My instructions are final and peremptory. You say we are not fighting for our spoil. Is it not agreed that Russia's part is to hang back and make no move till the moment comes—if ever such a moment needs to come? You forget, perhaps, that it is you, and not we, that have demanded this blow. You have been forced to action by the decline of your commerce, the decay of your trade, your imperative need of fresh markets, your lack of colonies. England has seized all that is fairest on earth, and you can no longer exist against so huge a monopoly. You are both in desperate straits, and the imperative voice of your suffering peoples forces you to close with this all-devouring race which is checking your growth, crushing your strength, and throttling your prosperity. That is why you have formed this alliance, is it not?'

He paused, but there was no answer. 'Russia, however,' he continued, 'has no such need. She has rich and fertile lands. Siberia alone adds a second empire to her throne. What she wants is, no doubt, a sea-coast. That sea-coast is India. If Russia helps you to secure the success of schemes she is not interested in, she demands that sea-coast. Gentlemen, you cannot oppose the resistless necessity of things. Russia must and will secure for herself the Indian Empire.'

His words fell inexorable and unanswerable. The acquiescence of Russia was essential to England's overthrow. It was essential to the peaceful division of spoil. Large though the price she asked, there could be no refusal.

Then rose a debate upon Gibraltar, and it well nigh brought to a close the temporary alliance between the powers. That impregnable fortress was coveted by all. But Count Holbach had not come unprepared for this. He had, that morning, had a long interview with the Spanish Minister, and it was in his power to outwit his French comrade. He proposed that Gibraltar be returned to Spain.

To his joy, the French Minister accepted this method of settlement as the most satisfactory way out of the difficulty. If the German could have seen a letter bearing the official stamp from Madrid that even then lay in M. Hanotaux's pocket, he would perhaps have been less satisfied with himself. Even now had the allies commenced to scheme against each other.

And thus the Conference went on, and by slow degrees all of the British Empire that remained was divided between the two countries. What was left of England was a crippled island under the heel of a despotic military government, a tributary state of less consequence than Bulgaria, and a people crushed, ruined, and enslaved.

'One point only,' observed Caprivi, as the Council was about to rise. 'Germany, of course, claims Belgium.' The Frenchmen started to their feet at this amazing announcement. 'Impossible!' cried the President. 'Not so,' replied Caprivi calmly. 'It is, no doubt, a prize of value, but we are prepared to pay for it.'

M. Hanotaux turned upon him a look of disdain.

'And what payment do you presume to consider adequate?' he said.

The German put his finger carelessly upon a map which lay on the table. Then quietly: 'We offer Alsace and Lorraine!'

It was a startling *dénouement* of the grim drama of hatred and selfishness that had just been played. But the German statesman knew his men. Before he returned to Paris that night he placed in his pocket a signed *précis*, in which Belgium figured as a German dependency.

It was almost dawn when the Council rose.

'Adieu, gentlemen,' said the President, with a bow. 'When we next meet, it will be in Whitehall.'

The French had not foreseen that the Germans would side with the British and that, with the aid of large German forces, Lord Roberts, 'the Hero of Kandahar', would take Paris and end the war with a great victory. The closing paragraphs proclaim the adaptability and continuing progress of the Anglo-Saxon peoples.

Thus, armed with all that discovery could yield her and owing allegiance only to herself, she poured her sons over the earth and upon the seas, and in remote regions founded another empire. America arose—that second England—new home of the Saxon race, and heir to her aspirations and destiny—America, which developed a new type of being, more versatile still, and still more strenuous. And the impulse went on, giving life to Canada, peopling the vast continent of Australia, carrying civilised arts to mysterious Africa, to venerable India, and on every continent, in every sea, stamping itself in eternal characters.

And how could such a race be resisted? For, wherever it penetrated, it did not languish under conditions unfavourable to its growth. With miraculous ease the Saxon remodelled himself to cover every variation of climate, every manner of sky, every form of life, till it became clear that he was no fixed irrevocable type, but of plastic mould, and reproducing himself in a hundred different shapes. The Saxon is content wherever he is; the instinct of his blood tells him that the earth is his home, and that his spirit must inform the nations and regenerate decaying peoples.

Commerce bent itself to Britain and all peoples intrusted to her their possessions. The Saxon tongue has become the speech of the world, the Saxon ensign—whether British or American—is the flag of the seas.

Thus, as life becomes more complex and harder grows the struggle, there is no escape for peoples not fitted to bear its strain. The Saxon race will absorb all and embrace all, reanimating old civilisations and giving new vigour to exhausted nations. England and America—their destiny is to order and rule the world, to give it peace and freedom, to bestow upon it prosperity and happiness, to fulfill the responsibilities of an all-devouring people; wisely to discern and generously to bestow.

This vision—far-off it may be—already dawns; and in the glory of its celestial light is the peace of nations.

The Spies of the Wight

As the number of these future-war stories increased year by year, they made their separate contributions to the growing myth of the invasion-to-come. Louis Tracy was the first popular writer to show that there were secret plans for a sudden strike against the United Kingdom—a theme that kept on reappearing in later fiction, most notably in Erskine Childers' Riddle of the Sands. *Another important element in this composite myth was the enemy spy, a character of some antiquity, who first saw service during the Channel Tunnel uproar of the early 1880s. In the pamphlets of that time—*The Battle of Boulogne, How John Bull Lost London, The Surprise of the Channel Tunnel, The Taking of Dover—*the enemy agent went to ground in Dover. There he spied out the land in readiness for the moment when he would give the signal for hundreds of highly trained French troops to come out of hiding and seize Dover Castle. This expression of total impotence—of the nation treacherously attacked from within—had the double advantage of exposing a perfidious enemy and of demonstrating the calamitous folly of building a Channel Tunnel. By the 1890s there was evidence enough, it seemed, to accept this notion of 'the enemy within' as a variant on the secret activities and violent methods of the Anarchist and Nihilist societies in Europe and of the Fenians in North America. Moreover, espionage had become a topic of great interest in the 1890s as a result of the startling disclosures that Major Henri Le Caron (Thomas Miller Beach, British Secret Service) made in his* Twenty-five Years in the Secret Service *(1892); and the immense publicity of the Dreyfus Affair—from condemnation in 1894 to rehabilitation in 1906—provided even more amazing revelations of secret agents and their activities.*

From this rich compost of treachery and deceit came the first flowering of British spy fiction in the activities of von Beilstein, 'an expert spy in the Secret Service of the Tzar'. He failed to do his worst in William Le Queux's serial,

The Poisoned Bullet, *which began on 23 December 1893 in* Answers. *The development of the spy story gathered pace in 1898 with the publication of* The Mysterious Mr Sabin *by E. Phillips Oppenheim. In a succession of stories, Oppenheim developed the essential features of spy fiction: the danger from without—secret societies or foreign powers—and the hero from within—the amateur who finds himself in time of peace suddenly committed to saving the nation from gravest peril. A year later Headon Hill used this formula in* The Spies of the Wight, *the first full-length account of German agents at work in the United Kingdom and an early indication that Germany had taken the place of France as the enemy in tomorrow's war. The notorious Kruger telegram of 3 January 1896 was read as a hostile act against the United Kingdom; and the new German fleet, sanctioned by the Navy Law of April 1898, suggested to many that the two nations had started on a collision course. Feelings of anger and contempt, once reserved for the French, are now concentrated on 'certain dirty little games of the German Emperor himself', as the hero is briefed for his secret mission.*

A SECRET MISSION

It was half-past six on a sweltering July afternoon, and the work of the day was nearly finished in the office of the *Evening Argus*. As I put my foot on the private spiral iron staircase that runs from the machine-room in the basement to the general offices, thence to the compositors' floor, and, higher still, to the editorial rooms above, the three great Marinoni presses down in the central 'well' of the building pulsed to a standstill, after tossing off the last of the damp sheets, which five minutes later the newsboys would be crying outside in Fleet Street as our 'special edition'.

The sudden cessation of the steady rumble of the machinery brought other noises into clearer relief, and, nearing the head of the stairs, I became conscious of a footstep on the stone gallery of the editorial floor to which I was ascending. The footsteps of all the members of our staff were familiar to me, and this tread, I knew, was not caused by one of my colleagues. The hesitating, shuffling footfall was that of a stranger who did not know his way about, and who was in all probability looking for means of exit.

Stepping on to the landing, I found that my surmise was correct. I stood face to face with a man who had evidently been about to descend by the way I had come, and upon whom I had certainly never set eyes before. He was shabbily dressed, and was unmistakably a foreigner. No Englishman of his years—he looked about

thirty—would have worn a threadbare black overcoat on that brilliant summer day; no Englishman would have permitted six inches
of frowsy auburn hair to well-nigh obscure the greasy velvet collar
of that unnecessary garment.

'Ach! but pardon!' he exclaimed, starting at my sudden appearance and removing a napless tall hat; 'Is it that this is the way out?
I have been the editor to see.'

'Your way is along the gallery, and turn to the right,' I replied.
'You will find the stairs there which will take you down through the
publishing offices into the street. This is a private staircase for the
use of the staff.'

The stranger wore a pair of heavily rimmed spectacles, under
whose thick lenses it was difficult to discern the expression or even
the colour of his eyes, but I thought that he blinked at me queerly
as I proffered this simple information. 'Ach! then it is to the staff of
this egsellent paper that you belong?' he exclaimed. 'I am proud—I
am happy to meet you, sir. For your kindness I am obliged, and I bid
you the good-day.'

He shuffled off to the staircase I had indicated, and I dived into my
own little writing den to put my things away and lock my desk
before going to say good-bye to my chief. On the morrow I was to
commence the first real holiday I had had for three years, and I did
not expect to be at the office again for a month. I swept my table
clear of stray flimsies, crammed into the drawers the penholders and
such-like tools of the craft as formed the every-day litter of my
workshop, and, going out on to the gallery again, knocked at the
editor's door.

He who bade me enter, and who, as I entered, looked up from a
map over which he had been poring, was one of the most remarkable personages of the day; yet so deeply had he merged his own
personality in the great journal which he controlled that, though he
wielded a more potent influence than a Cabinet Minister, the
outside public hardly knew him by name. For fame for its own sake
Shirley Wreford cared less than nothing. One glance at his square,
massive jaws and firm lips would have told anyone that love of
power was his leading characteristic; a second glance at the satisfied,
confident grey eyes would have shown that he had not failed to
attain it.

As an exponent of the 'new journalism'—that modern inquisition
which insists on getting to the back of things, on arraigning its
discoveries before public opinion, and on pronouncing judgment
before constituted authority has begun to move—the editor of the

Argus was without an equal. Though I was his most trusted lieutenant, I never knew quite how he gained and retained touch with
every social and international undercurrent; but whether it was the
first whispering of a Continental imbroglio that had to be caught and
sifted, or a new grouping of City financiers that had to be dissected,
he somehow and somewhere managed to get his information. Numberless were the sensations which he served up to an expectant
world, and, unlike those of his rivals, they did not fizzle out after the
first day, contradicted and discredited. They grew and grew in interest till they took their place as recorded facts of history.

'Ah, Monckton!' he said; 'you are come to make your adieus, I am
afraid. If you hadn't been worked to skin and bone lately over that
Pretoria conspiracy business, I should be almost inclined to ask you
to postpone your holiday. But I know you need rest, and you shall
have it.'

'Something in my line has cropped up?' I hazarded.

'Well, yes,' said Wreford, with the magnetic glint in his shrewd
eyes that made him so well served; 'considering that it is a piece of
detective journalism that, properly handled, may put a stopper on
certain dirty little games of the German Emperor himself, it may be
deemed very much in your line.'

'If I am not much mistaken,' said I, 'the informant has been with
you recently. I think I met him—a peculiar-looking foreigner—in
the gallery just now.'

My editor laughed genially. 'As ever, you take hold quickly,
Monckton,' he said. 'Yes, that was the fellow. By the way,' he added,
as though struck by a sudden afterthought, 'where are you going to
spend your holiday?'

I told him that I purposed joining my mother, who had taken a
furnished cottage near Alum Bay and Freshwater, in the Isle of
Wight. Wreford never allowed himself to be excited, but on hearing
my destination, he rather hurriedly consulted a memorandum
which lay at the side of the map before him.

'Then, by Jove, my dear boy, without curtailing or interfering with
your holiday, I may still be able to have you with me in this matter,'
he exclaimed. 'There is a chance—only a chance, mind—that the
focus of the trouble indicated by that tow-haired traitor may be in
the neighbourhood to which you are going. Just look outside the
door before I post you in the particulars; if ever man was charged
with a secret service, this is one.'

I obeyed his behest so swiftly that I must have surprised any
lurking eavesdropper had such a one been there, but the gallery was

clear from end to end. The last edition of the paper was on the streets, and the editorial staff had all gone home.

'Then you had better sit down, for I shall have to detain you a little,' said Wreford when I had reported the coast clear. 'The man you saw brought me news of the presence in England of a gang of spies, who have been commissioned to supply the German authorities with plans and all particulars relating to the new defence works that have lately been undertaken by our own Government. The chief of the gang is a *déclassé* nobleman—the Baron Von Holtzman—who, seeing that he is to be paid by results, will stick at nothing to carry out his purpose.'

'One moment,' I interrupted. 'What is your informant's object in betraying this to you?'

'The usual thing—money,' replied Wreford contemptuously. 'I have given him a trifle, and promised him more if the *Argus* is eventually the means of exposing the spies.'

'Are you satisfied that there is anything in it, that it is more than a try-on for the preliminary cash? This Von Holtzman may be a myth,' I said.

'That, of course, would occur to you,' laughed Wreford, 'as it would have occurred to me had there been any room for such a supposition. But, fortunately, I was able to confirm the informer's allegations, to some extent, from my own knowledge. I have very good reason for knowing that the Baron Von Holtzman is a stern reality—a reason which you must have noticed and wondered at, but which wasn't worth explaining till an occasion arose.'

He held up his right hand, and the mere motion sufficed to explain his meaning without any close scrutiny on my part. Everyone on the staff was aware that the editor was short of a little finger.

'I owe that trifling mutilation to the Baron Von Holtzman', he continued, 'or rather to the assassin whom he hired to put me away. It was better to grasp the dagger and lose a finger than lose my life. That was in Buda-Pesth in '79—before I had made my mark, when I was fulfilling a somewhat delicate mission—and I need hardly say that I have when possible kept a vicarious eye on the Baron since. I was aware that he was spying for the German Government; but I have lost track of him lately, and thought he was working in France. The miscreant who was with me just now, however, says that Von Holtzman is at present actively engaged in this country, though he professed ignorance of the locality.'

'But you have reason to believe that it is the Isle of Wight?' I said.

'If I had, it would all be plain sailing,' Wreford replied. 'No. The island is only one of at least a dozen places where he *may* be, and it is about the most unlikely of the lot. My impression is that the Baron will be found prospecting the Scilly Isles, Falmouth, Berehaven, or one of the other new ports of refuge for which Parliament voted money this year. But, on the other hand, there is the chance that he may turn up in the Isle of Wight, and it is against that chance that I want to prepare you in the event of his coming your way. A very important new fort has recently been completed on the lofty down above the Needles, and it is now receiving its armament, the number and weight of its guns being preserved a close secret.'

'And how should I recognize—?' I was beginning, when there was a knock at the door, and one of the messengers employed in the publishing office on the ground floor looked in.

'I beg your pardon, sir, but I have just picked this up inside the street door,' the man said, advancing and handing a small article to Wreford. 'It don't belong to any of the clerks, and I thought I'd best bring it straight to you. It looks valuable.'

Wreford took the object somewhat impatiently. I could see that he was annoyed at the interruption, and wanted to get it over; but as his keen eyes fastened on that which he held, he started visibly and examined the thing closely.

'Thank you, Simmonds,' he said at length. 'You did right in bringing it to me. It *is* very valuable, and I hope the owner will be found. What strangers passed through the offices in the last half-hour?'

'Only the foreign-looking gent as came up to see you, sir. He passed out a while back, but he didn't seem to be much in the way of wearing such things.'

'Ah, well, one never knows; that will do, thank you,' said Wreford. 'I will relieve you of all responsibility in the matter.'

After Simmonds had left the room my editor continued for a minute or more to examine the treasure-trove. Then suddenly he passed it to me, with the question:

'What do you make of it, Monckton?'

'It is a sleeve-link of unique design,' I said, after a brief scrutiny. 'It is fashioned in the form of a serpent for the gold setting; but, instead of having diamonds for eyes, as usual, this reptile has got a big ruby in his mouth. It is rather quaint; might be intended to represent the old original serpent tempting Eve with the apple.'

'Exactly,' said Wreford, holding out his hand for the link. 'I have never seen anything like it before but once.'

'And that was—?'

'On the shirt-cuff of the man who attempted to stab me at Buda-Pesth eighteen years ago,' replied Wreford coolly. 'As I was grasping his wrist I had every opportunity for inspecting his trinkets. It is wonderful what an impression trifles make when one's every nerve is on tension. If I am not very much mistaken, this sleeve-link is one of the identical pair that flashed in my face at the back of that ugly dagger. The man who was here to-day was not the man who wore it then, unless he is a past master in the art of disguise; but that is not of much importance. What really matters is, that it clearly establishes a connection between my late visitor and those who were working with Von Holtzman formerly. It puts an end to the theory of the man being a mere outsider, who, having got hold of the Baron's name, is trying to turn it into ready cash.'

It was impossible not to agree with every word of this, and I confess that the finding of the link considerably added to the interest I felt in the rather vague commission entrusted to me. Till the entrance of the messenger I had been inclined to the opinion that my editor might for once have been hoaxed, and it encouraged the sporting instinct with which I always approach my 'cases' to know that, whether the Baron was in the Isle of Wight or not, I was not hunting a shadow. I eagerly repeated my interrupted question about Von Holtzman's personal appearance.

'There I cannot help you,' said Wreford gravely. 'Some of the cleverest agents in Europe have done their best to furnish me with his true description, but one and all have utterly failed. He changes colour like a chameleon, and has a perfectly Protean faculty for disguise. I know, however, that he must be at least fifty years old, and rumours have reached me during the last year or two that he has a daughter who is very beautiful, and who aids him in his schemes. That has struck me as a weak point in his armour, and it might give you your clue, only you mustn't fall in love with the girl.'

'I shan't do that,' I said sturdily, as I thought of a face that was not to be eclipsed by the charms of any foreign adventuress.

'Well, if you come across these people or any traces of them, you will know what to do,' replied the editor, rising to grasp my hand in farewell. 'I shall have the other more likely coverts drawn by Philips and Bruton, but of all the members of our staff, Monckton, I would prefer that this case fell into your hands. It is no compliment to you to say that you would run the thing to earth more keenly and work it into a bigger "boom" than the others. Good-bye, and if you *should* cross Von Holtzman's path, do not forget that he is well served by men as unscrupulous as himself. It seems strange advice to give to anyone going for a holiday in this country, but in your place I should include a revolver in my luggage.'

Die Abrechnung mit England

The title of Karl Eisenhart's Die Abrechnung mit England *('The Reckoning with Britain') is both an angry cry from the subconscious— summoning Great Britain to a settlement of accounts with Germany—and an early warning sign of the great changes then beginning to affect the long friendship between the two nations. How did Karl Eisenhart imagine it was possible to balance the books when there were no debit entries on the British side? What had the British people done to offend the author and his countrymen? One answer came from a candid essay on 'Anti-English Sentiment in Germany' which appeared in* Blackwood's Magazine *for April 1901.*

Hatred of the British, the author thought, derived from the ambitions so forcefully expressed in two contemporary slogans: 'German Colonial Enterprise' and 'Germany: A World-Power'. It was a common complaint in Germany that Britain 'sets its face against the expansion of German energy in commerce and colonial enterprise, and strives in various ways, never cited explicitly or in detail, to thwart its world-power aspirations'. As Prince Bismarck had said in his usually candid way: 'Envy is the national vice of the German people.' The proof of that could be seen in ' the violent detestation of the bulk of the German people towards a nation and a race that have done them no wrong save that of being "greater than themselves"'.[8]

This detestation is the power that drives Eisenhart's carefully prejudiced account of the war-to-come between the Reich and the United Kingdom. Like his contemporaries across the North Sea, Eisenhart found that the end required him to tell a tale of good and evil. The narrative maintains a sharp division between the disgraceful actions of an ever-despicable enemy and the spotless honour, heroic actions and steadfastness that the defenders of the Fatherland display on all occasions. This episode describes:

THE BEGINNING OF THE WAR WITH BRITAIN

In the war with the Boers the British suffered a severe defeat. True to their antiquated and defective principles, they set out against their fearful enemy with forces that were too small. Half their Redcoats and more than seven-eighths of their officers lay dead on the battlefield; all their artillery and their entire equipment were lost. Their conduct of strategy and tactics had been pitiful; the discipline of their troops was non-existent. Their courage, the whisper went, was not beyond question, and their fire control was wretched. The causes of defeat were more humiliating than the defeat itself.

The jubilation which consequently broke out in France speeded up the pace of events: the French were full of themselves, but the British were sorely provoked. And so one fine day, before you could say Jack Robinson, they went to war again. Frau von Suttner and Frau Professor Selenka wrang their hands and sent imploring tear-stained protests to London and Paris.[9] There they met their inglorious end, unread in the ministerial waste-paper baskets.

Britain found itself in a far from brilliant situation; for just at this point the hidden enmity between Great Britain and the North American Union—always concealed beneath sycophantic, boot-licking verbiage—almost erupted into war. For the time being, however, matters did not go that far. Thanks to the compliance of the British, they resolved the differences between them; and amongst these the border dispute in Alaska played an important part. But a thorn remained in the flesh of the two nations; and Britain could hardly count on the benevolent neutrality of the Americans, let alone on any support from them.

However, the well-known Parisian loud-mouths very soon discovered that once again they had made a mistake: they had under-estimated the strength of their opponent, and in their foolish arrogance they had badly miscalculated the situation. Despite the many boastful announcements of the French press, it was some time before there was a major engagement at sea. During the first two months of the war French privateers seized a large number of British merchant ships, and the British took just as many French vessels. It was apparent that the two countries were engaged in old-style naval warfare without any concern for the spirit and the practice of international law. For a time there were only one-to-one engagements between armoured cruisers; and on these occasions the British displayed their usual naval superiority, whilst the French showed their limited capacity for sea warfare.

Vehemently and impatiently, the French lamented the inglorious inactivity of their fleet which fell so far short of their cherished expectations. The government, however, and the naval commander-in-chief were agreed that no decisive action should be taken before the occurrence of an event which they awaited in suspense and with an anxious hopefulness that increased from day to day. No one could speak openly about this, because any disclosure would immediately thwart the realization of what all had long desired. They were waiting for Russia to join in the war.

This timorous waiting for a third party would have left any other nation with a sense of humiliation; but, as everyone knows, the French have no feelings in these matters. For centuries servile French historians have known how to handle the assistance given by foreign troops in French wars so that their national vanity and their obsessive desire for glory never got short shrift. That was the way of it in the naval war they fought in alliance with the British against Holland, just as it was in the Napoleonic wars. One need only think of the despicable slandering of the brave Saxons in 1813; and it was the same during the Crimean War. And so, the French could rest completely easy in the expectation that history would repeat itself in the event of a Russo-French war against Great Britain.

Tsar Nicholas II, however, could not be persuaded to intervene in the war. The Russian politicians and military thought that the time had come to begin, sooner or later, the inevitable reckoning with England; and they would have been for immediate participation. But all attempts were foiled by key figures at court. Nicholas himself, who had a most unwarlike temperament and took against everything military, had an absolute aversion to warfare of any kind; and there was the female influence of his beautiful and noble-born wife. As a German princess she was opposed to a military alliance with France; and then there was the influence of his mother, sister of the Queen of England, who had no desire for a war with that country and did all she could to keep Russia from taking any part in the war.

As soon as the French had convinced themselves that they had nothing whatsoever to expect from the ally on whom they had heaped such sycophantic flattery, there were not only changes in government circles but there was also a sudden change in public opinion. That unfortunately came too late to put their senseless and erratic policies back on the rails. But it was now, at this point, that it was so desperately necessary that something should happen that would end the hitherto inglorious war with a victory, or at least with a not too shameful defeat. The French were certain that, without such a brilliant end to the war, France would be removed for ever from the ranks of the Great Powers. She would be reduced to the level of Italy, and before long would be mentioned in the same breath with Spain.

So, they prepared for action. Under the direction of the commanding admirals a plan was drawn up in the Ministry of Naval Affairs: they would bring their Mediterranean and their North Sea squadrons together; and in combination with their submarines they would make a joint attack on one of the British fleets which were blockading the French ports, just as they had done during the wars with the Republic and with Napoleon.

However, before these desperate plans could be implemented, something happened that, without any action on their part, gave the French an ally and at a stroke completely changed the course of the war. The British government—contrary to the definition of block-ades as laid down by international law—had declared that all of France and all the French colonies were blockaded, although their naval forces were by no means large enough to make the blockade totally effective. They laughed at the protests of the neutral coun-tries and filed them away in pigeonholes. Some they turned down; and they did not even respond to the smaller countries for whom they could have done something. Without more ado, British cruis-ers and privateers seized all neutral vessels bound for French ports; and these were condemned as prizes by the corrupt and mercenary British courts.

There was great delight in Britain that once again Britannia was ruling the waves; and in the middle of their jubilation there came news of the incident already mentioned, the first reports of which gave rise to an outburst of unrestrained rejoicing. However, when more detailed information came along later, the general euphoria was considerably dampened.

In spite of the risk of capture, the *Capella*, a Hamburg steamer, was proceeding on its way with a mixed cargo of goods to a small French port on the Gironde which everyone knew was not blockaded. Off the coast of Britanny, and still rather far from her destination, she saw two warships appear to the southwest as a third approached from the south. Their courses meant that all three ships would soon come close on one another.

The captain of the *Capella* thought it best to hold to his course, as though he was unaware of any transgression and, therefore, of any danger. To his great relief, he was happy to see that the vessel coming from the south displayed the German flag. The flag of St George flew on the other two; and all three were fast, big-gunned cruisers.

Their converging courses brought the ships ever faster and ever closer together. After half-an-hour there was a shot from the British cruiser, apparently as a signal that the German steamer was not to continue on its course. The captain hoisted the German colours, but paid no further attention to the signal, since he knew that in the presence of a German warship he was bound solely by German orders. Moreover, the German ship was somewhat closer to him.

When they came within signalling distance, the captain stopped engines and signalled the ship's number to the German warship. The commander of the *Freya*, as the German cruiser was called, ordered him to leave his ship and come across in a boat to him. The *Freya* belonged to a small squadron that cruised along the French coast with orders to protect German trading vessels from all arbitrary harassment. The squadron was, in particular, to establish to what extent the blockade was effective in order that, in the light of their observations, they could prepare for common action on the part of the neutral powers.

The *Capella* lowered a boat; the captain climbed in and took the helm. He had hardly got half-way across, however, when he stopped, since he had noticed that a boat had been lowered from the *Emerald*, the nearest British cruiser, and was making towards his ship.

There was great activity on board the *Freya*. The captain of the *Capella*, who had done his military service in the navy, guessed from all the activity, that they were clearly making ready for action. They called down to him from the deck that he should return to his ship. As he was carrying out this order, a boat was also lowered from the German cruiser; and with a full crew it sped away towards the *Capella*, powered by regular and powerful oar-strokes.

In the meantime a lively exchange of signals was going on between the two British cruisers. The second, the *Topaz*, steamed westwards at full speed round the stern of the *Freya*. The aim of the manoeuvre was clear: they wanted to attack the German from both sides. At such a moment many a fearless man might feel his heart beating; and yet no one really believed that there would be an engagement.

All three boats arrived almost at the same moment at the ladder of the *Capella*. The captain of the merchant ship leapt up on board and gave the order for the boat to be hauled up again. A midshipman piloted the British boat, and the first-lieutenant of the *Emerald* was in the boat with him. In the boat from the *Freya* the only officer was their first-lieutenant.

They greeted each other with casual courtesy. In the British navy the example of the uncouth arrogance of a certain Kautz and a Coghlan had not made a good impression—quite the contrary—and for a decade they had been at pains to remove all the Sturdee's and fill all commissioned ranks exclusively with gentlemen.[10] The ill-mannered boastfulness of Uncle Sam had not become the accepted thing.

A brief conversation followed. The German lieutenant stated, in precise terms, if very politely, that in the presence of SMS *Freya*, it was out of the question for a foreign warship to search and molest a German vessel. In answer to the British lieutenant's question—What would happen, if he followed orders and went on board to look at the ship's papers?—the German replied that he would resist such an attempt by every means in his power. He would oppose it, first, with this explanation, thereafter with a formal protest; but in the end, if need be, he would use force.

'I am very sorry,' was the British answer. 'I have to obey orders.' The lieutenant touched his cap in salute. 'So have I,' the German replied in the same courteous way, and then drove his boat right up against the ship's ladder.

The Englishman was about to commence hostilities, when a signal from the *Emerald* summoned him back. The two opponents left each other with chivalrous farewells. The Englishman went back to his ship, whilst the German, obeying orders, remained with his men on the *Capella*.

The boat from the *Emerald* pushed off again and made for the *Freya*. The lieutenant had a long exchange with the ship's commander, which appeared in a sombre and eerie light, as the *Topaz* approached on the starboard side of the German warship. Just before the Englishman came on deck, he heard the crew give three ringing hurrahs in response to a short speech by their captain. He told them that they were about to enter on an all-out struggle for the still untarnished honour of the German battle ensign. They could be defeated and destroyed, but surrender—never.

The entire navy had long hoped to see the day when they would once and for all take on the hated British. They had earned themselves immense hatred and bitterness, comparable with the feelings against France in 1813 which so astonished the French by the outburst of passionate emotions during the first hostile encounters.

When the English lieutenant demanded that they should let him have free sight of the ship's papers of the *Capella*, the German commander replied with a curt negative. His answer to a comment about the necessities of war was: the blockade was not effective, and of that the squadron to which he belonged was convinced. The blockade was, moreover, not recognized by the German government and could not be used as a pretext for molesting German ships. The

Englishman refused to discuss this point, but then made a final concession: if the German commander would agree to give his word of honour that the *Capella* was not destined for a French port, they would call off the search; or, if the commander did not wish to do this, he could promise to send the merchant ship back to port.

In keeping with his instructions, the commander refused the two points. Some uneasy moments followed as the British lieutenant left the *Freya* in order to return to the *Emerald*. A short time after he had returned on board, the two British cruisers exchanged signals; and the result was that a heavily manned boat pushed off from both of them and made for the *Capella*.

For his part, the captain of the *Freya* sent a signal to his lieutenant who was on board the *Capella*: 'You know your orders.' These stated that they were to resist by force any attempt by the British to come on board. Then he fired off a live round from his saluting gun which was so directed that the shot hit the water immediately before the bow of the *Emerald*. The answer came in a steel salute from one of the 21 centimetre guns of the *Emerald*. The elevation was too high and the shell came screaming over the German warship. At that the *Topaz*, which was on the starboard side of the *Freya*, immediately opened fire.

The German cruiser answered with the speed and accuracy that was to be expected from the splendidly trained crew. The *Emerald* and the *Topaz* discovered that an engagement with weaker German forces made far greater demands on their determination and their ability than an encounter with superior French opponents. There was painful admiration when, in the middle of the dreadful battle, the *Freya* did not forget the ship it was protecting and with a well-aimed shot shattered the boat sent from the *Emerald* to the *Capella*. Had the boat from the *Topaz* not already been masked by the merchant ship, it would have fared no better.

The British captain, who was the senior officer in command of both ships, had to abandon his intention to fire on the *Capella* if they resisted his boarding parties, because the *Freya* kept the two British vessels fully engaged. But their superiority was too great; and after an hour-long cannonade the fire of the *Freya* grew weaker and finally ceased altogether. The *Emerald* and the *Topaz* likewise ceased fire in order to repair damages and to take possession of the German vessel which was obviously defenceless. As the gun-smoke lifted, however, they saw that the *Freya* was a total wreck; but the German battle ensign still flew proudly from her masthead. As the vessel heeled over before sinking to the depths, a weary but absolutely fearless Hurrah for Germany and the Emperor sounded once again from the surviving crew.

In the meantime the crew of the *Capella*, with the help of the party from the *Freya*, had driven off the boarders from the *Topaz* in a short and furious hand-to-hand fight. Whereupon the *Capella* made good her escape at full speed; but the British cruisers were so badly damaged that it was impossible for them to give chase.

As the *Freya* went under, the British put out their only undamaged boat in order to save as many of the crew as possible. They fished out about ten sailors and the captain, who had been badly wounded by a shell splinter. The captain of the *Emerald*, a chivalrous gentleman, shook him silently by the hand and saw to it that he had all possible help; but the hero died an hour later. Together with the dead Britons, he went to a sailor's grave in the stormy waters of the Bay of Biscay.

In Britain the first news of the engagement appeared in an inaccurate account. It stated that a German warship, which had opposed the search of a German blockade-runner, had been compelled to strike its flag by the weaker cruiser *Emerald* after a brief exchange of fire. One can imagine the rejoicing that broke out in Old England, and the contemptuous, arrogant articles that appeared in the leading British newspapers. And then came the bad news; and the reports came so thick and fast that John Bull began to feel decidedly uncomfortable. The German warship had not surrendered. After an extraordinarily heroic resistance it had gone down with all flags flying. The victory had not been over a more powerful enemy, but over a weaker opponent which was less than half as powerful. The worst news was that the British losses were tremendously high: several guns had been put out of action, and the casualty list for the two ships together came to 94 dead and 237 wounded—twice as many as those lost on the *Freya*, apart from those who had been drowned. The precision of the German gunfire, which had hit the British ships again and again, had a special mention in the commodore's report. But that was still not the end of the bad news. There was one report which removed the right to talk about a British victory: the *Topaz* had been so badly damaged that it sank a few hours after the *Freya*. The crew were picked up by the *Emerald*, which returned to Britain in the most miserable condition.

The mood changed suddenly. The papers were very subdued in their reporting of all these details, and some of them even went so far as to speak of a 'fratricidal' battle. A mindless, vulgar cartoon in *Punch*, which only found approval with the crowd of cultured and

'A picture postcard by the Kaiser—not sent to Lord Tweedmouth.' The battle scene was painted by the Kaiser in 1895 and had recently been published for sale as a postcard in aid of the sick. Lord Tweedmouth, First Lord of the Admiralty, had exchanged indiscreet letters about the Navy with the Kaiser

uncultured hooligans, earned that crude and unamusing comic journal quite a number of angry letters.

Downing Street was still debating whether they should send a sharp note to Germany and threaten them with coercive measures or whether they should seek an amicable settlement, when Graf Hatzfeld presented his letter of recall together with the German declaration of war. Immediately after that Sir E. Lascelles, who was still representing Britain in Berlin, reported by telegram that he had been told to leave, and that an embargo had been placed on all British ships in German ports. This embargo would be lifted, if Britain declared that it would renounce all privateering operations against German merchant ships. In a complete misjudgment of their unfavourable position, the British declined to make such a statement, and they kept on with their old business of piracy.

The German Reichstag was summoned by telegram to an extraordinary session. Until the delegates met, however, the hysterical contingent, which had been gaining ground in Germany since 1899, continued to play its nauseating game.[11] Women in trousers—figuratively speaking—and men in petticoats—again figuratively speaking—arranged meetings at which female doctors of law and male professors of philosophy wailed and whimpered in every manner over the threat to peace. This unprincipled nonsense only came to an end when a short, sharp note in the *Reichsanzeiger* announced that the organizers of such gatherings and their principal speakers would be taken to court to be charged with treason.

At the same time, a known lickspittle from South Germany got a rude awakening. He ran a rag of a paper in which for years, unnoticed by the public prosecutor and unchecked by the law, he had conducted the most infamous rabble-rousing propaganda against Prussia and the Reich. He published one of his usual immensely vulgar articles, in which he rejoiced at the sinking of the *Freya*, and, amongst other things, he remarked: 'Even the Prussian swine could not stomach the shells from the British warships.' After a week had passed without any action from the public prosecutor, an inset appeared in a prominent position in the *Norddeutschen Allgemeinen Zeitung*. This expressed amazement that in a federal state such gross misconduct should have escaped the notice of the authorities who would normally be exceptionally sensitive if it concerned matters that might, for example, do harm at the court of the Tsar. This hint was enough for the ministers to discover that the citizen had duties not only to Russia but also to the Emperor and the Reich.

The terrible beating that the timeserver received from enraged students was in part-payment for the judicial punishment waiting for that miserable citizen; but he escaped it by fleeing to Austria.

The Emperor opened the Reichstag in person, where only three members were absent, for reasons of health, from the entire assembly. In his speech from the throne, when he spoke about the glorious end of the *Freya*, his voice faltered and he burst into tears, and only after a long pause did he recover his composure. The emotion in the chamber was indescribable.

The government demanded considerable funds for the conduct of the war. In his speech the Emperor observed that certain circumstances, on which for obvious reasons he could not expound in more detail, showed that the coming naval war against Britain was by no means as hopeless as it might seem to an outsider. He said that he counted on the patriotism of the nation, which had never failed him even in the most seemingly desperate situations. It guaranteed him in any case an honourable and, as he had the confidence to hope, a victorious outcome to the inevitable and bitter conflict.

The war opens with the British merchant navy suffering enormous losses by capture or sinking. However, the future in fiction of this kind is what the author makes it; and, since Karl Eisenhart aims at a great German triumph, he follows British and French future-war writers by inventing a secret weapon. A Heidelberg scientist, the late Professor M., has created an electric engine of great power: it allows their warships to operate without the need for coal or coaling stations. In consequence Germany has no difficulty in destroying two British fleets. Peace negotiations follow. In the usual manner there is an advantageous transfer of colonial possessions; and the Germans take the opportunity to make a secret agreement with the British behind the backs of their allies. Naturally, Graf Bülow tells the British plenipotentiary, Lord Muckelbarrow, with great good humour, that ...

Germany was animated by the most lively desire to restore good relations with Great Britain, and for that reason would not lay down any unreasonable peace terms. The terms themselves, however, were not open to discussion.[12] They were to be accepted or rejected in their entirety. The terms were as follows:

1. Territories to be ceded:
   a) in Europe: Gibraltar.
   b) in Africa: Walvis Bay, Zanzibar, Witu and the rest of North-east Africa, and the Niger area.
   c) in the South Seas: Tonga and the British territory in New Guinea.
2. To be renounced:
   a) the British right of pre-emption in Portuguese territory in Africa.
   b) British claims to the Fiji Islands.
3. No war reparations; but payment of the purchase price to the English companies which are to be expropriated by Germany in the ceded territories; additionally, payment to Holland for the Dutch part of New Guinea purchased by Germany—Holland, for reasons which it would take too long to elaborate here, had placed all her island empire in the Far East under German protection; and payment to Portugal for Goa and for the Portuguese part of Timor.

The settlements between the latter two states were soon completed: Portugal was to receive 16 million marks and Holland 12 million marks. Britain could not turn down so small a bill for war damages. Moreover, Germany could be pleased with it, since she could set her commercial losses against the enormous number of British prizes during the last weeks of the war. When the peace treaty was close to completion, the Kaiser found yet another way of making a courteous gesture to the British, since he presented them with Goa as a small exchange for their large territorial cessions. That was a bitter-sweet revenge for Heligoland. Just as Germany had once obtained that worthless island (only because it lay in German coastal waters) by paying a comparatively high price in Africa, in like manner Britain now gained the Indian enclave in exchange for large cessions of territory in other areas of the world. By this means the sting of humiliation was in some measure taken out of the treaty.

The two powers of Russia and France faced each other, ignorant of the transactions conducted in the greatest secrecy, and they repeated their demand for peace negotiations in a more pressing manner. On this occasion Germany refused in a positive, unequivocal, and indeed courteous manner. In Britain, where there was the need to repair war damages, the short answer to the would-be mediators was that their demand was seen as an unfriendly act.

Whilst they were considering how they should answer this shameful refusal in Paris and St Petersburg, the news arrived of the conclusion of the peace treaty, and with that the fervid activity of the Dual Alliance was at an end. They would gladly have responded with warlike measures to the provocative rejection from Britain, but they had to keep to the peace terms and to the attitude of the contracting powers, lest there should be yet another secret arrangement. On the Seine and on the Neva, they were convinced that Britain could count on an alliance with Germany in the event of a war with the Franco-Russians. They pointed to the analogy which was to be found in Bismarck's actions after 1866. At the time when the peace treaty was concluded, Germany had made it her aim to win over with forbearance the recently defeated enemy. So, they reckoned it might not be impossible to make a friend of Britain in the future.

IN THE BALTIC.

First British Tar (to Second Ditto). "'ERE, MATE, LET'S BREAK THE ICE. WOT'S THE GERMAN FOR 'ENTENTE'?"

Chapter Two
The Enemy Within and the Enemy beyond the Seas

By the first year of the twentieth century, the new myth of the coming war between the British and the Germans was in the making. As early as 1900 the authors of Die Abrechnung mit England *and* Wehrlos zur See *had shown their German readers that the United Kingdom would be the primary target in the Great War of the future. On the other side of the North Sea, however, there were uncertainties about the naming of the enemy. Although Germany had first appeared as the future foe in* Spies of the Wight *(1899) and in* How the Germans took London *(1900), the old war against the French still went on in stories like 'The Sack of London' in* The Great French War of 1901 *(1901). In fact, there was no immediate change for the military: in* The Campaign of Douai *(1899) Captain Cairnes described the role of Germany in the Anglo-German war against the Russians and the French; and Colonel F. N. Maude warned of the danger of a surprise raid by the French in* The New Battle of Dorking *(1901). In fact, the last stage in the slow decline and disappearance of the familiar French enemy came close to farce. By a seemingly innocent coincidence, two civilian writers—F. M. Allen in* London's Peril *(1900) and Max Pemberton in* Pro Patria *(1901)—squeezed the last drops from the golden orange of fantasy by producing accounts of a French plan to invade England by way of a secret tunnel under the Channel.*

These hesitations about the name of the enemy in tomorrow's war reflected contemporary uncertainties about the future of the United Kingdom at a time when the Boer War still had a year to run, when French resentment over the Fashoda incident of 18 September 1898 had not diminished, when the German Navy Bill of 12 June 1900 had doubled the size of Germany's battle fleet. It followed that the 'Kaiser's Navy', as it was known, would be 'numerically the mightiest naval power in the "narrow seas", with a double squadron of seventeen battleships and a number of cruisers always in commission'; and, in consequence, as the eminent naval historian and propagandist Archibald Hurd noted, the British had to recognize 'that Germany is making a bold bid for supremacy in the waters that we have been accustomed to regard as essentially British'.[1] So, the questions were:

*would the French attack while the British were entrapped in the Boer War,
or would the French join with the Germans for a combined descent on
England?*

The Invaders

*In 1901, Louis Tracy returned to future-war fiction with an original contri-
bution to the notion of 'the enemy within'. Terror and confusion mark the
opening of* The Invaders, *as French and German troops come out of hiding
in Liverpool and Birmingham. An eye-witness tells Major Forster, the hero,
of their sudden attack in the opening chapter ...*

THE IDES OF MARCH

'All I know is, that at six o'clock I was walking home from my office
when, as I passed the telegraph office, a large number of men
suddenly rushed into it. I heard shots within and shrieks. The police
came. A crowd gathered. Mounted men, in khaki uniforms, but
speaking German or French, seemed to drop from the sky and cut
down or shoot every policeman or other person in their way. At the
same moment I heard the booming of cannon in the river. I was

The 1907 Territorial and Reserve Forces Act established the new volunteer Territorial
Force, which many saw as a major safeguard against invasion

carried away by the crowd into South John Street, and managed, half-fainting, to reach this hotel. My friend here', for Mr. Colt had risen whilst he spoke, and now indicated a gentleman in the group near him, 'tells me that he actually saw thousands of men surrounding the *Servia* and other transport vessels in the docks and shooting soldiers and crew indiscriminately. I myself, in Lord Street, witnessed the cold-blooded butchery of a small detachment of the Army Service Corps which was escorting, unarmed, some commissariat waggons to the docks.'

'Yes,' broke in the man he had alluded to. 'I was coming up town by the Overhead Railway, and exactly at six o'clock I saw a large number of men, all wearing long overcoats, rush up the gangways of the *Servia*, which is berthed in the Clarence Dock, and begin shooting, apparently with Mauser pistols. The train passed Prince's Dock, and the same bloody work was evidently in progress on board other ships, but at Pierhead Station the train was unable to proceed further in safety. I passed through Water Street and Dale Street, in which there were scores of corpses—nearly all men in uniform, police, soldiers, and sailors—and only reached here five minutes before you.'

'In a word, Major Forster,' said Mr. Colt, 'Liverpool has been attacked and taken by an unknown enemy.'

Before the officer could utter a word of amazement or further inquiry, his trained ear caught the sound of passing cavalry and guns. Followed by the others, he ran rapidly into the hall-porter's office, from which the most immediate view of the street could be obtained. For an instant he could not believe his eyes. Riding at a walking-pace up Ranelagh Street, and passing towards Mount Pleasant to the left of the hotel, came a military parade of mounted men, escorting guns and waggons, not in much order, but alert and business-like, seemingly pressing forward to some definite goal.

The light of the street lamps revealed to him British horses and arms, British cannon and ammunition carts, portions of a howitzer battery, British commissariat carts, Army Hospital waggons—all the paraphernalia of war, and all unmistakably belonging to his own service. But the officers and men! They were clothed in khaki, but not of British cut. They were quite as unmistakably foreigners; trained soldiers, selected, according to his hasty judgment, for physique and intelligence. As he looked, spellbound and doubting his own senses, he thought he recognized some of the men in a troop of cavalry. He was not mistaken. They had been among his fellow-passengers from London, and one of them saw him. The light shone fair on both, and recognition was mutual. The man drew a revolver.

'Down for your lives,' shouted the Major. Those behind him ducked, and a sharp crack, followed by a thud in the woodwork of the office, showed that a shot had been fired. A loud order from a passing officer closed the incident, and the continuous clatter of the horses' feet showed that no halt was being made in front of the hotel.

There were similar reports from Birmingham. Of a sudden, enemy soldiers appeared and took over the communication installations.

Uphill and downhill mounted men in khaki suddenly came spurring, their rendezvous evidently being the open space bounded by the Council House, Town Hall, Post Office, and Christ Church. Once arrived here they neither waited for orders, nor assumed other than a very loose military formation. Many dismounted and threw the reins to their comrades, and, exactly as the Town Hall clock struck six, a rush was made for the post and telegraph offices.

Some fifty men burst in through the great double doors that admit the public, whilst two parties, of perhaps a dozen each, ran to the side doors of the telegraph office in Pinfold and Hill Streets respectively. The Birmingham Central Post Office is a fine building for its purpose. Its narrowest width provides the New Street front, whilst its length, gradually widening, runs down the two side streets already mentioned. At the two corners in New Street are the double entrance doors, and these lead into a spacious hall, its centre occupied with stands containing postal and other information, whilst the counters follow the side walls and the back of the hall. From the centre of the rear hall a door leads into the magnificent instrument room of the telegraph department, whence instant communication can be obtained with practically all parts of the kingdom.

The strangers—each of whom was seen, by the astounded postal officials and those members of the general public who happened to be in the post office at the time, to be armed with a Mauser pistol— swarmed over the middle counter and burst through the connecting door into the telegraph room. A commissionaire who ran forward to stop them was fired at and fell severely wounded. The chief counter clerk, too, who strove to bar their progress, dropped with a bullet through his brain.

When they reached the telegraphists, who, startled by the sound of firing without, had momentarily ceased work, a man, who appeared to be the leader of the intruders, cried in a loud voice:

'Anyone who touches an instrument without my orders will be instantly shot.'

Outside could be heard some firing, the shouting of men, the screams of terrified women, the neighing and trampling of horses, but for the instant there was dead silence in the vast operating department. Then the telegraph master spoke, 'Who are you that dares to interrupt—?'

The poor fellow was allowed to say no more. The leader of the gang fired at him and smashed his right shoulder, the force of the blow at such a short distance spinning him round twice before he lurched unconscious to the floor.

'My orders must be obeyed,' he shouted again. 'The remaining employees will be unharmed, but they must communicate with no one, and above all not attempt to touch an instrument.'

Even amidst the alarm and confusion of the moment some of the clerks noted that though using perfect idiomatic English the man spoke with a foreign accent, and that he motioned to some of his followers to remove the body of the unfortunate telegraph master, the sight of which seemed to annoy him. The clerks were then marshalled into two ranks down each side of the room.

'Now,' said the foreign officer, addressing them, 'I want to know the different lines which communicate with Liverpool, Sheffield, Derby, and Goole. The senior official present will indicate these to me.'

Instinctively a number of the operators turned to look at a Mr. Robertson, who was in actual charge of the room during the day. Robertson was Scotch, and cautious. 'What will happen if I canna fall in with your wishes?' he said.

'You will be shot dead immediately,' was the calm reply. 'Failing you I will call upon the next, and the next, until I am obeyed or you are all dead. Moreover, it will be useless to try to deceive me, as the offices in those towns are now in the possession of my friends, and they will soon be in communication with me.' As if to give effect to his words one of the receivers commenced clicking rapidly with the Birmingham call.

'See what it is,' was the order, and Robertson obeyed.

'It's from Sheffield,' he said, after some interrogatory taps on the sounder.

'What is it saying?'

Click, tick, click, tick, tick went the machine, rattling out the morse alphabet, whilst the hundred or more men in the room kept perfectly still, the Englishmen feeling that Sheffield was about to announce the advent of the Day of Judgment.

'The message from Sheffield says this,' said Robertson, '"Successful in all directions. Have you a German operator in the room? If so, send him to the instrument—Gebhardt."'

'Good!' exclaimed the German. 'Here Schmidt,' he continued,

PUNCH, OR THE LONDON CHARIVARI.—September 14, 1910.

" I SPY ! "

Both (*together*). " PEEP-BO ! I SEE YOU ! "

A graphic *reductio ad absurdum* for the German spy stories

speaking German, 'take charge here and note carefully in writing what General Gebhardt has to say . . .'

'Now,' said the officer to Robertson, 'get into touch with Liverpool.'

Robertson had been thinking hard during this comparatively quiet interlude. He gathered that the German could not follow his manipulation of the telegraph instruments, and that he was intensely anxious to prevent communication with other towns than those he had named. It was risky, but Robertson resolved to try it, for even in the few minutes that had elapsed since the first inrush of the enemy it was evident that a large part of the country was in their hands. Crossing over the room, he called up London on the direct wire. Of course every Englishman present knew instantly what their plucky leader was doing, and it speaks well for their grit that none of them betrayed his knowledge by involuntary sign or look. But London would not answer, and the expert soon knew that the wire had been damaged.

'There is interference somewhere,' he explained to the German, and he moved to another route, via Northampton.

Here, again, he met with failure, though the Coventry office broke in upon his call, and said that the circuit was disconnected near Northampton. With perfect self-possession, he told the watchful officer that the Stockport route was blocked with messages so he must try Chester, which to his listening compatriots told its full story. It was impossible to communicate with London, and there was no resource left but to call up Liverpool in dead earnest.

He did so, but was obliged—this time quite honestly—to inform the German that the Chester route was, for some reason, interfered with, as the Chester office said they could not get through to Liverpool, owing to an extraordinary disturbance that was taking place there. The German smiled. 'We will soon be in possession of the Chester office,' he said, 'and then it will be all right.' He was turning away to read the communication from Gebhardt when a thought seemed to occur to him suddenly. 'Here, you,' he said, selecting at random a youngster from the ranks of the telegraphists, 'show me which of these instruments governs the direct London wire.'

For an instant Robertson's heart throbbed tumultuously, for he realized the possible motive of the question. But the lad, though terribly frightened, nevertheless kept his wits sufficiently collected to appreciate the result to his chief if he answered correctly, so he pointed out the connection with Worcester and Bristol. Quite satisfied, the German picked up the first slip of Gebhardt's message, and Robertson took a long breath.

Meanwhile strange and terrible scenes were being enacted in the streets of Birmingham. Simultaneously with the attack on the telegraph office, parties of armed foreigners seized the central telephone office, the joint station at New Street of the London and North Western and Midland Railways, the cavalry barracks in Great Brook Street, the central police and fire brigade stations, and the headquarters of the volunteer corps. Nearly all the main thoroughfares were patrolled by mounted troops, who seemed to have sprung fully armed from the earth, and a general gathering-ground for the cavalry was the open space at the top of New Street, already alluded to, and Chamberlain Square at the back of the Town Hall. Every 'bus and cab horse in the city seemed to have been promptly requisitioned, and the saddlers' shops were quickly gutted of their saddles and bridles when the stores found in the cavalry barracks were exhausted.

Throughout the city the *modus operandi* was invariably the same. Every man in uniform, mostly policemen of course, with a few soldiers and a sprinkling of sailors on leave, was shot at sight, and civilians were butchered remorselessly if they showed the least resistance or even accidentally interfered with the operations of the invading forces. Their policy was to strike terror into the hearts of the people, and, armed as they were, this was a comparatively easy task with defenceless men taken utterly by surprise.

The Enemy in our Midst

The myth of the 'Secret Army in Waiting', also known as the 'Alien Army', grew with the telling. The more detailed the statements, the greater was the readiness to believe in fabrications like the 'Committee of Secret Preparations', here described as they plot and plan in The Enemy in our Midst *in 'one of the back rooms of a house in Soho'* ...

THE PLAN OF WAR

Only half-a-dozen men were present. Each was dressed as a workman, and for their present purpose the thin disguise was enough. The leader was Captain Mahler, and the other five were also German officers. They formed what was known, in certain high

German quarters, as the Committee of Secret Preparations. Their purpose was simple and definite—to make England ready for invasion and capture. The meeting had been in progress for some time. Mahler and Schussler had joined it after leaving the police station.

'When we strike, it must be at the heart—and the heart is London!'

It was Captain Mahler who spoke; and, as he uttered the words, the weals on his face once more became livid. He spoke confidently, for he knew that he was in a dwelling which was as safe a gathering-place as any which could have been found in London. There were no police to watch their movements, no detectives to ferret out their objects. Even they, in a free country, aliens all, were as untrammelled as if they had been the native-born Englishman whom it was their deliberate purpose to supplant.

'And when will London be ready for the death-wound?' asked a dark, silent man, named Captain Roon.

'She is ready now. At last!' replied Mahler. 'And could there be a better beginning than this riot?' There was a gleam of exultation in his eyes. 'Listen,' he continued, passionately, 'we have reached the culmination of the work which we have been doing since the glorious and victorious war with France. Until then, we were satisfied to be a leading Power amongst the Continental nations! But we have changed all that! We must be a great Colonial Power, and we can do it only by taking the place of Great Britain! We have done well in Asia Minor and Brazil; with better fortune we could have had South Africa. If we did not succeed it was not for want of planting poison! We have increased our wealth enormously, and our population is rapidly becoming too large for Germany. There must be an outlet for our surplus riches and people—and the outlet is in the Empire in whose capital we stand. And only here! There is no other way!'

'You would come into the very lion's den?' asked Roon. 'You would walk into the very jaws of the brute?'

'Yes,' said Mahler, unhesitatingly.

'What of the British Army?' asked Roon. Mahler laughed contemptuously.

'The British Army!' he exclaimed. 'Has it not been damned repeatedly out of the mouths of its own rulers? Was not the truth revealed by South Africa?'

'It won in the end,' observed Roon, gravely.

'But only against a handful of farmers!' declared Mahler. 'England's forces could not meet and fight a Power of equal military strength. They would be destroyed.'

'Their history does not teach us that,' said Roon. 'They may fall sometimes, but they rise again from the very ashes of their dead. History is a teacher of truths.'

'Have we a traitor in our midst?' asked Mahler, furiously, appealing to his companions; and there was a murmur of sympathy for him.

'I am not a traitor, I am not an unbeliever in the power of Germany—I am simply looking at both sides of the question,' said Roon, quietly.

'There is only one side, and that is the downfall of England, and her utter and lasting humiliation!' continued Mahler, enthusiastically. 'Look at what we have done. We have successfully competed against them in their own markets, and we are driving their merchant ships off the seas. Only a few years ago our fastest steamers were built in English yards by English labour; now, in German yards, with German material and German labour, we are building vessels which have beaten their own at sea. We have the supremacy of the Atlantic, and there is not a sea in the East or West on which the splendid steamers of the Fatherland are not sailing. And it is the doing of his Imperial Majesty—the Kaiser. And what he has done with the Army and the Mercantile Marine, he is doing with the Imperial German Navy. The day of reckoning is at hand!'

'And because we have so easily conquered some of the British trade, cut into their industries, and are acquiring their shipping, we are to conquer the people themselves?' continued Roon.

'It is all planned, even to the last round of ammunition for the Alien Army!' said Mahler. His exultation had reached its climax; but an oppressive silence fell on the meeting. It was as if some ill omen had unexpectedly come amongst them.

Mahler looked craftily around him, and lowered his voice to a whisper, as he continued: 'Because of the blindness of these English fools, we have been for years draining our country of some of its worst and surplus population, and allowing it to settle here in London. Hints of what has been happening have been given to the British Government, and the British Government has sneered and shown contempt, after its ancient custom—has refused to believe that it can be possible for aliens in its midst to be secretly armed and drilled, that stores of arms and ammunition can be got together, that with the machine-like precision of the German Army everything can be mapped out like a railway time-table, and the very hour arranged at which the opening blow shall be struck! The hour has come! Never will there be a more favourable chance than now, when the labour crisis has come to a head, and the very working-classes are divided against themselves!'

His voice vibrated with triumph and rancorous hate.

'There is much that we have yet to learn,' said Roon, almost coldly. 'What of the cost? What if we fail?'

'There can be no failure!' declared Mahler, passionately. 'The German Army is invincible!'

'So we believe,' said Roon, 'being Germans; but even against a tribe of African savages it has not won much renown!'

'It will become a question for the Imperial German Navy,' continued Mahler, ignoring the implied taunt.

'And of the British Navy!' retorted Roon. 'Have you thought of its history? Do you know its record? Do you remember that it can make a boast like no other navy or army in the world—that it has never been beaten?'

For a moment Mahler was silent. Again, it seemed as if some cold wave had passed over and damped the enthusiasm of the meeting.

'You talk of blows,' continued Roon, earnestly. 'Cannot the British Navy strike the most terrible blow that ever a weapon of war struck since the world began?'

'We have thought of that,' replied Mahler, recovering. 'But the English people have not the necessary courage. They would gladly strike, but they are afraid to fail. It will be one swift and sudden descent upon them which will destroy them in their own waters. Even the details for that are planned. It is to be a war of ruthless crushing, and in carrying it out we shall hesitate at nothing. But before I can go on, I must have the guarantee of Captain Roon's loyalty to his Imperial master.'

'That loyalty has never been called in question,' answered Roon, still quietly, 'but, since you have spoken, I will be silent. As a German soldier, my sole duty is obedience. Pray continue your explanation.'

He leaned back in his chair, and for the rest of the meeting did not speak. Sometimes his lip curled, and there was a questioning look in his eye, but the question was not put into words. In low, passionate tones, Captain Mahler continued his explanations, and while he showed his own inveterate and insensate hatred of the country in which he had long resided, and whose people had shown him numberless kindnesses, he laid bare the plans which had been made in Germany for an invasion of England.

Years had been spent in preparing and perfecting it, and amongst all the secret agents who had been at work in England, none had striven more zealously and ruthlessly than Captain Mahler. His own personal ambition was boundless, and he saw in this projected descent, and in that alone, a means of fully realising it. He it was who had inspired the scheme which was now to be put into operation.

Steadily, year after year, German aliens had been flowing unchecked into London. Many were supposed to be on their way to other countries, merely passing through as a part of their journey; but they never got beyond the capital. That was their original destination, and there they remained. They gradually over-ran and captured Stepney, and other parts of the East End, and from that centre they began to radiate to every point of London. Soho was riddled with them. There, as in Stepney, entire streets were held by aliens; in Bloomsbury itself, quiet, sleepy, respectable Bloomsbury, the German alien was a menace. In almost every boarding-house, in the hours which he could steal from work—and they were many— there was a German waiter, and the man was known, and his record kept, by Mahler and his secret service agents.

Every registered alien German—registered by Mahler and his staff —was an authority on the topography and resources of the district in which he dwelt. If there was a *cul-de-sac* into which an enemy could be driven, or trapped, and butchered, he knew of it; if there were mews, or garages, he was acquainted with them and their accommodation for horses and vehicles; he knew the resources of every grocer's shop, every public-house, every dairy, every fruiterer's, every butcher's, every telephone call office, and every post-office. The capacities of the railways were known to a truck; the tubes were understood throughout every yard of their length, and their possibilities for an appalling sacrifice of English people calculated and put down on paper.

And another thing had been done. Careful statistics had been compiled of the London hospitals, their capacity for dealing with the wounded and sick, and, more ruthless still—for war is war, and its business must be carried out as business—the cemeteries themselves were apportioned to respective districts. Butchery there was to be, and it was to be conducted on the most modern and sanitary principles, as existing and preached and made in Germany.

There was not a square yard of London's vast area which was not as accurately known in Germany as it was in England, not an acre of Great Britain with which some German officer, as a part of his professional training, had not been made acquainted. He spoke the language of the people as understandably as they spoke it themselves, and knew that when the time for action came he would score enormously over the English military man, whose leisure had been given over to feeble social functions, and not to making even a bowing acquaintance with a language on the knowledge of which his very life might depend.

'One of our great soldiers taught us', continued Mahler, breathlessly, when he had set these things forth, 'that we might get an army corps into England, but that we could not get it out. We have profited by his meaning, and, without so much as a shot or a blow, we have got our army here! We have a hundred thousand men in London who are ready to spring to arms! They will seize the capital and hold it, our troops will pour into England at every necessary point, and before the first and paralysing blow has been recovered from, the Empire is ours! Ours to do with as we please! And it is all to be done at once, at a single blow! And the very people themselves, these foolish rioters, have paved the way for us! Hurrah!'

His voice rose to a subdued cry of triumph, but even in his intense excitement, he was careful to restrain the tones, so that they were inaudible outside the door. Fired by the picture he had drawn, and his complete assurance and enthusiasm, his hearers joined in his expressions, but Roon did not lift his voice. He also saw a mental picture; but it was not a burning British capital, a city of dead, wounded, and defeated people, a fallen Empire, a vanquished army, and a crippled fleet.

It was a picture of another capital which had collapsed, another throne which had been shattered, another army which had proved an unpricked bubble, and another fleet which had been destroyed, and which was lying, with its dead, below the dark waters of the Narrow Seas. And with it all there was still a fleet floating proudly, whose white ensigns were unscorched by battle-flames, whose guns were untarnished by powder, and whose crews were still unscathed; and this was the surplus of the mighty navy which could still be spared, despite the calls of war, to carry out its peaceful policing of its country's sea-borne commerce north and south, and east and west.

Captain Roon alone, then, remained silent when the applause was murmured of Mahler's words, and it seemed as if he only, of all the enthusiasts in the room, felt the strange chill of the Unseen which they had already jointly known. His mind, indeed, reverted to Germany, away to a village on the Rhine, where he had been born and bred, and where a fairhaired German maiden impatiently awaited his coming; for the date of the wedding, which had long ago been arranged by the two families, was rapidly approaching. He had had countless kindnesses shown him, too, in England; he had many friends amongst the English people.

And this was to be the return for their friendship and hospitality! His soul revolted from the mere contemplation of his act, but he was helpless. Like his countrymen, he was over-ridden by the God of War, the military idol whom all, from Emperor to private, fell down and worshipped; and he knew that the god was one which showed no mercy.

The meeting broke up at last, but not until the hour of midnight had been struck from many melancholy steeples. And it did not disperse until every detail which had been entrusted to the Secret Preparations Committee had been thoroughly discussed and agreed upon.

'Nothing now remains to be done except to help the fire to which the spark has been already set!' whispered Mahler, as they pushed their chairs away, and prepared to separate. 'Gentlemen, we may already congratulate ourselves on conquest! There are many honours to be won, and his Imperial Majesty the Kaiser is not forgetful of his faithful servants!'

Mahler was the first to creep stealthily down the dark, creaking staircase and into the street, along which he walked rapidly and unobserved towards the west, avoiding Oxford Street. His confederates followed singly, and at intervals, and all finally separated without arousing suspicion or attracting notice, for every policeman had been withdrawn from his beat to take a hand in quelling the rioting.

Captain Roon, alone, walked steadily onward until he reached the Embankment. He was still, to all appearances, an honest workman, and as such he easily passed in the darkness. He hurried on until he arrived at Waterloo Bridge, then he paused to look up and down the wondrous river, on the banks of which, rising ghost-like, were the colossal structures which told of the world's greatest power, luxuries, and miseries, for here were the Houses of Parliament, the huge hotels, and St Thomas's Hospital.

He noticed the glare of the fires, and already began to imagine the destruction of the noble pile of Westminster, the sacking of the hotels and other haunts of wealth, and was dwelling on the more sinister side of the picture which was suggested by the hospital.

'Can it be done?' he almost whispered aloud. 'Even now, with all our vast and careful preparations, with all this rich and splendid city honey-combed with our tools, with its very cellars sheltering our arms and ammunition, with the people actually in revolt, can we succeed?'

And by way of answer, there came that strange, cold feeling, which had oppressed him at the secret meeting. Was it answer, too, that caused the image of his betrothed, in the far-away village on the Rhine—an image which had been radiant and clear—fade slowly away, as if an opaque curtain had been drawn between the lovers? He turned and, regardless of the trouble in the streets, walked quickly to his own rooms near Buckingham Palace.

No such gloomy forecasts troubled Mahler, as he also hastened homeward to the West. His exultation had reached its climax. The hour for which he and many others like him had patiently plotted and intensely yearned had come at last, for it was on the unanimous recommendation of the Secret Preparations Committee that the German Government was prepared to act, and that recommendation had been made.

It was now Mahler's duty to convey the decision to his country's Ambassador, and he hastened joyously, for he knew that the Ambassador was a more intense hater of England than he was, and was a man even more ambitious of his own country's advancement.

Mahler presented himself at the Ambassador's private door, and, late though the hour was, there was no difficulty or delay in securing admission, for the holding of the meeting in Soho was known, and this further meeting with the Ambassador had been arranged, whatever the hour might be.

'You are late,' said the Ambassador, in a low voice.

'We have had much to consider and talk about, your Excellency,' said Mahler, standing rigidly upright.

'And I see the result by the fire in your eyes,' said the Ambassador; 'to say nothing of the fire in the sky!'

'Everything is ready, your Excellency! At last! The infinite preparations, which are the result of years of work, are completed. The Alien Army is ready to rise, and the sacrifice is waiting to be made!'

'There can be no turning back when once we start,' said the Ambassador.

'There will be no occasion for retreat, your Excellency,' replied Mahler.

'It is victory or—'

'Death, your Excellency,' interposed the captain, quietly. 'But the issue is assured. The British Army is a proved failure, the British people are utterly untrained in war, and such Volunteers as they possess are useless for want of official encouragement. And even they are absent just now, at their annual camps of exercise, while the Regular troops themselves have been withdrawn from London for manoeuvres. Some of the ablest officers are absent, too, either in the far North or abroad, holiday-making. As for the people, the dear people, who are supposed to be so loyal and devoted to their country—well, does not that lurid sky tell its own story! It is as if the Fates had played into our hands! On the other side there is the omnipotent German Army, and the now invincible German Fleet! And your Excellency knows that there are huge ocean liners even now cruising in the Channel with German troops aboard, and within instant reach of the coast by wireless telegraph!'

The Ambassador paced the thickly-carpeted room for a few moments before he replied. 'Then we must hurry matters on. The necessary act of war is in readiness for perpetration—the English people will be easily goaded into it, and then!'

Mahler did not answer. His feelings were too overwhelming.

'You will send this by telegraphic cypher to Berlin,' said the Ambassador. 'It is for the eye of his Imperial Majesty alone. But *you* may see it!'

He showed a single sheet of plain note-paper on which was written, in cypher, without signature, the simple sentence, 'Everything is ready for the first blow!'

Within a few hours, Captain Mahler had returned with the Imperial answer, in the Imperial cypher.

It was even simpler than the original message, for it consisted of one word only:

'Strike!'

The Riddle of the Sands

The early years of the twentieth century saw a rapid consolidation of the 'German Invasion' story—from the appearance of the 'Alien Army' in The Invaders *in 1901 to the serial publication of William Le Queux's notorious* Invasion of 1910 *in the* Daily Mail, *20 March to 4 July 1906. The stories found their justification in the abundant evidence of the German dislike— hatred, many said—for the British people. The first reports on the nature and extent of German animosity appeared about 1902 in lengthy, well-informed accounts from* The Times *correspondent in Germany, and in* articles in the major journals: 'Anglophobia in Germany', 'The Anti-British Movement in Germany', 'Great Britain and Germany'. These all argued that, although the Boer War was undoubtedly one reason for the contemporary anti-British mood in Germany, the most important factor was the German push for expansion—for colonies, for a place in the sun, for a greater share in world trade.

British observers pointed to the foundation of the Flottenverein, the German Navy League created by Krupp in April 1898. Two years later there were 600,000 members; there had been more than 3,000 lectures, and 7 million pamphlets had been distributed. Then, there were those ominous speeches from the Emperor William II, who talked about the need 'to further our interests overseas'; and he went further on 1 January 1900, when he announced his determination to create a powerful navy: 'As my grandfather reorganized the army, so I shall reorganize my navy, without flinching and in the same way, so that it will stand on the same level as my army, and that, with its help, the German Empire shall reach the place which it has not yet attained.' To British ears that sounded like fighting talk; and from that time onwards, his often belligerent speeches and his function as supreme commander made the Kaiser the principal figure in Punch cartoons and gave him a leading role in future-war fiction.

The Emperor William II made his first entrance in the classic tale of The Riddle of the Sands (1903), where Erskine Childers added two new elements to the myth of the German Invasion: the secret German preparations for transporting a landing force across the North Sea, and the command function of 'one who in Germany has better right to insist than anyone else'.

Early in the cruise of the Dulcibella, the narrator talks with respect of Germany: 'her intense patriotic ardour; her seething industrial activity, and, most potent of all, the forces that are moulding modern Europe, her dream of a colonial empire, entailing her transformation from a land-power to a sea-power ... our great trade rival of the present, our great naval rival of the future ... ' The image of that future takes on a fateful shape in the penultimate chapter, where Carruthers finally unravels the mystery of Dollmann, 'an Englishman in German service', and of the naval activity about the island of Norderney off the coast of East Friesland.

THE LUCK OF THE STOWAWAY

It was nine o'clock of a fresh wild night, a halo round the beclouded moon. I passed through quiet Esens, and in an hour I was close to Bensersiel, and could hear the sea. In the rooted idea that I should find Grimm on the outskirts, awaiting visitors, I left the road short

'It was one who, in Germany, has a better right to insist than any one else.' The German
Emperor lends a hand in *The Riddle of the Sands*

of the village, and made a circuit to the harbour by way of the sea-wall. The lower windows of the inn shed a warm glow into the night, and within I could see the village circle gathered over cards, and dominated as of old by the assertive little postmaster, whose high-pitched, excitable voice I could clearly distinguish, as he sat with his cap on the back of his head and a 'feine schnapps' at his elbow. The harbour itself looked exactly the same as I remembered it a week ago. The post-boat lay in her old berth at the eastern jetty, her mainsail set and her twin giants spitting over the rail. I hailed them boldly from the shore (without showing them who I was), and was told they were starting for Langeoog in a few minutes; the wind was off-shore, the mails aboard, and the water just high enough. 'Did I want a passage?' 'No, I thought I would wait.' Positive that my party could never have got here so soon, I nevertheless kept an eye on the galliot till she let go her stern-rope and slid away. One contingency was eliminated. Some loiterers dispersed, and all port business appeared to be ended for the night.

Three-quarters of an hour of strained suspense ensued. Most of it I spent on my knees in a dark angle between the dyke and the western jetty, whence I had a strategic survey of the basin; but I was driven at times to relieve inaction by sallies which increased in audacity. I scouted on the road beyond the bridge, hovered round the lock, and peered in at the inn parlour; but nowhere could I see a trace of Grimm. I examined every floating object in the harbour (they were very few), dropped on to two lighters and pried under tarpaulins, boarded a deserted tug and two or three clumsy rowboats tied up to a mooring-post. Only one of these had the look of readiness, the rest being devoid of oars and rowlocks; a discouraging state of things for a prospective boat-lifter. It was the sight of these rowboats that suggested a last and most distracting possibility, namely, that the boat in waiting, if boat there were, might be not in the harbour at all, but somewhere on the sands outside the dyke, where, at this high state of the tide, it would have water and to spare. Back to the dyke then; but as I peered seaward on the way, contingencies evaporated and a solid fact supervened, for I saw the lights of a steamboat approaching the harbour mouth. I had barely time to gain my coign of vantage before she had swept in between the piers, and with a fitful swizzling of her screw was turning and backing down to a berth just ahead of one of the lighters, and not fifty feet from my hiding-place. A deck-hand jumped ashore with a rope, while the man at the wheel gave gruff directions. The vessel was a small tug, and the man at the wheel disclosed his identity when, having rung off his engines, he jumped ashore also, looked at his watch in the beam of the side-light, and walked towards the village. It was Grimm, by the height and build—Grimm clad in a long tarpaulin coat and a sou'-wester. I watched him cross the shaft of light from the inn window and disappear in the direction of the canal.

Another sailor now appeared and helped his fellow to tie up the tug. The two together then went aft and began to set about some job whose nature I could not determine. To emerge was perilous, so I set about a job of my own, tearing open my bundle and pulling an oilskin jacket and trousers over my clothes, and discarding my peaked cap for a sou'-wester. This operation was prompted instantaneously by the garb of two sailors, who in hauling on the forward warp, came into the field of the mast-head light.

It was something of a gymnastic masterpiece, since I was lying—or, rather, standing aslant—on the rough sea-wall, with crannies of brick for foothold and the water plashing below me; but then I had not lived in the *Dulcibella* for nothing. My chain of thought, I fancy, was this—the tug is to carry my party; I cannot shadow a tug in a rowboat, yet I intend to shadow my party; I must therefore go with them in the tug, and the first and soundest step is to mimic her crew. But the next step was a hard matter, for the crew having finished their job sat side by side on the bulwarks and lit their pipes. However, a little pantomime soon occurred, as amusing as it was inspiriting. They seemed to consult together, looking from the tug to the inn and from the inn to the tug. One of them walked a few paces inn-wards and beckoned to the other, who in his turn called something down the engine-room sky-light, and then joined his mate in a scuttle to the inn. Even while I watched the pantomime I was sliding off my boots, and it had not been consummated a second before I had them in my arms and was tripping over the mud in my stocking feet. A dozen noiseless steps and I was over the bulwarks between the wheel and the smoke-stack, casting about for a hiding-place.

The conventional stowaway hides in the hold, but there was only a stokehold here, occupied moreover; nor was there an empty apple-barrel such as Jim of *Treasure Island* found so useful. As far as I could see—and I dared not venture far for fear of the skylight—the surface of the deck offered nothing secure. But on the further or starboard side, rather abaft the beam, there was a small boat in davits, swung outboard, to which common sense and perhaps a vague prescience of its after utility, pointed irresistibly. In any case, discrimination was out of place, so I mounted the bulwark and gently entered my refuge. The tackles creaked a trifle, oars and seats impeded me; but well before the thirsty truants had returned I was settled on the floor boards between two thwarts, so placed that I could, if necessary, peep over the gunwale.

The two sailors returned at a run, and very soon after voices approached, and I recognised that of Herr Schenkel chattering volubly. He and Grimm boarded the tug and went down a companion-way aft, near which, as I peeped over, I saw a second skylight, no bigger than the *Dulcibella*'s, illuminated from below. Then I heard a cork drawn, and the kiss of glasses, and in a minute or two they re-emerged. It was apparent that Herr Schenkel was inclined to stay and make merry, and that Grimm was anxious to get rid of him, and none too courteous in showing it. The former urged that tomorrow's tide would do, the latter gave orders to cast off, and at length observed with an angry oath that the water was falling, and he must start; and, to clinch matters, with a curt good-night, he went to the wheel and rang up his engines. Herr Schenkel landed and strutted off in high dudgeon, while the tug's screw began to revolve. We had only glided a few yards on when the engines stopped, a short blast of the whistle sounded, and, before I had had time to recast the future, I heard a scurry of footsteps from the direction of the dyke, first on the bank, next on the deck. The last of these new arrivals panted audibly as he got aboard and dropped on the planks with an unelastic thud.

Her complement made up, the tug left the harbour, but not alone. While slowly gathering way, the hull checked all at once with a sharp jerk, recovered, and increased its speed. We had something in tow—what? The lighter, of course, that had been lying astern of us.

Now I knew what was in that lighter, because I had been to see, half an hour ago. It was no lethal cargo, but coal, common household coal; not a full load of it, I remembered—just a good-sized mound amidships, trimmed with battens fore and aft to prevent shifting. 'Well,' thought I, 'this is intelligible enough. Grimm was ostensibly there to call for a load of coal for Memmert. But does that mean we are going to Memmert?' At the same time I recalled a phrase overheard at the depôt, 'Only one—half a load.' Why half a load?

For some few minutes there was a good deal of movement on deck, and of orders shouted by Grimm and answered by a voice from far astern on the lighter. Presently, however, the tug warmed to her work, the hull vibrated with energy, and an ordered peace reigned on board. I also realised that having issued from the boomed channel we had turned westward, for the wind, which had been

blowing us fair, now blew strongly over the port beam. I peeped out
of my eyrie and was satisfied in a moment that as long as I made no
noise, and observed proper prudence, I was perfectly safe until the
boat was wanted. There were no deck lamps; the two skylights
diffused but a sickly radiance, and I was abaft the side-lights. I was
abaft the wheel also, though thrillingly near it in point of distance—
about twelve feet, I should say; and Grimm was steering. The wheel,
I should mention here, was raised, as you often see them, on a sort
of pulpit, approached by two or three steps and fenced by a breast-
high arc of boarding. Only one of the crew was visible, and he was
acting as look-out in the extreme bows, the rays of the masthead
lights—for a second had been hoisted in sign of towage—glistening
on his oilskin back. The other man, I concluded, was steering the
lighter, which I could dimly locate by the pale foam at her bow.

And the passengers? They were all together aft, three of them,
leaning over the taffrail, with their backs turned to me. One was
short and stout—Böhme unquestionably; the panting and the thud
on the planks had prepared me for that, though where he had
sprung from I did not know. Two were tall, and one of these must be
von Brüning. There ought to be four, I reckoned; but three were all
I could see. And what of the third? It must be he who 'insists on
coming', the unknown superior at whose instance and for whose
behoof this secret expedition had been planned. And who could he
be? Many times, needless to say, I had asked myself that question,
but never till now, when I had found the rendezvous and joined the
expedition, did it become one of burning import.

'Any weather' was another of those stored-up phrases that were
apropos. It was a dirty, squally night, not very cold; for the wind still
hung in the S.S.W.—an off-shore wind on this coast, causing no
appreciable sea on the shoal spaces we were traversing. In the
matter of our bearings, I set myself doggedly to overcome that
paralysing perplexity, always induced in me by night or fog in these
intricate waters; and, by screwing round and round, succeeded so far
as to discover and identify two flashing lights—one alternately red
and white, far and faint astern; the other right ahead and rather
stronger, giving white flashes only. The first and least familiar was, I
made out, from the lighthouse on Wangeroog; the second, well
known to me as our beacon star in the race from Memmert, was the
light on the centre of Norderney Island, about ten miles away.

I had no accurate idea of the time, for I could not see my watch,
but I thought we must have started about a quarter-past eleven. We
were travelling fast, the funnel belching out smoke and the bow-

wave curling high; for the tug appeared to be a powerful little craft, and her load was comparatively light.

So much for the general situation. As for my own predicament, I was in no mood to brood on the hazards of this mad adventure, a hundredfold more hazardous than my fog-smothered eaves-dropping at Memmert. The crisis, I knew, had come, and the reckless impudence that had brought me here must serve me still and extricate me. Fortune loves rough wooing. I backed my luck and watched.

The behaviour of the passengers struck me as odd. They remained in a row at the taffrail, gazing astern like regretful emigrants, and sometimes gesticulating and pointing. Now no vestige of the low land was visible, so I was driven to the conclusion that it was the lighter they were discussing; and I date my awakening from the moment that I realized this. But the thread broke prematurely; for the passengers took to pacing the deck, and I had to lie low. When next I was able to raise my head they were round Grimm at the wheel, engaged, as far as I could discover from their gestures, in an argument about our course and the time, for Grimm looked at his watch by the light of a hand-lantern.

We were heading north, and I knew by the swell that we must be near the Accumer Ee, the gap between Langeoog and Baltrum. Were we going out to open sea? It came over me with a rush that we *must*, if we were to drop this lighter at Memmert. Had I been Davies I should have been quicker to seize certain rigid conditions of this cruise, which no human power could modify. We had left after high tide. The water therefore was falling everywhere; and the tributary channels in rear of the islands were slowly growing impassable. It was quite thirty miles to Memmert, with three watersheds to pass; behind Baltrum, Norderney, and Juist. A skipper with nerve and perfect confidence might take us over one of these in the dark, but most of the run would infallibly have to be made outside. I now better understood the protests of Herr Schenkel to Grimm. Never once had we seen a lighter in tow in the open sea, though plenty behind the barrier of islands; indeed, it was the very existence of the sheltered byways that created such traffic as there was. It was only Grimm's *métier* and the incubus of the lighter that had suggested Memmert as our destination at all, and I began to doubt it now. That tricky hoop of sand had befooled us before.

At this moment, and as if to corroborate my thought, the telegraph rang and the tug slowed down. I effaced myself and heard Grimm shouting to the man on the lighter to starboard his helm, and to the look-out to come aft. The next order froze my very marrow;

it was 'lower away'. Someone was at the davits of my boat fingering the tackles; the forward fall-rope actually slipped in the block and tilted the boat a fraction. I was just wondering how far it was to swim to Langeoog, when a strong, imperious voice (unknown to me) rang out, 'No, no! We don't want the boat. The swell's nothing; we can jump! Can't we, Böhme?' The speaker ended with a jovial laugh. 'Mercy!' thought I, 'are *they* going to swim to Langeoog?' but I also gasped for relief. The tug rolled lifelessly in the swell for a little, and footsteps retreated aft. There were cries of *'Achtung!'* and some laughter, one big bump and a good deal of grinding; and on we moved again, taking the strain of the tow-rope gingerly, and then full-speed ahead. The passengers, it seemed, preferred the lighter to the tug for cruising in; coal-dust and exposure to clean planks and a warm cuddy. When silence reigned again I peeped out. Grimm was at the wheel still, impassively twirling the spokes, without a glance over his shoulder at his precious freight. And, after all, we *were* going outside.

Close on the port hand lay a black foam-girt shape, the east spit of Baltrum. It fused with the night, while we swung slowly round to windward over the troubled bar. Now we were in the spacious deeps of the North Sea; and feeling it too in increase of swell and volleys of spray.

At this point evolutions began. Grimm gave the wheel up to the look-out, and himself went to the taffrail, whence he roared back orders of 'Port!' or 'Starboard!' in response to signals from the lighter. We made one complete circle, steering on each point of the wind in succession, after that worked straight out to sea till the water was a good deal rougher, and back again at a tangent, till in earshot of the surf on the island beach. There the manoeuvres, which were clearly in the nature of a trial trip, ended; and we hove to, to tranship our passengers. They, when they came aboard, went straight below, and Grimm, having steadied the tug on a settled course and entrusted the wheel to the sailor again, stripped off his dripping oilskin coat, threw it down on the cabin skylight, and followed them. The course he had set was about west, with Norderney light a couple of points off the port bow. The course for Memmert? Possibly; but I cared not, for my mind was far from Memmert to-night. *It was the course for England too.* Yes, I understood at last. I was assisting at an experimental rehearsal of a great scene, to be enacted, perhaps, in the near future—a scene when multitudes of sea-going lighters, carrying full loads of soldiers, not half loads of coal, should issue simultaneously, in seven ordered fleets, from seven shallow outlets, and, under escort of the Imperial

Navy, traverse the North Sea and throw themselves bodily upon English shores.

Indulgent reader, you may be pleased to say that I have been very obtuse; and yet, with humility, I protest against that verdict. Remember that, recent as are the events I am describing, it is only since they happened that the possibility of an invasion of England by Germany has become a topic of public discussion. Davies and I had never—I was going to say had never considered it; but that would not be accurate, for we had glanced at it once or twice; and if any single incident in his or our joint cruise had provided a semblance of confirmation, he, at any rate, would have kindled to that spark. But you will see how perversely from first to last circumstances drove us deeper and deeper into the wrong groove, till the idea became inveterate that the secret we were seeking was one of defence and not offence. Hence a complete mental somersault was required, and, as an amateur, I found it difficult; the more so that the method of invasion, as I darkly comprehend it now, was of such a strange and unprecedented character; for orthodox invasions start from big ports and involve a fleet of ocean transports, while none of our clues pointed that way. To neglect obvious methods, to draw on the obscure resources of an obscure strip of coast, to improve and exploit a quantity of insignificant streams and tidal outlets, and thence, screened by the islands, to despatch an armada of light-draught barges, capable of flinging themselves on a correspondingly obscure and therefore unexpected portion of the enemy's coast; that was a conception so daring, aye, and so quixotic in some of its aspects, that even now I was half incredulous. Yet it must be the true one. Bit by bit the fragments of the puzzle fell into order till a coherent whole was adumbrated.

The tug surged on into the night; a squall of rain leapt upon us and swept hissing astern. Baltrum vanished and the strands of Norderney beamed under transient moonlight. Drunk with triumph, I cuddled in my rocking cradle and ransacked every unvisited chamber of the memory, tossing out their dusty contents, to make a joyous bonfire of some, and to see the residue take life and meaning in the light of the great revelation.

My reverie was of things, not persons; of vast national issues rather than of the poignant human interests so closely linked with them. But on a sudden I was recalled, with a shock, to myself, Davies, and the present.

We were changing our course, as I knew by variations in the whirl of draughts which whistled about me. I heard Grimm afoot again, and, choosing my moment, surveyed the scene. Broad on the port-beam were the garish lights of Norderney town and promenade, and the tug, I perceived, was drawing in to enter the See-Gat. Round she came, hustling through the broken water of the bar, till her nose was south and the wind was on the starboard bow. Not a mile from me were the villa and the yacht, and the three persons of the drama—three, that is, if Davies were safe.

Were we to land at Norderney harbour? Heavens, what a magnificent climax!—if only I could rise to it. My work here was done. At a stroke to rejoin Davies and be free to consummate our designs!

A desperate idea of cutting the davit-tackles—I blush to think of the stupidity—was rejected as soon as it was born, and instead, I endeavoured to imagine our approach to the pier. My boat hung on the starboard side; that would be the side away from the quay, and the tide would be low. I could swarm down the davits during the stir of arrival, drop into the sea and swim the few yards across the dredged-out channel, wade through the mud to within a short distance of the *Dulcibella*, and swim the rest. I rubbed the salt out of my eyes and wriggled my cramped legs ... Hullo! why was Grimm leaving the helm again? Back he went to the cabin, leaving the sailor at the helm ... We ought to be turning to port now; but no—on we went, south, for the mainland.

Though one plan was frustrated, the longing to get to Davies, once implanted, waxed apace.

Our destination was at last beyond dispute. The channel we were in was the same that we had cut across on our blind voyage to Memmert, and the same my ferry-steamer had followed two days ago. It was a *cul-de-sac* leading to one place only, the landing stage at Norddeich. The only place on the whole coast, now I came to think of it, where the tug could land at this tide. There the quay would be on the starboard side, and I saw myself tied to my eyrie while the passengers landed and the tug and lighter turned back for Memmert; at Memmert, dawn, and discovery.

There was some way out—some way out, I repeated to myself; some way to reap the fruit of Davies's long tutelage in the lore of this strange region. What would *he* do?

For answer there came the familiar *frou-frou* of gentle surf on drying sands. The swell was dying away, the channel narrowing; dusky and weird on the starboard hand stretched leagues of new-risen sand. Two men only were on deck; the moon was quenched under the vanguard clouds of a fresh squall.

A madcap scheme danced before me. The time, I *must* know the time! Crouching low and cloaking the flame with my jacket, I struck a match: 2.30 a.m.—the tide had been ebbing for about three hours and a half. Low water about five; they would be aground till 7.30. Danger to life? None. Flares and rescuers? Not likely, with 'him who insists' on board; besides, no one could come, there being no danger. I should have a fair wind and a fair tide for *my* trip. Grimm's coat was on the skylight; we were both clean shaved.

The helmsman gazed ahead, intent on his difficult course, and the wind howled to perfection. I knelt up and examined one of the davit-tackles. There was nothing remarkable about it, a double and a single block (like our own peak halyards), the lower one hooked into a ring in the boat, the hauling part made fast to a cleat on the davit itself. Something there must be to give lateral support or the boat would have racketed abroad in the roll outside. The support, I found, consisted of two lanyards spliced to the davits and rove through holes in the keel. These I leaned over and cut with my pocket-knife; the result being a barely perceptible swaying of the boat, for the tug was under the lee of sands and on an even keel. Then I left my hiding-place, climbing out of the stern sheets by the after-davit, and preparing every successive motion with exquisite tenderness, till I stood on the deck. In another moment I was at the cabin skylight, lifting Grimm's long oilskin coat. (A second's yielding to temptation here; but no, the skylight was ground glass, fastened from below. So, on with the coat, up with the collar, and forward to the wheel on tiptoe.) As soon as I was up to the engine-room skylight (that is to say, well ahead of the cabin roof) I assumed a natural step, went up to the pulpit and touched the helmsman on the arm, as I had seen Grimm do. The man stepped aside, grunting something about a light, and I took the wheel from him. Grimm was a man of few words, so I just jogged his satellite, and pointed forward. He went off like a lamb to his customary place in the bows, not having dreamt—why should he? of examining me, but in him I had instantly recognized one of the crew of the *Kormoran*.

My ruse developed in all its delicious simplicity. We were, I esti-mated, about half-way to Norddeich, in the Buse Tief, a channel of a navigable breadth, at the utmost of two hundred yards at this period of the tide. Two faint lights, one above the other, twinkled far ahead. What they meant I neither knew nor cared, since the only use I put them to was to test the effect of the wheel, for this was the first time I had ever tasted the sweets of command on a steamboat. A few cautious essays taught me the rudiments, and nothing could hinder the catastrophe now.

I edged over to starboard—that was the side I had selected—and again a little more, till the glistening back of the look-out gave a slight movement; but he was a well-drilled minion, with implicit trust in the 'old man'. Now, hard over! and spoke by spoke I gave her the full pressure of the helm. The look-out shouted a warning, and I raised my arm in calm acknowledgement. A cry came from the lighter, and I remember I was just thinking 'What the dickens'll happen to her?' when the end came; a *euthanasia* so mild and gradual (for the sands are fringed with mud) that the disaster was on us before I was aware of it. There was just the tiniest premonitory shuddering as our keel clove the buttery medium, a cascade of ripples from either beam, and the wheel jammed to rigidity in my hands, as the tug nestled up to her resting-place.

In the scene of panic that followed, it is safe to say that I was the only soul on board who acted with methodical tranquillity. The look-out flew astern like an arrow, bawling to the lighter. Grimm, with the passengers tumbling up after him, was on deck in an instant, storming and cursing; flung himself on the wheel which I had respectfully abandoned, jangled the telegraph, and wrenched at the spokes. The tug listed over under the force of the tide; wind, darkness, and rain aggravated the confusion.

For my part, I stepped back behind the smoke stack, threw off my robe of office, and made for the boat. Long and bitter experience of running aground had told me that that was sure to be wanted. On the way I cannoned into one of the passengers and pressed him into my service; incidentally seeing his face, and verifying an old conjecture. It was one who, in Germany, has a better right to insist than anyone else.

As we reached the davits there was a report like a pistol-shot from the port-side—the tow-rope parting, I believe, as the lighter with her shallower draught swung on past the tug. Fresh tumult arose, in which I heard; 'Lower the boat' from Grimm; but the order was already executed. My ally the passenger and I had each cast off a tackle, and slacked away with a run; that done, I promptly clutched the wire guy to steady myself, and tumbled in. (It was not far to tumble, for the tug listed heavily to starboard; think of our course, and the set of the ebb stream, and you will see why.) The forward fall unhooked sweetly; but the after one lost play. 'Slack away,' I called, peremptorily, and felt for my knife. My helper above obeyed; the hook yielded; I filliped away the loose tackle, and the boat floated away.

A New Trafalgar

*From the beginning there was a marked contrast between the sensational
tales of 'the Enemy in our Midst' and the accounts of the coming clash at sea.
These were far more restrained, since their arguments—the strength, disposition, and battle readiness of the Royal Navy—limited their authors to
tolerable suppositions about the capabilities of the British and German fleets.
The problem for the prophets was: Given the undoubted naval superiority of
the British, how could the two fleets be brought to battle? The answer, both
in fact and in fiction, was the could-be nightmare of a nation left defenceless—'the absence of the fleet'. As Chesney had shown in* The Battle of
Dorking, *the enabling clause in the conflict-to-come began with the phrase:
'The fleet was scattered abroad.' If the Channel Squadron, the home defence
force of the early 1900s, was to be on manoeuvres or at some distant station,
then a powerful enemy fleet would have little difficulty in landing an army
corps anywhere on the south coast.*

That is the central proposition in A New Trafalgar *(1902); and the
author is quick to make the point that, with the Channel Squadron away 'on
its usual autumn cruise at Gibraltar', the defence of the United Kingdom
depended on antiquated vessels. 'Such splendid men in such wretched warships, the pity of it!'—the cry was a plea for a naval building programme
that would counter the German Navy Bill of 1900. By the day and by the
month, naval observers pointed out that, when the Navy Bill had run its
course by 1920, the German Fleet would be most powerful: 'The Prospect is
that not only will Germany be the second greatest naval Power in the world,
but in numerical strength her battle squadrons will compare with ours, and
will certainly exceed in fighting value such ships as we will be able to allo-
cate to the defence of the "near seas".'[2] Then the news comes suddenly in the
fiction of* A New Trafalgar: *the German fleet is heading across the North
Sea; and a flotilla of destroyers—a British invention which came into service
in 1893—has made the first contact with the enemy ...*

SUCH SPLENDID MEN IN SUCH WRETCHED WARSHIPS!

It must be said that the Germans had chosen the time well for their
raid; the Channel Squadron was on its usual autumn cruise at
Gibraltar, so that the first brunt of the storm would fall on a British
battle-line of nearly obsolete ships. One alteration of practice, made
but a year or two before by the Admiralty, proved of immense
advantage to England; the coastguard and port-guard ships forming
the reserve squadron had full crews on board, and indeed had but

just returned from one of their newly instituted quarterly cruises, so that when the news which the *Bat* brought home was received, there was assembled in the Thames a number of ships efficient at least as regards their crews. Such splendid men in such wretched warships, the pity of it! The situation, however, might have been far worse, as several recently completed ships had relieved some of the *Royal Sovereign* class, which in their turn had displaced some hopelessly obsolete vessels in the reserve. The battleships assembled at the Nore were:

Ramillies	*Royal Oak*	*Collingwood*
Repulse	*Benbow*	*Camperdown*
Resolution	*Anson*	*Nile*
Revenge	*Howe*	*Trafalgar*

A few years earlier, and this would have been considered a powerful fleet indeed, but the march of invention has been rapid in naval affairs,[3] and with the exception of the quickfirers on the *Nile* and *Trafalgar*, and four six-inch guns only on each of the *Royal Sovereign*s, the crews of the secondary armaments of these huge ships were bare to even small-bore shell-fire.

In addition to the above ships, there were a number of cruisers, some hastily mobilized, and some drawn from the training squadron with seasoned crews. In the dockyards a number of ships were refitting, and under repair, which could not possibly be ready for the sudden emergency.

The news brought by the *Bat* sent a thrill through the country, and a sense of exultation too; it was felt that the destroyers had worthily vindicated the sea-queen's children.

As Barlow with his squadron sailed up the Medway, they were everywhere greeted by cheering knots of people and the hooting and whistling of steamers. Barlow shook his head: 'They are a bit too previous with their cheers, Nevil,' he said. The people indeed trusted their sailors, and not without cause, but the sailors alone knew the true gravity of the situation.

That morning, as the destroyers passed the British battle squadron, Barlow had turned gravely to his friend, and laying his hand on his shoulders, an unwonted display of feeling on his part, had said:

'Look yonder, Harry, it is we—the torpedo men—who must save old England. Go below, and write to whoever you love best—it may be the last letter she, or the old admiral you talk of, may ever have from you.'

Admiral Dobson, in the *Revenge*, had received Barlow's report, and directed him to coal, and make good what deficiencies he could in the time, and rejoin him within twelve hours.

From every British war port, a stream of small craft of every description was steadily flowing up-channel. On shore the country itself was not idle; men sprang to arms, broken veterans of the Boer War, men who had seen and therefore knew the value of irregular corps, formed nuclei round which bands of rifle-men collected; and various volunteer regiments, stiffened now by men who had been shot at, were mobilized at every railway centre, where long rows of empty trains waited in the sidings for news of the place of the enemy's landing.

The night of the 3rd October is a black, panic-stricken memory even yet for London's citizens. The evening papers announced all sorts of contradictory reports, and Fleet Street and its environs were a seething black mass of people afflicted with a dreadful attack of nerves. The crowd reached a state of excitement when it might do anything and commit any excess; but, strange to say, the definite official news that the enemy had landed at Harwich, and that the Government was taking every measure for their expulsion, had an instantaneously soothing effect, and, though excited knots of people stayed in the streets all night, the larger bulk of the crowd melted away on learning the worst.

The *Falcon*'s crew had a hard job to patch up their boat, and indeed if Macfarlane, the engineer—or rather, chief engine-room artificer, who acted as engineer—had not possessed a valued friend and compatriot in the Yard, they would not have managed it in time; as it was, by dint of a good deal of faking, and a judicious application of paint, she looked almost new when the admiral inspected her. He had a conveniently short-sighted eye, that good admiral.

'I suppose she can steam?' he asked.

'Yes, sir, Macfarlane says he will answer for twenty-five knots,' Barlow replied.

'Well, you may take her out.'

The crew were as pleased as if they had been granted a fortnight's leave.

Barlow made arrangements for them to have a few hours' rest, and never were tired men more thankful for a little sleep.

Just before going below, Nevil was watching a destroyer steaming down the river, when an old petty officer standing near touched his cap.

'Beg pardon sir, that's the *Thrasher*.'

'Oh! she's a long way from home. A Plymouth boat, isn't she?'

'Yes sir, this is her last voyage sir.'

'"Her last voyage"; what do you mean Haines?'

'Well sir, she's always been an unlucky craft, and there ain't a man aboard her at this minute as don't know that this is her last voyage. And I pities the Dutchman as gets across her bows to-morrer, they just means to give 'em hell all they knows sir.'

Pondering this bit of seaman's logic, Harry went below to his berth.

The German strategists had indeed showed but scant respect for the 'fleet in being', and were proceeding on a plan long projected and openly discussed in their service papers; they were determined, having evaded our fleet by a surprise attack, to carry London by a sudden overwhelming rush.

It was no part of the British admiral's policy, however, to allow their landing to go undisturbed, and by dawn on the 4th, the *Falcon* found herself steaming steadily forward into the North Sea, with the huge bulk of the *Revenge*, the leading ship in the British battle-line, lying on their starboard bow.

The cruisers were spread out in a long line across the front of the fleet, to act as scouts, and the battleships steamed in a compact double 'line ahead', each with a destroyer under her port quarter. It was a beautiful autumn morning, the clouds to the east being blown away in ragged clusters, leaving a pale golden sky, up which the sun was quickly climbing. There was a fresh breeze stirring, and though the sea had fallen since the previous day, it was still in a restless mood, and the translucent grey-green waves were often flecked with foam, which caught the early morning sunshine, and flashed back a thousand jewelled points of light through the brisk, keen, kindly air.

Tired and worn as the struggles of the past few days had left him, Nevil breathed the strong air with a sense of exhilaration, and felt that life was well worth living on a morning such as this; and when the signal, 'enemy in sight' came twinkling down the line in a flutter and dance of flags, his heart beat high with hope and resolution, and, looking down the deck of the little craft, he could see the same feelings reflected in the faces of his fellows.

From the position of the *Falcon*, it was fairly easy to make out the German fleet, and to a certain extent their formation, which was, they afterwards heard definitely, two lines ahead, in fact, in the same disposition as the British ships. The nearest German line was composed of eight large and powerful battleships, of which four were of the magnificent Kaiser class. The eight ships of the second line were all of the comparatively small, but well-protected Odin class.

The relative power of the two opposing fleets may well be stated by the comparison of their heavy guns, the British battleships carrying forty-nine to the Germans' sixty-four. But the British sailor is not apt to count odds too closely; moreover, the Navy knew Admiral Dobson as a man with a head on his shoulders, and a will to use that head, and trusted him.

The first manoeuvre of Admiral Dobson was a subtle one; he leaned over the taffrail of the *Revenge* and called to Barlow:

'Destroyers are to take cover, and lie concealed close under the lee of the battleships, until they receive further orders.'

Barlow made the necessary signals to his command, and the *Falcon* crept close under the port side of her huge companion. The British had one great advantage, in the fact that their united fleet speed was quite three knots more than their opponents', and they had been exercised at their full speed in manoeuvres. Another great gain to the British was that the Germans had, at all costs, to protect their transports, a second fleet of which, containing most of their artillery and about forty thousand men, were just within sight of the British coast. Of these two facts the British admiral took full advantage.

The cruiser divisions, now that touch was obtained between the hostile battle-fleets, drew off, and were engaged in a desperate encounter to the north-east.

But the British battleships concern us most, and we have seen that for them the fight really began with the ambuscading of the destroyers. Then followed a personal duel between two highly trained players; the fleets were many miles apart, and no shot had been fired, yet each admiral manoeuvred for victory. Steaming at about eleven knots, which is the utmost speed for fleet tactics in every navy but the British, the fleets were swung this way and that in long flexible lines, drawing now nearer, now further apart.

The sailors half humorously grumbled under their breath, 'they weren't out for bloomin' steam tattics, they could 'ave them at 'ome any day'. But at last Admiral Dobson's object was attained, and the signal was made for 'fifteen knots' speed', and, with a steady rush, the British fleet drove straight for the German transports, some fifteen miles off.

The German admiral now made a fatal move. He determined at every cost, to try and head the British line away from their apparent objective, and the result was, that the two fleets were steaming at a wide angle for the same point some eight miles ahead of the *Revenge* and ten miles from the *Kaiser Wilhelm II*, the leading German ship.

Then Admiral Dobson did a daring thing. With his fleet actually steaming at the pace they were, he ordered the lee line to fill up the intervals, and Nevil saw, almost with a shiver, the huge bows of the *Resolution* bearing down, apparently full for the broadside of the *Falcon*. On she came, a towering object, and as if by magic slipped astern and swung round in the wake of the flagship, with the *Thrasher* destroyer close under her port beam, held there as though by some invisible bond.

Looking back along the line now, the fleet formed a magnificent spectacle, a long dark line of huge hulls close together, forcing wild foam surges from their bows in which their attendant destroyers danced and tumbled. Scarcely any smoke came from their funnels in spite of their speed; the stokers were using Welsh coal, and using it well—the admiral's least signal could be seen far down the line. Far to the eastward lay the low line of the Essex coast, right ahead could be seen a confused mass of transports, while on the starboard bow was the German fleet, black smoke-clouds pouring from the funnels, which the westerly wind blew straight over the bows of the fol-lowing ships, so that when the British executed their last manoeuvre, and the German admiral seemed for a moment to hesi-tate, a certain amount of confusion was apparent in their lines.

It was the British admiral's intention to cross the bows of the Germans, and so concentrate the full broadsides of successive ships on the leading German vessel, thus ever bringing fresh ships, with gun fire undiminished by loss, to bear on partially shattered foes. Nevil, standing outside the after steering-shelter, had been able to guess with fair accuracy the meaning of the various manoeuvres, and he turned with a cheerful smile to Haines:

'Well, the admiral has got the weather-gauge of the Dutchmen at last, Haines, and now the little game is going to begin; I must say, I'm jolly well glad I'm not on the German flagship.'

The news went round the destroyer's dingy deck that 'the loote-nan' thought as 'ow the old man 'ad pretty well sewed up the damned Dutchman awready', and the men in threes and fours, lying behind coal-bags stacked round guns and torpedo-tubes, began to chaff each other, and make humorous remarks in low-toned growls on the seamanship of the enemy.

Meanwhile no shot had been fired, and the only indication of the approach of the enemy to be observed on the destroyer's deck was the slow movement of the huge barbette guns on their consort as they swung steadily round, keeping their muzzles full on the foe. So, for many minutes, the long line of ships rushed silently through the

green seas. The feeling of suspense grew and grew, till suddenly a
wild, weird, wailing scream tore through the air over their heads,
and, rattling away to port, like some gigantic aerial railway train,
went the huge German shells, followed by the heavy report of guns
from the invisible sea beyond the flagship. Nevil's eyes followed
almost unconsciously the course of the shots as they leaped in wild
foam-spouts mile after long mile from wave to wave. Then there
came an awful concussion, that for a moment almost stayed his
breathing; the *Revenge* and the four ships next astern had fired their
concentrated broadsides simultaneously at the unfortunate German
flagship. Twenty 13-inch guns, each firing a shot weighing half a
ton, and twenty-five 6-inch quickfirers were concentrated in one
awful discharge on one vessel; the result could not be doubtful. The
Kaiser Wilhelm II simply withered up under the fire. Her forward
barbette was pierced by more than one shot, while heavy shell
bursting between decks wrecked casemate supports, and ammuni-
tion-tubes, and even drove great masses of metal through her
protective deck into the engines and boilers; she drifted out of the
line a steam-clad, scalding wreck.

Once begun, the fire never ceased; fresh ships continually coming
up added their quota to the awful din. The Germans too were not
idle, but took advantage of the exposed masses of the big guns on
the British ships, whose long muzzles showed a perfect target, as
they turned to their only loading position fore and aft. From this
cause, the after barbette guns of both the *Resolution* and *Repulse* were
put out of action, after they had fired but one round apiece. The
unprotected batteries of the British ships too suffered, the loss of life
being frightful at some of the 6-inch and 12-pounder guns. But
undeterred by losses, and encouraged by their first success, the
British held on with a never-faltering pace, repeating their tactics as
fresh German ships came to the head of their line.

When four of his best ships had been rendered *hors de combat* in
almost as many minutes, by this successive concentrated fire, the
German admiral made his second error; he loosed his destroyers on
his enemies. Had he but waited a few minutes longer, until the light
quickfirers on the British ships had been put out of action, he might
have been successful, but he made this desperate effort to escape
from a desperate position, ignorant as he was of the presence of
destroyers with the British.

Admiral Dobson saw the movement with joy. 'Keep where you
are,' he ordered Barlow; and by gun-fire alone were the German
boats crushed out of existence.

'Wars are over! Everything is now done by manoeuvres. The British are in control of the North Sea, and Graf Zeppelin drops dynamite on them by way of experiment. Magnificent results!'

Then at last came the welcome order, 'destroy those transports and return!' Like hell-hounds slipt from leash, the boats leapt forward.

Ten minutes' steaming took them among the German troop-ships. A stern lesson did the British seamen teach the soldiers who would tempt the seas, their Queen unwilling; torpedo and gun-fire did their awful work, the soldiers raining ineffectual bullets on their foes lying behind their shields of coal-bags. For weeks after, ghastly relics of the fight strewed the long beaches and mud flats of the Essex coast, so that to walk there was a thing of horror. The few survivors surrendered to some cruisers coming up, and the destroyers returned to the battle still raging to the south east.

They reached the fight in time to see two disasters befall the British. The *Anson* and *Benbow*, most inefficiently armoured ships, had their upper works riddled and almost blown to bits; the former, struck on her water-line by several shells, gave a couple of heavy rolls, and turned turtle going down with all hands; while the *Benbow*, very much down by the head, and evidently sinking fast, swung out of the line, and went straight for a knot of German ships. Struck repeatedly by shell, the water foaming with the storm of shot rained at her, still she held one, and with a crash caught the *Wörth* amidships, and fired her 100-ton guns point-blank into the *Weissembourg*. The *Thrasher*, following in her wake, fired two torpedoes at the latter, but, struck by a shell, she herself blew up, the *Benbow* and her tiny consort going down in splendid company.

The *Falcon* had not steamed many yards into the fight when she was fiercely engaged with two German division boats; a small shell struck the pedestal of the after 6-pounder gun close by Nevil, and killed two men instantly. Nevil sprang to the gun, and helped the remaining gunner to send shot after shot at one of their opponents; the range was almost point-blank, and a lucky shell struck the German's bow torpedo—the boat was simply blown to bits. Meanwhile their second opponent had not been idle, and an explosion forward on the *Falcon* caused Harry to leave his gun, and with set teeth step to the steering-shelter: the conning-tower was a wreck. He scarcely gave a thought to his friend, but, with every energy bent on the problem before him, took command of the destroyer. A rapid twist of the helm brought her broadside guns bearing on the *German*, who had already been a good deal knocked about, and shell after shell struck her in quick succession. Leaving her sinking in his wake, Harry steered straight to where the fight still raged. No time for pity or for thought; could Peggy have seen her sweetheart then, she would scarcely have known him, in the bleeding white-faced fierce-eyed baerseker, going straight where death was reaping his greedy harvest.

Harry felt that he was passing through some fearful waking night-mare. A huge shape loomed up grey and battered, with heavy, ungainly masts, and they swept past her, leaving ruin behind; a swift destroyer flying across their bows towards the British battleships, and the 6-pounder guns would bark out their vicious protest; this way and that they raged, till suddenly the din ceased, and Nevil with the rest found himself cheering hoarsely, as he held on to a splin-tered tangle of steel which had once been a gun-mounting. It was victory!

How many hours—*years*—lay between that bright fresh dawn and the greyness now hanging over a leaden sea whereon battered ships rolled heavily in far-scattered confusion? Here a ship was sinking, and there another sorely hurt was creeping shore-wards. They bore down to the *Camperdown*, and rescued some eighty of her crew; she had lost three hundred men from gun-fire alone, and now was sinking slowly. The *Falcon* stayed by her to the last, and only drew clear just in time to escape sharing her fate.

The remnants of the British cruiser division, which had been engaged with the German light ships, and in destroying the trans-ports, now steamed slowly up with a few prizes in tow, and the British admiral collected his fleet and their conquered foes for the homeward voyage. The *Royal Oak, Benbow, Anson, Howe, Collingwood*, and *Camperdown* would fly the white ensign never more, and there were but seven shattered prizes still afloat of the German fleet of sixteen ships. It was victory, but at what a cost!

At last Nevil remembered, as through a dream, the ruined conning tower, and with sickening heart went forward. Amid the ruin he found Barlow lying under a mass of iron jammed across the narrow space; from under this they drew him, and Nevil often says that the low moan of pain which came from the lieutenant's lips was the sweetest music he had ever heard: his friend lived!

The author had not read the future accurately enough. He describes how the French side with Germany against the British. With the limitless facility of fiction he introduces the latest secret weapon in the last pages of his story. The new British vessels are 'immense, squat terrible-looking leviathans, each carrying four huge and lofty turrets, from each of which projected the long black muzzles of four heavy guns'. They destroy the French fleet:

Far to the south-east the French cruisers were fleeing towards their own coast, while scattered over a wide space lay the shattered, semi-sinking remains of the proud battle squadron that but a short half-hour before had gone into action confident of almost certain victory, and ignorant of the new forces that have been launched to control the seas.

The Invasion of 1910

The defeat of the German fleet and the sinking of their troop transports was one way of presenting the case for bigger and better ships. Other writers chose the harder way for their warning stories—defeat, invasion, and national humiliation. That was the formula for the most notorious of all the future-war stories, William Le Queux's The Invasion of 1910 *(1906). The extraordinary success and the world-wide notoriety of that alarmist story have their origins in the 1890s, when Alfred Harmsworth commissioned William Le Queux to write a serial,* The Poisoned Bullet, *for* Answers. *This tale of future warfare taught Harmsworth a lesson he never forgot: there was nothing like a good war to send up the circulation figures. The corollary was: if the world is at peace, then an editor can always invent an imaginary war.*

By the time Harmsworth had become Lord Northcliffe, his Daily Mail *had revolutionized both the contents and the layout of the daily newspaper, and he was well on his way to establishing the largest periodical business in the world. From 1900 onwards he exercised a growing influence on politics, especially on relations with Germany. Under his direction, the* Daily Mail *kept readers informed on the need for a stronger navy and for universal military service. To this end, he organized the writing and serial publication of Le Queux's* Invasion of 1910 *in the* Daily Mail. *The ludicrous strategy in that story, the inflammatory language, and the narrative that goes at the gallop—these reveal the editor's assessment of* Daily Mail *readers. Le Queux tells the familiar tale of the successful German invasion: 'The Surprise', 'How the Enemy Dealt the Blow', 'Desperate Fighting in Essex', and so on to the 'Bombardment of London'. The bad news begins ...*

STATE OF SIEGE DECLARED

As the sun sank blood-red into the smoke haze behind Nelson's Monument in Trafalgar Square, it was an ominous sign to the panic-stricken crowds that day and night were now assembled there. The bronze lions facing the four points of the compass were now mere mocking emblems of England's departed greatness. The mobilization

Speaking in the House of Lords on the 10th July 1905, I said :– "It is to the people of the country I appeal to take up the question of the Army in a sensible practical manner. For the sake of all they hold dear, let them bring home to themselves what would be the condition of Great Britain if it were to lose its wealth, its power, its position." The catastrophe that may happen if we still remain in our present state of unpreparedness is vividly and prettily illustrated in Mr. Le Queux's new book which I recommend to the perusal of every one who has the welfare of the British Empire at heart.

29. Nov: 1905   Roberts. F.M.

Field-Marshal Lord Roberts warns the nation of 'The catastrophe that may happen if we still remain in our present state of unpreparedness'

muddle was known; for, according to the papers, hardly any troops had, as yet, assembled at their places of concentration. The whole of the East of England was helplessly in the invader's hands. From Newcastle had come terrible reports of the bombardment. Half the city was in flames, the Elswick works were held by the enemy, and whole streets in Newcastle, Gateshead, Sunderland, and Tynemouth were still burning fiercely.

The Tynemouth fort had proved of little or no use against the enemy's guns. The Germans had, it appeared, used petrol bombs with appalling results, spreading fire, disaster, and death everywhere. The inhabitants, compelled to fly with only the clothes they wore, had scattered all over Northumberland and Durham, while the enemy had seized a quantity of valuable shipping that had been in the Tyne, hoisted the German flag, and converted the vessels to their own uses. Many had already been sent across to Wilhelmshaven, Emden, Bremerhaven, and other places to act as transports, while the Elswick works—which surely ought to have been properly protected—supplied the Germans with quantities of valuable material.

Panic and confusion were everywhere. All over the country the railway system was utterly disorganized; business everywhere was at a complete deadlock, for in every town and city all over the kingdom the banks were closed. Lombard Street, Lothbury, and other banking centres in the city had all day on Monday been the scene of absolute panic. There, as well as at every branch bank all over the metropolis, had occurred a wild rush to withdraw deposits by people who foresaw disaster. Many, indeed, intended to fly with their families away from the country. The price of the necessities of life had risen further, and in the East End and poorer districts of Southwark the whole population was already in a state of semi-starvation. But worst of all, the awful truth with which London was now face to face was that the metropolis was absolutely defenceless.

Would not some effort be made to repel the invaders? Surely if we had lost our command of the sea the War Office could, by some means, assemble sufficient men to at least protect London? This was the cry of the wild, turbulent crowd surging through the City and West End, as the blood-red sun sank into the west, flooding London in its warm afterglow—a light in the sky that was prophetic of red ruin and of death to those wildly excited millions.

Every hour the papers were appearing with fresh details of the invasion, for reports were so rapidly coming in from every hand that the press had difficulty in dealing with them. Hull and Goole were known to be in the hands of the invaders, and Grimsby, where the Mayor had been unable to pay the indemnity demanded, had been sacked. But details were not yet forthcoming.

Londoners, however, learnt late that night more authentic news from the invaded zone, of which Beccles was the centre, and it was to the effect that those who had landed at Lowestoft were the IXth German Army Corps, with General von Kronhelm, the Generalissimo of the German Army. This Army Corps, consisting of about 40,000 men, was divided into the 17th Division, commanded by Lieutenant-General Hocker, and the 18th, by Lieutenant-General von Rauch. The cavalry was under the command of Major-General von Heyden, and the motor infantry under Colonel Reichardt.

According to official information which had reached the War Office and been given to the press, the 17th Division was made up of the Bremen and Hamburg Infantry Regiments, the Grand Duke of Mecklenburg's Grenadiers, the Grand Duke's Fusiliers, the Lübeck

Regiment No. 162, the Schleswig-Holstein Regiment No. 163, while the cavalry brigade consisted of the 17th and 18th Grand Duke of Mecklenburg's Dragoons. The 18th Division consisted of the Schleswig Regiment No. 84, the Schleswig Fusiliers No. 86, the Thuringen Regiment, and the Duke of Holstein's Regiment, the two latter regiments being billeted in Lowestoft; while the cavalry brigade forming the screen across from Leiston by Wilby to Castle Hill were Queen Wilhelmina's Hanover Hussars and the Emperor of Austria's Schleswig-Holstein Hussars No. 16. These, with the smart motor infantry, held every communication in the direction of London.

As far as could be gathered, the German commander had established his headquarters in Beccles, and had not moved. It now became apparent that the telegraph cables between the East coast and Holland and Germany, already described in the first chapter, had never been cut at all. They had simply been held by the enemy's advance agents until the landing had been effected. And now von Kronhelm had actually established direct communication between Beccles and Emden, and on to Berlin.

Reports from the North Sea spoke of the enemy's transports returning to the German coast, escorted by cruisers; therefore the plan was undoubtedly not to move until a very much larger force had been landed. Could England regain her command of the sea in time to prevent the completion of the blow?

The *Eastminster Gazette*, and similar papers of the Blue Water School, assured the public that there was but very little danger. Germany had made a false move, and would, in the course of a few days, be made to pay very dearly for it. But the British public viewed the situation for itself. It was tired of these self-satisfied reassurances, and threw the blame upon the political party who had so often said that armed hostilities had been abolished in the twentieth century. Recollecting the Czar's proposals for universal peace, and the Russo-Japanese sequel, they had no further faith in the pro-German party or in its organs. It was they, cried the orators in the streets, that had prevented the critics having a hearing; they who were culpably responsible for the inefficient state of our defences; they who had ridiculed clever men; the soldiers, sailors, and writers who had dared to tell the plain, honest, but unpalatable truth. We were at war, and if we were not careful the war would spell ruin for our dear old England.

That night the London streets presented a scene of panic indescribable. The theatres opened, but closed their doors again, as nobody would see plays while in that excited state. Every shop was closed, and every railway station was filled to overflowing with the exodus of terrified people fleeing to the country westward, or reserves on their way to join the colours. The incredulous manner in which the country first received the news had now been succeeded by wild terror and despair. On that bright Sunday afternoon they laughed at the report as a mere journalist sensation, but ere the sun set the hard, terrible truth was forced upon them, and now, on Tuesday night, the whole country, from Brighton to Carlisle, from Yarmouth to Aberystwyth, was utterly disorganized and in a state of terrified anxiety. The Eastern counties were already beneath the iron heel of the invader, whose objective was the world's great capital—London. Would they reach it? That was the serious question upon everyone's tongue that fevered, breathless night.

THE BOMBARDMENT OF LONDON

Day broke. The faint flush of violet away eastward beyond Temple Bar gradually turned rose, heralding the sun's coming, and by degrees the streets, filled by excited Londoners, grew lighter with the dawn. Fevered night thus gave place to day—a day that was, alas! destined to be one of bitter memory for the British Empire.

Alarming news had spread that Uhlans had been seen reconnoitring in Snaresbrook and Wanstead, had ridden along Forest Road and Ferry Lane at Walthamstow, through Tottenham High Cross, up High Street, Hornsey, Priory Road, and Muswell Hill. The Germans were actually upon London!

The northern suburbs were staggered. In Fortis Green, North End, Highgate, Crouch End, Hampstead, Stamford Hill, and Leyton the quiet suburban houses were threatened, and many people, in fear of their lives, had now fled southward into central London. Thus the huge population of greater London was practically huddled together in the comparatively small area from Kensington to Fleet Street, and from Oxford Street to the Thames Embankment.

People of Fulham, Putney, Walham Green, Hammersmith, and Kew had, for the most part, fled away to the open country across Hounslow Heath to Bedfont and Staines; while Tooting, Balham, Dulwich, Streatham, Norwood, and Catford had retreated farther south into Surrey and Kent.

For the past three days thousands of willing helpers had followed the example of Sheffield and Birmingham, and constructed enormous barricades, obstructing at various points the chief roads leading from the north and east into London. Detachments of Engineers had blown up several of the bridges carrying the main roads out eastwards—for instance, the bridge at the end of Commercial Road, East, crossing the Limehouse canal—while the six other smaller bridges spanning the canal between that point and the Bow Road were also destroyed. The bridge at the end of Bow Road itself was shattered, and those over the Hackney Cut at Marshall Hill and Hackney Wick were also rendered impassable.

Most of the bridges across the Regent's Canal were also destroyed, notably those in Mare Street, Hackney, the Kingsland Road, and New North Road, while a similar demolition took place in Edgeware Road and the Harrow Road. Londoners were frantic, now that the enemy were really upon them. The accounts of the battles in the newspapers had, of course, been merely fragmentary, and they had not yet realized what war actually meant. They knew that all business was at a standstill, that the City was in an uproar, that there was no work, and that food was at famine prices. But not until German cavalry were actually seen scouring the northern suburbs did it become impressed upon them that they were really helpless and defenceless.

London was to be besieged!

This report having got about, the people began building barricades in many of the principal thoroughfares north of the Thames. One huge obstruction, built mostly of paving-stones from the footways, overturned tramcars, wagons, railway trollies, and barbed wire, rose in the Holloway Road, just beyond Highbury Station. Another blocked the Caledonian Road a few yards north of the police station, while another very large and strong pile of miscellaneous goods, bales of wool and cotton stuffs, building material, and stones brought from the Great Northern Railway depot, obstructed the Camden Road at the south corner of Hildrop Crescent. Across High Street, Camden Town, at the junction of the Kentish Town and other roads, five hundred men worked with a will, piling together every kind of ponderous object they could pillage from the neighbouring shops—pianos, iron bedsteads, wardrobes, pieces of calico and flannel, dress stuffs, rolls of carpets, floorboards, even the very doors wrenched from their hinges—until, when it reached to the second storey window and was considered of sufficient height, a pole was planted on top, and from it hung limply a small Union Jack.

[In] Finchley Road, opposite Swiss Cottage Station; in Shoot Up-Hill, where Mill Lane runs into it; across Willesden Lane, where it joins the High Road in Kilburn; [in] Harrow Road, close to Willesden Junction Station; at the junction of the Goldhawk and Uxbridge roads; [and] across the Hammersmith Road in front of the hospital other similar obstructions were placed with a view to preventing the enemy from entering London. At a hundred other points, in the narrower and more obscure thoroughfares, all along the north of London, busy workers were constructing similar defences, houses and shops being ruthlessly broken open and cleared of their contents by the frantic and terrified populace.

London was in a ferment. Almost without exception, the gunmakers' shops had been pillaged and every rifle, sporting gun, and revolver seized. The armouries at the Tower of London, at the various barracks, and the factory out at Enfield had long ago all been cleared of their contents; for now, in this last stand, every one was desperate, and all who could obtain a gun, did so. Many, however, had guns but no ammunition; others had sporting ammunition for service rifles, and others cartridges, but no guns.

Those, however, who had guns and ammunition complete mounted guard at the barricades, being assisted at some points by Volunteers who had been driven in from Essex. Upon more than one barricade in North London a Maxim had been mounted, and was now pointed, ready to sweep away the enemy should they advance.

Other thoroughfares barricaded, beside those mentioned, were the Stroud Green Road, where it joins Hanley Road; the railway bridge in the Oakfield Road in the same neighbourhood; the Wightman Road, opposite Harringay Station, the junction of Archway Road and Highgate Hill; the High Road, Tottenham, at its junction with West Green Road; and various roads around the New River reservoirs, which were believed to be one of the objectives of the enemy. These latter were very strongly held by thousands of brave and patriotic citizens, though the East London reservoirs across at Walthamstow could not be defended, situated so openly as they were. The people of Leytonstone threw up a barricade opposite the schools in the High Road, while in Wanstead a hastily constructed but perfectly useless obstruction was piled across Cambridge Park, where it joins the Blake Road.

Of course, all the women and children in the northern suburbs had now been sent south. Half the houses in those quiet, newly-built roads were locked up, and their owners gone; for as soon as the report spread of the result of the final battle before London and our crushing defeat, people living in Highgate, Crouchend, Hornsey,

Tottenham, Finsbury Park, Muswell Hill, Hendon, and Hampstead saw that they must fly southward, now the Germans were upon them.

Think what it meant to those suburban families of City men! The ruthless destruction of their pretty, long-cherished homes, flight into the turbulent, noisy, distracted, hungry city, and the loss of everything they possessed. In most cases the husband was already bearing his part in the defence of the metropolis with gun or with spade, or helping to move heavy masses of material for the construction of the barricades. The wife, however, was compelled to take a last look at all those possessions that she had so fondly called 'home', lock her front door, and with her children join in those long mournful processions moving ever southward into London, tramping on and on—whither she knew not where.

Touching sights were to be seen everywhere in the streets that day. Homeless women, many of them with two or three little ones, were wandering through the less frequented streets, avoiding the main roads with all their crush, excitement, and barricade building, but making their way westward, beyond Kensington and Hammersmith, which was now become the outlet of the metropolis.

All trains from Charing Cross, Waterloo, London Bridge, Victoria, and Paddington had for the past three days been crowded to excess. Anxious fathers struggled fiercely to obtain places for their wives, mothers, and daughters—sending them away anywhere out of the city which must in a few hours be crushed beneath the iron heel.

The South-Western and Great Western systems carried thousands upon thousands of the wealthier away to Devonshire and Cornwall—as far as possible from the theatre of war; the South-eastern and Chatham took people into the already crowded Kentish towns and villages, and the Brighton line carried others into rural Sussex. London overflowed southward and westward until every village and every town within fifty miles was so full that beds were at a premium, and in various places, notably at Chartham, near Canterbury, at Willesborough, near Ashford, at Lewes, at Robertsbridge, at Goodwood Park, and at Horsham, huge camps were formed, shelter being afforded by poles and rick-cloths. Every house, every barn, every school, indeed every place where people could obtain shelter for the night, was crowded to excess, mostly by women and children sent south, away from the horrors that it was known must come.

Central London grew more turbulent with each hour that passed. There were all sorts of wild rumours, but, fortunately, the Press still preserved a dignified calm. The Cabinet was holding a meeting at Bristol, whither the Houses of Commons and Lords had moved, and all depended upon its issue. It was said that Ministers were divided in their opinions whether we should sue for an ignominious peace, or whether the conflict should be continued to the bitter end.

Disaster had followed disaster, and iron-throated orators in Hyde and St James's Parks were now shouting 'Stop the war! Stop the war!' The cry was taken up but faintly, however, for the blood of Londoners, slow to rise, had now been stirred by seeing their country slowly, yet completely, crushed by Germany. All the patriotism latent within them was now displayed. The national flag was shown everywhere, and at every point one heard 'God Save the King!' sung lustily.

Two gunmakers' shops in the Strand, which had hitherto escaped notice, were shortly after noon broken open, and every available arm and all the ammunition seized. One man, unable to obtain a revolver, snatched half a dozen pairs of steel handcuffs, and cried with grim humour as he held them up: 'If I can't shoot any of the sausage-eaters, I can at least bag a prisoner or two!'

The banks, the great jewellers, the diamond merchants, the safe-deposit offices, and all who had valuables in their keeping were extremely anxious as to what might happen. Below those dark buildings in Lombard and Lothbury Street, behind the black walls of the Bank of England, and below every branch bank all over London, were millions in gold and notes, the wealth of the greatest city the world has ever known. The strong rooms were, for the most part, the strongest that modern engineering could devise, some with various arrangements by which all access was debarred by an inrush of water; but, alas! dynamite is a great leveller, and it was felt that not a single strong room in the whole of London could withstand an organized attack by German engineers. A single charge of dynamite would certainly make a breach in concrete upon which a thief might hammer and chip day and night for a month without making much impression. Steel doors must give to blasting force, while the strongest and most complicated locks would also fly to pieces.

The directors of most of the banks had met, and an endeavour had been made to co-operate and form a corps of special guards for the principal offices. In fact, a small armed corps was formed, and was on duty day and night in Lothbury, Lombard Street, and the vicinity. Yet what could they do if the Germans swept into London? There was but little to fear from the excited populace themselves, because matters had assumed such a crisis that money was of little use, as there was practically very little to buy. But little food was reaching London from the open ports on the west. It was the enemy that the banks feared, for they knew that the Germans intended to enter and sack the metropolis, just as they had sacked the other towns that had refused to pay the indemnity demanded.

Small jewellers had, days ago, removed their stock from their windows and carried it away in unsuspicious-looking bags to safe hiding in the southern and western suburbs, where people for the most part hid their valuable plate, jewellery, etc., beneath a floor-board, or buried them in some marked spot in their small gardens.

The hospitals were already full of wounded from the various engagements of the past week. The London, St Thomas's, Charing Cross, St George's, Guy's and Bartholomew's were overflowing; and the surgeons, with patriotic self-denial, were working day and night in an endeavour to cope with the ever-arriving crowd of suffering humanity. The field hospitals away to the northward were also reported full.

The exact whereabouts of the enemy was not known. They were, it seemed, everywhere. They had practically overrun the whole country, and the reports from the Midlands and the North showed that the majority of the principal towns had now been occupied.

The latest reverses outside London, full and graphic details of which were now being published hourly by the papers, had created an immense sensation. Everywhere people were regretting that Lord Roberts' solemn warnings in 1906 had been unheeded, for had we adopted his scheme for universal service, such dire catastrophe could never have occurred. Many had, alas! declared it to be synonymous with conscription, which it certainly was not, and by that foolish argument had prevented the public at large from accepting it as the only means of our salvation as a nation. The repeated warnings had been disregarded, and we had, unhappily, lived in a fool's paradise, in the self-satisfied belief that England could not be successfully invaded.

Now, alas! the country had realized the truth when too late.

That memorable day, September 20, witnessed exasperated struggles in the northern suburbs of London, passionate and bloody collisions, an infantry fire of the defenders overwhelming every attempted assault; and a decisive action of the artillery, with regard to which arm the superiority of the Germans, due to their perfect training, was apparent.

A last desperate stand had, it appears, been made by the defenders on the high ridge north-west of New Barnet, from Southgate to

PUNCH, OR THE LONDON CHARIVARI.—May 26, 1909.

AN EARLY SILLY SEASON.

The Sea-Serpent. "WELL, IF THIS SORT OF THING KEEPS ON, IT'LL MEAN A DULL AUGUST FOR ME."

Once again *Punch* makes fun of the mysterious flying machines, one of the many scares of the 1906–10 period

near Potters' Bar, where a terrible fight had taken place. But from the very first it was utterly hopeless. The British had fought valiantly in defence of London, but here again they were outnumbered, and after one of the most desperate conflicts in the whole campaign—in which our losses were terrible—the Germans at length had succeeded in entering Chipping Barnet. It was a difficult movement, and a fierce contest, rendered the more terrible by the burning houses, ensued in the streets and away across the low hills southward—a struggle full of vicissitudes and alternating successes, until at last the fire of the defenders was silenced, and hundreds of prisoners fell into the German hands. Thus the last organized defence of London had been broken, and the barricades alone remained.

The work of the German troops on the lines of communication in Essex had for the past week been fraught with danger. Through want of cavalry the British had been unable to make cavalry raids; but, on the other hand, the difficulty was enhanced by the bands of sharpshooters—men of all classes from London who possessed a gun and who could shoot. In one or two of the London clubs the suggestion had first been mooted a couple of days after the outbreak of hostilities, and it had been quickly taken up by men who were in the habit of shooting game, but had not had a military training.

Within three days, about two thousand men had formed themselves into bands to take part in the struggle and assist in the defence of London. They were practically similar to the Francs-tireurs of the Franco-German War, for they went forth in companies and waged a guerilla warfare, partly before the front and at the flanks of the different armies, and partly at the communications at the rear of the Germans. Their position was one of constant peril in face of Von Kronhelm's proclamation, yet the work they did was excellent, and only proved that if Lord Roberts' scheme for universal training had been adopted the enemy would never have reached the gates of London with success.

These brave, adventurous spirits, together with 'the Legion of Frontiersmen', made their attacks by surprise from hiding-places or from ambushes. Their adventures were constantly thrilling ones. Scattered all over the theatre of war in Essex and Suffolk, and all along the German lines of communication, the 'Frontiersmen' rarely ventured on an open conflict, and frequently changed scene and point of attack. Within one week their numbers rose to over 8,000 and, being well served by the villagers, who acted as scouts and spies for them, the Germans found them very difficult to get at. Usually they kept their arms concealed in thickets and woods, where they would lie in wait for the Germans. They never came to close quarters, but fired at a distance. Many a smart Uhlan fell by their bullets, and many a sentry dropped, shot by an unknown hand.

The announcement, in September 1908, of a state visit by King Edward VII to the German Emperor caused a German artist to find international harmony in the future

Thus they harassed the enemy everywhere. At need they concealed their arms and assumed the appearance of inoffensive non-combatants. But when caught red-handed, the Germans gave them 'short shrift', as the bodies now swinging from telegraph poles on various high roads in Essex testified.

When the Eagle Flies Seaward

The extraordinary success of Le Queux's Invasion of 1910 *encouraged more writers to have their say in the contemporary debate about the size and the efficiency of the armed forces. The creation of a Home Fleet—six battleships, six cruisers, forty-eight destroyers—in October 1906 did much to satisfy those who wanted to see a naval force immediately available to respond to any move by Germany; and the start on the Dreadnought construction programme in 1906 added greatly to the general satisfaction. The new battle-ships were a prodigious advance: a technological innovation that signalled 'obsolete' to the warships of the world's navies. Their new turbine engines gave them a higher speed in their class than anything seen before; and their big guns— eight twelve-inch guns on the* Dreadnought—*allowed them to act outside the range of the dreaded torpedo.*

The army, in a far less satisfactory condition, merited to some extent the judgement of 'inept and antiquated' that the authors of When The Eagle Flies Seaward *passed in 1907. Although the regiments were efficient, an antiquated command system was an effective break on their mobilization and direction. The blunders of the Boer War had revealed the folly of trying to manage a war without a general staff and without a comprehensive intelligence service. Reforms began with the establishment of the Committee of Imperial Defence in 1904; and these encompassed the entire army after that managerial genius, Richard Burdon Haldane, became Secretary for War in the Campbell-Bannerman Cabinet of 1905. He started from first principles: 'The first question was what must be our objective, and what was required for its attainment? In almost every period the peril to be provided against is different from what it is in another period.' His conclu-sions undoubtedly had a major effect on the initial engagements during the Fist World War: a friendly nation in the ports from Dunkirk to Boulogne 'was therefore an objective on which to concentrate. The accomplishment of this implied that we should have an Expeditionary Force sufficient in size and also in rapidity of mobilising power to be able to go to the assistance of the French Army in the event of an attack on the Northern or North-Eastern parts of France.'[4]*

Others wanted more than an efficient Expeditionary Force. Nothing less than a conscript army on the continental scale would satisfy them. That is the point the authors make in their tale of invasion repulsed, When the Eagle

Flies Seaward. *They open their account of the invasion with an attack on the proponents of the Blue Water School, who argued that a large and efficient navy was the surest safeguard against the possibility of invasion.*

THE ALL BUT IMPOSSIBLE HAD TAKEN PLACE

'Not even the crew of a dinghy could be landed on our shores.'

These were the boastful words of a British Minister, an ardent disciple of the Blue Water School, when speaking from his place in Britain's Parliament on the momentous and much discussed question of home defence. And though less extreme adherents to the same famous theory admitted—just as postulated by Lillinge to Lieutenant Malcolm and Mr Gunning—that a raid was possible, no one had contemplated it save as a remote possibility. Already the course of the war had made most of the nation feel absolutely safe.

The greater then came the shock of alarm, of sickening dreads and fears. Britain had suddenly learned that the all but impossible had taken place. Her inviolability—that charm seducing her these hundred years back from fulfilling her true military functions—was now become but the myth of a renegade past; a past in which the 'impossibility of an invasion' had gone to cocker the hearts of too many native Britons bent on evading their obligations in the defence of Home and Empire!

The most succinct and unbiased account of the 190– invasion is that written by a noted military authority for the important USA monthly, *World Events*, Washington DC, in its April number, 190–. By permission, it is now given for the first time to British readers, minus certain excisions relating to purely theoretical details regarding the pros and cons of the military strategies concerned.

I

…On the forenoon of January 5th, close on 12 a.m., when the City was engrossed in the business of the day, and early habitués at the clubs up west were settling down to discuss the Borkum disaster, the *Pall Mall Gazette* rushed out an early edition. Its startling poster caused a temporary stoppage of traffic in almost every street within the five mile radius from Charing Cross.

ENGLAND INVADED
60,000 GERMANS MARCHING ON THE MIDLANDS

Notwithstanding most people were still incredulous, the copies of the paper sold at sixpence each. Excited crowds gathered magically in Throgmorton Street, and amidst wild shouting sent the prices of everything running down. Another crowd collected before the Mansion House; to what end no one in it exactly knew—they had stopped just as the others had stopped, expecting something to happen. More unruly crowds poured into Trafalgar Square and along Whitehall, already thronged by peace demonstrators, and tried to charge into and break them up; but were thwarted by the strong patrols of mounted and foot police who were speedily reinforced by the military.

Here and there in the streets, stump orators harangued wildly, but the constabulary always pushed forward, and checked their flow of turbid eloquence.

Meanwhile, editions of all the newspapers, morning and evening, poured forth, and the newsboys drove a roaring trade.

Yes, the impossible had really happened.

The invaders had landed on the Lincolnshire coast—that was indubitably the case. It was conjectured their immediate object was the Midlands—was to plant themselves astride on the very backbone of Britain, and deal irreparable injuries to the spinal cord of her.

From Louth came a report of a German force landed at Skegness. Then from Spalding a reporter of the *Boston Guardian* wired the news that the old historic town was in the hands of the enemy, a huge fleet was in Boston Deep on the Lincolnshire side of the Wash, and transports were disembarking alongside Boston quays. From Grantham came tidings that German troops had seized Sleaford with its important network of railway junctions. And from Kirkstead, through Lincoln, was telephoned the information of German gunboats working up the Witham River, and that the enemy had arrived at Tattershall and Coningsby.

The *Westminster Gazette*, also *The Tribune*, in their special editions argued that the invaders were between 50,000 and 60,000 strong, gauging these numbers by the large circle held by the enemy's advanced posts. The *Globe*, *Pall Mall Gazette*, and other journals, however, pointed out that no considerable force could have been landed as yet, and protested against panic-mongering. It was a raid, not an invasion, so panic-stricken Londoners were assured by them, and would be at once effectively quashed.

'No!' screamed the alarmists, among whom were Government organs, 'it is the great vanguard of a great invasion. Our North Sea and Atlantic fleets are lured away on a wild-goose chase. If you had not jeered at our army reforms the enemy would never even have attempted this.'

In the afternoon, however, an official communication was issued stating the Government had instantly taken steps to deal with the enemy's 'expedition'. An overwhelming force was being hurried to the front to destroy or capture the invaders; and the home defence squadron was already close upon the Wash to intercept further disembarkation, to destroy all supplies, and prevent even a fragment of the enemy's force from re-embarking. No further descent could possibly occur. What had really happened was known to very few except the Committee of Defence and at the headquarters of the services, military and naval.

II

On that eventful morning, at many a hamlet and farm on the south uplands of the Lincoln wolds, and along the Witham where it flows through the undulating country west of the Boston Fens, and across the marshy levels towards Sleaford, hinds, when turning out to their work, saw in the dim winter dawn small parties of soldier cyclists riding steadily inland and so intent on making progress that they seldom exchanged even a nod in passing. Those who saw them, khaki-clad, their features similar to their own, merely thought they were some of the militia mobilized for winter training, though, afterwards, they recalled some unfamiliar details on their persons.

At Sleaford, where a half company of cyclists dashed up to the station, there was no doubt about their character. They seized the telegraph offices in the town and on the railway. They stopped a train going towards Grantham, but sent on a goods and passenger train to Boston; and, after they were passed, displaced the rails at the various junctions, disconnected the telegraph wires east and south, and placed guards to hinder anyone from leaving the town. Here, as elsewhere, it may be said, the officers in command seemed to know the names and occupations of the chief residents.

The screen of cyclists thus thrown out from Boston, together with a strong patrol from the Skegness detachment, halted after a bold dash inland and sent back some of their men who, with the help of the country folk impressed at the point of the bayonet, drove all the horses, wagons, cattle and motor cars that they could lay hands upon, back as rapidly as practicable into the invaded area.

In the course of the morning there was some skirmishing here and there with British irregulars—companies of volunteers and squads of rifle-club men who had turned out at the first words of alarm. Sometimes they were severely repulsed in their attacks on the enemy's outposts; but in other cases they cut up far-flung patrols and recaptured some of the booty.

On the Witham, two flat-bottomed gunboats (centreboard—as now used along the East Frisian coast), flying the German flag, pushed far inland, their draft being only between 4 and 5 feet. Near Kirkstead, a militia officer, who had got together a handful of volunteers and rifle-club men, took up his position on a rising ground overlooking the river, and opened a hot fusillade on both vessels; but in less than five minutes his command was scattered with heavy losses, by the withering blast of shell and machine-gun fire from the river. He had too recklessly exposed his men. The collapse of their resistance comes as no slur on their courage and staunchness.

A half-company of Jägers, disembarking from the barges towed by the *Memmert* and *Rother* up the Witham, pursued the defeated irregulars for three miles and picked up some prisoners; but were brought to a stand by the desperate resistance offered them at the first village, the villagers burning their houses in their unexpected defence. Before this, five unfortunate clubmen, who wore no uniform, had been shot by a squad just outside the village not far from the school; but a sixth, a mere lad, was released, and given copies of a proclamation warning irregular and un-uniformed levies that under the laws of war they incurred the penalty of being shot at sight.

The invaders had thrown ashore at Skegness a rifle battalion and a company of cyclists. However, their principal striking force had disembarked in the small hours of the morning at and close on Boston, where improvements to the port and waterway allow steamers up to 2,500 tons to run up to the town. The two gunboats and a small cruiser, the *Hela*, had led the way.

Just on 3.30 a.m. the few night watchmen on the quays had been surprised at seeing a number of vessels emerge from the mist and send off boatloads of armed men, who swiftly set about shifting the few vessels berthed alongside the quays. Within half-an-hour the landing parties had seized the telegraph and other offices, and were effectively patrolling the streets and approaches to the town, thus compelling the startled townsfolk to remain quiescent. The local volunteers they had also promptly squashed, by seizing the drill hall and destroying all arms and ammunition.

The senior officers in command all spoke English well. They informed the local authorities, when convened at the Town Hall, that they would interfere as little as possible with the ordinary life of the town and district, and though they had to requisition supplies, these would be settled for by bonds payable at the end of the war, and in the case of small traders by cash down against the receipt.

At the quays, men were already frantically busy with crane and derrick, guns and stores were smartly being swung ashore, and horses were walking down the gangways with well-trained ease. Below the harbour, troops were pouring out of the crammed transports, ship after ship having been moored broad-sides in contact with each other, with bridges of barges (stores) extending from the most landward vessel to the shore.

Those who saw in the grey light of that eventful morning the unending stream of soldiery pouring westward and northward through the town, judged that at least an army corps was being disembarked.

With stalwart bearing and eager air, the thousands of invaders stepped on British soil: infantry, riflemen (Jägers), cavalry, cyclists, horse artillery, field artillery, light guns and departmental troops. They were all picked men of the VII and X Army Corps. At the Town Hall, the officer in command, General von Loevw, informed the Mayor they were only the vanguard of a much larger force. Descents, he hinted, were being made on other parts of the east coast.

By dawn, the enemy's vanguards were marching out towards Lincoln, by the roads on the left or north bank of the Witham. The left of the advance was covered by the fen-lands beyond the Witham, with their network of water-courses, all the passages across them being now held by the enemy's cyclist companies, their extreme point Sleaford. In fact, the invaders were moving forward as rapidly as practicable in order to extricate themselves from the Boston fens before any resistance could be organized in their front. The Skegness detachment protected their right flank.

For some hours they had nothing to fear.

The blow had come so suddenly and unawares—so little was known to the British War Office beyond vague and exaggerated rumours—that no combined defensive measures were possible.

By mid-day on the 5th, the German headquarters were at Kirkstead. Supplies were coming up along the roads that, owing to the wintry weather, were heavy for vehicular traffic. Laden goods trains crowded the railway between the higher grounds and the river, while on the Witham itself a flotilla of barges, escorted by the two gunboats, was being towed up abreast of the advance.

The Battle of the
North Atlantic—German
airships against American
warships—in H. G. Wells,
The War in the Air, 1908

At 6.40 p.m., when Boston, to her intense relief and joy, at last
heard the guns of the naval engagement between Vice-Admiral
Dacres' and the German squadrons covering the disembarkation,
the enemy's force in the town immediately left, and formed rearguard to their land convoy laden with transhipped and requisitioned
supplies. Their comrades in the transports and store ships they abandoned to their fate.

The Germans, in true raiding spirit, cut themselves off from the
sea, and not they, but the British Navy 'burned the boats'.

III

At Lincoln there was a British cavalry regiment, the 8th Hussars, not
up to strength, for they had lately had to supply a draft to another
Hussar regiment. Many of the Lincolnshire Imperial Yeomanry reinforced them; and in the dusk of the afternoon they reconnoitred the

German position. The 1st battalion of the Lincolnshire Regiment, that had been rapidly mustered and turned out, unfortunately short of transport and field equipment owing to the curtailment of them by the ruling powers of the War Office, and without a reserve of cartridges, followed in support of the hussars.

Towards sunset, the sound of firing was heard away to the front. The battalion had halted, but now it instantly was reformed, and pushed forward for a couple of miles. But though the reports of quick-firing field guns came down with the wind, no signs of hostilities were discovered till the hussars joined them.

The horse had fallen back.

They had had sharp skirmishing with a very long line of the enemy's outposts, infantry and cavalry, and some of the enemy's horse artillery had galloped to the front and engaged them with shrapnel. Patrols to the north-west had tried to work round the German flank; but they had been checked and driven in by cyclists and dragoons.

Immediately the senior officer commanding the British troops reported per telegraph to headquarters that the extent and the strength of the enemy's line of outposts suggested a very large force had been landed; that he had been able to make no impression on the enemy; and, though the hussars had taken risks freely and lost a number of men, they had neither penetrated nor been able to turn the line of outposts. If the enemy's advance was resumed he proposed to retire on Lincoln, and to the best of his powers hamper the German van.

Many of the volunteers found shelter for the night in the villages and barns at hand. Others, more heroically endued, wrapped themselves up in their service great-coats, and lay around the bivouac fires, a long line of which were kept burning all night to mislead the enemy's scouts.

The hussars, strengthened by some companies of militia, who arrived by train after nightfall, formed the advanced outposts of the home army.

IV

On the afternoon of January 5th, a great defensive movement had begun. And late in the night wirelessed information from Vice-Admiral Dacres—transmitted by the Admiralty to the War Office and thence to the Supreme Committee of Defence formed of members of the Cabinet—relating to the number and destruction of the transports on the west side of the Wash, led the authorities to conclude that their impression of the enemy numbering between 35–40,000 troops was wholly erroneous.

The invaders' actual force, including the Skegness detachment, was three infantry brigades (each of six battalions), two rifle battalions (Jägers), a regiment of cavalry, six companies of cyclists, embarked to remedy the deficiency in cavalry, one battery of horse artillery, six batteries of field guns, twenty machine-gun sections, and various departmental troops: in all, 20,432 men, of whom over 3,000 were yet on board the transports when they sank, hashed and riddled, most of them burning fiercely, under the fire directed on them by the cruisers and destroyers of Britain's first home defence squadron.

Yet for Great Britain to launch an overwhelming strength of troops against even this minor body of invaders was an impracticable matter for the next four and twenty hours. The enemy's capture of Sleaford Junction and his rapid destruction, by means of cyclists, of the bridges south of Grantham, Billingborough, and Spalding, delayed any swift enflanking movement of the defensive troops from the eastern counties. However, a battalion of the 2nd Coldstream Guards detrained on arriving at the destroyed communications, and reached Grantham late in the evening. Here they formed the nucleus for a muster of local levies, militia, volunteers, and riflemen.

Already engineers and railway gangs were repairing with frantic energy the broken bridges along the Great Northern and Great Eastern railroads, and replacing the deranged rails. Peterborough had been secured against a raid by a battalion from Newmarket; and all that night, the cavalry, of which there was but a small brigade at Newmarket, was being moved by a steady service of trains towards the vicinity of Grantham for the advance on Lincoln next day; while the two divisions in camp and quarters about Cambridge and Newmarket were *en route* in the rear.

A division of militia in winter training at Aldershot was being moved up by rail on Sheffield to protect that great British centre of munitions of war; and the volunteers throughout the Midlands were alertly responding to the call of mobilization. Already their cyclist companies—half mobilized as they were—had thrown forward strong scouting parties towards the crossings of the Trent, which had been indicated as the line to be held on the enemy pushing rapidly westward into the heart of England; while the famous London Volunteer corps, together with the few regulars and militia units that could be spared from the southern garrisons, were being massed, ready to reinforce the Midlands or the columns moving through the eastern counties on the invaders.

All over the British Isles, I may say, tens of thousands of military units were travelling backward and forward on the railways. Troop trains and supplies for the front took precedence even of the mails, which in many cases were sent on by automobile service *via* the highway.

The difficulties and contrarieties existent in the mobilization scheme of the British army have, perhaps, never been more acutely presented. It might have occurred to any individual save a Britisher, with his seemingly inherent love of a muddle when fate is striking her hardest at him, to have had reorganized, not so much the strength and material of his so-called striking forces, but his details for extending and reinforcing them in mobilization. Yet the same system prevails as of old. To give an authentic instance—authentic like many other thousands of cases which I am not acquainted with—is, however, more significant than exposition. A reservist of the Liverpool Regiment, who was employed as head railway porter at *Clacton*, read the proclamation just after it was posted up at the local post office. He forthwith told the station master he had to rejoin, and after an exchange of telegraphic messages with the office of the chief constable of the county, was ordered to report himself at *Colchester*. Arriving there early on January 6th, he was presented with a 'travelling warrant' and some money, and next forenoon found himself travelling with some fifty comrades to the depôt at *Liverpool*. Here he got part of his kit. Together with sixty-eight units under charge of a junior officer, he was then sent up to *Scotland*, to *Glasgow*, where his battalion, the 2nd Liverpool, was stationed. On arrival it was found that the battalion had moved off by troop train for the eastern counties; the Liverpool depot had been warned, but the information had arrived half an hour after our friend had started for Scotland. There was then another long journey south for him before he joined his battalion late on the 8th at *Gainsborough*, a temporary base in the line of defence.

Multiply the movements of this one man by tens of thousands—and keep in mind that every unit signifies so much writing, signing, counter-signing and initialling, and filing the duplication—and it may be possible for one to have a glimmering of an idea of how Great Britain marshals her military strength so tardily and ill-organized, even while the enemy is ravaging Lincolnshire.

Great Britain's scheme for army mobilization is as inept and antiquated, for immediate purposes, as is Germany's present scheme for mobilizing her reservists who serve in the British Mercantile Marine!

V

When day dawned on the 6th of January, it found Lincoln in a wild panic. The enemy were in her market-place and streets, and engaging the volunteers, driving in their sentries, and surprising the battalion of them asleep in the railway sheds, the drill hall, and schools, and also those billeted on hotels and private houses.

During the course of the night, two squadrons of German dragoons, two guns of the horse artillery, and sixty cyclist-riflemen had made a daring march in the snow and the sleet and over the heavy, if not unknown, roads through Staunton and Nettleham, and had raided the old cathedral town.

As one publican afterwards said, his first customers that morning 'wore the enemy, an' they didn't take no 'alf an 'alf in the shape of all comestibles'.

The battalion of volunteers that had come in from Doncaster on the previous night, had hardly realized what was happening before they were cut down or captured. The majority of the men were made prisoners as they rose from their sleep, and were huddled together in the slushy market-place below the cathedral. The enemy then quickly destroyed all arms and stores, blew up two of the railway bridges outside the town, set fire to the truck loads of supplies at the station; effectually damaged all the instruments in the telegraph offices, carried off a mass of Government correspondence from the post office, and, taking five senior officers with them as prisoners, told the rest that they were at liberty, having exhausted every attempt to parole them. Then, despite the heavy snow falling, they rode out of the town, apparently in the direction of Langworth.

It seemed as if they did not know what fatigue was. Later on in the forenoon they suddenly engaged the 8th Hussars and volunteers, who were retiring stubbornly in steady fighting formation before the enemy's vanguard of one Jäger battalion, six guns of the horse artillery, and six squadrons of dragoons and cyclist riflemen.

Caught between the two fires at the hamlet of Gautby, the little force of defenders made a fierce stand, though most of them were hearing the whistle of bullets for the first time.

But at 11.30 a.m. two German batteries came galloping up, having been detached in reinforcement from the main body of the invaders, and their volume of fire speedily decided the encounter. At 11.43 a.m., as the British force had not a single gun in action, and their fusillade was dropping fast owing to lack of ammunition, they had no other recourse but to surrender.

A hussar lieutenant and a sergeant of the volunteers, managing to escape before the cessation of hostilities, brought the news of the disaster to Market Rasen.

Unimportant as this encounter was in intrinsic results, when it was made known in the evening press, it produced a widespread depression throughout the Isles, and this was accentuated by the knowledge of the Germans' successful dash upon Lincoln. Late though the hour was, and in spite of the inclement weather, men gathered in crowds and talked of the disasters in the first days of the Boer War, or the train trapped by Delarey north of Kimberley on the morrow of the outbreak of hostilities, and the other 'regrettable incidents' that followed so quickly.

But great had been the joy in Lincoln itself when in the afternoon the 2nd Coldstream Guards had reached the city, after a forced march from the point where the broken bridges had stopped transit. They had worked forward with great caution for the first few hours, with patrols well in the van, for the temporary cessation of all intelligence from Lincoln had led to conjectures of grave disaster and defeat.

More troops came in as the day went on, including the brigade of cavalry from Newmarket. One brigade of the line also had been brought up from Newmarket, together with two batteries of field artillery, within striking distance of Sleaford; and the troops from the Midlands were moving fast upon the line of the Trent.

Late that night, two British cyclist scouts reached Lincoln in a state of exhaustion with the news that they had been fired at near Staunton by a strong force of the enemy, and had seen camp fires blazing on the hills away towards the head-waters of the Ancholme river.

The raiders had turned northward.

VI

Next day, January 7th, the fugitives from outlying hamlets and farms told of the broad columns of men making north-west over the wintry wolds, and their huge train of wagons, mostly requisitioned motors and carts, that dragged along the upland roads and lanes.

Along the Witham Valley, the wrecked transport trains and barges scuttled in the river indicated that the Germans had been thwarted in their advance south of Lincoln into the Midlands, and had abandoned all they could not transport by road. The two gunboats, *Rother* and *Memmert*, had retired down-stream to meet the small flotilla of steamboats from the British home defence squadron just above Holland Fen, and had been destroyed in their gallant attempt to break through down-river to the sea.

The same afternoon, the British force advancing on Sleaford found it was evacuated, though the German rearguard of cyclist riflemen held on there till the British patrols were in touch with them.

Sleaford, Tattershall, Horncastle, and town and house alike, the enemy, it may be said, had literally swept clean of food and provender. In payment, neither cash nor pay-notes, 'redeemable at the conclusion of the war', were now proffered; a blow with a rifle butt or a prog with a bayonet sufficed!

That evening the country grew more sanguine, and public prayers for the safety of the Realm began to be put up less frequently. Indeed, it now seemed as if the enemy's enterprise had miscarried from the first, except in so far as he had created national confusion and alarm, that in several instances, most notably at the great centres of commerce, had heightened into panic, financial crises, and savage recriminations in Parliament.

The British defence was hour by hour growing stronger; the line of the Trent bristled with rifle bayonets and the batteries of the artillery volunteers pouring in from northward, westward, and southward, to become stiffened with Royal Artillery batteries hurried up from the south. The two divisions of regulars, with four volunteer brigades, the cavalry, and 3,387 Imperial Yeomanry, had pushed north from Lincoln, leaving militia and volunteer battalions to hold Boston and Lincoln and the Witham Line.

From Spalding to Goole and Howden, the call of the bugle and the flicker of bivouac fires now went up into the thick drizzling night. The invaders were caught in a net. The British striking forces were fast closing in on them.

With the British cavalry and cyclist riflemen hanging on the German flanks, often to be trapped and despatched with no mercy, the foe pushed as far north as Brigg. Their vedettes were now being driven back constantly upon the van. The Trent being found impassable, it was on the fifth day of their brief campaign that they turned south on their pursuers, and worked along the upland ground of the Lincoln heights.

Next day, the 10th of January, Kirton gave its name to a battle on English soil—a battle fought for the most amidst blinding showers of sleet and snow and a continuous January mizzle. The figures in this momentous battle are small. In round numbers there were 14,832 invaders with forty-two guns, against a mixed force of British regulars, militia, and volunteers, mustering in all 38,000 bayonets and seventy-one guns, the majority of these much heavier in metal than anything the Germans had been able to transport. Yet, outnumbered as they were, they fought with a valour and obstinacy incomparable in the annals of even their splendid army.

Early that afternoon, on their vanguard being impetuously driven in upon its supports by an overwhelming British force, the Germans rapidly entrenched themselves, notwithstanding the severe fire soon brought to bear upon them; and, though their artillery was gradually crushed out in the ensuing cannonade, they were not the men to yield to a mere threat of bombardment. By nightfall they were partly surrounded; and had been driven with great loss from two points commanding the west flank of their position. Yet they still doggedly held out, their line now thrown back so as to form their array into a great circle.

Searchlights from the British positions soon distinctly lit up the trenches, parallels, and casemates, hastily formed by the enemy on every available fold of ground. Hour after hour the British artillery, strengthened by five fresh batteries hurried up from the Trent, accurately ranging with shrapnel and shell, cracked and splashed their tremendous blasts of bullets and shells without intermission into the vast mob of combatants, crouching unseen, in their earthwork shelters.

Close on midnight, the Germans made a desperate attempt to break through the weakest zone of fire, away towards Redbourne; but it was as if they had been trapped.

Like some immense display of fireworks, hundreds of star-shell, fired from the adjacent British positions, burst overhead, as the heavy column of British infantry, over whose head the artillery was firing, charged with fixed bayonets to the attack. The two columns met with a shock that shivered their fronts; but the neck of the British column, the Cameronians (2nd battalion), remained solid. It drove like a wedge, that jagged mass of human steel, into the heart of the assault. More terrible than even the sleet of lead and steel and nickel sweeping their entrenchments, came the thrust, dull jab, and wrench of British steel. The German column hesitated, quivered; its rear sections broke into a broad dribble back towards the defence, to wither away under the swish of metal from the batteries of auto-matic quick-firers. Of officers and men, 845 were taken prisoners.

At dawn, General Detternhelder, who had succeeded in command General Loevw, killed early in the fight by bursting shell, found his decimated forces ringed by entrenched firing lines, rifle and artillery, 'sniping' on a gigantic scale for human game. At 8.52 a.m. a staff officer, his head bare and his right arm in a sling, together with an orderly waving the white flag, came walking slowly into the British lines near Waddingham. The invasion of 190– was at an end.

There come, it has to be noted, in the course of hostilities, times and opportunities when the sleepless vigilance of the most active and strenuous seamen in the world cannot act as safeguard against invasion.

If the British observation flotilla before Emden had not been destroyed, thus affording for nearly fourteen hours the unimpeded egress of the transports and convoying warships; if the weather had not been wintry North Sea weather—had not been adverse to the employment of small craft as advanced scouts; if a sufficiently large number of them had been flung out, and if the easternmost craft had carried wireless apparatus; if, indeed, as the *Judge* has phrased it, in contempt of the numerous reasons put forth by the British Press, there had been no war—there would have been no invasion!

Not till the potential element of Chance be eliminated will Britain lie secure from invasion; the more, when encountering such an adversary as Germany. She has counted her loss but as her gain. She has successfully proved England can be invaded, even with her strong navy sweeping the seas. And greater consequences may follow as years roll on.

The decisive British victory followed on the fleet action fought southwest of the Skager Rak, when the new Dreadnoughts (recommended in 1904 and first laid down in October 1905) prove to be the perfect fighting machine of that time. The authors make this very clear in their final pages.

Germany's High Seas Fleet was doomed. Heavier gun-fire, superior speed, were speedily to turn their heroic effort into mere self-demoli-tion—suicide. The vast bulk of the later Dreadnoughts not only gives them increased steadiness in a heavy seaway; but, too, their remark-able adjustments in gun mechanism maintain the constant alignment of their guns on the target in storm as well as in calm. In the latest development of British gunnery, only sheer aberration on the part of the gunner may prevent him from hitting his mark.

The Death Trap

The formula for the tale of the 'War with Germany' had evolved rapidly—from the appearance of the German spy in The Spies of the Wight *(1899) to the entrance of the Kaiser in* The Riddle of the Sands *(1903). By 1906 all the elements were well-established: the barges ready to cross the North Sea, the sudden raid that almost catches the Navy off guard, the landing in force, the ritual capture of London, and the Emperor William II in his role as the Kaiser. This figure of the dark invader appears from time to time as the originator and director of the plan to conquer the United Kingdom. He is shown to have all the malevolence and almost as much power as the demon scientists, anarchists, and nihilists who preceded him in the tale of terror. A double-take makes the Kaiser bigger than the sum of all his parts: although a figure of caricature with his upswept moustache and piercing eyes, he is close enough to the contemporary British perception of the German monarch to be taken for the man himself; and by becoming larger than life—vehement in language, all demanding, intolerant of opposition, impatient for immediate success, a primal force of unnature—he manifests the most dangerous corruption of supreme power. Let the nations tremble!*

Behind the malign image of fiction there was a real and growing anxiety about German intentions and about the role of the Emperor in his office as Supreme War Lord. There were many failures in understanding. The British sense of the appropriate did not quite chime with such statements of absolute authority as: 'I am the sole master of German policy and my country must follow me wherever I go.'[5] Again, William II had a gift for making unfortunate speeches, so it seemed to the world outside the Reich. There was that address to the German troops about to embark for China and the Boxer Rebellion on 27 July 1900: '... no pardon will be given, and prisoners will not be made. Anyone who falls into your hands falls to your sword! *Just as the Huns under their King Etzel created for themselves a thousand years ago a name which men still respect, you should give the name of German such cause to be remembered in China for a thousand years that no Chinaman, no matter whether his eyes be slit or not, will dare to look a German in the face.'[6] That speech was the origin of the pejorative use of 'Hun' as a means of indicating all that was believed to be wrong in German military action.*

The author of The Death Trap *opens with a touch of the Gothic: a dark night, high-ranking German officers, 'a man of commanding appearance', and a carriage for three. When the Kaiser speaks, he pours out a carefully edited version of the more belligerent ideas known to be in circulation in the Germany of 1907.*

I

It was nearly midnight. The night was dark and stormy, the wind howled, and driving rain beat against the windows of a pair-horse landau, which slowly and laboriously rolled westwards, through mud and darkness, across the Franco-German frontier. On the box were two men, wearing the great-coats and helmets of German soldiers. Inside sat three officers of the German army, evidently high in command, but so muffled up as to be almost unrecognizable. They were stern, silent, and forbidding. One, who sat facing the horses, was a man of commanding appearance. His face was deadly pale, but every feature betokened intense ambition and selfishness, supported by unconquerable energy and resolution. His moustache was brushed away from his mouth, the ends curling upwards. He was evidently the leader of the party, to judge from the deference and respect with which the other men treated him.

Opposite the Chief, and on the right hand side of the carriage, was a stout, heavily-built man, with dark eyes, massive, brooding brow, and a terribly firm and cruel mouth, denoting merciless devotion to purpose. This was Prince Hohenhaus, Chancellor of the German Empire, a man hated and feared throughout Europe and the world for his subtle policy and the deadly strokes of aggression he had dealt in Bismarckian fashion at the countries standing in his way. Now his brow was sombre and lowering, for he was thinking out, by the wish of his Imperial Master, the final details of what was to be the last crowning act of Germany's career of robbery and aggression.

The third occupant of the carriage sat next the Chancellor. He was tall, thin, and clean-shaven, his eyes steel-blue, and his face seamed with a fine network of lines. His lips were thin and firm, and his mouth appeared to be even more cruel than that of the Chancellor. He was Field-marshal von Prankhe, the great German strategist, of world-wide fame, on account of his vast military genius. These three men were the ruling chiefs of Germany, the skilful engineers who controlled the vast pent-up forces of the mighty German Empire; three Fates, who plotted with relentless determination the ruin of rival states.

The carriage had rumbled for miles through flying mud and blinding rain, whilst none of the three spoke. They were still silent when it crossed the frontier and entered French territory. But a few moments later, the man who faced the horses spoke.

'Yes, my mind is quite made up,' he suddenly exclaimed, in a harsh voice. 'There must be no turning back now we have put our hand to the plough—no faint-heartedness. I have determined to make this great venture, and I will shrink from no sacrifice to bring it to a successful conclusion. I can do nothing else; there is no other line of policy open to me.'

'There is not, Your Majesty,' assented the Chancellor. 'I have thought everything over very carefully, and I can suggest no other way out of the difficulty.'

'Wherever we go, whatever we want to do,' continued the pale man in quick, sharp sentences, 'England stands in our way. She is our rival in the sea-carrying trade, in manufactures, in commerce, in empire, in everything. We can touch nothing inside or outside Europe without England interfering. If we want a country to colonize, England is there before us. We can do nothing but sit still in Europe and twiddle our thumbs as long as England dictates to the world with her fleet and her power. It is England, England everywhere. Germany cannot have a world-wide policy whilst this British Empire exists.'

'Your Majesty is right,' assented the Chancellor. 'England prevents our legitimate expansion; England crushes us.'

'But the end must come,' continued the other. 'My empire cannot bear the strain much longer. Its commercial prosperity is declining. Its population is too great, and there is no outlet for it in any quarter of the globe. The United States will not let us take part of South America on account of the Monroe doctrine. England has the cream of Africa and all India and Australia. England, and her yellow servant Japan, forbid the partition of China. It is England, England all over the world corking up my people in their narrow bottle, suppressing their legitimate aspirations, thwarting the mission of expansion which God has given them. But relief *must* be found somehow. The Socialists are increasing in numbers and influence. Industrial troubles accumulate daily. Sufficient food cannot be found in this barren Central Europe to support my teeming people. Germany must increase. It is her divine destiny to expand, and eventually become a world-empire; it is my heaven-sent mission to become Emperor of the West. By the grace of God, and the power of my sword, I shall rule over the greatest and most mighty empire the world has ever seen. But what obstructs the legitimate expansion of Germany? England, always England! She throttles us; she murders us; she must be blotted out.'

While he was speaking his eyes flashed and his pale face flushed with excitement. The other two nodded in silence. 'The first thing necessary is a coalition,' he continued. 'We don't require soldiers, but warships and sailors. France and Russia have plenty. Russia has already promised to join us in crushing England on condition that we give her a free hand in India and Manchuria. We can make France join by threatening war. There is nothing she dreads more than a conflict with my army. The German army crushed her in 1870, and it could crush her as easily now. We shall have to promise her North Africa as her reward.'

The Kaiser directs operations in the entirely imaginary Battle of Erquelinnes

'I don't like the idea of giving up North Africa,' interrupted the Chancellor. 'We can easily repudiate that part of the bargain when England is crushed and prostrate on the ground. I have thought everything over, and success seems certain. The British Empire is merely a colossal fraud, held together by weak bonds, and ready to fall to pieces at any moment. It is even more rotten than the Roman Empire at the time of its fall. I have received secret information of vast importance regarding this terrible British navy, before which all the world trembles. The shooting is very bad, the gun sights are defective, the guns tear their rifling after a few rounds, and the armour-plating is not what it is believed to be. The British public has been deluded and defrauded for years by that delightful Unionist Government it trusts so much.

Now I *know* that the ships of my navy are the soundest and best obtainable. The British Government knows nothing whatever about its numbers. I have dozens of submarines, destroyers, and torpedo-boats secretly laid up in the dockyards, and ready to be commissioned at a moment's notice. At the present time, the private shipbuilders have battleships and cruisers ready in every detail, and it has been announced that they were built to the order of certain South American republics. I have arranged that all the finest vessels of the mercantile marine will be handed over to me in the event of war, to act as cruisers or transports. France has several powerful squadrons, and the Russian navy has vastly improved since the Russo-Japanese war. England will be without her Far Eastern and East Indian squadrons, and the great number of cruisers required to escort her food ships. British auxiliary ships cannot be mustered at a moment's notice, for they are scattered over the globe. The French and German vessels, added to the hosts we can muster, will outnumber the British fleet by nearly two to one. We will fall on it suddenly and annihilate it, and then the road will be clear for the invasion of England.

'The fact that England is not a self-supporting country is the principal factor that will determine her fate. Five-sixths of her food is imported, and there is never sufficient in the country to last for more than six weeks. Food will go up to famine prices directly war is declared. That will not touch the rich, but will be an unbearable hardship to the masses. We shall do everything to keep food away from them. When the proper time arrives, agents of the German Government will buy up all the available supplies of wheat in Russia, Argentine, Canada, and the United States. For weeks beforehand, there will be German agents in Britain to buy up and hold under assumed names all the food they can lay hands on. When war is declared, they will be instructed to hold back all the food under their control. That will be bad enough for the British public. But when the naval crash comes, the price of food will be prohibitive to the masses. The great towns will be filled by raving, starving mobs. Maddened by hunger, they will riot and demand peace at any price. The law-abiding, staid, and stodgy English citizen will become a lunatic when he sees his wife and family starving. What can the British Government do against vast hordes of starving savages?

'Meanwhile, my invincible army will cross the Channel, and land on the south-eastern coast of England. The wise British public has been living in a fool's paradise as regards the possibilities of an invasion. Its Prime Ministers have cajoled it into thinking that the invasion of England is absolutely impossible. The state of the British army was bad enough then, but it has been allowed to grow worse since. It cannot muster many more than three hundred thousand all told, probably not nearly so many. The officers are very badly trained and educated. Promotion goes by petticoat influence and money. There is not even a single general fit to command a division. The physique of the rank and file is very poor. The militia and volunteers are totally inefficient. The artillery is armed with out-of-date weapons. The British magazine-rifle is much inferior to ours. The coast fortresses are not even worthy of the name; they will fall without firing a shot.

'Once the British navy is out of the way, we will prove that the theories of eminent British strategists are wrong, by landing eight hundred thousand men, with full equipment of guns and horses, in a few weeks. The road from the coast to London is quite open, and the country as defenceless as a garden. The British have only their regulars and auxiliaries to depend upon, between three and four hundred thousand altogether. They cannot obtain more soldiers, because they have no compulsory military service or universal military training. The stolid British cannot fight on empty stomachs. Even supposing the whole nation flies to arms, which is quite unlikely, of what use would it be? The British masses are quite untrained, and know nothing of soldiering. Soldiers are not made in a day, or even in a month, and by that time we shall have thrust our sword into the heart of the British Empire. Even supposing they had the men, who is to organize a huge levy? who drill the men? and where are the trained officers capable of directing a gigantic army of raw levies? Then they have not sufficient arms and ammunition. There are not half a million rifles in the country, and scarcely sufficient field-guns for the regulars. As at the time of the Boer War, their arsenals are nearly depleted of ammunition. We shall find no opposition beyond the three or four hundred thousand men of all arms. My army will surround the British army somewhere on the borders between Surrey and Kent, and annihilate it once and for ever. Then we shall march on to London, and fight our way through the defenceless suburbs. If the British Government does not yield then, we shall bombard London from the suburbs, fight our way through the streets, and capture the Houses of Parliament, Government offices, and public buildings. We shall have previously captured Chatham, Sheerness, and Woolwich. Then, with the War Office, Admiralty, Foreign Office, Bank of England, Stock Exchange, Post Office, and Houses of Parliament in our hands, the British Government will not have the power of further resistance. The mob of starving people will insist on peace at any price, so that the horrors of invasion may cease, and they can get food.

'We shall then dictate out terms of peace at London. All British colonies to be handed over to Germany, all British warships in any port to be surrendered, the payment of an indemnity of four hundred millions, the Mediterranean and Baltic to be closed to British warships, and the march of my army in triumph through London. Everything *must* succeed as I have arranged it. But very probably we shall not have to bombard London. After the first great battle, when the British army has been destroyed, the mob may make the Government surrender unconditionally. They must have food, and they will have it at any price. If the Unionist Government is turned out, as it probably will be after the first disaster, the Liberals, Irish, and Little Englanders will let all the empire go without a struggle. My scheme cannot fail to be successful. Starvation, unpreparedness, incapacity, lack of patriotism, deficient physique, and love of ease, everything will conspire to help it forward.'

'Excellent!' commented the Chancellor. 'If the British fleet is cleared away, and twenty of Your Majesty's army corps landed,' said Prankhe, 'I will guarantee to annihilate the British army in three or four weeks.'

'Good,' exclaimed the German Emperor. 'But now listen again, both of you. Crushing England is only the beginning of my great scheme for founding a world-wide German Empire. When I have made terms with England, I shall seize Holland, Belgium, Denmark, and part of Austria without much difficulty. Then I shall join Russia in crushing the naval power and commerce of Japan. Germany and her Kaiser will no more brook a rival in the East than in the West. I shall make Japan keep to her island home. Then I shall attack and annex the republics of South America. If the United States has anything to say to the contrary, she will have to fight my ever-victorious fleet. No country of the earth will be able to stand against my power.'

He paused for breath, and looked at his two hearers with flashing eyes. As he finished speaking, the carriage rumbled and jolted over the rough paving-stones of the French frontier town, Rodelles. It was a little insignificant town, boasting one street and one inn. The three arbiters of the destinies of Germany and the world were silent while the carriage rolled down the street of the sleeping town. There was not a living being visible anywhere;

there was no sound but the roar of wind and the patter of rain. All the inhabitants of Rodelles, at least nearly all, were sleeping the sleep of the just. Little did the humble peasants or petty trades-people guess that the first scene of a terrible drama would be played in their midst on that very night!

The inn was the only house in Rodelles where there appeared to be any life. There were lights at the windows and at the open doors. Evidently visitors were expected, for a small stout man ran down the steps when the carriage approached. As it pulled up at the door, the clock of a neighbouring church tolled the hour of midnight.

'Punctual to the minute!' exclaimed the Kaiser, as he stepped to the ground. 'I hope the French are here.' The party walked into the hall, followed by the bowing landlord. 'Is the room upstairs ready?' inquired Prince Hohenhaus. 'Certainly, the room is prepared. Will the gentlemen walk upstairs?' 'Have the other gentlemen arrived?' continued the Prince. 'We are about to meet some French excise officials. We anticipate smuggling trouble.'

'The other gentlemen are already upstairs. They have inquired for the German officials.'

'Are we quite alone here?'

'Quite alone. There are no other guests in the house. It has been reserved in accordance with instructions.' 'Well, to business!' exclaimed Hohenhaus, with a meaning look at his Imperial Master.

The landlord led the way up the creaking staircase. The German Emperor, carefully muffled in an overcoat, followed him, then the other two, and lastly an aide-de-camp, who had ridden on the box with the driver. The landlord opened the door and ushered in the three Germans. Then he withdrew, and the aide-de-camp closed the door and remained on guard outside.

II

Two Frenchmen rose and bowed as the newcomers entered. They were Monsieur Donaine, the President of the French republic, and Monsieur Chauvier, the French Minister for Foreign Affairs. The former was the first to speak.

'Good evening, gentlemen,' he said. 'We are here as you desired. We have considered your proposals carefully, and regret that we cannot accept them.'

The Kaiser's brow darkened, and his eyes flashed angrily.

'We will talk about that presently,' he exclaimed with an impatient wave of his hand. 'Where are the Russians? Have they not arrived?'

'Not yet.'

'They should be here by now. They left Berlin an hour before we departed; I saw them before I started, and they accept all our proposals. India and Manchuria are to be their reward.'

As the Kaiser spoke, there was a rumbling of wheels outside, and another closed carriage was driven up to the door at a smart pace. There was a noise of shuffling feet on the pavement, and the bang of a carriage door. Then heavy footsteps were heard ascending the creaking stairs, and the aide-de-camp ushered two tall, bearded men into the room. These were Prince Zeidsomsky, the Russian Foreign Minister, and the Grand Duke Alexis Alexandrovitch. Bows were exchanged with the newcomers, and the door was closed. There were a few moments of intense silence, broken only by the heavy breathing of the seven men. The air seemed to be pervaded by a fearful nervous tension. At last the Kaiser advanced to the table and spoke.

'Well, gentlemen,' he exclaimed abruptly as he glanced at the four statesmen with his flashing eye, 'you all know my proposals?'

The Frenchmen and Russians nodded silently. Prince Hohenhaus drew apart, and looked out of the window, but von Prankhe surveyed the Frenchmen with his glittering steel-blue eyes.

'Russia agrees to everything,' continued the Kaiser in a meaning voice.

'That is so,' said the Grand Duke. 'We assent to everything.'

'And what reply does France give?' he asked sharply, turning to the two Frenchmen.

'France declines,' replied the President in a voice that trembled slightly in spite of his efforts to keep it firm. 'She will not act against the *Entente Cordiale*. She has no cause for quarrel with Great Britain, and does not wish to find one.'

The air seemed surcharged with electricity as the President finished speaking.

'So those are your views?' asked the Kaiser in an icy tone.

'They are.'

The Kaiser's face became whiter and whiter with savage passion. 'Now listen!' he exclaimed fiercely, as he brought his clenched fist down on the table with a bang. 'Do you know what the alternative is? If you will not fight Great Britain, you will be compelled to fight the mighty German Empire. I shall make a pretext for war at a suitable time, and send my armies over the frontier. They are larger, better organized, more highly trained, and more skilfully led than yours. I shall swamp France with my soldiers. I shall crush your wretched republic once and for all time with the ever-victorious sword of my never-to-be-forgotten ancestors. What help will your England give you then? Of what use will your *Entente Cordiale* be? Even your friend and ally, Russia, barters you for India and Manchuria. You did not help Russia in her struggle with Japan, and she will not help you against me. Russia has been husbanding her resources, and making vast preparations for campaigns in India and Manchuria since the termination of the Russo-Japanese War. Her *amour propre* was wounded by the successes of the Japanese, and she will not rest until her army and navy have recovered her prestige. Hence she falls in with every detail of my plans, and throws France over; you may go to the dogs for what she cares. Even now she is massing vast hordes of troops in Central Asia.

'As usual, the inefficient and lazy British Intelligence Department knows absolutely nothing of the concentration of hostile troops on the borders of the British Empire. Directly war is declared against Great Britain, these troops will be marched across Afghanistan; they will swamp the wretchedly-led Indian army, and take India. With her sea-power gone, England can do nothing to retrieve the disaster. She will have lost India for ever.'

The German Dictator of Europe paused a moment to take breath. Then he continued the same savage menacing language.

'If you refuse my terms, what do you suppose England can or will do to save France from my armies? She can help you on the sea; together you might destroy my navy, harass my commerce. But what of that? The conflict will be decided on land, and on French soil, and I shall dictate my terms of peace at Paris. Can England help you there? What advantage will you gain if she sends over her puny army of two or three hundred thousand men? Her army will be like a mouse between the paws of a cat. Small, ill-trained and ill-led, we shall crush the British army like matchwood. One German army can settle *that*. The rest of my armies will crush you, *you*! They will take Paris, and dictate terms of peace to your republic. One-third of France to become German territory, a huge indemnity; that is what we shall demand. Refuse it, and my armies overrun and bleed France until she yields. England may ruin our over-sea trade, but it is *you*—*you* who will have to pay the bill in money and territory. The more damage England does to us, the more *you* pay; that is the logic of gunpowder and steel. Remember 1870! You escaped lightly then; the next time you will be crushed once and for all time! Think well before you refuse my terms. It is impossible for you to resist my mighty armies.

'Accept my terms, and you gain all Northern Africa, and the nightmare of British power is laid for ever. Refuse, and you seal your ruin, your utter and irretrievable ruin! You can never recover from it! Glorious France will become a feeble and insignificant republic like Switzerland; she will be the laughing-stock of Europe and the world. What country in Europe will be able to help you? Austria? Russia can spare an army to keep her under observation. Italy? I can fight her as well as you. America only worships the dollar, and cares nothing for European politics. But if she does raise any objection, I shall bribe her with Canada.'

'A war with Great Britain would not be popular in France now,' remarked the President, who was making a great effort to restrain his outraged feelings. 'All Frenchmen would be dead against it.'

'Bah!' exclaimed the Kaiser roughly. 'Of what use governing a country if you cannot bend it to your will? You have your news-papers and politicians. You must start a Press campaign against England, make out that the English are the rivals of French citizens in everything, that they are plotting a deadly blow at French independence. You must make bad feeling. Remind the French of Waterloo and Fashoda. Stir up jealousy. You can easily break up that *Entente Cordiale* if you try. It is easy enough to make two nations hate one another if you only go the right way to work. I have been thoroughly successful in making my people hate the English. Where there is a will, there is a way, Monsieur le Président.'

'I should like to confer with my colleague for a few minutes,' said Monsieur Donaine, after considering for a moment.

The two Frenchmen withdrew to the bay window and conversed in low tones, while the Kaiser strode restlessly to and fro in front of the fireplace, and the other plenipotentiaries stood in a group at the further end of the room. Monsieur Donaine and Monsieur Chauvier looked pale and harassed as they conferred in low hurried whispers. At the end of half an hour, they again approached the table. The Kaiser paused in his restless walk and faced them, the light from the overhanging lamp illuminating his pale features and gleaming eyes.

'Well, gentlemen,' he inquired, 'is it peace or war between France and Germany?'

'We agree to Your Majesty's proposals,' replied the President quietly.

'Good!' exclaimed the Kaiser, his eyes flashing fire.

'That seals our friendship and England's doom! The hour of

England's downfall is at hand! Prince,' he added, turning to his Chancellor, 'be so good as to read out the Articles of the Agreement.'

Despite the initial German successes and the enemy occupation of London, there is a national uprising directed by Lord Eagleton, the Military Dictator; and then help comes with the arrival of a Japanese fleet—a convenient, fictional activation of the Anglo-Japanese Treaty of 1905. Tens of thousands of Japanese troops land in Liverpool and hasten south to assist the British insurgents. The beginning of the end for the invaders starts with news of heartening events.

Great Naval Victory
The French Desert Germany
Arrival of Japanese Fleet
Thousands of Japanese Officers Landed at Liverpool

The Japanese officers have come to lead British units in the great task of reconquering the United Kingdom. When the enemy have been defeated, easily and rapidly, the story closes with the high drama of the Kaiser in the moment of capitulation:

The Kaiser staggered, gasped, turned whiter and whiter as sentence after sentence of that terrible document smote his ears like the knell of Doom. The Kaiser, the princes of the empire, the imperial statesmen, the members of the imperial entourage were all without exception to be surrendered as prisoners of war. The whole army, all officers and men, to be prisoners. All guns, weapons, and munitions of war to be surrendered. All German overseas possessions to be ceded to Great Britain. Alsace and Lorraine to be given to France. A war indemnity of five hundred million pounds to be paid. The Kaiser, the royal princes, and the statesmen to remain in England as prisoners of war until a substantial part of the terms had been carried out.

The Child's Guide to Knowledge

By 1909, when packed audiences were cheering every episode in Guy du Maurier's play, An Englishman's Home, *the 'German invasion' had become an established fact in British folklore. Even the young had their accounts of the day when the Germans would arrive and be repelled, or would conquer, in the gripping narratives that appeared frequently in the boys' magazines. There was, for instance, the occasion in 1909 when the pupils of Aldeburgh Lodge preparatory school in Suffolk were introduced to their future as subjects of the Pan-Teutonic Empire. In the Spring number of the* Aldeburgh Lodge Magazine *an anonymous adult set down the consequences of 'the great war of 1915–17' in a brief catechism.*[7]

A SMALL ISLAND OFF THE WESTERN COAST OF TEUTONIA

(*As commanded to be used in all schools of the province of England in the Teutonic Empire in the year 1930.*)

Question: What is England?
Answer: England is a small island off the western coast of Teutonia, and became part of the Pan-Teutonic Empire in 1917.
Q: What language is spoken there?
A: The official language is German. In remote parts of the country the original dialect called English still survives, although the use of it is by severe penalties discouraged. A new simplified language called Teutonic, scientifically formed from the word-roots common to German, Dutch, English, and Scandinavian is being, for use all over the Empire, introduced.
Q: When was England to the Teutonic Empire annexed?
A: After the great war of 1915–17, when Germany after uniting to herself Austria-Hungary, Holland, and Denmark, to complete her grand and noble scheme of a Pan-Teutonic Empire, was by the English Press on the pretext that the balance of power was being disturbed, wantonly attacked.
Q: To what was the signal success of the Teutonic Empire in this war due?
A: To the fact that the admirable and far-seeing plans of Marshal von Greinitz had secretly for many years matured been.
Q: To what was the complete collapse of the British Empire due?
A: To the fact that the English nation had an over-weening and totally unfounded confidence in its powers and had neglected the all-important subject of self-defence for trivial matters, so that they were taken by surprise and never really recovered from the initial blow dealt them.
Q: What was this blow?
A: The great and glorious victory of the 26th December 1915, when all the most important vessels of the British Home Fleet were simultaneously before the declaration of war by the so-called-invisible-then-newly-by-Capt.-Vogt-invented torpedoes destroyed.

Q: What further naval engagements took place?

A: The sea-fights of the war were numerous, and continued even after the official surrender of the English Government, but they had little effect on the general issue of the war.

Q: What were the important land-battles?

A: Numerous minor engagements took place, but there was only one battle of importance, the magnificent-still-in-all-parts-of-the-Empire-annually-celebrated victory of Canterbury when the hastily organized English forces after a prolonged and sanguinary engagement were by the combined armies of the Teutonic Empire completely crushed.

Q: Did this victory end the war?

A: No, as the English very obstinately and foolishly kept up a guerilla warfare of a most ferocious character for upwards of two years, and measures of the utmost severity had to be taken in order to compel them into submission.

Q: What is the present extent of the Teutonic Empire?

A: It comprises Germany, Austria-Hungary, Switzerland, Denmark, Holland, England, and many other smaller dependencies. It is in fact the greatest empire of the globe.

Q: What advantages are possessed by citizens of this Empire?

A: A just and paternal Government which regulates with scientific accuracy every event of their lives, and the honour of serving in the mightiest army in the world. The various nationalities have also been for the present permitted to use their own languages, and have been given a certain limited amount of local self-government under the control of German governors. These latter privileges are however not as yet enjoyed by the province of England.

SOLID.

GERMANY. "DONNERWETTER! IT'S ROCK. I THOUGHT IT WAS GOING TO BE PAPER."

The German attempts to split the *Entente Cordiale* at the time of the Agadir Crisis in 1911
come up against the solid rock of unity

Chapter Three
'Denn wir fahren, wir fahren gegen England!'

The Coming Conquest of England

The first German tale of the Zukunftskrieg *to attract European attention in the new century was* Der Weltkrieg—Deutsche Träume *('World War—German Dreams') by August Niemann, as Carl Siwinna noted in his survey of future-war fiction (p. 298). When* Der Weltkrieg *first appeared in 1904, the all-too-evident signs of* Schadenfreude *were read as an indication of German intentions. So* Der Weltkrieg *was immediately translated into English and given a title that said what the author had in mind:* The Coming Conquest of England. *The publishers (G. Routledge—a solid, reputable firm) were evidently confident that the book would speak for itself. They presented Niemann and his ideas as they came straight from the German with the briefest of pointers to the reader: 'The translator offers no comment on the day-dream which he reproduces in the English language for English readers. The meaning and the moral should be obvious and valuable.'*

The Niemann story would undoubtedly have given British readers good reason to believe that some Germans looked forward to the day when there would be 'a new division of the possessions of the earth' after the forces of the Reich had destroyed the British Empire. Many must have concluded that Niemann's jubilant recollections of the notorious Kruger telegram were the expression of a determined animosity. Some may have noted that the grandiloquent language of the exalted personalities set the right opening tone in a great, Wagnerian scene. The 'Author's Preface', which follows, is a prose variation on 'Deutschland Über Alles', a wish-fufilment fantasy of world conquest.

MY DREAMS, THE DREAMS OF A GERMAN

The map of the world unfolds itself before me. All seas are ploughed by the keels of British vessels, all coasts dotted with the coaling stations and fortresses of the British world-power. In Britain is vested the dominion of the globe, and Britain will retain it; she cannot permit the Russian monster to drink life and mobility from the sea.

'Without England's permission no shot can be fired on the ocean,' once said William Pitt, England's greatest statesman. For many, many years Britain has increased her lead, owing to dissensions among the continental Powers. Almost all wars have, for centuries past, been waged in the interests of Britain, and almost all have been incited by England. Only when Bismarck's genius presided over Germany did the German Michael become conscious of his own strength, and wage his own wars.

Are things come to this pass, that Germany is to crave of Britain's bounty—her air and light, and her very daily bread? or does their ancient vigour no longer animate Michael's arms? Shall the three Powers who, after Japan's victory over China, joined hands in the treaty of Shimonoseki, in order to thwart Britain's aims, shall they—Germany, France, and Russia—still fold their hands, or shall they not rather mutually join them in a common cause?[1]

In my mind's eye I see the armies and fleets of Germany, France, and Russia moving together against the common enemy, who with his polypus arms enfolds the globe. The iron onslaught of the three allied Powers will free the whole of Europe from Britain's tight embrace. The great war lies in the lap of the future. The story that I shall portray in the following pages is not a chapter of the world's past history; it is the picture as it clearly developed itself to my mind's eye, on the publication of the first despatch of the Viceroy Alexieff to the Tsar of Russia. And simultaneously, like a flash of lightning, the telegram which the Emperor William sent to the Boers after Jameson's Raid crosses my memory—that telegram which aroused in the heart of the German nation such an abiding echo.[2] I gaze into the picture, and am mindful of the duties and aims of our German nation. My dreams, the dreams of a German, show me the war that is to be, and the victory of the three great allied nations—Germany, France, and Russia—and a new division of the possessions of the earth as the final aim and object of this gigantic universal war.

The opening chapter, 'The Council of State', describes the decision of the grand alliance—France, Germany, and Russia—to make war on the British Empire. The author must have put this most ambitious scheme together before the announcement of the Anglo-French Treaty on 8 April 1904. That did serious damage to his best of all possible futures; and the Anglo-Russian Convention of 31 August 1907 made it a total impossibility.

Cover illustration for Seestern (F. H. Grautoff), *Der Zusammenbruch Der alten Welt*, 1906

THE COUNCIL OF STATE

It was a brilliant assemblage of high dignitaries and military officers that had gathered in the Imperial Winter Palace at St Petersburg. Of the influential personages, who, by reason of their official position or their personal relations to the ruling house, were summoned to advise and determine the destiny of the Tsar's Empire, scarcely one was absent. But it was no festal occasion that had called them here; for all faces wore an expression of deep seriousness, amounting in certain cases to one of grave anxiety. The conversation, carried on in undertones, was of matters of the gravest import.

The broad folding-doors facing the life-size portrait of the reigning Tsar were thrown wide open, and amid the breathless silence of all assembled, the grey-headed President of the Imperial Council,

Grand Duke Michael, entered the hall. Two other members of the Imperial house, the Grand Dukes Vladimir Alexandrovitch and Alexis Alexandrovitch, brothers of the late Tsar, accompanied him.[3]

The Princes graciously acknowledged the deep obeisances of all present. At a sign from the Grand Duke Michael, the whole company took their places at the long conference table, covered with green cloth, which stood in the centre of the pillared hall. Deep, respectful silence still continued, until, at a sign from the President, State Secretary Witte, the chief of the ministerial council, turned to the Grand Dukes and began thus:[4]

'Your Imperial Highnesses and Gentlemen! Your Imperial Highness has summoned us to an urgent meeting, and has commissioned me to lay before you the reasons for, and the purpose of, our deliberations. We are all aware that His Majesty the Emperor, our gracious Lord and Master, has declared the preservation of the peace of the world to be the highest aim of his policy. The Christian idea that mankind should be '*one* fold under *one* shepherd' has, in the person of our illustrious ruler, found its first and principal representative here on earth. The league of universal peace is due solely to His Majesty, and if we are called upon to present to our gracious Lord and Master our humble proposals for combating the danger which immediately menaces our country, all our deliberations should be inspired by that spirit which animates the Christian law of brotherly love.'

Grand Duke Michael raised his hand in interruption. 'Alexander Nicolaievitch,' he said, turning to the Secretary, 'do not omit to write down this last sentence *word for word*.'

The Secretary of State made a short pause, only to continue with a somewhat louder voice and in a more emphatic tone:

'No especial assurance is required that, in view of this, our noble liege lord's exalted frame of mind, a breach of the world's peace could not possibly come from our side. But our national honour is a sacred possession, which we can never permit others to assail, and the attack which Japan has made upon us in the Far East forced us to defend it sword in hand.[5] There is not a single right-minded man in the whole world who could level a reproach at us for this war, which has been forced upon us. But in our present danger a law of self-preservation impels us to inquire whether Japan is, after all, the only and the real enemy against whom we have to defend ourselves; and there are substantial reasons for believing that this question should be answered in the negative.

'His Majesty's Government is convinced that we are indebted for this attack on the part of Japan solely to the constant enmity of Britain, who never ceases her secret machinations against us. It has been Britain's eternal policy to damage us for her own aggrandizement. All our endeavours to promote the welfare of this Empire and make the peoples happy have ever met with resistance on the part of Britain. From the China Seas, throughout all Asia to the Baltic, Britain has ever thrown obstacles in our way, in order to deprive us of the fruits of our civilizing policy. No one of us doubts for a moment that Japan is, in reality, doing Britain's work. Moreover, in every part of the globe where our interests are at stake, we encounter either the open or covert hostility of Britain. The complications in the Balkans and in Turkey, which Britain has incited and fostered by the most despicable methods, have simply the one object in view—to bring us into mortal conflict with Austria and Germany.

'Yet nowhere are Great Britain's real aims clearer seen than in Central Asia. With indescribable toil and with untold sacrifice of treasure and blood our rulers have entered the barren tracts of country lying between the Black Sea and the Caspian, once inhabited by semi-barbarous tribes, and, further east again, the lands stretching away to the Chinese frontier and the Himalayas, and have rendered them accessible to Russian civilization. But we have never taken a step, either east or south, without meeting with British opposition or British intrigues. Today our frontiers march with the frontier of British East India, and impinge upon the frontier of Persia and Afghanistan. We have opened up friendly relations with both these states, entertain close commercial intercourse with their peoples, support their industrial undertakings, and shun no sacrifice to make them amenable to the blessings of civilization. Yet, step by step, Britain endeavours to hamper our activity. British gold and British intrigues have succeeded in making Afghanistan adopt a hostile attitude towards us.

'We must at last ask ourselves this question: How long do we intend to look on quietly at these undertakings? Russia must push her way down to the sea. Millions of strong arms till the soil of our country. We have at our own command inexhaustible treasures of corn, wood, and all products of agriculture; yet we are unable to reach the markets of the world with even an insignificant fraction of these fruits of the earth that Providence has bestowed, because we are hemmed in, and hampered on every side, so long as our way to the sea is blocked. Our mid-Asiatic possessions are suffocated from want of sea air. Britain knows this but too well, and therefore she devotes all her energies towards cutting us off from the sea. With an insolence for which there is no justification, she declares the Persian Gulf to be her own domain, and would like to claim the whole of the Indian Ocean, as she already claims India itself, as her own exclusive property.

'This aggression must at last be met with a firm "Hands off", unless our dear country is to run the risk of suffering incalculable damage. It is not we who seek war; war is being forced upon us. As to the means at our disposal for waging it, supposing Britain will not spontaneously agree to our just demands, His Excellency the Minister of War will be best able to give us particulars.'

He bowed once more to the Grand Dukes and resumed his seat. The tall, stately figure of the War Minister, Kuropatkin, next rose, at a sign from the President, and said:[6]

'For twenty years I served in Central Asia and I am able to judge, from my own experience, of our position on the south frontier. In case of a war with Britain, Afghanistan is the battleground of primary importance. Three strategic passes lead from Afghanistan into India: the Khyber Pass, the Bolan Pass, and the Kuram Valley. When, in 1878, the British marched into Afghanistan, they proceeded in three columns from Peshawar, Kohat, and Quetta to Cabul, Ghazni, and Kandahar respectively. These three roads have also been laid down as our lines of march. Public opinion considers them the only possible routes. It would carry me too far into detail were I to propound in this place the 'pros and cons' of this accepted view.

'In short, we *shall* find our way into India. Hahibullah Khan would join us with his army, 60,000 strong, as soon as we enter his territory. Of course, he is an ally of doubtful integrity, for he would probably quite as readily join the British, were they to anticipate us and make their appearance in his country with a sufficiently imposing force. But nothing prevents our being first. Our railway goes as far as Merv, seventy-five miles from Herat, and from this central station to the Afghan frontier. With our trans-Caspian railway we can bring the Caucasian army corps and the troops of Turkestan to the Afghan frontier. I would undertake, within four weeks of the outbreak of war, to mass a sufficient field army in Afghanistan round Herat. Our first army can then be followed by a ceaseless stream of regiments and batteries. The reserves of the Russian army are inexhaustible, and we could place, if needs be, four million soldiers and more than half a million of horses in the field.

'However, I am more than doubtful whether Britain would meet us in Afghanistan. The British generals would not, in any case, be well advised to leave India. Were they defeated in Afghanistan, only small fragments of their army at most would escape back to India. The Afghans would show no mercy to a fleeing British army and would destroy it, as has happened on a previous occasion. If, on the other hand, which God forbid!, the fortune of war should turn against us, we should always find a line of retreat to Turkestan open, and be able to renew the attack at pleasure.

'If the British army is defeated, then India is lost to Great Britain; for the British are, in India, in the enemy's country; as a defeated people they will find no support in the Indian people. They would be attacked on all sides by the Indian native chieftains, whose independence they have so brutally destroyed, at the very moment that their power is broken. We, on the other hand, should be received with open arms, as rescuers of the Indian people from their intolerable yoke. The Anglo-Indian army looks on paper much more formidable than it really is; its strength is put at 200,000 men, yet only one-third of this number are British soldiers, the rest being composed of natives. This army, moreover, consists of four divisions, which are scattered over the whole great territory of India. A field army, for employment on the frontier or across it, cannot possibly consist of more than 60,000 men; for, considering the untrustworthiness of the population, the land cannot be denuded of its garrisons. As a result of what I have said, I record my conviction that the war will have to be waged in India itself, and that God will give us the victory.'

The words of the general, spoken in an energetic and confident tone, made a deep impression upon his hearers; only respect for the presence of the Grand Dukes prevented applause. The greyhaired President gave the Minister of War his hand, and invited the Minister for Foreign Affairs to address them.

'In my opinion,' said the diplomatist, 'there is no doubt that the strategical opinions just delivered by His Excellency the Minister for War are based upon an expert's sound and correct estimate of the circumstances, and I also am certain that the troops of His Majesty the Tsar, accustomed as they are to victory, will, in the event of war, soon be standing upon the plain of the Indus. It is also my firm conviction that Russia would be best advised to take the offensive as soon as ever the impossibility of our present relations to Britain has been demonstrated. But whoever goes to war with Britain must not look to one battleground alone. On the contrary, we must be prepared for attacks of the most varied kinds, for an attack upon our finances, to begin with, and upon our credit, as to which His Excellency Witte could give better information than I could. The

Bank of England, and the great banking firms allied with it, would at once open this financial campaign. Moreover, a ship sailing under the Russian flag would hardly dare show itself on the open seas, and our international trade would, until our enemy had been crushed, be absolutely at a standstill.

'Moreover, more vital for us than considerations of this sort would be the question: What of the attitude of the other great Powers? Britain's political art has, since the days of Oliver Cromwell, displayed itself chiefly in adroitly making use of the continental Powers. It is no exaggeration to say that Britain's wars have been chiefly waged with continental armies.

'This is not said in depreciation of Britain's military powers. Wherever the British fleet and British armies have been seen on the field of battle, the energy, endurance, and intrepidity of their officers, sailors, and soldiers have ever been brilliantly noticeable. The traditions of the English troops who, under the Black Prince and Henry V, marched in days of yore victorious through France, were again green in the wars in the eighteenth century against France and Napoleon. Yet infinitely greater than her own military record has been Britain's success in persuading foreign countries to fight for her, and in leading the troops of Austria, France, Germany, and Russia against each other on the Continent. For the last two hundred years very few wars have ever been waged without Britain's co-operation, and without her reaping the advantage. These few exceptions were the wars of Bismarck, waged for the advantage and for the glory of his own country, by which he earned the hatred of every good Briton.

'While the continent of Europe was racked by internal wars, which British diplomacy had incited, Great Britain acquired her vast colonial possessions. Britain has implicated us too in wars which redounded to her sole advantage. I need only refer to the bloody, exhausting war of 1877–78, and to the disastrous peace of San Stefano, where Britain's intrigues deprived us of the price of our victory over the Crescent. I refer, further, to the Crimean War, in which a small British and a large French army defeated us to the profit and advantage of Britain. That Britain, and Britain alone, is again behind this attack upon us by Japan has been dwelt upon by those who have already addressed you. Our enemies do not see themselves called upon to depart in the slightest degree from a policy that has so long stood them in such good stead, and it must, therefore, be our policy to assure ourselves of the alliance, or at least, where an alliance is unattainable, of the benevolent neutrality of the other continental Powers in view of a war with Britain.

'To begin with, as regards our ally, the French Republic, a satisfactory solution of our task in this direction is already assured by the existing treaties. Yet these treaties do not bind the French Government to afford us military support in the case of a war which, in the eyes of shortsighted observers, might perhaps be regarded as one which we had ourselves provoked. We have accordingly opened negotiations through our Ambassador with M. Delcassé, the French Minister for Foreign Affairs, and with the President of the Republic himself. I have the supreme satisfaction of being in a position to lay before you the result of these negotiations in the form of a despatch just received from our Ambassador in Paris. It runs, in the main, as follows:

> I hasten to inform Your Excellency that, in the name of the French Republic, M. Delcassé has given me the solemn assurance that France will declare war upon Britain at the moment His Majesty the Tsar has directed his armies to march upon India. The considerations which have prompted the French Government to take this step have been further explained to me by M. Delcassé in our conference of this day, when he expressed himself somewhat as follows:
>
> "Napoleon, a hundred years ago, perceived with rare discernment that Britain was the real enemy of all continental nations, and that the European continent could not pursue any other policy but to combine in resisting that great pirate. The magnificent plan of Napoleon was the alliance of France with Spain, Italy, Austria, Germany, and Russia, in order to combat the rapacity of Britain. He would, in all probability, have carried his scheme through had it not been that considerations of domestic policy determined the Tsar Alexander I, in spite of his admiration for Napoleon's ability, to run counter to the latter's intentions. The consequences of Napoleon's defeat have shown themselves sufficiently clearly during the past hundred years in the enormous growth of the British power. The present political constellation, which in many respects is very similar to that of the year 1804, should be utilized to revive Napoleon's plan once more. Russia has, of course, the first and most vital interest in the downfall of Britain, for, so long as Great Britain controls all the seas and all the important coastlines, it is like a giant whose hands and feet are fettered. Yet France is also checked in her natural

Cover illustration for
Michael Wagebald, *Europa
in Flammen*, 1908

development. Her flourishing colonies in America and the
Atlantic Ocean were wrested from her in the eighteenth
century. She was ousted by this overpowering adversary from
her settlements in the East Indies, and—what the French
nation feels perhaps most acutely—Egypt, purchased for
France by the great Napoleon with the blood of his soldiers,
was weaned away by British gold and British intrigues. The
Suez Canal, built by a Frenchman, Lesseps, is in the possession of the British, facilitating their communications with
India, and securing them the sovereignty of the world. France
will accordingly make certain stipulations as the price of its
alliance—stipulations which are so loyal and equitable that
there is no question whatever of their not being agreed to on
the part of her ally, Russia. France demands that her posses-

sions in Tonking, Cochin China, and Cambodia, Annam, and Laos shall be guaranteed; that Russia be instrumental in assisting her to acquire Egypt, and that it pledges itself to support the French policy in Tunis and the rest of Africa."

In accordance with my instructions, I felt myself empowered to assure M. Delcassé that his conditions were accepted on our side. In answer to my question, whether a war with Britain would be popular in France, the Minister said:

"The French people will be ready for any sacrifice if we make Fashoda our war-cry.[7] British influence never showed itself more brutal and insulting than over this affair. Our brave Marchand was on the spot with a superior force, and France was within her rights. The simple demand of a British officer, who possessed no other force but the moral one of the British flag, compelled us, however, under the political circumstances which then obtained, to abandon our righteous claims, and to recall our brave leader. How the French people viewed this defeat has been plainly seen. The Parisians gave Marchand a splendid ovation as a national hero, and the French Government seriously contemplated the possibility of a revolution. We are now in a position to take revenge for the humiliation which we then endured, probably out of excessive prudence. If we inscribe the word *Fashoda* on the tricolour there will not be in the whole of France a man capable of bearing arms who will not follow our lead with enthusiasm."

It appeared to me to be politic to assure myself whether the Government or the inspired press would not perhaps promise the people the recovery of Alsace-Lorraine as the price of a victorious issue of the war. But the Minister replied decidedly,

"No. The question of Alsace-Lorraine", he declared, "must remain outside our view as soon as we make up our minds to go in for practical politics. Nothing could possibly be more fatal than to rouse bad blood in Germany. For the German Emperor is the tongue of the balance in which the destinies of the world are weighed. Britain in her own esteem has nothing to fear from him. She regards him more as a Briton than a German. Her confidence in this respect must not be disturbed; it forms one of the props on which British arrogance supports itself. The everlasting assurances of the German Emperor, that he intends peace and nothing but peace, appear, of course, to confirm the correctness of this view. But I am certain that the

Emperor William's love of peace has its limits where the
welfare and the security of Germany are seriously jeopar-
dized. In spite of his impulsive temperament, he is not the
ruler to allow himself to be influenced by every expression of
popular clamour, and to be driven by every ebullition of
public feeling, to embark on a decisive course of action. But
he is far-seeing enough to discern at the right moment a real
danger, and to meet it with the whole force of his personality.
I do not, therefore, look upon the hope of gaining him for an
ally as a Utopian dream, and I trust that Russian diplomacy
will join with ours in bringing this alliance about. A war with
Britain without Germany's support would always be a
hazardous enterprise. Of course we are prepared to embark
upon such a war, alike for our friendship with Russia and for
the sake of our national honour, but we could only promise
ourselves a successful issue if all the continental great Powers
join hands in this momentous undertaking."'

Although the fact of an offensive and defensive alliance with France
in view of a war with Britain could not have been unknown to the
majority of the assembled company, yet the reading of this despatch,
which was followed with breathless attention, evidently produced a
deep impression. Its publication left no room for doubt that this war
had been resolved on in the highest quarters, and although no loud
manifestation of applause followed its reading, the illustrious assemblage now breathed freely, and almost all faces wore an expression
of joyous satisfaction.

Only one man, with knitted brows, regarded the scene with
serious disapproval. For decades past he had been regarded as the
most influential man in Russia—as a power, in fact, who had
constantly thwarted the plans of the leading statesmen and had
carried his opinions through with unswerving energy.

This solitary malcontent was Pobedonostsev, the Chief Procurator
of the Holy Synod, who, despite his grey hairs, was detested only
less than he was feared. His gloomy mien and his shake of the head
had not escaped the presiding Grand Duke, and the latter evidently
considered it to be his duty to give this man who had enjoyed the
confidence of three successive Tsars an opportunity of recording his
divergent opinion.

At his summons the Chief Procurator arose, and amid complete
silence said:

'It cannot be my duty to deliver an opinion as to the possibility or on the prospects of an alliance with Germany, for I am as little acquainted as any here present with the intentions and plans of the German Emperor. William II is the greatest sphinx of our age. He talks much, and his speeches give the impression of complete sincerity; but who can guess what is really behind them? That he has formulated a fixed programme as his life's work, and that he is the man to carry it out, regardless whether public opinion is on his side or not—thus much appears to me to be certain. If the subjection of Britain is a part of his programme, then the hopes of the French Minister would, in fact, be no Utopia, only supposing that the Emperor William considers the present the most suitable time for disclosing to the world his ultimate aims. It would be the task of our diplomatic representative at the Court of Berlin to assure himself on this point.

But it is quite another question whether Russia really needs an alliance either with Germany or with the Western Power just referred to, and my view of the case leads me to answer this question in the negative. Russia is, at the present time, the last and sole bulwark of absolutism in Europe, and if a ruler called by God's grace to the highest and most responsible of all earthly offices is to remain strong enough to crush the spirit of rebellion and immorality which here and there, under the influence of foreign elements, has shown itself in our beloved country, we must, before all things, take heed to keep far away from our people the poison of the so-called liberal ideas, infidelity, and atheism with which it seems likely to be contaminated from the West. In like manner, as we, a century ago, crushed the powerful leader of the revolution, so also shall we today triumph over our foe—we single-handed! Let our armies march into Persia, Afghanistan, and India, and lead throughout all Asia the dominion of the true faith to victory. But keep our holy Russia uncontaminated by the poison of that heretical spirit, which would be a worse foe than any foreign power can be.'[8]

He sat down, and for a moment absolute silence reigned. The Grand Duke made a serious face, and exchanged a few whispered words with both his nephews. Then he said: 'All the gentlemen who have here given us their views on the situation are agreed that a declaration of war upon Britain is an exceedingly lamentable but, under the circumstances, unavoidable necessity; yet before I communicate to His Majesty, our gracious Lord, this view, which is that of us all, I put to you, gentlemen, the question whether there is anyone here who is of a contrary opinion. In this case I would beg of him to address us.'

He waited a short while, but as no one wished to be allowed to speak, he rose from his chair, and with a few words of thanks and a gentle bow to the dignitaries, who had also risen in their places, notified that he regarded the sitting, fraught with momentous consequences for the destiny of the world, as closed.

The Russian plan works like a charm. The allied powers—Russia, Germany, and France—declare war against the United Kingdom. The combined Franco-German fleet inflicts a crushing defeat on the Royal Navy in the Battle of Flushing; and allied troops begin landing in Scotland. Read on:

THE LANDING IN SCOTLAND

The ninth and tenth army corps had collected at the inlet of Kiel harbour. The town of Kiel and its environs resounded with the clattering of arms, the stamping of horses and the joyful songs of the soldiers, who, full of hope, were expecting great and decisive events. But no one knew anything for certain about the object of the impending expedition.

From the early hours of the morning of the 13th of July an almost endless stream of men, horses, and guns poured over the landing-bridges, which connected the giant steamers of the shipping companies with the harbour quays. Other divisions of troops were taken on board in boats, and on the evening of the 14th the whole field army, consisting of 60,000 men, was embarked.

Last of all, the general commanding, accompanied by the Imperial Chancellor, proceeded in a launch on board the large cruiser *König Wilhelm*, which lay at anchor in the Bay of Holtenall. Immediately afterwards, three rockets, mounting brightly against the dark sky, went up from the flagship. At this signal, the whole squadron started slowly in the direction of the Kaiser Wilhelm Canal.

The transport fleet consisted of about sixty large steamers, belonging to the North-German Lloyd, the Hamburg-America, and the Stettin companies. They were protected by the battleships *Baden*, *Württemberg*, *Bayern*, and *Sachsen*, the large cruisers *Kaiser* and *Deutschland*, the small cruisers *Gazelle*, *Prinzess Wilhelm*, *Irene*, *Komet*, and *Meteor*, and the torpedo divisions D5 and D6, accompanied by their torpedo-boat divisions.

The last torpedo-boat had long left the harbour, when, about eleven o'clock in the forenoon of the 15th of July, the dull thunder of the British ironclads resounded before the fortifications of the inlet of Kiel, answered by the guns of the German fortress.

Bright sunshine was breaking through the light clouds when the *König Wilhelm* entered the Elbe at Brunsbüttel. The boats of the torpedo division, hastening forward, reported the mouth of the river free from British warships, and a wireless message was received from Heligoland in confirmation of this.

The squadron proceeded at full speed to the north-west. The torpedo division D5 reconnoitred in advance, the small, swift boats being followed by the cruisers *Prinzess Wilhelm* and *Irene*, which from their high rigging were especially adapted for scouting operations and carried the necessary apparatus for wireless telegraphy. The rest of the fleet, whose speed had to be regulated by that of the *König Wilhelm*, followed at the prescribed intervals.

When the sharp outlines of the red cliffs of Heligoland appeared, the German cruiser *Seeadler* came from the island to meet the squadron and reported that the coast ironclads *Ægir* and *Odin*, the cruisers *Hansa*, *Vineta*, *Freya*, and *Hertha*, together with the torpedo-boats, had set out from Wilhelmshaven during the night and had seen nothing of the enemy. The sea appeared free. All the available British warships of the North Sea squadron had advanced to attack Antwerp.

Since the transport fleet did not appear to need reinforcements, it proceeded on its way west–north-west with its attendant warships, the Wilhelmshaven fleet remaining at Heligoland.

What was its destination?

Only a few among the many thousands could have given an answer, and they remained silent. The red cliffs of Heligoland had long since disappeared in the distance. Hours passed, but nothing met the eyes of the eagerly gazing warriors, save the boundless, gently rippling sea and the crystal-clear blue vault of heaven, stretched above it like a huge bell.

'What is our destination?'

It could not be the coast of England, which would have been reached long ago. But where was the landing to take place, if not there? To what distant shore was the German army being taken, the largest whose destinies had ever been entrusted to the treacherous waves of the sea?

When daylight again brought a report from the scouts that the enemy's ships were nowhere to be seen, the Commander-in-Chief of the army could not help expressing his surprise to the Admiral that the British had apparently entirely neglected scouting in the

North Sea, and further, that they did not even see any merchant vessels.

'The explanation of this apparently surprising fact is not very remote, Your Excellency,' replied the Admiral. 'We should hardly sight any merchantmen, since maritime trade is now almost entirely at a standstill, owing to the insecurity of the seas. We have not met a flotilla of fishing-boats, since in this part of the North Sea there are no fishing-grounds. We see none of the enemy's ships, since the British have most likely calculated every other possibility except our attempting to land in Scotland.'

'Your explanation is obvious, Herr Admiral; nevertheless, it seems to me that our enemy must have neglected to take the necessary precautions in keeping a look-out.'

'Your Excellency must not draw an offhand comparison between operations on land and on sea. The conditions in the latter are essentially different. I do not doubt for a moment that there is a sufficient number of British scouts in the North Sea; if we have really escaped their notice, the fortune of war has been favourable to us. I may tell Your Excellency that, even during our manoeuvres in the Baltic, where we know the course as well as the speed and strength of the marked enemy, he has sometimes succeeded in making his way through, unseen by our scouts. Perhaps this will mitigate your judgement of this apparent want of foresight on the part of the British.'

At last, on the evening of the 16th of July, land was reported by the *König Wilhelm*. The end of the journey was in sight, and the news spread rapidly that it was the coast of Scotland rising from the waves.

'We are going to enter the Firth of Forth,' was the general opinion. Even the brave soldiers, who perhaps heard the name for the first time in their lives, repeated the word with as important an air as if all the secrets of the military staff had been all at once revealed to them.

In the red light of the setting sun, both shores appeared tinged with violet from the deep-blue sky and the grey-blue sea, the north shore being further off than the south. Favoured by a calm sea, the squadron, extended in close order to a distance of about five knots, made for the entrance of the Firth of Forth.

Full of expectation, the expeditionary army saw the vast, bold undertaking develop before its eyes. For nine hundred years no hostile army had landed on the coast of Britain. Certainly, in ancient times Britain had had to fight against invading enemies: Julius

Cæsar had entered as a conqueror, Canute the Great, King of Denmark, had subdued the country. The Angles and Saxons had come over from Germany, to make themselves masters of the land. Harold the Fair-haired, King of Norway, had landed in England. But since the time of William of Normandy, who defeated the Saxons at Hastings and set up the rule of the Normans in England, not even her most powerful enemies, neither Philip of Spain nor the great Napoleon, had succeeded in landing their troops on the sea-girt soil of Britain.

Would a German army now succeed?

The outlines of the country became clearer and clearer; some even believed they could see the lofty height of Edinburgh Castle on the horizon. But soon the distant view was obscured and darkness slowly came on.

Hitherto not a single hostile ship had been seen. But now, when the greater part of the squadron had already entered the bay, the searchlights discovered two British cruisers whose presence had already been reported by the advance boats of the torpedo division.

In view of our great superiority, these cruisers declined battle, and by hauling down their flag, signified their readiness to surrender. From the sea, nothing remained to hinder the landing of the troops. The transports approached the south shore of the bay, on which Edinburgh and the harbour town of Leith are situated, and, after casting anchor, landed the troops in boats by the electric light. The infantry immediately occupied the positions favourable to meet any attack that might be made. But nothing happened to prevent the landing. The Scottish population remained perfectly calm, so that the disembarkation was completed without disturbance.

The population of Leith and the inhabitants of Edinburgh, who had hurried up full of curiosity, beheld, to their boundless astonishment, a spectacle almost incomprehensible to them, carried out with admirable precision under the bright electric light from the German ships.

The people had taken the keenest interest in the great war of Britain against the allied Powers—Germany, France, and Russia—but with a feeling that it was a matter which chiefly concerned the Government, the Army, and the Navy. They were painfully aware that things were going worse and worse for them, but were convinced that the Government would soon overthrow the enemy. Everyone knew that the Russians had penetrated into India, but the great mass of the people did not trouble about that. It could only be a passing misfortune, and trade, which was at present ruined, would soon revive and be all the more flourishing. But the idea that an enemy, a continental army, could land on the coast of Great Britain, that German or French soldiers could ever set foot on British soil, had seemed to Scotsmen so remote a contingency that they now appeared completely overcome by the logic of accomplished facts.

About noon on the following day the two army corps were already south of Leith. A brigade had been pushed forward towards the south; the rest of the troops had bivouacked, that the men might recuperate after their two days' sea journey.

The quartermasters had purchased provisions for ready money in the town, the villages, and the scattered farmhouses. The warships filled their bunkers from the abundant stock of British coal, guard-ships being detached to ensure the safety of the squadron. The Admiral had ordered that, after coaling, the warships should take up a position at the entrance to the bay, the transports remaining in the harbour. In the possible event of the appearance of a superior British squadron, the whole fleet was to leave the Firth of Forth as rapidly as possible and disperse in all directions. Certainly in that case the army would be deprived of the means of returning, but the military authorities were convinced that the appearance of an army of 60,000 German troops on British soil would practically mean the end of the war, especially as an equally strong French corps was to land in the south. The military authorities consequently thought they need not trouble themselves further about the possibility of the troops having to return.

The garrison of Edinburgh had surrendered without resistance, since it would have been far too weak to offer any opposition to the invading army. Accordingly the German officers and soldiers could move about in the town without hindrance. A number of despatches and fresh war bulletins were found which threw some light upon the strategic position, although they were partly obscure, and partly contained obvious falsehoods.

A great naval battle was said to have taken place off Flushing on the 15th of July, ending in the retreat of the German and French fleets with heavy losses. It was further reported that the British fleet had destroyed Flushing and bombarded several of the Antwerp forts. Lastly, according to the newspapers, the British fleet which had been stationed before Copenhagen had entered Kiel harbour and captured all the German ships inside, the loss of the British battle-ships at the Kieler Föhrde being admitted. The German officers were convinced that only the report of the loss of the two battleships deserved credit, since the British would hardly have invented such

7. Auflage.

Der deutsch-englische Krieg

Vision eines Seefahrers
von
Beowulf.

1906.

Verlag von Hermann Walther G. m. b. H. in Berlin.

Cover illustration for
Beowulf (pseud.), *Der
deutsch–englische Krieg*, 1906

bad news. Everything else, from the position of things, bore the stamp of improbability on the face of it.

The trumpets blew, the soldiers grasped their arms, the battalions began their march. The batteries clattered along with a dull rumble. In four columns, by four routes, side by side the four divisions started for the south.

Armageddon 190–

The other, more acceptable account of the Zukunftskrieg *appears in the anonymous tale of 1906,* Der Zusammenbruch der alten Welt. *Although the author—F. H. Grautoff—argued for a stronger German navy, he deplored the possibility of a war in Europe. Grautoff is the bright opposite of*

August Niemann, that eager devastator of nations: he foresaw that 'a great war' would be a disaster for all the combatants. Ninety years ago this German writer began his tale of the war-to-come with an unusual lamentation for the destructiveness of war and, even more unusual, a plea for a union of the European nations.

THE MOST TERRIFIC WAR IN HISTORY

The end has come at last. The awful year in which the Old World ran blood is over. 'Glad, refreshing war'—well, we have had it now. European armies are still in the field, trying to win back, step by step, all that has been buried beneath the crash and ruin of the recent devastating war. It will take a decade to restore the work of peaceful civilization that has been annihilated. And the men who are returning from the enemy's country are a people who have lost the habit of work. Hearts have grown harder during this year in which the world has reeked of blood. Countries have grown emptier; too many are sleeping under the green mounds yonder.

We have come to the end of the most terrific war that the world has ever seen; the year 190– has been recorded on the scroll of History in letters of blood. We have come to the end of it, and now it is the duty of the historian to unfold in sequence the scenes of the fearful drama that had its commencement on those fateful March days of 190– in Samoa, and which dragged all the nations of the Old World with it in its relentless course. All those irresponsibles who in Parliaments, popular assemblies, and the Press on both sides of the water, had kept stirring up hatred between two nations, who had thought that a passage of arms between Britain and Germany would clear the air, like a thunderstorm, and that either side would be able, today or tomorrow, or whenever they pleased, as soon as the tension was relieved, to call a halt—over all these the march of events swept remorselessly.

They had not stayed to consider that a war in Europe, with its manifold intricate relations with the new countries over the seas, the millions of whose populations obeyed a handful of white men, but grudgingly, must necessarily set the whole world ablaze. A bora, a fiery storm across the desert, lashing all slumbering feelings into activity, rushed through the countries of Islam, an electric current flowed through the apparently indolent masses of the Asiatic races, when the ground of Europe was shaken with the noise of arms. The diplomats of the Berlin Congress are now endeavouring to put the new wine into new bottles; as yet nothing is finished, nothing decided, but the outlines of their endeavours are sketched in.

Let us, then, look back, and, passing the whole in review once more, trace its development. Here we shall show only a section of events, bring forward only the main points, the milestones that mark the year 190–.

The *union* of the European peoples alone can win back for them the undisputed political power and the dominion of the seas that they have lost. Today the centre of political gravity is in Washington, St Petersburg, and Tokyo.

The first chapter sets the scene in the harbour of Apia, where 'the German flag fluttered limply over the Imperial Government Buildings'. The German inhabitants are apprehensive after they have had news that the British Mediterranean Fleet seemed to be preparing for war. Their sole defence is the antiquated survey ship, Möwe, *anchored in the harbour.*

THE INCIDENT OF SAMOA

On the afternoon of March 13th a curl of smoke appeared on the western horizon, and shortly before five o'clock the British cruiser *Katoomba*, an old acquaintance at Apia, arrived from Sydney and cast anchor some 200 yards from the *Möwe*. After the prescribed salutes, the British commanding officer had himself rowed ashore to pay a visit to the Governor. Mentioning that the same regulation was in force on board the *Möwe*, Dr Solf asked the Englishman not to allow shore leave to the crew of the *Katoomba* so long as the present strained relations, which had made themselves felt even as far as Apia, should last, and to this Captain Hopkins readily agreed. He next spent half an hour—a longer visit would have attracted attention—at the British consulate, and then presented himself on board the *Möwe*.[9]

The conversation, at first strictly formal, grew somewhat more cordial when the two commanding officers found that they had been comrades in the Seymour expedition to Pekin. Kapitän-leutnant Schröder returned the visit on board the *Katoomba* the same evening. The evening of the same day, the Governor was informed that an American missionary had been half-killed for attempting, by means of liberal gifts of spirits and freely scattered dollars, to stir up some former adherents of Malietoa against the Germans. This excellent shepherd of souls—it was said that before his 'conversion' he had passed a lengthy holiday in the well-known American prison of Sing-Sing—had been surprised in his dirty work by two of the military police, who promptly took upon themselves the administration of Lynch law, and gave the 'reverend' gentleman a sound thrashing.

The American consul immediately sent an official note: 'I hope sincerely that American subjects, even under existing circumstances, are under the protection of the German Government.' The situation was delicate on account of the implication of the two policemen.

Dr Solf informed the consul that the two offenders had already been placed under arrest, but asked him to use his influence to restrain American subjects from all political agitation, as only in that case could he offer any guarantee.

On March 15th the British consul complained that drunken natives—the spirits had emanated from the American minister—had broken into a British store during the night. Thereupon Dr Solf issued an order prohibiting under the severest penalties any gift or sale of spirituous liquors to natives or Chinese. During the afternoon the American cruiser *Wilmington* and the British cruiser *Wallaroo* from Sydney appeared in the harbour and anchored near the *Katoomba*. Late in the evening a boat from the *Wilmington* put ashore; an officer went up to the consulate and returned only after some considerable time to his ship. A subordinate customs officer declared that two heavy chests had been carried from the boat into the consulate; in his opinion they could only have contained rifles.

Dr Solf called upon the American consul at nine o'clock next morning, in order to clear up the matter. He informed him of the communication he had received and called his attention to the fact that the prohibition of the importation of arms was still in force. The consul, Mr Schumacher, indignantly repudiated the imputation of any chests having been brought ashore, much more rifles.

Two hours later a suspicious-looking parcel was taken from a native on an American plantation, and proved to contain three American naval carbines. The fellow was allowed to escape, and the arms were brought into the Governor's house. Dr Solf sent an official note to the American consul, in which he reiterated his caution.

In the afternoon Dr Solf invited all the naval commanding officers and the two consuls to a conference at his residence. He briefly outlined the political position, and begged the representatives of the foreign powers to do their utmost to avoid a breach of the peace. A sultry atmosphere pervaded the little room. There was a forced tone about the conversation, and mutual confidence was lacking. Suddenly a shot was heard outside, followed by wild shouts. The captain of the *Wilmington* hurried to the window. Outside, helped along by their clubs, a Chinaman was being driven into the outer court of the Government buildings by the native police. An orderly came in and announced that the Chinaman, after a few words with a policeman, had shot at him in the open street.

'Shot?'

'Here is the rifle,' said the orderly, producing it.

A quiver ran across Dr Solf's clean-shaven face. He struck the floor sharply with the butt end of the rifle, walked up to the table with his hand on the barrel and, fixing meanwhile a penetrating glance on Mr Schumacher, said:

'This is the second time today that American naval rifles have been brought into this house. In half an hour's time two pairs of sentries will be posted outside the doors of the American consulate so that no more articles may be—stolen from the building.'

The Americans rose and icily took their leave. The British followed them. Kapitänleutnant Schröder and Dr Solf remained in eager consultation for a few minutes, then the former returned to his ship.

Half an hour later the *Möwe* had landed thirty marines, who moved into temporary quarters near the Government House, and immediately took over police duty in the streets of Apia. The activity of the native Samoan police was restricted to the Samoan quarter. Dr Solf issued an order that no one was to be allowed in the streets after sunset without a pass, and this order was immediately communicated to the foreign consuls.

The sun sank crimson into the sea. The slender white silhouettes of the four ships rocked gently on the calm water. The harsh roll of the drums and the long drawn out bugle notes of the tattoo came clearly and distinctly over to land. Slowly and jerkily, the white anchor-light of the *Möwe* climbed, like a pale star, to the forestay. With her high rigging, she looked like a toy ship, compared with the grave, unreservedly warlike-looking foreign cruisers. Only two gun ports broke her gunwale, only two large guns to the two dozen British and American. Behind the *Möwe* rose the grotesque figure of the *Wilmington*, a floating flat-iron with a factory chimney on top, suggesting, with her overgrown funnel, one of those earlier, helpless, disproportioned steam-boats come to life again, that are rusting away here and there in forgotten corners of harbours.

The British monarch has a nightmare vision of the menace of the Zeppelin

The tropical night fell quickly. Under its cover, two American boats approached the shore; the officers from both went up to the American consulate. Only a watch remained on the beach. At about two o'clock in the morning, several hopelessly intoxicated American sailors were placed under arrest by German marines. While the latter were engaged in subduing these fellows—there were two negroes among them—wild scenes of disorder were being enacted in Apia proper. A company of American sailors, excited by whisky, had broken into some of the native huts, and a row developed into a regular fight. Shots were fired on both sides. The Samoans, from whom all arms had been taken, that is to say, bought up, years before by the German authorities, had suddenly, in some inexplicable manner, become possessed of American carbines; as was ascertained later, they had come from the supply of arms in the American consulate. Two American sailors were killed, four wounded, eight, speechlessly drunk, were placed under arrest. Eight Samoans were dead and fourteen wounded. Active official communication was in progress even before daybreak between the Governor and the consuls. It was an evil night.

On March 17th, at seven o' clock in the morning, Dr Solf received a note from the American consul, and immediately afterwards one from the British consul, to the effect that, armed natives having attacked American marines, they, as the representatives of their Governments, felt it incumbent upon them to request permission to land detachments for the protection of the consulate.

Dr Solf replied that the consulates were under the protection of the German Government, but that this protection certainly did not extend to persons who attacked the huts of peaceful natives, as had happened the previous night. He could not permit the landing of foreign troops. He would consult his Government by cable concerning the case. For the time being he must hold to his decision. The cables, for the present, might be used only for the despatch of ordinary telegrams, not for cipher telegrams. The incarcerated Americans must remain temporarily under arrest.

Both consuls replied that, if no assent were received from the Governor before nine o'clock, the landing of two detachments would be effected without his permission. To this Dr Solf replied that he would oppose an armed landing by force. The commander of S.M.S. *Möwe* would be instructed to fire upon any boat containing armed men.

The clock struck eight; all work in Apia was suspended. Everywhere the events of the night were being discussed. Groups engaged in eager conversation stood about the streets. The British and American colonists assembled in the neighbourhood of their respective consulates. The hills behind Apia were crowded with natives; it was like a Roman amphitheatre, with the Europeans as gladiators.

At five minutes past eight the Governor's boat, rowed by eight native policemen, shot swiftly from the quay. Dr Solf was on his way to the *Möwe*. A quarter of an hour later he took a silent leave of Kapitänleutnant Schröder at the accommodation ladder with a long hand pressure. On his way back, Dr Solf met the American consul's boat, which reached the *Wilmington* a few minutes later, and shortly afterwards returned. It was said on shore that Mr Schumacher had conveyed a very important communication to the commander of the *Wilmington*.

Half-past eight. A thousand eyes gazed anxiously out to sea. Apia was flung entirely on her own resources. After the American consul had sent off one final telegram, the cable had ceased to act, so that she was cut off from the rest of the world. Outside lay the three white ships with their glittering, threatening guns—the enemy; near them, facing the shore, the little *Möwe*.

The minutes fled. Proudly the Imperial flag floated in the fresh breeze over the Governor's House. The funnels of the warships emitted thick clouds of smoke, which sank again upon the surface of the water, and dissolved into a thin, brown mist. Occasionally a signal came across. Click, click, clack; click, click, clack—sharply and evenly—the anchors were weighed and a foaming wave appeared astern—the propeller began to move.

And the minutes fled. The little *Möwe*, the poor *Möwe*! Her fate was sealed. Alas! for the brave fellows on board! Apia was wrapped in death-like silence. All the Germans on the farthest outpost of the Empire gazed out with bated breath and eager eyes. The marines stood on shore, with rifles ordered, in the courtyard of the Government House.

'I say, you fellows, this is horrible. If we could only be on board and have a go at the damned hounds!' hissed the lieutenant in command between his teeth.

Men counted the seconds now. The Germans gathered round the Government House. Men wrung each other's hands in silence, conversation was carried on in a whisper, and the seconds raced on. Then suddenly the screech of a steam whistle came across the water and a white cloud of steam appeared from the long funnel of the *Wilmington*. The water spurted up about her bows. Slowly she glided between the two British vessels, and left the harbour under full steam, describing a curve to eastward far out at sea, and then steering her course for Pago-Pago. The American consul had been able in time to pass on a telegram from his Government, directing that a conflict was to be avoided *under any circumstances*, and should hostilities break out, the *Wilmington* was to quit Apia, leaving the rest to the Government of the United States. The two British boats remained where they were.

A quarter to nine. Was that the sound of a steam-siren wafted across by the wind? The crew of the *Möwe* assembled on the after-deck. Kapitänleutnant Schröder made a short speech:

'Comrades! The commanding officers of the British and American ships have demanded the right to land men for the protection of their consulates. Foreign consulates on German soil are under German protection and require no other. Our Governor has consequently flatly refused the demand, and declared that he will be compelled to oppose a landing by force. As the *Wilmington* is putting out to sea, the American appears to have withdrawn his request. The two British, however, will doubtless stick to their point. Comrades! We cannot permit German soil, soil on which so much German blood has been shed, to be calmly appropriated by the foreigner. If a landing be attempted, our guns must speak. Men, I wish we had a better ship beneath our feet, for if the first shot be fired at nine o'clock, in all probability a quarter of an hour later the *Möwe* will have ceased to exist. But, comrades, let us show the world that German sailors know how to defend their flag. Never yet has a German warship lowered her flag to the foe; let the last of us take it with him into his grave. And now let us sum up all that is in our hearts in one cry together: Our most gracious Sovereign Commander! Hurrah! hurrah! hurrah!'

The stormy hurrah was echoed a thousandfold on shore; choked feelings gave vent in the old war cry.

Five minutes to nine. Dr Solf appeared on the verandah of the Government House. The corps of marines marched up. Arms were shouldered with a jerk. Dead silence. Nerves at utmost tension. Alas! poor *Möwe*. Someone pointed towards the western horizon where a curl of smoke lay across the water. Who was that, talking of help and rescue? Boom! boom! nine o'clock.

A signal was displayed on the flagstaff of the British consulate, just below the national ensign. The decision! All eyes were turned upon Dr Solf, whose set features betrayed nothing. He took off his feathered hat, walked across to the front of the verandah, and grasped the rail with both hands, fixedly watching the sea.

A boat was lowered from the *Wallaroo* and another from the *Katoomba*. Men could be seen standing at every gun, behind the gun-shields, and at the machine guns. Now the boats' crews bend to the oars. The boats shoot out with a jerk, they are out of the shadow of the ships, describe a slight curve, are in open water. You almost fancy that you hear the rhythmic beat of the oars. Ruck! ruck! ruck!

All eyes are upon the *Möwe*. The ducks of the seamen stand out against the dark guns. A shrill whistle, then a blue cloud appears from the forward revolving gun, a flash—a second cloud, a second flash—Splash! the projectiles strike the water in front of the two boats. They seem to hesitate. No, they are pulling on. Splash! the oars dip into the water. Splash! splash! splash!

Who struck up the old battle-song of the *Iltis*?[10]

> From our vessel's mast
> Proudly waves our flag
> The red-white-red.

The *Möwe's* stern is covered with foam. Her funnels belch dense volumes of smoke. The gunner's orders are to count twenty after the first warning shot.... Twenty. A blue cloud hides the revolving gun. Splinters and planks shoot up from both boats. The water spurts high in dozens of jets.

Then a few planks floating about in the water, and here and there a head or an arm, were all there was to be seen, for the moment the machine guns of the *Möwe* came into play, pandemonium was let loose. All three ships disappeared from view in a grey-white veil of smoke, pierced by red and yellow flashes. Then came dull, reverberating shocks, shrieking whistles, the sharp crash of rending steel, the roll of heavy guns, thundering explosions, and above all the harsh, metallic chatter of machine guns. Isolated missiles reached the shore, here a palm tree snapped off short, there a bursting shell cut up the ground, there a house took fire. In the harbour, columns of water leapt up in a hundred places at once.

After ten minutes things became quieter; now and again a shot or a bugle call, the shriek of a siren, or the roar of cheers came across, but the tortured ear-drum was hardly sensible of the sudden relief, and the hellish din echoed in the ears for hours. The thick wall of smoke crumbled, the light breeze tore great pieces of it away.

Tops and smoking funnels came into sight again. At last a gust of wind split the smoke, sweeping it away like a bank of fog, and the sun shone down on a terrible scene of devastation. The *Möwe* had disappeared; only her masts still rose above water; but on her fore topmast head the Imperial flag waved proudly. Her crew had gone down with her. Two or three men, only, had taken refuge in the rigging. A boat put off from the *Katoomba* to bring away the survivors.

The *Katoomba* appeared to be hardly damaged; one 4-inch gun had been flung off the carriage and lay slanting across the ship's side. The gun-shield had been dented in at the side like a biscuit box. The *Wallaroo*, on the other hand, seemed to have suffered a good deal. She lay athwart the wreck of the *Möwe*, which had sunk about thirty yards from the reef that was a continuation of Cape Mulinuu. The *Wallaroo* was evidently on the reef up to her waist—how she had got there was an enigma—and was clearly making water fast, as her pumps were throwing out tremendous streams of water to both sides. The annihilation of the *Möwe* had cost the enemy dear.

While the volunteer corps (about 160 strong), that had been formed two days before, were getting arms under the walls of the Government House (towards half-past ten) a boat put off from the *Katoomba*, flying a flag of truce. The first lieutenant of the ship brought to the Governor a request that he would haul down the German flag, and surrender Apia to the British captain. Dr Solf answered coolly that if they wanted the German flag, they had better fetch it.

At 11 o'clock to the minute, the *Katoomba* opened a vigorous but ineffectual bombardment of Apia. The result of it was practically nil; several natives were killed and wounded, and a few buildings wrecked; that was all. At 12 o'clock the steam pinnace of the *Katoomba* took three boats crowded with marines in tow and, under the fire of the ships, approached the shore. As there was danger of hitting their own people, however, the bombardment had to cease, and small-arms fire commenced, supported by the gun of the British pinnace. The German volunteer corps joined valiantly in the fight, and the thirty marines, under good cover, managed to give the enemy a good deal of trouble. The boats had already lost several men, but would nevertheless, in a few minutes, have reached the shore; several of the marines had jumped overboard, and were wading towards the land.

Suddenly the siren of the *Katoomba* gave a long, warning shriek; the advance of the landing party was arrested, simultaneously a dull report rang out from the sea, and two seconds later a shell burst on the afterdeck of the *Katoomba*.

It was one of the moments that afterwards seem simply inconceivable to all that have been concerned. The enemy's attention had been so taken up by the operations on land, while there, people had had eyes only for the attacking boats, and had, moreover, been obliged to keep under cover from the well-aimed shells, that hardly any one had noticed the approach of two ships to seaward. As though suddenly risen out of the water, the two German cruisers, *Thetis* and *Cormoran*, that had been announced the week before, came into sight two geographical miles away and opened an energetic and well-directed fire. Dr Solf had been watching the arrival of the two saviours in need for two hours, but only those immediately round him were aware of their approach. People drew long breaths of relief when at half-past seven, through good glasses, they recognized the German flag flying astern of them both. And yet the final issue had hung on a few minutes.

The enemy was in a bad way. One half of the efficient crews were in the boats, others were engaged in repairing damages—though on the *Wallaroo* it was more a case of saving the lives of the men—so that the guns, for the time being, were under-manned. The boats were hastily recalled. Still, the enemy took up the new fight with commendable smartness. Matters looked ugly only on board the *Wallaroo*, which hung on the coral reef like a stranded whale. Sides were pretty equal. The *Katoomba* and the *Thetis* were evenly matched, and the little *Cormoran* was about on a level with the injured *Wallaroo*. But the severe losses that the enemy had sustained reduced the balance.

One lucky shot struck the returning steam pinnace, piercing the boiler, which exploded, so that in half a minute the vessel was swallowed up by the waves; another boat, too, was hit by a shell. Their abortive attempt at landing cost the enemy over sixty men in less than five minutes, the rapidly nearing Germans, too, concentrating the fire of their light guns on the boats. The details of the fight could not be followed exactly on account of the black smoke from the British ships, the *Thetis* and the *Cormoran*, with their almost smokeless powder having very much the advantage.

The *Wallaroo* suffered terribly. The *Cormoran*'s fire swept her deck and mowed down her gunners—by now, few in number. The superstructures and the funnels were shot away. Still, the Britons showed that the men under the Union Jack had not forgotten their old traditions. Towards half-past one all was silent on board the *Wallaroo*, which lay a smoking ruin on the reef. The wind kept the smoke low, the machine guns chattered ceaselessly, the 4-inch guns, with pauses of barely a second, spat out their screeching projectiles. But already the intervals between the enemy's shots were growing longer. The *Katoomba* had only one funnel left; one of the masts of the *Cormoran*, which showed the effects of many a well-aimed shot, had gone overboard. The searchlight and the standard compass were a confused mass of splinters.

The fight raged on. The *Katoomba* then abandoned her position and made a brilliant turn to starboard, all but grazing the *Cormoran* as she flew past. The keen eye of a British gunner seized the chance, and a shell hit the muzzle of the *Cormoran*'s port torpedo tube. A white flash, a deafening detonation—the foam swirled up and in the *Cormoran*'s broadside yawned a breach a yard wide, extending below her water-line, through which the water poured, splashing and gurgling. One of her port boilers was likewise shattered, and steam rushed up on deck through every opening.

The ship was heeling perilously over to port; the situation was critical. With quick presence of mind her commander ordered 'Full steam ahead'. The *Cormoran* passed the threatening coral reefs at full speed, reached the inner bay of Apia and, steered by a sure hand, ran on the soft, muddy bottom of the harbour. The cruiser then righted herself and lay where she was, like a block, the waters breaking gently against her sides.

The *Cormoran*, it is true, was thus put out of action, but the ship and her crew were saved; and, moreover, the *Thetis* had now only to deal with the much-damaged *Katoomba*, whose engines, through the bursting of one boiler and the damaging of another by a German shell which had crashed through the thin-armoured deck, were considerably reduced in efficiency. At the moment of the explosion on board the *Cormoran*, the *Katoomba* had forged slightly ahead of the *Thetis*. The latter was now following her, and a running fire was kept up on both sides, which, however, could not last long, as the *Thetis* was still practically intact.

The intention of the British commander was evident: he wished to bring the hopeless conflict to an end with honour. He kept his course parallel with the coast, about a sea mile from shore. The *Thetis* gave chase for all her engines were worth, and soon overhauled her. The *Thetis* had six 4-inch guns in action to the *Katoomba*'s two stern guns, and this circumstance decided the action in twenty minutes, especially as the service of the British guns, thrice relieved, quickly melted away under the hail of the machine guns. Shortly after two o'clock the *Katoomba* sheered off to starboard, and ran on the coral reef. The forepart of the ship reared up, almost burying the stern under water, while the terrific impact threw all off their feet.

The battle was over. The *Thetis* stopped her engines a hundred yards from the *Katoomba* and the latter struck her flag. At the same moment the last two available boats were lowered from the *Thetis* to take off the survivors of the *Katoomba*, all her own boats, as could be seen, having been shot away.

As the British commander set foot on the *Thetis*, the drums beat the salute and the crew presented arms. Kapitänleutnant Hartmann shook hands with his defeated opponent, and, with a silent gesture, declined his proffered sword. Then, as the *Thetis* put about and set her course towards Apia again, the wreck of the *Katoomba* slipped off the reef and sank in the waves—a giant coffin for her unburied dead.

The victors were met with acclamations from on shore, but the note of the greeting was grave and dignified. Dr Solf had himself rowed across to the *Thetis* without delay. He wrung Kapitänleutnant Hartmann's hands again and again in silence. Apia was saved, but at what a cost! and for how long? For this meant war. Perhaps even now the storm had broken loose.

The author had two good reasons for choosing Samoa, a German colony at that time, for the opening stage in his tale of the war-to-come. First, a far-away island allowed him to demonstrate that, given the 'intricate relations' of the European powers and their colonies, an incident anywhere in the world could set the nations on the road to war. Second, the remoteness of Samoa made it possible for him to by-pass the initial problem of all future-war fiction—inventing a history to show how hostilities could follow out of contemporary disagreements and discord. The naval engagement, far away in the Southern hemisphere, touched off the Great European conflict. At an early stage in the war, a British naval force attacks Cuxhaven, then a new port on the west bank of the Elbe, some 70 miles north-west of Hamburg. The new harbour was completed in 1892, and it would be a prime target for British naval vessels in 1906.

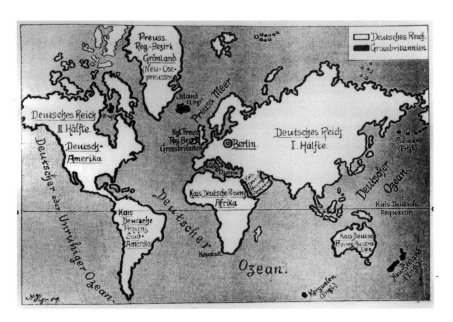

A German map of the world in 1907 as it should be in the near future

THE BOMBARDMENT OF CUXHAVEN

A service had been arranged for the garrison of Cuxhaven at nine o'clock on the morning of March 21st—the day, as previously observed, having been set apart as one of General Confession and Intercession. Every seat in the garrison church was occupied. The preacher had hardly begun his discourse when the blare of bugles and the rolling of drums crashed out from the street. The general alarm was being sounded, and, as the preacher paused a moment to listen to the unwonted sounds, the door was flung open and some-one shouted into the church: 'The British are coming.' No one stopped to listen to the peaceful words from the pulpit, but a sharp order was given, and officers and men trooped out through the church doors. Outside, the men fell in quickly, and while the bugle call rang out from every corner of the streets of the little town, companies of marine artillery were already hurrying at the double in the direction of the two batteries of Kugelbaake and Grimmerhörn.

From all the houses people came with anxious faces into the street, apparently not yet fully grasping the meaning of the sudden alarm; but the report of the enemy's approach spread like lightning. Then, in frantic haste, men and women rushed back into their houses, snatching up their valuables, and, in their excitement, saving and stowing away the merest trifles. There might be hours yet, but perhaps the enemy was already at hand, and the inhabitants of Cuxhaven began to leave the town without delay. From the harbour could be heard the hooting of the steam whistles, and the sirens of the tugs that were towing the fishing boats—broad lighters and slender cutters—on which the fisher folk had packed away their belongings the day before, in long processions, upstream. Police offi-cers went from house to house, requesting the people, in view of a possible bombardment, to leave their houses. At the railway stations trains were being brought up continuously, and a busy, nervous activity reigned over the little town. All sorts of household stuff was being loaded on waggons, some were shouting themselves hoarse for carts and other means of transport, and despairingly wringing their hands at being obliged to leave their property behind. The station was soon besieged by dense crowds, perpetually reinforced from the streets. Although a detachment of Hamburg police did their utmost to maintain a semblance of order, there were fearful scenes when the people learnt that any extensive conveyance of luggage by the trains that had been waiting in readiness since the day before was out of the question. And the bugles never ceased their call.

A group of Hamburg gentlemen had gathered together on the 'Alte Liebe',[11] and were watching the harbour, and following events in the batteries, with their field-glasses. Towards eleven o'clock the port and the beach were completely deserted. The streets lay silent and empty, and no sound was heard but the hooting of the locomotive whistles and the drawing up of the trains.

All eyes were directed out to sea, whence distant firing was already audible. On the horizon a long line of ships was seen approaching slowly. First came the two coast defence ships *Odin* and *Hagen*, which steamed quickly past Cuxhaven. Then four small cruisers appeared far out, between the sandbanks, where, as a rule, the red lightships indicated the navigable channel, and then six battle-ships filed slowly into the estuary. The yellow flashes from the guns could be clearly distinguished amid the thick brown clouds of smoke belched from their funnels. Of the enemy nothing was as yet to be seen, but the spurting jets between the German ships, and to landward of them, showed that a fight was in progress. Slowly the German ships drew back into the wide Elbe estuary, and louder and louder pealed the thunder of the heavy artillery.

Towards eleven o'clock, to seaward, farther out even than where a grey shadow indicated the position of the squat, square Neuwerk lighthouse, appeared a line of fire-spouting battle-ships, and over them a light blue veil of smoke: the British fleet. The six German battle-ships were about opposite Kugelbaake. Behind them hid a swarm of torpedo craft. The four small cruisers and the *Kaiserin Augusta*, as well as the two heavy armoured cruisers, had already retired from action and were steaming up the Elbe. The forward funnel of the *Friedrich Karl* was shot away, and lay, broken off in front, near the bridge. The *Gazelle* had two great holes in her side, just above her water line. On the *Kaiserin Augusta* a port gun had been thrown off its carriage and was pointing straight upwards. There was no further serious damage to be perceived on the ships. Each one, as she arrived, was greeted with loud hurrahs! from the 'Alte Liebe', which was now being slowly cleared of curious onlookers by the military.

The guns of the shore batteries were still silent, as the distance from the enemy was too great for their fire to be effective, nor did the enemy's shells as yet reach the batteries. But more and more British ships were coming into sight. Apparently they were advancing to the attack. Then, the six German ships of the line steered in file—evidently through a gap in the mine barricade—past Cuxhaven, and anchored up the river, a little above the new port.

Then the battery of Fort Kugelbaake burst into flame. The heavy 12-inch guns came into play, and, with a roar, the battery sent its first salute to the enemy. The vibration from the firing rattled every pane of glass in the town. The German shots only succeeded each other at long intervals. A quarter of an hour later there was a flash between the green traverses of Fort Grimmerhörn. The fight was being carried on, on the German side, by the shore batteries only; the battle-ships, their largest calibre guns, 9.5-inch, no longer reaching the enemy, being forced, at this distance, to look on, inactive. The enemy, on the contrary, having numerous 12-inch guns (the same calibre as those in the German shore batteries), and their battle-ships having greater engine power, were able to compel the maintenance of the distance. If the German ships had pressed forward to within firing-range of their 9.5-inch guns, they would have been obliged—if indeed the British ships had not retreated out of range again—to cross a zone during the passage of which they would have been exposed, defenceless, to the fire of the enemy's heavy artillery, especially as the British, in possession of accurate charts, at every attempt at an advance made by the German ships, kept the very narrow navigable channel under brisk fire with their largest calibre guns. The Admiral, therefore, issued orders for a preliminary retreat, and, as above mentioned, went a little way up stream and anchored beyond the range of the enemy's fire.

In the meantime the firing proceeded with unabated fury. All the small calibre guns were silent, as only the heaviest were effective at the distance. Still, shots were succeeding each other at longer and longer intervals; for both sides, in view of the restricted firing capacity of the heavy 12-inch guns, were anxious to be careful with their ammunition. As soon as the *Kaiserin Augusta* had passed the 'Alte Liebe', her steam pinnace was lowered, and steered for the harbour. An officer went ashore and presented himself to the commandant of the shore batteries, to communicate to him his more exact observations concerning the strength and composition of the enemy's fleet. The latter tallied on the whole with the most recent reports received from the observation station on the Neuwerk lighthouse, before its lantern and signalling apparatus had been destroyed by a shell. Only, from Neuwerk four more heavy battle-ships, with extraordinarily high superstructures, had been signalled, ships, consequently, that were not of the characteristically low build of the British ships of the line. Judging from this, a French battle-ship division must already be with the British fleet. As was learnt later, it included the French battle-ships *Charlemagne*, *Gaulois*, *St Louis*, and *Bouvet*.

Fort Kugelbaake suffered less, but the first of the enemy's shells aimed at Fort Grimmerhörn fell right in the middle of the battery, and, sighted with mathematical accuracy, more than a dozen others followed. The artillerymen fell by rows, and between the guns, protected only by earthwork traverses and not by any armour, the splinters of the enemy's shells swept the platforms with ghastly thoroughness. Fresh men kept taking the places of the fallen, who had been literally cut to pieces. The loading-platforms were slippery with blood and fragments of flesh. The next gunners, whose fate was to be the same, stood in the sickening mess and manipulated with machine-like regularity the loading of the guns, their sinewy arms thrusting one charge after another into the hot tubes. Shot after shot rent the air, and in the fiendish, deafening noise of their own and the enemy's fire, the men could only understand each other by signs.

At two o'clock half the Grimmerhörn guns were out of action. The linings of two of the guns were no longer air-proof, owing to sand and stones having flown in. Another was flung out of position by a shot that took it full on the carriage, and had crushed several gunners under its heavy bulk. Inside the battery a horrible scene of carnage presented itself to the eye. Bleeding lumps of flesh, burnt and torn scraps of uniform, and steaming pools of blood were where living men had stood just before. An ambulance corps, braving the splinters from the enemy's shells which flew all round them, dragged a few of the severely wounded into the covered-in, bomb-proof rooms. But fresh relays of gunners stepped undauntedly from the inside of the fortress onto the loading-platform, and the rolling and flashing of guns came ceaselessly from between the earthwork traverses, which gradually, demolished by bursting shells, lost their regular form and became mere shapeless heaps of soil.

Outside, in the roadstead, the dark silhouettes of the British warships were drawing closer and closer together. The enemy were only firing from fore turrets, with their heaviest calibre guns, pressing slowly forward, in a semicircle, towards the mouth of the Elbe, thus turning their best protected front to the German defenders. The lofty signal masts and tall funnels, on some ships placed in pairs (which showed them to belong to the *Majestic* class), were now clearly distinguishable, and yellow lightning spat and flashed unceasingly from the grey hulls, pouring death and destruction into the German shore batteries. It was now possible, with the glass, to see columns of water shoot up where German shells fell between the enemy's ships. But not every missile sank thus ineffectual into the waves. On the forepart of the decks of several British ships explosions could be seen to take place. On board one of the *Majestic* class a black cloud of smoke rose, after which the fore signal mast pitched sideways overboard. Another ship veered suddenly to port, thus exposing her whole starboard side to the German gunners, whereupon a second British boat steamed up to drag the ship, which had, in the meantime, been struck two or three times on her water line, and was heeling over badly, out of the line of battle.

The naked eye could only perceive all this in outline on the horizon. From the Cuxhaven lighthouse, however, with good field-glasses, it was possible to observe more closely the shots that told. It could be seen thence that several of the British ships had swung round and were fighting from their stern turrets.

The French suffered very much more than the British, affording the German gunners, with their tall, easily damaged, and only lightly protected superstructures, better targets than did the low-built British war-ships. Two of the French battle-ships (one of them had apparently taken fire) were obliged, after the battle had lasted only two hours, to retire from the fight and steam seaward. A third French ship, the *Bouvet*, had ceased firing and was drifting about, pitching helplessly.

As was ascertained later, what had happened was that a German shell, striking between the fore turret and the somewhat higher conning-bridge, had not only cut many telegraph signalling connections, but, piercing the fore turret diagonally, had also penetrated the armoured deck and, bursting in the engine-room, destroyed the whole of the port machinery, and burst all the boilers. As the British Admiral did not wish to take a battle-ship out of the fighting line to tow off the *Bouvet*, she was simply let lie, in the hope that the task of rescuing her could be carried out as darkness fell.

Towards five o'clock in the afternoon the *Bouvet*, hit by three more German shells, became quite incapable of manoeuvring. The two heavy turret guns had fired off a shell occasionally, but towards five o'clock the top of the forward turret was pierced by a shell which, exploding inside the turret, simply made mincemeat of the gunners. As, simultaneously, a number of shells that were lying in readiness blew up, a sort of panic seized the crew. Then the *Bouvet*, with only her starboard engine still working, and her helm useless, drifted about for a time, lay for ten minutes exposed diagonally to the German fire, was hit again several times, and then stranded on a sandbank, a helpless wreck.

It could not fail to strike the observer that the enemy, though unable to do much harm to Fort Kugelbaake, and putting no gun there permanently out of action, had struck the Grimmerhörn battery with the very first shot. The riddle was easy to solve. Acting as pilots for German waters, and especially for the mouths of the Elbe and Weser, were British steamship captains and helmsmen who, on their regular journeys to Hamburg and Bremen, had become so accurately acquainted with the navigable channels that even after the removal of the sea marks they were able to guide the British fleet between the sands and shallows of the sea bottom. These British captains naturally also knew the position of the German shore batteries, and, for an eye in any degree schooled, it was sufficiently plain that the gunner who wished to aim at Fort Grimmerhörn had nothing more difficult to do than to take the tower of the garrison church immediately behind it as his target. The war breaking out with such surprising suddenness, this circumstance, which was of course well known in the German Navy, had been quite overlooked, and at the approach of the enemy's fleet the necessary precautionary steps had been neglected.

This omission was now rectified through the enemy's fire blowing up the tower. Towards two o'clock in the afternoon the church tower was suddenly enveloped in a cloud of dust, and it, and the walls of the church, collapsed with a terrific roar. The enemy was thus deprived of a very convenient point of aim, and the number of shots striking Fort Grimmerhörn was quickly much reduced. Unfortunately, just before, one of the enemy's shells had carried off the bomb-proof roof of an ammunition chamber, blowing up the magazine and all its contents. The falling fragments of masonry and explosives caused great damage amongst the Cuxhaven houses.

By four o'clock in the afternoon Cuxhaven was on fire in several places. As the town had been cleared of inhabitants, this was not a matter of vital importance. In order to avoid any unnecessary sacrifice of life, the salvage work was reduced to a minimum and the fire was allowed to take its course, under the assumption, correct as it proved, that the flames would perhaps give the British an exaggerated idea of the havoc wrought by the bombardment. With the same object, at half-past five in the evening, one after another of the German guns ceased fire, and only two kept up the defence. And it really seemed as though the enemy believed that, not only had the batteries been silenced, but that the town itself, and the port, had been reduced to a heap of ashes, the more so as the warehouses and the depôt of the Hamburg–America line were ablaze.

All at once the enemy's ships began to move, signals were interchanged, thick clouds of smoke poured out of every funnel, and only the injured *Bouvet* remained motionless. The enemy's fleet was advancing, reducing the fire from the heavy guns, and soon after stopping it altogether. A pause ensued in the land fire as well.

The German gunners stood with smoke-grimed faces at their posts. The last charge was in the guns, and in breathless expectation they followed the approach of the enemy's fleet, waiting for the word of command that was to open the murderous giant mouths once again. It was already possible to distinguish with the naked eye the spray at the bows of the foremost ships, cast up by the high speed at which these steel colossi, urged by thousands of horse-power, were being driven forward. It was a majestic and a thrilling, but at the same time a terrifying, sight, this row of foreign ships steaming up.

The silence that ensued was strange in its effect; the thunder of the guns so suddenly mute, still rang in the ears with such intensity that every sound, even the slightest, immediately made one fancy that the din of battle was about to recommence. Now that in the unwonted stillness they could hear the crackling of the fire in the little town behind the batteries, it was curious to note how many of the artillery-men abruptly turned round, quite prepared to find machine-guns directed upon them from the rear.

A dense cloud of smoke lay over Cuxhaven, coloured fiery red beneath from the flames, and bordered above, from the rays of the setting sun, by a halo of yellow light. The waves broke in soft spray upon the beach. The enemy was still about a geographical mile from the first barrier of mines. A few more minutes would unavoidably bring the first of the British ships in contact with the submarine mines, when a ringing blast issued from the siren of the British Admiral's ship, and almost simultaneously, as the British war-ships slackened speed, a white, foaming mountain of water, like a giant fountain, shot up on the centre of the navigable way, and near it another, and yet another, and amongst these swirling, writhing pillars, two black bodies rose to the surface, flung hither and thither, like pieces of wreckage, among the angry, lashing waves. And fresh and ever fresh fountains and columns of foam dashed up to heaven.

The witnesses of this marvellous and startling spectacle could not at first explain what had happened. When, however, a mighty wave broke on the beach, scattering clouds of spray as high as the stone quay, was then sucked back again and succeeded by a fresh foam-thrashed billow, and one of the above-mentioned black objects was flung high on the flat beach, where it lay like a capsized boat; it became clear that the British, with their submarines, which they had sent in advance of the fleet, had laid counter-mines and caused them to explode near the German mines, thus annihilating the outer barrier. The crews of the four British submarines had thereby been sent to certain death, however, for not one man escaped, and what had taken place beneath the water remained for ever untold.

As the first column of water rushed up, the silent, grey iron-clads were transformed into fire-spouting volcanoes. From every port-hole the yellow flames gushed forth. From every corner and from every cranny, from every level of the superstructures, from every aperture in the turrets, death flashed and quivered. The shots flew like hail from all the enemy's guns of every calibre, hurling inch-deep layers of sand and showers of stones over the batteries: the enemy's shells were exploding everywhere, and the heavy broad-sides from the enemy's guns were cutting the men to pieces. The German artillerists, with no iron walls to protect them, sank down, some silently, some uttering horrible cries. The thundering and the roaring of the guns was like a very witches' Sabbath; it was as though the earth itself were opening and vomiting forth her red-hot fires. Here, in front of the burning town—the fire-breathing sand-heaps of the German forts! yonder—the steel monsters belching with flame on the heaving bosom of the sea!

The enemy enter London in triumph

Now that the enemy was so near, the moment had arrived for the German mortar batteries, with their plunging fire, to enter the fray, and, protected by thick steel walls, they commenced. Look where you might, nothing was to be seen but lurid flashes, dancing, palpitating, sputtering flames.

And they were taking some effect out at sea. The enemy's echelons were undoubtedly well ordered, but they were getting into confusion. On the battle-ship *Ocean* a white cloud of steam flew up suddenly between the funnels, and one of them went overboard. A howitzer shell had pierced the armour deck, and, exploding in the engine-room, had burst several of the boilers. On the *Glory*, likewise a first-class battle-ship, a shell burst behind the after turret, flinging the two long gun bores forward across the deck. The *Glory* slackened speed, sheered to starboard, collided with the *Albion*, which was following her almost abreast, and both ships then became targets for the shore batteries. On the flagship, the after fighting-top fell shattered overboard, apparently fouling one propeller with the wire ropes of the topmast rigging, for the ship stopped short and described a circle.

This unexpected effect of the German plunging fire, which the British armour decks were not thick enough to resist, spread confusion among the enemy. In the comparatively narrow navigable way their original fighting formation could no longer be maintained, and several of the ships were touching one another. The *Ocean* was making water and, through damage to her engines, was out of action. Thick streams of water from the pumps poured out from her hull on the opposite side to the leak. Then the vessel was towed away by a comrade, but, not far from the spot where the *Bouvet* had stranded, ran aground on the sands.

The moment had come for the German battle-ships to re-engage in the fight. Carefully passing in line the second barrier of mines, they steamed straight ahead against the enemy. But, more quickly than had been expected, the latter had re-formed, turned round, and were steaming full speed out to sea. As the German battle-ships masked the fire of the shore batteries, this ceased, and the pursuit of the enemy after their unsuccessful attack was left to the fleet.

The fight in the roadstead, which could not be kept up any longer by the Germans against such unequal odds, could, as dusk fell, no longer be followed from the shore. Owing to their greater speed, the enemy, with their larger calibre guns, were very easily able to keep out of range of the six German battle-ships. At eight o'clock the latter re-entered the estuary of the Elbe, leaving behind them a

chain of look-outs, in the shape of fast cruisers, to guard against any
further attack by the enemy, their number, in the course of the
afternoon, having been increased by the arrival from Brünsbuttel of
the *Lübeck*, *Berlin*, and *München*.

On the German battle-ships the engagement had told severely.
The tall super-structures in particular had been badly battered, and
splinters from bursting shells had run up the death roll high. Still,
the damage, to the lay eye, looked worse than it really was. Vital
parts had scarcely been injured, and all the German battle-ships
were still able to fight. March 21st, however, had indubitably established what, during the past few years, had been urged again and
again by different naval writers, namely, that the lower build of the
British battle-ships was better adapted for warfare than that of the
German, with their lofty, and certainly very martial-looking superstructures, which, however, afforded the enemy too good a target.

Worst of all were the French, with their gun-platforms and bridges
piled up one above another on the unwieldy, floating fortresses, to
the extreme limit of navigability.

While the low-built British ships offered a mark very difficult to
hit, the French had paid for their predilection for grotesque shapes
with terrible losses in men and horrible mutilation of their structures above the water line.

The German squadron once more took up its position inside the
second row of mines. Two additional torpedo divisions took their
places during the evening in the advanced line of look-outs. The
position of the enemy's fleet, which had apparently fallen back with
its main body on Heligoland, was still recognizable in that direction
from the searchlight signals interchanged between the ships. In the
course of the night, news by wireless arrived to the effect that the
enemy had provided against a torpedo attack on the part of the
Germans by several lines of cruisers and torpedo craft.

After the enemy's retreat, sapper divisions began, by the light of
electric arc lamps, to repair as quickly as might be the devastation in
the coast forts, that next day the enemy should find all ready to
repel attack again. During the evening two trains of the Hamburg
fire brigade arrived by the coast railway, and, with their steam-hose
and fire-engines, energetically took in hand the putting out of the
fire in the town; nevertheless, until early next morning, a fiery red
cloud hung over the unfortunate place. The enemy's first attack had
been repulsed, but at a heavy cost. All night severely wounded men
were being carried in ambulances from the forts to the railway
station, to be conveyed thence to the Hamburg hospitals.

All the major European powers are involved in this war-to-come, and all their efforts end in total failure. Armies collapse, great fleets are destroyed, whole nations know despair and misery. The author gives the last admonitory words to A. J. Balfour, who was the British prime minister in 1902–05. He reappears in the fiction of 1907 in the unlikely role of Secretary of State for Foreign Affairs. When he addresses the House of Commons at the end of the great war-to-come, he transmits the verdict of future-history on the follies of great power competitiveness, all in capitals to make the author's point that a great war will not bring any benefits to the nations of Europe:

THE DESTINY OF THE WORLD NO LONGER LIES IN THE HANDS OF THE TWO NAVAL POWERS OF THE GERMANIC RACE, NO LONGER WITH BRITAIN AND GERMANY, but on land it has fallen to Russia, and on sea to the United States of America. St Petersburg and Washington have taken the place of Berlin and London.

Die 'Offensiv-Invasion' gegen England

By 1906, British and German tales of the war-to-come had become so numerous and so bellicose that many considered their chauvinism was a positive menace to good relations between the two nations. William Le Queux's Invasion of 1910 (1906) had presented the German invaders in the worst possible light—as ruthless, reckless enemies who would not hesitate to bombard London into surrender. German writers responded with equally frightening tales of British naval attacks in Hamburg und Bremen in Gefahr (1906) and of coming German victories in Mit deutschen Waffen über Paris nach London (1906).

However, the journalists and the propagandists did not have it all their own way. In May 1906 the Anglo-German Friendship Committee—an influential body—arranged for a visit from the chief burgomasters of Berlin, Aachen, Dresden, Cologne, and Charlottenburg. They were welcomed by King Edward VII and they were guests at a banquet given by the Lord Mayor of London. On that occasion the young Winston Churchill spoke out against 'the attempts of alarmist journalists to set up strife between the nations'; and the Annual Register noted the visit as 'an important step ... towards dissipating the fears of an eventual Anglo-German conflict, which was fostered, both in Germany and Great Britain, by a section of the "patriotic press".'[12]

The authors of the coming-war stories, however, got on with the business *of describing the worst possible future for the other side. In 1907, for example, Karl Bleibtreu published* Die 'Offensiv-Invasion' gegen England, *which showed how the German fleet could make a successful surprise attack upon the British.*

TO TAKE THE BRITISH NAVAL BASES BY SURPRISE

From the Norddich-Emden signal station and from the lofty signal tower on Heligoland wireless messages rattled off incessantly, as night fell across the ominously thundering sea. Of a sudden, late in the evening of 4 May 19– –, a long line of grey ships snaked their way one after the other across the North Sea. They poured out unceasingly from the Wilhelms Canal, and from the Wilhelmshaven–Jahdebusen station another division made out towards the open sea. Off Borkum both divisions joined with the battle-ships and the best cruisers of the German Navy which had, for no apparent reason, been carrying out manoeuvres in the Heligoland area during the last two days. Bugles rang out across the raging sea.

Throughout the world and in all imaginable areas of conflict, after all the slogans about peace and disarmament, British hostility towards Germany had become so pronounced that those responsible for German policy did not delude themselves that not even the most conciliatory disposition could prevent a serious confrontation. Because the Bagdad Railway was most unwelcome for the British, it followed that sooner or later they would provoke a war as soon as they reckoned that an appropriate opportunity had arisen. The *Entente Cordiale* with France was undoubtedly cooling off, so that the French alliance against Germany—should the latter not attack—was seriously questioned, especially since France alone would have had to carry the whole burden of a war west of the Vosges. Yet, in the case of a war with Britain there was no question of a military invasion, as it had been imagined and described by fantasists on both sides of the North Sea; it was solely a matter of a naval confrontation. And here, despite all the efforts of German shipyards, Britain was still in such a dominant position that even the combined European navies could not do that country any harm; but in the normal course of events they would have been the losers. Germany could not count on any support at sea, and in this only the United States fleet would be decisive. So, Germany was left to look after herself and a hard struggle was unavoidable. Thus, two divergent roads for naval operations opened up.

The first and most obvious of these called for a strong defence: the Imperial Navy would simply have had to remain in harbour. It would have limited duties to allow it to operate as a kind of superior coastal defence unit, so that in combination with coastal fortifications, and relying on mines and torpedoes, it would ward off British bombardments. Was a defence strategy of this kind at all possible, and was it feasible on purely naval and tactical grounds? Did the poor navigational conditions of the Elbe or the Wilhelms Canal (unsuitable for vessels of the deepest draught) provide a good basis for a system of defence? Definitely not. Even remaining in harbour is tactically inadvisable because of modern long-range gunfire from an enemy force disposed around the Bay of Heligoland; and then, there is the greater danger from torpedo-boats which are here more difficult to evade than they are out at sea. Furthermore, would we not be making a pointless and inevitable sacrifice of the island fortress of Heligoland, if we did not risk a naval engagement for its protection?

It was unfortunately only too easy to predict how a battle of that sort would end in the face of such overwhelming superiority. What would be the consequences of this kind of defensive arrangement? Not only would such a timorous strategy endanger Germany's prestige and depress the general morale of the Navy and of the nation, but at the same time we would also be trapped in a merciless blockade with all the harm that might cause. Without a fight the entire merchant navy would then be left in the lurch; for its ships would not reach neutral ports, and certainly not German havens, in good time. Since all that meant an horrific end, would it not be better to have an end with horror?

This conclusion opened up in the second instance; for, even if the offensive against such superior force was unthinkable rashness, did not the possibility of a sudden all-out offensive fall within the range of the feasible? Whenever it was purely a question of our existence or non-existence as a naval power, we had to play our trump cards, if we hoped to have some sort of a chance in the face of an otherwise unavoidable defeat. The British navy, lulled in the complacent conviction of its immeasurable superiority, would never expect a preventive action of such boldness. Could we not seize a favourable opportunity to take the British naval bases by surprise and destroy their maritime commerce far and wide in a two-day raid? It was known that British mobilization was too cumbersome to respond immediately to a sudden attack. Of course, there was always the deadly peril that we could be cut off from behind, if we advanced

down the Channel and moved too far from our own Wilhelmshaven–Cuxhaven base. To counter this, it was necessary to devise
counter-measures. At any rate, this gave us a hint of success. Yet, it
was quite another matter if we slunk away fearfully into our ports,
and thus from the start announced to the whole world that we were
not ready to do battle.

Again, it was quite different if—sooner or later—as could be foreseen, one had to return from out there, having struck a blow against
Britain. By keeping up a strict defence, we had no more tricks up our
sleeve for harming Britain herself. Only by means of an offensive did
this seem possible—and only an offensive in the form of a sudden
attack, as preferred by the British themselves and of the sort recommended by Admiral Campbell, which he made in a public lecture at
that very moment when the fraternizing after-dinner speeches rose
up to a patient heaven, on the occasion when the German burger-
meisters were welcomed as guests.[13]

Once it became absolutely clear that Britain herself would do
down Germany at the given opportunity by playing her well-known
game of suddenly Copenhagening the opposition, it was decided—
after careful consideration of the pros and cons—to go for the
audacious option of making a surprise attack. Once the decision had
been confirmed, all set tirelessly to work on preparations for mobilization in great secrecy and with every sort of subterfuge so that,
should the occasion arise, everything would be ready for action
within twenty-four hours. Accordingly, when they had determined
on the approximate time of the attack, they let the directors of the
major shipping lines into the secret in the greatest confidentiality.
They saw to it that their most valuable ships were in German
harbours by the end of April; and that the rest had sealed orders: on
the first wireless message they were to hasten to neutral ports. As for
the question of getting the troops on board with the greatest speed—
that was tried out carefully in special exercises and in various places.
The loading of the troops and the artillery was effected under the
cover of military exercises. At the same time everything was carried
through in good order and according to a previously arranged
scheme. Large stocks of coal had been stored in secret so that the
bunkers on all the naval vessels were filled completely; and in the
Elbe a considerable flotilla of colliers lay waiting. Naval tugs joined
them, too, in order to tow away any steamers from the line of fire.

So, everything then went ahead to make success possible; and for
the rest luck had to play a part. Foggy conditions, as forecast by the
meterological stations, made it possible to reach the Channel unob-

served. The ships' engines, all of them in first-class condition, went to maximum revolutions which in the big new cruisers (35,000 horsepower) and in the battleships reached a very considerable level. They had observed the movements of the British fleet with great care; and they had established that, in addition to the main cruiser force which was away on operations in foreign stations, a whole group of first-rate battleships had been sent away and were not in position. Moreover, the reserve group based in Devonport was engaged in exercises in the northern waters of the Irish Sea; and—above all—the mighty Rosyth squadron was away on manoeuvres to the north of Scotland. *Triumph, Cornwallis, Vengeance*—these had already been sighted and reported up there in the north-western area of the Atlantic. This was all the more important, because the best known and most able British admiral, Lord Charles Beresford, had been appointed to command the crack Rosyth North Sea squadron and had moved North with some of the best vessels in the Mediterranean fleet.[14] He had previously commanded the British fleet in the Mediterranean, where at that time the display of the greatest naval power in Malta, Port Said, and Gibraltar still seemed necessary. The news that this most dangerous opponent was away for the time being came as further encouragement to the planners. However, the Channel Fleet (Portsmouth–Plymouth–Devonport) and the Reserve Fleet (Chatham–Sheerness) added up to a superior number of ships. Yet the most powerful armoured vessels and cruisers belonged to the North Sea bases of Rosyth and Clyde; and at the start these were not engaged in the action.

Moreover, the British ships, most of which had difficulty in bringing their crews up to full strength, were all still at their usual peace-time stations. For that reason it was hoped they could be blockaded and prevented from leaving port until maximum damage had been done to their harbours, and the blockaded vessels themselves had been weakened by torpedo attacks. All this happened so quickly that Beresford could not come to their aid in time. After that our forces retired with equal speed from the action, before Beresford could threaten their line of retreat. During the naval manoeuvres of 1906 the former commander of the Channel Squadron, Admiral Wilson, had shown that, although the Mediterranean vice-admiral, May, had far greater speed, he was not in the same class since he was too slow and too cautious.

Only with a heavy heart was it decided to copy the British practice of making a sudden attack without a declaration of war. There was no other choice, if one did not wish to experience exactly the same thing. How eagerly we wanted to live in peace with the British, if only they had been sensible and had seen that to weaken Germany as well as Britain was to play into the hands of American and Japanese interests. But the British would not be told. By 'friendship' they understood that Germany was to look on patiently at all British encroachments, that Germany had to stand back like a lamb, never take advantage from British difficulties anywhere in the world, but in addition give Britain a free hand to ruin the importance of the Bagdad Railway.

Had the Reichstag—where wheeling and dealing always comes before the national good—sanctioned a swifter rate of construction for the German fleet, we would at least have been better equipped. For that reason, we had to resort to unusual means of warfare in order to go some way towards evening out the differences between the two naval forces, and so reducing the great superiority of the British. In Britain itself, where the campaign against Germany went on relentlessly, they deluded themselves with the pious belief that Germany would seek peace at any price, even at the cost of national humiliations, and obedient to the peremptory demands of Britain, would patiently agree to stop work on the building of the Bagdad Railway. There did not seem to be any fear of an initiative on the part of their opponents, and so they thought there was time enough, should they themselves wish to resort to any sudden action. If a sudden upheaval in the colonies did not provide an opportunity, then one only had to wait for a suitable moment to risk a European encounter. Hitherto Germany had only used colonial disturbances to make diplomatic protests about Egypt (where German commercial interests were supposedly threatened) and to give the British something bitter in their Abyssinian soup. There they were slowly eating up Menelik's kingdom, like the Congo, in the well-used cooking pot of imperial annexation. Diplomatic needling only stings; it never wounds. Diplomatic chicanery rarely makes an impression, as the Algeciras Conference made clear at the time. Germany would rather talk, not haggle. At best she would bestir herself too late, when Britain had settled her overseas difficulties.

That was how the world appeared to the British. For the rest, Admiral Wilson, the charming author of the *The Invasion of 1912*, sang his old song in every number of the *National Review*: 'Carthage must be destroyed.'[15] It followed that, since Britain stood for Rome, all that remained for Germany was the amusingly unsuitable comparison with that ancient maritime trading state, as though Germany herself rather more resembled Rome and Britain was like Carthage, if one has to make such lame comparisons. No one was thinking of attacking Germany, and Germany was taking things calmly as the French advance went on into Morocco and the agreements of the Algeciras Conference were shot through and through.

For the rest, however, there were rather mixed feelings in the recently founded General Staff, the War Office in London. Indeed, the commander-in-chief of the Home Army, Sir John French, felt comfortable reading the report from the new Corps Commander at Aldershot in which he pompously assured him that everything was in perfect order and not a thing was out of place. Bethune, the Chief-of-Staff, submitted plans for horse transportation, should an invasion of Holland be attempted in the following year. The Volunteer manoeuvres in Salisbury Plain had apparently gone off magnificently and in the course of that gratifying exercise the so-called Post Office Rifles (London) had earned themselves boundless praise.

Great naval battles follow with heavy losses on both sides, all described in detail by Bleibtreu. The shattered German fleet takes shelter in Bremerhaven under the protection of the Weser forts, and the remnants of the British squadrons arrive at dawn next day to begin a blockade …

The British had themselves suffered such immense losses that at the time only eighteen armoured ships were actually ready for action (eight from Rosyth; five from the Reserve; and five from the Channel Squadron). However, six large armoured ships and many first and second-rate cruisers were away in foreign stations and could endeavour to reach the mother country from all parts of the world, and in addition there were twenty-one armoured ships in the Mediterranean.

There was no doubt about the end of the war. In fact, it was already decided. Heligoland, Cuxhaven, and probably Kiel as well were bound to fall one after the other; and nothing could venture out of the Weser. Even if twenty-two British battleships and many cruisers had been destroyed or put out of action, the final reckoning for the Germans came to twenty battleships and most of their cruisers. Of 144 mostly first-class torpedo-boats (99 on permanent alert), 71 remained in service. What, then, was the result of the offensive, even though it had been pursued with the greatest energy and quite exceptional luck? Inevitable defeat. But what had Britain gained from this? Severe damage for her harbours and her fleet, to the delight of the Yankees and the French who now saw the British command of the sea itself reduced at Germany's expense.

Even with the help of the French and Italian navies, on which it was always difficult to rely, the German naval war against Britain would have had to end in ever greater misfortune. And even if, in the unlikely event that the American navy should ever at some future date come in on the side of Germany, America would gain the most and would press hard on Britain—all without any change to the partly destroyed German maritime trade, to the coastal blockade that has badly damaged Hamburg, Bremen, and Kiel. To be condemned to the defensive means a useless loss of power; and the offensive remains equally pointless. It is a permanent necessity that Germany must arm without pause for such a necessity and bring its fleet to the highest possible level; and yet to to make every sacrifice in re-arming is without profit, if at the same time Britain increases its sea power more and more. The disarmament talk of the Liberal Government, which deceives both the foreigner and the grumbling British taxpayer, makes a laughable contrast to the reality of the secret contracts that for years have concealed the constant growth in battleships and in cruisers. Only fear of a general rising in India, and of Panislamic and Ethiopian entanglements, has hitherto kept Britain from taking aggressive action against Germany.

What is the only thing that could alone guarantee peace in Europe? The strongest moral and intellectual pressure on the political outlook of the British: to understand that every European war could only benefit the other continents of the world; that Napoleon's old statement is truer than ever today—'Every war in Europe is always a civil war.'

The nations do not want to hear the voice of reason that says: a naval war between the British and the Germans will be the beginning of the end—the collapse of the British Empire and of European supremacy in Asia and Africa. Only a lasting friendly union of the two great Germanic races can save Europe. All warnings fade away to no purpose—Cassandra always preaches to deaf ears that the prophecy will be fulfilled: 'The day will come when proud Ilium falls.' Poor Europe, poor blinded nations! Peace, peace, peace! Only a peacefully united Europe can maintain itself against the growing strength of other races and against the economic dominance of America. Unite, unite, unite!

Berlin–Bagdad: Das Deutsche Weltreich im Zeitalter der Luftschifffahrt, 1910–1931

The Bleibtreu account of a successful surprise attack upon the Royal Navy was a modest affair in comparison to Rudolf Martin's extravagant fantasy of 1907, Berlin–Bagdad. *The sub-title promised to tell the tale of the dominant role of German air power in establishing 'The German World-Empire in the Age of Airship Travel, 1910–1931'.*

The book may have given H. G. Wells the idea of writing The War in the Air *(1908); for Wells explained the rapid development of German air power in his own story by saying that: 'A considerable literature of military forecasts beginning as early as 1906 with Rudolf Martin, the author not merely of a brilliant book of anticipations, but of a proverb, "The future of Germany lies in the air", had, however, partially prepared the German imagination for some such enterprise.'[16]*

The tribute from Wells is suspect: it was far too convenient a way of making the characteristic Wellsian leap of the imagination from the realities of 1907 to 'a pleasant summer day in the year 191–', when the great air war is about to begin in Wells's story. Indeed, as he wrote his words of praise, Wells knew very well that his story was already developing into a repudiation of everything that Rudolf Martin admired. Martin wrote for the greater glory of his nation, whereas Wells dedicated his tale of terror to the salvation of mankind. The German gave his readers a future history of technology in the service of the Greater Reich: the rapid advances in airship construction lead to easy victories and to a world in which Germany will be the dominant power. Wells wrote his admonitory account of the war-to-come for a world audience. Like Martin, he starts from the base of an advanced technology— the enormous German airships, 'monsters capable of ninety miles an hour in a calm', which speed across the Atlantic and destroy New York.

There is no mistaking the warning: 'As the airships sailed along they smashed up the city as a child will shatter its cities of brick and card.' Indeed, Wells is so intent on delivering his final warning to the world that he makes the reader face all the horrors of world-wide destruction: 'The great nations and empires have become but names in the mouths of men. Everywhere there are ruins and unburied dead, and shrunken yellow-faced survivors in a mortal apathy.' The imagination had proved equal to the intention. In the final chapter on 'The Great Collapse', Wells was once again ahead of his times; for his projection of the last days—a commonplace in future-war fiction after 1918—was most unusual before 1914. In that far-off time the general belief held that, although 'the Next Great War' could prove a disaster for some, it would never be a final catastrophe for all.

Rudolf Martin's version of things-to-come in Berlin–Bagdad *is an old-*

style story of victory and empire that had the rare distinction of appearing in condensed form in the Review of Reviews. *The translation, together with a somewhat testy commentary, was the work of W. T. Stead, a most original and successful editor, a pioneer in the business of investigative journalism, a resolute supporter of the peace movement, a friendly and temperate critic of Germany.*

THE FANTASY OF RUDOLF MARTIN

Here is an outline of this preposterous prophecy of things to come when men have achieved the conquest of the air.

Germany's Future Lies In the Air

On January 1st, 1910, the German Generals and Admirals being assembled in Berlin to offer New Year's greetings to their Sovereign, the Kaiser made them a sonorous speech on the transcendent importance of air-ships to the world in general and to the German Empire in particular. The invention of the steerable motor air-ship, he declares, is only comparable in importance to the discovery of gunpowder. Every German army corps in the future, he announces, is to have an air sailors' brigade attached to it. The Imperial Chancellor had been ordered to demand the sum of £500,000 to hasten the building of the German air-fleet. There must be 30,000 swift flying-machines for the transport of 300,000 infantry. Krupp is to fit out 1,000 flying-machines at once with artillery, and by means of the 400 transport air-ships (Zeppelins) already ordered it will be possible between the hours of twelve and three to transport from Germany 400,000 men into England. 'Germany's future', concluded the Emperor, 'lies in the air!' The history of the next twenty years is one long proof of his Majesty's sagacity and foresight.

The First Great Air-Battles

The year 1913 found Russia still muddling along in much the same way as in 1907. Continual revolutionary dripping, however, had worn away even the Russian governmental stone; and just when the tension between the Parliament and the people was at breaking point the Japanese found a pretext for a quarrel with Russia that they had been seeking since 1905, and the second Russo-Japanese War was declared (October, 1912). In March, 1913, after a murderous battle in the desert of Gobi the whole Russian army capitulated, the Japanese battle air-ships, transport air-trains, and war-motors being altogether too much for them. Zeppelin motor air-ships drew the trains and in reality decided the Japanese victory. This catastrophe made even the Russian worm to turn. 'Down with Tsarism!' is the universal cry. The Tsar and his family prepare to fly; but, had it not been for the kindness of the commander of the German torpedo flotilla, then at Cronstadt, who sent two battle air-ships to the rescue, they would never have got away at all. The battle air-ships *Pomerania* and *Westphalia*, however, conveyed the Imperial family and all the Grand-Ducal families, with their suites, nearly 10,000 feet up into the air, and so to safety and oblivion.

Suwarow, the Napoleon of the Air

Russia at once declared herself a Republic. Next day she was split into two Governments; a fortnight later into twenty, *plus* ten independent States. Civil war raged, the scaffolds ran red with blood, and half the population was reduced to the verge of starvation. Things might have gone on thus indefinitely had not a new Napoleon Bonaparte, one Michael Suwarow, arisen, and induced Sacharow, the most bloodthirsty of the Russian tribunes, to provide Russia with a first-class air-fleet and put him in command of it.

Suwarow–Napoleon decided to begin his career of conquest by reconquering Central Asia for Russia. In April, 1913, at twelve (midnight), therefore, he left with the Russian air-fleet for Bokhara. At 5 a.m. the Emir was awakened by the noise of the first bomb from Suwarow's battle-ship. In an hour the conquest of Bokhara was complete. With the Emir's wealth Suwarow in a year built an air-fleet of 40 battle-ships, 200 flying-machines, and 12 transport air-trains. The first use to which these were put was to reconquer the Caucasus. Suwarow was fully alive to the immense possibilities opened up by aerial navigation. He introduced aerial transport and wireless telephony into the smallest villages and remotest mountain valleys. As for himself, he positively lived in his air-ship. His flying-machine, heavier than air, was the fastest in the world; and his aluminium motor air-ship, a Zeppelin, lighter than air, was a flying palace.

250 Miles an Hour

Suwarow was President of the world-famous Aero-Auto Club in Baku, whose air-races attracted crowds from all parts of the world.

These races, being generally in the direction of China, suggested to Suwarow the conquest of that Empire. In 1914 and 1915 aeronautics made amazing progress. By 1915 motor air-ships had attained a speed of 187½ to 250 miles an hour. From Suwarow's air-ship station in Khokand to Peking was not quite 2,200 miles—a nice little air-trip of ten hours. So it came about that the summer of 1915 saw Michael Suwarow with three battle air-ships (one being a supplementary air-ship filled with benzoin and oil) and one Zeppelin air-train, hovering at 5,000 feet above the golden roofs of Peking. Leaning on the gilded aluminium bulwarks of his stately air-ship, he planned his conquest of the age-old Chinese Empire.

The Battle Air-ship

But this project had perforce to be postponed on account of the outbreak of the Russo-German War of 1916. In the six years since the Kaiser's stirring air-ship speech Germany had been steadily creating a superb aerial navy, till she was now the first aero-naval power in the world, France being the second.

The war with Russia came about in this wise. Germany's heart had long been wrung by the sorrows of the three Republics of Poland, Lithuania, and Ruthenia in their struggle with Russia. The subject had come up more than once in the British Parliament also, and Mr. Geoffrey Drage, the Prime Minister, had promised to intervene, if possible. Meanwhile Russia, knowing things could not continue as they were, piled battle air-ship on battle air-ship. One great advantage of such ships over the old-fashioned type was their extreme cheapness, a first-class Zeppelin air-cruiser in 1915 only costing £15,000, and being capable of carrying 600 men. On the 19th April, 1916, therefore, diplomatic relations ceased between Germany and Russia.

Air-ships v. Infantry

Suwarow at the outbreak of hostilities was in Warsaw. He at once ordered five battle-ships up aloft, at varying heights. Presently he sent up his air-fleet to cruise about and make reconnaissances at 29,500 feet, for which of course they had to carry proper air-oxidising plant. The look-out air-ships from time to time announced that various German air-fleets were to be seen scurrying about in different directions. These fleets rained down torpedoes and bombs on the Russian infantry, slaughtering masses of them; while the Russian field-guns were powerless to harm a single German air-vessel, more especially as the German officers kept their ships well above the Russian fire-zone. Generally the German air-ships sailed at 6,500 to 9,000 feet, only descending to 4,500 feet when they found themselves directly above a Russian regiment on the march. Then they took up positions at some distance apart along the line of march, and poured down fearful discharges of bombs and torpedoes on the luckless soldiers beneath, destroying whole companies at a time. Even if a stray shot did reach one of the Zeppelins of 100,000 cubic metres gas-burden and make a hole in three or four gas-balloons, what did that matter? There were 150 of these gas-balloons, every one independent of all the others. Even a hole or two in the aluminium itself had no effect.

Air-ships' Raid on Berlin

Meanwhile Suwarow was planning a bold enterprise. This was nothing more nor less than the bombardment of Berlin before sunrise the next morning. An air-fleet on the defensive, as he well knew, is 'nonsense'. Naval air-tactics are essentially offensive, and will ever remain so. Therefore, leaving young Kuropatkin in charge at Warsaw, Suwarow ordered all lights in or near the city to be put out by ten o'clock, and in the thick darkness 20 battle air-ships went up every two minutes, besides three transport air-trains full of ammunition and benzoin. They went via Petersburg, so as to mislead any German air-fleets which might catch sight of them. The admiral's flag-ship (or what corresponded to it) was the *Tiflis*, an aluminium battle air-ship of the latest pattern. Suwarow's sitting-room was nearly as large as the admiral's cabin on an old-fashioned sea battle-ship. Every window was defended by cannon, and the whole place bristled with torpedoes. All the air-ships communicated with one another by wireless telegraphy, which was absolutely necessary in order to dodge the enemy's air-cruisers. The giants of Suwarow's fleet were 9,843 feet long and 120,000 cubic metres gas-burden. The battle-front of the fleet was nearly four miles long, although there were only 20 air-ships.

The Air Battle above Berlin

Presently the sun rose. The *Tiflis*, with Suwarow on the bridge, finally reviewed the air-fleet before beginning the attack on Berlin. There was no time to be lost, for far away the German air-fleet of

125 ships was already sighted. Somehow or other they had got wind of Suwarow's movements. Just then a shrapnel shell nearly hit the *Tiflis*. Other air-ships telegraphed that their aluminium hulls were pierced; but no harm was done. Then suddenly a torpedo from the *Caucasus* hit the aluminium hull of a gigantic German battle air-ship. There was a fearful explosion, and the proud air-ship sank rapidly. Meanwhile the Russians hailed shots on the German ships. Four German air-ships tried to rise, but sank riddled with shots, and those of their crews who had not their fall-lifebelts on were smashed to pieces. In a few moments almost all the 125 German air-ships were struck with torpedoes. They could not rise, but as many as were able fled in all directions, about five going towards Berlin. The Russians pursued them, firing all the time.

The Bombardment of Berlin

Then, at a sign from Suwarow, fifty of the Russian ships assembled for the bombardment of Berlin. With lightning speed they distributed themselves over the city, the *Tiflis* with Suwarow taking up its post at 6,500 feet over the Imperial residence. Torpedoes and bombs rained down. Thousands soon lay dead or grievously wounded. The living meanwhile scuttled in every direction. The great Alexander Barracks was destroyed by torpedoes, and its inmates annihilated. The railway stations were reduced to heaps of ruins. Nearly all the military trains were cannonaded. In fact, nothing of Berlin would have been left at the end of half an hour had not two great columns of air-ships come rushing up. Up shot the Russian ships; but it was too late. A German shrapnel struck the *Tiflis*, and she sank rapidly. Suwarow, however, jumped out, having his fall-lifebelt on. The little battle-ship *Tibet* threw him a rope, which, when he had nearly reached the earth, he managed to catch. A strong pull, and he was on board. But she, too, was badly hit, and was sinking fast. The *Volga*, a giant of the air, was telephoned to (wirelessly), and took him on board by a spring-bridge. Then, pop! she is away 16,500 feet up in the clouds, going at such a pace that none of the German ships can possibly come up with her. A few hours afterwards she has landed Suwarow in the Pamir Mountains, and before the sun has risen next morning over the Himalayas all the other air-ships of the line are safely at home in the Pamirs also.

The German Empire in 1930

Suwarow retires to his wonderful air-ship station in the inaccessible fastnesses of the Pamirs, and there plans future conquests, but for the present lies very low and says nothing. He has married a daughter of the Emir of Bokhara, and the two take many agreeable little jaunts together in a private air-ship de-luxe. Communication with the outer world is kept up by wireless telegraphy and telephony; and air-ships come every day from Central Asia and India with all sorts of provisions. Suwarow is immensely busy. Not only is he perfecting air-ships, but his aerial fortifications are slowly overcoming the protection afforded in the past to British India by the Himalayan chain. He also has his eye constantly on China as well as on India.

The German Emperor, duly victorious, concludes the Peace of Warsaw (May 10th, 1916). A Pan-German Empire becomes daily

One hundred years of the German future

more desirable; and shortly after the declaration of Peace the draft of an Austro-German Commonwealth is published. Petersburg, Warsaw, and Kieff soon beg for its protection. Two days before the signing of the treaty of Peace, the Kaiser had agreed in the name of this Commonwealth to take the Sultan, the whole Balkan Peninsula, and Greece under his protection. A huge Imperial Parliament—the Staatentag—displaces the former humble Reichstag. It is amazing with what wisdom this vast Empire is governed. The whole Commonwealth, from Hamburg to Bussorah on the Persian Gulf, is united in a vast Customs Union. Air-ships and flying-machines had long made mock of customs and tariffs by facilitating the smuggling in vast quantities of all manner of articles, both luxuries and necessaries. Cargo air-ships could already carry up to 100 tons. In remote districts of the Turkish Empire the Albanians and Bedouins had long been selling everything direct to tramp airships, which smuggled the goods into the different countries; so that the taking off of customs duties was rather a necessity than a virtue. Innumerable benefits flowed from the formation of the Austro-German Commonwealth upon all the lands included under its beneficent sway.

4,000,000 Air-sailors

In 1930, the German Empire reached from Berlin to Bagdad, and beyond. In the 14 years after the Peace of Warsaw, civilization in the German Empire had advanced more than in the preceding 1,400 years. Nowhere were the changes more amazing than in Mesopotamia, where truly the desert was blossoming like the rose. Here, as elsewhere in this polyglot Empire, were to be found thousands of German teachers. It was quite easy to keep up the vast supply of them, as they were only a few hours by air-ship from home, and as every year they and their families were conveyed home free by a stately air-liner for a two-months' holiday. Tolerance was the guiding principle of the Commonwealth. German, though taught, did not stamp out the other languages. In December, 1930, the Commonwealth numbered 215,000,000 souls. There were three standing armies—land, marine, and air—of 17,000,000 men, the most important of which was that of the 4,000,000 trained airsailors. Moreover, the young German idea was diligently educated in the importance of the air-ship, and almost every boy wanted to be in the air-sailors' division of his regiment. Suwarow since 1917 had been Tsar of Russia, which, in spite of losses, was still one of the greatest world-Powers. Finland had joined hands with Sweden. The Peace of Tomsk (1916) gave to Japan all Siberia east of the Yenesei, which kept that Power quiet. France meanwhile seemed to be looking on; Italy, lost in amazement; and the British lion either lashing his tail or inarticulate with rage.

Crossing the Atlantic in Ten Hours

Wireless telephony and aerial navigation have made the United States and the pan-German Commonwealth much better acquainted with each other. Although the number of Hamburg–American liners is much greater than before, and they have not stood still in the matter of improvements, yet most travellers now cross the Atlantic by air-ship. There are, however, still a certain number of conservative old fogies who prefer some other method of locomotion to flying along up aloft at 250 miles an hour. The time of an air-journey varies, but between Bremen and New York is generally from ten to twenty hours. The best liner takes five days. With increased speed, liner collisions had become more frequent, and the rarity of these accidents on air-ships is a great argument in their favour. In 1930 the air-ships de-luxe of the Hamburg–American line have reached 180,000 cubic-metres gas-burden, with 300 separate gas balloons and eight to twelve motors. They can carry more than 1,000 passengers. The great aluminium air-ships can not only fly but also float, the reason for this being that they may be able to assist sea-vessels in distress, if need be. Moreover, should any air-ship itself be in distress, it can at once summon another to its aid by wireless telephony. With all its comfort, a first-class air-ship de-luxe carrying 1,000 passengers costs only £250,000—a fourth of the price of a fast liner. By air-ship, doing it in ten to twenty hours, the passage to America costs, first class, food and all included, only £10 per person.

Consumption Cured

Moreover, air-ship voyages across the ocean are extraordinarily healthful. Most air-ships de-luxe of the Hamburg–American line would, for 10 per cent of the passage money extra, sail by the upper air (9,843 to 16,400 feet). Some ships would even go much higher, for very soon after the coming of steerable air-ships it had been discovered that a stay of from 12 to 20 hours at a height of 19,000 to 20,000 feet was a certain cure for tuberculosis. Those threatened with consumption are therefore sent to spend several days or weeks in an air-ship cruising about at between 16,000 and 18,000 feet above the ocean.

Berlin to Bagdad by Air-ship

Nothing gives a better notion of the wisdom and beneficence of German Imperial Government and the changes which have been brought about by the coming of the air-ship than a journey taken in 1930 on the air-ship de-luxe, *Mecca,* by a party of Germans, Americans, and Englishmen. She left Berlin at 10 a.m. for Bussorah, on the Persian Gulf, via Bagdad. She was one of the most elegant air-ships of the Hamburg–American line, so luxuriously fitted up that she could only carry 80 passengers, so that travelling by her was, of course, remarkably dear, three times as dear as by ordinary air-ship. From Berlin to Bagdad by the *Mecca* cost £15; on an ordinary airship it costs £5 first-class and £2 10s. second-class. The distance of over 2,000 miles was covered in eleven hours. By electric railway it could not be done in less than twenty-one hours, and cost £20.

News by Wireless Telephony

On board the *Mecca* half the travellers were Americans, and the rest mostly German officers, who, being with their families, had not gone by the troop air-ship. Five or six times an hour the latest Berlin Stock Exchange news comes by wireless telephony. At luncheon-time by the same means the most interesting items are communicated from the Berlin and Viennese midday papers. The wireless telephone prints everything clearly on paper in the air-ship, like the old-fashioned telegraph used to do. A rumour arrives that German women are to be allowed to sit in the Staatentag. They already have the vote, which, by the way, has been very bad for the Social Democrats. The German officers think the Chancellor can hardly be foolish enough to allow them in the Staatentag. Meanwhile the air-ship speeds on over the Black Sea. Down below there are whole groups of flying-machines, at about 3,200 feet above the sea, going towards Constantinople. Being telephoned to, the fliers reply in English that they are having a jaunt from Egypt to the Crimea via Constantinople and back again. The *Mecca* descends to talk to them, and they prove to be Americans, many of the machines having only one young girl on board. An American on the *Mecca,* one Mr. White, the Standard Oil Company director, relates how his two daughters travelling with him, aged 18 and 20, had together already driven a flying-machine from New York to San Francisco, and how every day they did little runs like that from the Crimea to Constantinople and back.

Picknicking at the North Pole

His wife, he says, was the first woman to set foot on the North Pole, fifteen years ago. At that time the newspapers still recorded every visit to the North Pole. This, of course, was no longer possible, as in summer hundreds of persons, especially Americans, visited it every day in air-ships and flying-machines. Mr. White's daughters had had two picnics there already, and the last time had also visited the Magnetic Pole, the way to which the captain of the air-ship remembered, having been there once before, a fortunate circumstance, since the compass was useless, doing nothing but whirl round and round. In American sporting circles, according to the Miss Whites, it was only a visit to the South Pole which was now thought anything of, and then only because its great distance from New York made it rather inaccessible. Mrs. White had only been there once, and thought it a delightful place.

The following year the members of the New York Sport Club meant to build a comfortable club-house at the North Pole, and to celebrate its opening they proposed great air-ship races between the North and the South Poles. The competitors were only to stop on the way ten times, at places agreed upon beforehand. It was becoming highly necessary to have a proper club-house and restaurant at the North Pole, because of the crowd of picnickers, who never swept or tidied up at all, so that the place was becoming nothing but a heap of empty champagne bottles.

The Paradise of Mesopotamia

During the journey the Americans have time to gaze with admiration on the wonderfully fertile and verdant plains of Asia Minor, now one vast garden of cotton plantations and other crops. Irrigation works are everywhere. Mesopotamia, under German rule, has become a paradise. And Babylon is another! 'Is not this great Babylon?' has now quite another meaning. The two provinces together have 12,000,000 inhabitants. As for the Sultan, instead of being an impecunious monarch, about whom everyone delighted to say rude things, he has become the richest sovereign in the world, enjoying the utmost consideration.

The day after the arrival of the party in Bagdad they charter a number of excellent flying-machines (which, by all but nervous old ladies and gentlemen, are much preferred to staid gas-borne airships), and go off to see the beauty of the land. Bagdad from a distance positively bristles with public and private air-ship landing-stages. Never before had even the Americans seen such a number and variety of air-vessels. Many of these lay from 3,200 to about 12,000 feet above the town, for in summer many persons slept up aloft in their air-ships. Many others slipped over to the Taurus Mountains to sleep, or spend a few hours daily. In the height of summer the whole population lived in the high mountains.

Berlin in 1930

Berlin, the capital of this great empire, has in 1930 a population of 6,000,000. In Berlin in 1930 there were more air-vessels than in 1907 there were motor-cars. Flying-machines and air-ships are subjected to strict regulations. Drivers of them must pass an examination, and tens of thousands have done so. Within the city radius it is strictly forbidden to sail over the houses in flying-machines, and even air-ships must keep a proper distance. The air-police preserve order in the air, and are a terror to aerial evil-doers, whom they spy out from incredible distances. It is useless for the transgressor to dash up into higher regions; he will only find there more air-police ready to pounce upon him. In all directions there are roads free from houses, which are, of course, flying-ship-tracks. Numbers of the Berlin citizens live in Thuringia and the Hartz Mountains, and spend Saturday to Monday on top of the Jungfrau.

Season-tickets by air-ships cost only a third of what the railway tickets had cost. Heligoland has become so favourite a Saturday-to-Monday and picnic resort that it is absolutely invisible for the air-ships, and you have to wait an hour to an hour and a half before being able to land.

In Berlin it must be nearly pitch-dark because of the crowds of flying-machines, air-trains, commercial and other air-ships. Four colossal towers in the four directions of the compass stand outside Berlin. They are police and military observation posts, from which, day and night, photographs are constantly taken of the heavens, so that the approach of all air-ships to Berlin is at once known, for air-pirates have sometimes been rather a nuisance, even descending on villas in the dead of night and stealing the air-ships. In the German Commonwealth 10,000 air-ships were launched in 1930.

Hanging Gardens

In 1907 Berlin still bristled with telegraph wires, and even the railway lines were cumbered up with them. In 1930 these have vanished. Every house has two poles for wireless telephony. Express letters and parcels go by express air-ships. The London morning papers arrive by the second post. On Sunday afternoon, instead of every railway and tram being packed to suffocation, the Berlinese go comfortably about in their air-ships. They take great delight also in their four hanging-gardens, on pontoons built of steel and aluminium, suspended from 3,000 to 6,000 feet above the city. Each garden has a motor-track, cycle-tracks, tennis-courts, and little look-out towers. In winter they are turned into skating-rinks, and are even used for ski-ing. In the suburbs curious tower-like excrescences may be observed on the roofs of the villas. These are the dwelling-places of the flying-machines. Bank managers, artists, and deputies can fly straight from their own roofs into the country. In the grounds of many villas may be found, instead of stables, a lofty erection in which to house the aluminium air-ship. All the hospitals also have specially fitted-up air-ships.

A German Ultimatum

Holland and Antwerp, feeling rather lonely, have asked to be gathered to the all-embracing arms of Germania. Switzerland, up to the present outside the German Empire, is important, because the Alps form the only possible aerial jumping-off place for Morocco. Great deliberations take place accordingly at Berlin, the result of which is that France is offered the remains of Belgium, and England the Congo, in return for which they are to declare their approval of the incorporation of Holland, her colonies, and Flemish Belgium, and also of Switzerland as an independent State like Turkey, in the German Commonwealth. Morocco and Persia are to be taken over and administered by Germany for the benefit of the world.

The British Ambassador, however, cannot agree to the German Chancellor's proposals, especially as regards Switzerland and Persia. Thereupon the German Ambassador replies that, if Germany cannot do what she has made up her mind to do with Great Britain's approval, she will do it without. Mobilization of the German air-fleet will begin at once. The German air-navy is superior to the British and French combined. The Kaiser's transport air-ships can land 2,000,000 soldiers in England within three hours. They can keep their air-ships for the upper air strata only, and tackle the British aerial-fighting forces in the lower strata with their 4,000,000 flying-machines, each of which is so heavily armoured that one shot will sink a British battle-ship of the *Prince of Wales* type (a great advance on the old-fashioned Dreadnought). Moreover Suwarow, Tsar of Russia, it is pointed out, will profit by the occasion to fetch 2,000,000 Russians from the Pamirs in forty-eight hours and conquer India. After the war with Britain, Germany will, with regret, be forced to let Russia keep India. She herself will be content with Egypt, South Africa, and British East Africa. Japan can have all of China that she can get; and the United States shall have Canada if they like. Will the British Ambassador let the German Ambassador have an answer by one o'clock?

The Conquest of India

The British Ambassador took his leave at 10 a.m. By 11.30 the reply of the British Government was received, accepting the Congo State, and agreeing to all the annexations which Germany proposed. At the same time Great Britain humbly enquired how far mutual understanding was possible between herself and Germany as to their respective interests. Germany, therefore, gets Switzerland, which soon has the good sense to appreciate the Fatherland at its true worth. Air-ships and flying-machines now sprint through the air from the Jungfrau and the other high Swiss peaks into Morocco, where torpedoes and bombs speedily instill wholesome awe and order into the Moors.

Suwarow, with 400,000 transport air-ships and 800,000 flying-machines, sails off from the Pamirs on a glorious conquering expedition to India, and by eight o'clock next morning is proclaimed Emperor of India in Calcutta. The British make but the feeblest resistance, and apply to Germany for her intervention to save India. They have already applied to the Mikado, who replies that to his great sorrow he was just then too busy to be able to help John Bull. (N.B.: He has been told by Germany that she will respect his Chinese conquests, so that he is now in China conquering away for dear life.) Germany at first politely excuses herself also, but offers, should the British nation consent to hand over her British South African possessions from the Cape almost to Cairo, to reinstate British rule in India, as before. The consent of Parliament to Germany's proposal on these generous conditions being easily obtained, the two nations proceed to draw up a convention respecting their mutual interests.

THE NEW HAROUN AL RASCHID.

A DREAM OF BAGHDAD, MADE IN GERMANY.

The German Emperor dreams of the day when the Baghdad Railway has been completed

Chapter Four
Views, Reviews, and Downright Ridicule

By 1906 the German invasion story had grown into a new publishing indus-try which went on expanding in response to an apparently insatiable demand for large doses of instant terror. As the success of The Invasion of 1910 *shows, the tale of the war-to-come had become a marketable commod-ity. It was a necessary, patriotic fiction for the many. For those, however, who could perceive the golden nexus between book sales and a sometimes frantic nationalism, the tale of 'the Next Great War' was a subject for ridicule. It seemed as if an undeclared consensus worked to sort out the reprehensible from the responsible. No one ever mocked* The Riddle of the Sands *and comparable stories, since Erskine Childers and writers like him showed a patent sincerity and a moral earnestness that put them beyond suspicion. The derision of A. A. Milne, Heath Robinson, and P. G. Wodehouse was kept for the exaggerated language and most improbable plots of writers like William Le Queux.*

The Real Le Queux

As fabulator-in-chief to Lord Northcliffe, the most successful publishing entrepreneur of the day, Le Queux was the major suspect. He had made a business out of the future-war story; and he sought sensation at all times, as he revealed in a candid article on 'How I Write my Sensational Novels'. His first principle was that: 'Today the reader has no use for descriptions of scen-ery or weather. We live in the age of the motor-bus, and the sensational story must be so written that the reader once commencing it cannot lay it down until the last word is reached.' According to Le Queux, the author of sensat-ional stories had to have a good knowledge of the world and an intimate knowledge of the police forces of all countries: 'I count among my friends all the chiefs and many of the agents of the secret police of Italy, France, Russia, and Austria.'[1]

Had Le Queux told the whole truth, he would have added that the ulti-mate secret was to have a close relationship with Alfred Harmsworth, later Lord Northcliffe. That began for Le Queux soon after Harmsworth had founded Answers *in 1888, when he learnt from the success of Admiral Colomb's serial tale of* The Great War of 189– *(pp. 30–71) that an exciting future-war story would do wonders for his sales figures. The Franco-Russian Treaty of 1893 seemed a good starting point for a tale of consequences; and, in his imperious way, Harmsworth sent for William Le Queux. Together they planned* The Poison Bullet, *an invasion story (by the French and Russians) which opened in* Answers *on 23 December 1893. The new experiment in mass publishing profited from the latest innovations in publishing techniques: short paragraphs, the frequent use of headlines, and an almost unbroken succession of exciting episodes. From that Le Queux went on to write other future-war stories according to the Harmsworth/ Northcliffe specifications; and of these, the most successful was undoubtedly* The Invasion of 1910.

There was, however, far more to his sensational stories than Le Queux chose to reveal. In fact, it was left to his biographer, N. St Barbe Sladen, to give a full account of the ways in which Le Queux set out to reveal why he 'claimed that he was the first person to warn Great Britain that the Kaiser was plotting a war against her ...'

THE KAISER'S SPY BUREAU

As long ago as 1906 he discovered, through a friend who was an official in the Kaiser's Spy Bureau, a vast network of German espionage in the United Kingdom. He frankly informed Le Queux of what was happening. Le Queux promptly returned from Germany and endeavoured to rouse public opinion regarding the peril. The view commonly taken was to the effect that the Kaiser had assured Lord Haldane of his peaceful intentions.[2] Practically nobody paid any heed to Le Queux, 'writer of romances'; no newspaper would print any of his articles, even without payment! Four editors of London daily newspapers, who received Le Queux's letters of warning, returned them. The Editor of one of the most powerful newspapers wrote:

> My Dear Le Queux,
> We cannot publish this! Spies exist only in your imagination.
> We don't want to alarm the public.

Le Queux therefore related what he had discovered to the late Field-Marshal Earl Roberts of Kandahar, who paid great attention to the matter and said that he was also suspicious. Le Queux introduced the late Lord Northcliffe to Lord Roberts and the three individuals discussed the peril for over an hour. Le Queux next consulted Colonel Lockwood, MP (subsequently Lord Lambourne). After being fully informed, the Colonel made his own investigations in Essex and three weeks later entirely agreed with the views of Le Queux. The Colonel put a question in the House of Commons and the House laughed at the idea. Le Queux with a bee in his bonnet again!

Le Queux visited the late Rear-Admiral Prince Louis of Battenberg (later the Marquis of Milford Haven) and the late Charles Beresford (later Lord Beresford), who, on being furnished with the information, which Le Queux had obtained at his own expense, fully agreed that a serious peril existed. People declared that Lord Roberts, Lord Northcliffe and Le Queux were scaremongers.

When nobody would publish anything regarding the spy peril, an old friend of Le Queux's—D. C. Thomson, proprietor of the *Dundee Courier* and a group of influential newspapers in Scotland and England—heard Le Queux's contentions and, after consulting one of his editors, G. B. Duncan, decided to make investigations. Le Queux and Duncan travelled in Scotland together for some weeks, gathering information. Thomson then decided, in view of the apathy of the public, that Le Queux should write a series of articles, based upon the information obtained. This story, *Spies of the Kaiser*, was published by Thomson in the *Weekly News*, a journal with a large sale in the United Kingdom. It was also published in book form (Hurst & Blackett), and, when at last the public realized what was happening, others copied the idea of writing about spies and made money out of it.

Le Queux claimed that he had obtained a full report of a secret meeting in Potsdam: the Kaiser presided, and those present included the Chiefs of Staff for the Army and Navy, the representatives of the Federal States, and Prince Henry of Prussia. The Kaiser told them that, at the right moment, he intended to begin a European war: 'I have given orders for the hurried construction of more airships of the improved Zeppelin type, and when these are ready we shall destroy England's North Sea, Channel and Atlantic Fleets, after which nothing on earth can prevent the landing of our army on British soil and its triumphant march to London.' According to his biographer, Le Queux determined to write a book in order to reveal the German military intentions. He had little success until he turned to Lord Roberts.

THE INVASION OF 1910

In despair Le Queux told Lord Roberts about his despondency and of his denunciation as a scaremonger, adding that he was a novelist and would return to his profession.

'If you prefer your fiction to your fact, why not write a work of fiction—a description of what would happen if a great war came and we were invaded?' suggested the Field-Marshal. The idea seemed feasible, but Le Queux pointed out that he was not a military man and would make technical errors.

'I have the country's welfare at heart, just as you have. I will prepare the scheme of attack and defence, and give you hints, if you will write the books.'

'And who will publish it?' queried Le Queux. 'Try Lord Northcliffe,' advised Lord Roberts.

The next day Le Queux saw his old friend, Lord Northcliffe, and within an hour Northcliffe had given him an open commission. Le Queux was to write, regardless of expense, a forecast of *The Invasion* for the *Daily Mail* (of which he was formerly Correspondent and War Correspondent in the first Balkan War), with a very handsome payment.

'I know your pocket has suffered very much, Quex'—this was Northcliffe's invariable nickname for Le Queux—'write a good stirring forecast. Tell Lord Roberts we will both try and wake up the country to a sense of its peril.'

Greatly encouraged, Le Queux returned to Portland Place and told the veteran Field-Marshal, and that same evening they started to plan an imaginary German invasion. Having *carte blanche* in the matter of expense, Le Queux enlisted the assistance of Colonel Cyril Field, RMLI, and Major Matson, military experts, and H. W. Wilson, the well-known naval expert gave every help in his sphere. For four months they reconnoitred the whole of East Anglia from the Tyne to the Thames, finding out the most vulnerable points—including Weybourne Gap, in Norfolk—and they travelled altogether 10,000 miles by car. On his return to London, Le Queux was appalled to find that he had spent over three thousand pounds. Lord Northcliffe promptly paid this sum, remarking that if the forecast were well done, he would not mind the expense.

Le Queux then took a flat at Queen Anne's Mansions, Westminster, and began to write. It was a colossal task. In point of fact the book contained 550 pages! After a year's work Le Queux completed the manuscript and Lord Roberts read it *in toto*, and one morning the pages of the leading London daily newspapers, and of certain leading provincial newspapers, bore a map of England, showing the districts that would be invaded and announcing that publication of Le Queux's forecast, *The Invasion of 1910*, would commence in the *Daily Mail* on the following day.

That same afternoon the Prime Minister was asked if his attention had been directed to the advertisements. The campaign against Le Queux had started! Sir Henry Campbell-Bannerman replied that he had seen the advertisements and, denouncing Le Queux as a scare-monger, declared that such work was pernicious literature 'calculated to inflame public opinion abroad and alarm the more ignorant public at home'.

Le Queux at once wrote to the Prime Minister, asking how he could criticize a work which he had never read, and why he accused the British public of being more ignorant than their Continental neighbours—a poser. On the next day Sir Henry sent Le Queux a note in his own handwriting, by special messenger and marked *Strictly Private*. In this letter the Prime Minister apologized for the words which he had used. He meant to say 'the more ignorant *section* of the public at home' and hoped that Le Queux would not, in the exigencies of politics, take any word of his as being personally offensive. He concluded by asking Le Queux to call at Downing Street, when convenient, as he desired to make a full explanation!

On the following day the opening chapters of Le Queux's work duly appeared in the *Daily Mail* and proved a huge success. Le Queux was congratulated by a large number of members at the Savage Club, the Devonshire Club, Boodle's and the Reform Club, and at his friends' houses. Amongst the first letters Le Queux received was one which gave him great pleasure; it was from his staunch supporter, Lord Roberts:

47, Portland Place,
London, W.
22nd August 1906

Dear Mr. Le Queux,

I return with many thanks the enclosure of your letter of 2nd August.

The imaginary scheme seems carefully thought out, and it forcibly illustrates the risk we should run under present military conditions, if, owing to the temporary absence or inferiority of our fleet, a Continental power [meaning

Germany] were able to seize an opportunity for landing a large force of picked soldiers in this country.

The maintenance at home of an adequate number of well-trained and organised troops and reservists would not only set free the navy for offensive action and the protection of our sea-borne commerce, by relieving it to an appreciable extent of the onerous obligation which it has lately undertaken of defending these shores without military cooperation, but would also enable such reinforcements to be despatched to our Colonies and dependencies as might be required to preserve the integrity and safeguard the interests of the British Empire.

I therefore wish you every success in your endeavour to impress upon the people of this country that the possession of a world-wide Empire carries with it defensive obligations commensurate with the commercial and other advantages which it confers, and that, without concerted and patriotic effort, we *may not improbably lose what our ancestors won.*

> Believe me,
> Yours very truly,
> Roberts

Le Queux was inundated with letters from (among others): the Duke of Northumberland, the Duke of Argyll, the Duke of Fife, the Earl of Derby, the Earl of Rosebery, the Earl of Wemyss, Viscount Milner, Viscount Hardinge, Lord Brassey, Lord Tweedmouth, Field-Marshal Sir George White, VC, distinguished generals and members of parliament, many of whom became his supporters and personal friends.

Shortly afterwards a meeting to consider national defence was convened by the London Chamber of Commerce and the Lord Mayor presided at the Mansion House. Lord Roberts made a vigorous speech, showing the country's insecurity and advocating that the country should be roused to the danger of apathy. Lord Brassey proposed a vote of thanks, making a fine speech, and afterwards, when Lord Roberts introduced Le Queux to him, he congratulated Le Queux on *The Invasion*.

Although some of the staff had been sceptical regarding the public reaction to the forecast, the *Daily Mail* certainly achieved a notable success for its enterprising 'scoop'. When Eveleigh Nash published *The Invasion of 1910* in book form, it at once went through many editions. The book aroused widespread attention, which was partly due to the fact that one of the greatest strategists of that time had designed it and that in consequence no critic could find fault with the invasion scheme. Le Queux's book was translated into no fewer than twenty-seven languages, including Arabic, Urdu, Syrian, Japanese and Chinese, and the total sales amounted to about a million copies. This gave Le Queux the utmost satisfaction, as he felt that he had roused the British public at last.

The Introduction to the book was the following letter from Lord Roberts, which Countess Roberts and the publishers (Eveleigh Nash and Grayson) kindly permit me to reproduce.

> Speaking in the House of Lords on the 10th July 1905, I said: 'It is to the people of this country I appeal to take up the question of the Army in a sensible, practical manner. For the sake of all they hold dear, let them bring home to themselves what would be the condition of Great Britain if it were to lose its wealth, its power, its position.'
>
> The catastrophe that may happen if we remain in our present state of unpreparedness is vividly and forcibly illustrated in Mr Le Queux's new book, which I recommend to the perusal of everyone who has the welfare of the British Empire at heart.
>
> Roberts.
F. M.

Curiously enough, however, the results of this publication were quite different from what was anticipated. After enjoying the descriptions of how Great Britain was invaded and the accounts of battles in Essex, Lancashire and Yorkshire and also of the enemy's advance on London, many readers, after finishing the book, cast it aside. The climax was reached when a German came over from Berlin, interviewed Le Queux's literary agent, Mr. A. P. Watt, and arranged with him to pay a handsome sum for the German rights of the book. Le Queux was in Naples when the agent's letter was received, and accepted the terms of the Concordia Press of Berlin by telegram. He rejoiced, however, too soon, for six months later Le Queux saw an illustrated edition of *The Invasion* in German, the conclusion of which had been entirely rewritten, making the result of the invasion *a German success*! The new version even had pictures of the Germans sacking London! Furthermore—crowning humiliation—the book was published, bound in gilt, as a prize for German schoolboys![3]

Bouquets for Fleet Street

Although St Barbe Sladen was correct enough in his statement that 'one of the greatest strategists of that time' had drawn up the invasion plan, a somewhat different version came from another distinguished editor, Bernard Falk. He wrote that: 'One could pick on no more characteristic period to illustrate the Fleet Street scene of my younger days than 1906, the year in which the Daily Mail *was proclaiming a sale five times as large as any morning contemporary ...'*

Tired of the exploits of adventurous clerics, people were disposed to turn their attention to the warnings of men able to read correctly the signs of the times—men who were convinced that Germany was preparing a day of reckoning for Britain. To allow these warnings to sink in, the *Daily Mail* ran a serial *The Invasion of 1910*, the main feature of which was a description of the siege of London. The actual story was written by William Le Queux, but several chapters came from the pen of H. W. Wilson, who had played an important part in designing the serial. He and 'Bobs' (Lord Roberts) in consultation had sketched the probable route which an invading German army landing in England would take, their ideas being subject to the approval of Lord Northcliffe. Shown the German line of march according to Wilson and Lord Roberts, the great newspaperman caustically remarked that from a military point of view it might be all right, but from a circulation point of view it was all wrong. 'Bobs' or no 'Bobs', the Germans must pass through towns of size, not keep to remote one-eyed country villages, where there was no possibility of large *Daily Mail* sales. That, thus transformed to suit his argument, the invaders' route became a little zigzag and a bit of a chase round the mulberry bush, and not at all what the astute Von Moltke would have planned, did not unduly strain the credulity of the bulk of the *Daily Mail* readers, nor prevent the serial from being an enormous success. Lord Northcliffe was justified in his objections, and the voluble protests of doddering generals in Pall Mall clubs—'By Gad, sir! The thing's preposterous'—was so much wasted splutter.

Before the Lights Went Out

Another contemporary observer, Esmé Wingfield-Stratford, recollected that their 'Edwardian paradise was under an ever darkening shadow of swords, or more precisely, of Dreadnoughts ...'

For the future war of the novels was beginning to take a new shape, in a most uncomfortably imminent future. In the 'nineties it had always been France and Russia, with the emphasis on Russia, and our German cousins lining up with us, according to historic precedent. But on one fine morning—I think in 1906—the startling portent was seen of a long file of veterans in spiked helmets and Prussian-blue uniforms parading moodily down Oxford Street. Perhaps their slouching appearance, so strangely at variance with the Potsdam tradition, was due to the fact that they carried sandwich boards to inform all whom it might concern that the great William Le Queux, already famous as the historian (in 1894) of the Great War in England (in alliance with Germany against France and Russia) in 1897, was now about to add to his laurels by reporting day by day in the columns of England's most wideawake newspaper the progress of her Great Invasion (by Germany) in 1910. And didn't he just! Overwhelming forces of unsuspected Dreadnoughts sending the British North Sea Fleet to the bottom on the opening night; people digging their own graves in genteel suburbs; a beautiful girl, selected for the firing squad in Hyde Park, flinging herself at the feet of Herr Kommandant who turns on his heel—however that rather difficult balancing feat may be performed.

And though one consoled oneself by saying that the Kaiser would never allow his officers to indulge in quite such heartless gyrations, reports from other self-guaranteed informed sources supplied only too ominous confirmation. It appeared that the whole of East Anglia was swarming with German spies who, with characteristic thoroughness, instead of purchasing the large-scale Ordnance Survey maps, were doing the whole job again for themselves and whose activities were known to everybody but the police. I was even informed by a writer of some excellent detective stories that they had taken to marking gates; and certainly, if you came to examine the gates, markings could be discovered—often in the form of somewhat indelicately selected code words.

And then the First Sea Lord, Jackie Fisher, who was engaged in out-trumping his rival Charlie Beresford's hearty old nautical card, brought the nightmare to the couches of hitherto peaceful slumberers, by bawling at them, from the Lord Mayor's table, that they had all got to sleep quietly in their beds.

But it is no part of my business to record, as I have tried to do elsewhere, by what strange ways the consciousness of the German peril (invariably in the form of a sudden treacherous invasion, and never in that of our being forced to intervene in a Continental war) was generated in the public mind. I am merely trying to make you understand how, like the motor and the aeroplane, it had begun to enter into the pattern, and quicken the tempo, of all our lives.

Even as I was writing this last paragraph, there came up to the surface, out of some limbo of long-discarded memories, a close-up of a scene at some late hour in one of the streets just behind Piccadilly. A gathering crowd composed of late revellers, prostitutes, and in fact an assortment of all nocturnal types except the police, was bunched in a delighted half-moon round the steps of a restaurant that a small but intensely bellicose man was seeking to re-enter. His way was blocked by a much larger man in a boiled shirt. The little man was shouting repeatedly, like a war-cry:

'My name is Tompkins! I tell you my name is Tompkins!' to which the large one would keep on replying, in the richest patois of Hoxton:

'Oo cares whatyer nime is? You gotter oppit outer this, see?'

Finally the little man found a way of ending the stalemate. Thrusting his jaw nearly into the other's shirt, he spat out the words,

'German spy!'

The effect was electric. The large man, who had hitherto carried off the situation with imperturbable restraint, hurled himself with a roar down the steps on his traducer, and but for the arrival at this precise moment of the arbitrator from Vine Street, I should have looked with confidence for the name of Tompkins in the day after tomorrow's obituary columns.

About German Spies

Although the unrestrained and unreflecting sensationalism of Le Queux's Invasion of 1910 *was well calculated to persuade the more simple-minded readers of the* Daily Mail *in 1906 that the Germans were ready to invade the United Kingdom, the story soon lost its power to convince. Indeed, had Le Queux's credulous biographer looked for a reason to explain why 'many readers, after finishing, cast it aside', he would have found that, no matter what the sensational power of these future-war stories might have been, they all vanished from the bookshops as soon as another crisis led to a new variant on the stock theme of invasion. The debate about German intentions during the first Moroccan crisis 1905–06 had been an ideal prelude to the appearance of* The Invasion of 1910, *just as the Casablanca incident of 1908–09 renewed the general questioning of the future and so set the scene for the spectacular success of Guy du Maurier's play,* An Englishman's

Home, *in 1909: packed audiences, a lengthy note on 'a sensational, though short-lived success' in the* Annual Register, *and then the silence of the tomb.*

These stories left behind them their contributions to the theme of 'the German invasion'. The most persistent and the most extraordinary element in that composite myth was the German spy, labouring secretly and so industriously to prepare for 'the Day' when the troop-landing craft would make their dash across the North Sea. It was too much for an expert like Charles Lowe, who had been a well-known Times *correspondent in Berlin and was Admiral Colomb's principal collaborator in* The Great War of 189–. *In 1910 he protested at some length and with great effect in the* Contemporary Review *at 'the baneful industry' of the future-war stories. He made a frontal attack on the myth of the German spies.*

Among all the causes contributing to the continuance of a state of bad blood between England and Germany, perhaps the most potent is the baneful industry of those unscrupulous writers who are for ever asserting that the Germans are only waiting for a fitting opportunity to attack us in our island-home and burst us up. In this country, where the power of the printed word is still great over the popular mind, such wicked assertions are readily believed by those who have neither the knowledge nor the critical acumen to dissect them; while, on the other hand, in Germany, where those charges are known to be false and calumnious, they only create anger and resentment. Nevertheless, the mill of misrepresentation on this side of the water goes grinding on as merrily as ever.

Thus it is that one of the most remarkable signs of the times is the number of works of fiction dealing with the invasion of England—works in which pen and pencil vie with each other in the production of luridly life-like pictures of aggression from across the German Ocean. In every case these invaders are Germans—one can soon see that—even if some writers have the decency to refer to them simply as 'foreigners': there is no mistaking the massive build and masterful ways of those alien intruders—even if those who know the Germans best may fail to recognize them from the brutal manners with which they are generally debited, and which are just as little characteristic of them as of our own brave soldiers.

Such pernicious works of fiction have been positively pouring from the press for the last few years—works like *The Invasion of 1910* (though there is no sign of it yet); *The War Inevitable*; *The Swoop of the (Teutonic) Vulture*; *The Great Raid*; *How the Germans took London: Forewarned, Forearmed*; *The Invaders: A Story of the Coming War*; *While*

Britain Slept: A Story of Invasion that will stir Britain to its Depths, with dozens of others—most of them concocted so crudely, and with such technical ignorance of the subject, that one of the writers brings his army of invaders across the North Sea 'in large flotillas of lighters firmly lashed together and towed by shallow-draught tugs and torpedo-boats'—and all in one calm night!—while Horse Artillery is made to co-operate with Infantry, and cavalry conflicts take place on ground where you couldn't find room enough to swing a squadron cat. Moreover, the penny weekly which palmed off all this preposterous stuff on its credulous readers boasted to them that it had received 'three great opinions of our invasion story'—from Lord Esher and Sir Evelyn Wood, and from Colonel Lockwood, MP for the Epping Division of Essex, who had been making himself conspicuous as the spokesman of the spy-alarmists in and out of Parliament.

For you are to understand that there is one character inherent in all those silly invasion-stories, and that is the young, well-born, well-spoken, and attractive German who settles down somewhere in our eastern counties—the main line of invasion—to cultivate social relations and even lay claim to the heart and hand of the vicar's daughter. What he really is, and how he spends his time, is not at all clear to his wondering friends; but it all comes out when at last he boldly throws off the mask and appears before his fiancée in the hated garb of our Teutonic invaders, whose landing and whose passage through our intricate country he has facilitated by the information which he has been secretly accumulating all the time.

This leading character of a German spy, common to the invasion stories of all our writers of fiction, is not the individual creation of their fertile imaginations, but has been taken by them from the serious statements of members of Parliament and of countless 'Letters to the Editor' in the daily Press. According to these alarmist statements of speakers and writers, this country is now enmeshed by an elaborate system of German spies, more effective even than the network of the Spanish Inquisition, whose function it is to prepare the way for the invasion which is declared to be inevitable and impending.

Well, now, let us try and discover what truth there is in this assertion, this assumption. It may readily be granted that, if the Germans really and truly contemplated an early invasion of this country, they would be utter fools not to do their best to make themselves masters of all the means of success. But, on the other hand, if it cannot be shown that there is any solid ground for believing that they are now acting in the manner imputed to them by our spy alarmists, then there can be no reason for continuing to cherish the belief, or even the suspicion, that they are only waiting for the fitting moment to launch their legions upon our ill-defended shores.

First of all, then, let it be granted that no General Staff would be worth the name which did not include among its functions the collection of statistics about the military organization and resources of other countries, more particularly of those with which it might possibly one day be at war. The organization of our own General Staff lays it down that one of its duties is the 'collection, preparation (including strategical and tactical consideration), and distribution of information concerning the military geography, resources, and armed forces of *all* foreign countries'; and our General Staff has simply been modelled, like most of our other military institutions, on that of the Germans. This General Staff work, in time of peace, is akin to the laborious industry of the compiler of an encyclopedia, while, of course, it must assume a more extended, and also, perhaps, a more underground form in prospect of an intended or impending war. It is then that secret investigators are actually sent into the probable area of warlike operations to—well, to spy out the land, as was done by Caleb and Joshua.

In spite of all popular belief to the contrary, it would astonish the general public to know to what extent we ourselves practise the kind of espionage which we are now so indignantly imputing to the Germans. To speak of nothing else, this may be gathered from the military memoirs and biographies published in recent years—such as the lives of Sir John Ardagh, Sir Charles Wilson, Sir Henry Brackenbury (*Some Memories of my Spare Time*), and other scientific officers, where the reader will find in almost every chapter refer- ences to secret service missions on the Continent and elsewhere. Before retiring from the Grenadier Guards, in circumstances which may be remembered, Mr. H. C. Woods undertook several such tours in the Near East (*vide* his *Washed by Four Seas*) for the ferreting out of information that would be useful to our War Office.

But the most interesting, because the most candid, of all our confessions of this kind is to be found in the *Recollections of Forty Years' Service* by Major-General Sir A. Bruce Tulloch, which relates in detail how, on war in Egypt becoming inevitable owing to the rebel- lious attitude of Arabi, he hastened out to the Nile Delta as a private sportsman to indulge his favourite passion for snipe-shooting, and in this way, among other things, made a thorough survey of Arabi's lines at Tel-el-Kebir—his estimate of their strength being so accurate that, after their capture, it was 'found that the number of guns was exact to a single piece'.

On several occasions, also, previous to that, Major Tulloch had been dispatched on secret military service to the Continent, and once he was sent to survey the Yorkshire coast with reference to suitable landing-places for an invading force of all arms. In this connection he writes:

> When doing the Yorkshire coast I heard of a German officer staying at a hotel in Scarborough, which he had made his headquarters while doing work which, on inquiry, turned out to be precisely that on which I also was engaged, and my headquarters were close to—viz., at Bridlington Quay. My regret was that I did not hear about my German colleague until my work was just finished. We might have done it together.

On 6 July 1908 Colonel Lockwood MP told the House of Commons that he had discovered 'German spies, charged with the mission of securing photographs of Epping Forest'

Now, be it noted that Major Tulloch did not with his own eyes positively see and have speech with this Prussian officer; he only 'heard of him', which is a very different thing; and the same remark applies to almost all the allegations of German espionage in our midst which, for some time back, have been deluging the columns of our Yellow Press. For the last two years I have made a point of collecting as many of those statements as I could lay my hands upon, and all of them suffer from the taint of being in the nature of indirect and second-hand evidence, which would not be accepted in any court of law. 'A friend told me,' 'One of the ladies of the party said', 'Another gentleman made the following statement', 'A lady friend of mine not long ago in Germany,' 'One of my constituents told me', 'The proprietors of a good boarding-house informed me,' 'A most trustworthy authority states', 'The following definite statements were made to me,' 'In two cases I have received statements from people who believe', etc.—such are but a few of the authorities who vouch for German espionage in our midst, and I could find nothing of a more definite kind in support of the charge.

But what, then, it may be asked, about the evidence of such an egregious patriot of the Teutophobe type as Mr. L. J. Maxse, who has done more than any other man in England to embitter the relations between the two countries, and who keeps the breakfast-table of the Kaiser as liberally supplied with libels as his uncle, Admiral F. Maxse, kept the luncheon-table of Bismarck richly provided with lobsters from Heligoland, of which he was for years the Governor.[4] The burden of the gallant and hero-worshipping Admiral's editorial nephew's Tyrtæan song is always the same, namely (speech at Deepdene, Surrey):

> The portentous and sinister preparations of their false friend, the German Emperor, to make war upon this country when they least expected it ... Side by side with Germany's amazing preparations, which were known to all our responsible politicians, ... the German Emperor was engaged in manoeuvres to bamboozle the British people and throw them off their guard until it was too late. German officers trooped to England on staff rides, or disguised themselves as waiters and hairdressers, and our eastern counties were studded with spies. Mr. Maxse is, of course, too high and mighty a publicist to condescend to details, and his fellow-alarmist, Colonel Lockwood, is no better. The latter was always heckling Mr. Haldane about the dangerous activity of German spies—more particularly in his own county of Essex, but could never extract the least confirmation of his fears from our Minister of War, who was consequently pronounced by the Yellow Press to be supine, ignorant of what everybody knew, and over-complaisant to

his friend the Kaiser. At the same time Colonel Lockwood continued sticking to his guns. 'I say,' he declared, 'without the possibility of contradiction, that the thing is "going on".' Then, if so, why did he not prove it by some evidence? So far as I know, he has not only not done so, but not even attempted to do so. Neither Colonel Lockwood nor Mr. Maxse ever tells us where he gets his information; but possibly the latter derived his knowledge 'of the German officers who trooped to England on staff "rides"', from a letter-writer in the *Standard* signing himself 'Watch-dog', in which connection, be it noted, it is rather the exception than the rule for these alarmists to publish their discoveries under their own names. Well, then, this was 'Watchdog's' warning bark:[5]

'Not only was there the recent (1908) German staff ride through the eastern counties, but last year (1907) a number of German officers, including a General of the Staff, rode from Scotland to Cornwall, practically ranging the country from John o' Groat's to Land's End. Now I hear that Ireland has had a visit from our Teutonic cousins, the survey including even the wilds of Connemara. How long is this German military activity in our midst to be allowed to continue?'

'How long', indeed? *Quousque Tandem*? But why did not 'Watchdog'—and there are few of his breed that bark at mere shadows—why didn't he first inquire into the reality of the danger which he set himself to proclaim? A staff-ride carried out by several German officers, even in mufti, is not a thing than can easily escape observation. But not one tittle of positive evidence was produced in support of those silly assertions. No one came forward who, with his own eyes, had seen the alleged staff-riders, or could describe their horses, or their motor-cars, or where they put up, and what their hotel bills amounted to. These wild and whirling statements were unsupported by a single scrap of evidence beyond, perhaps, the assertion of some silly hotel-keeper that his guests included one or two visitors who spoke German, and that he could only account for their presence on the supposition of their being spies. They looked to him like spies, therefore they were spies.

Colonel Lockwood was fortunate enough to find a powerful ally in Mr. Courtenay Warner, MP, who at Walthamstow, in March last, roused the feelings of his audience by descanting on our unpreparedness for war. The German Government, he said, spent considerable sums of money, not only in making maps and surveying England, but in sending people over to mark out places in the eastern counties to see what they had to provide for. It was true; *he had seen one of them himself.* The more's the pity, then, that he didn't tell us more about him. It almost savours of insanity for anyone to ask us to believe that German officers give themselves the trouble to make sketches and maps of the Epping neighbourhood, when for a few shillings they can buy as many sections as they like of our ordnance survey maps, which would more than satisfy the wants of any invaders, if, indeed, a good cycling map did not better serve their turn, while a county directory would do the rest.

But such explanations fail to satisfy philosophers like Mr. Frederic Harrison, who, in a letter to *The Times* last March, committed himself, among other things, to this very positive statement:

> The German Navy is not built for distant voyages. It is built to act only as the spearhead of a magnificent army. This army, as we know, has been trained for sudden transmarine descent on a coast; and for this end every road, well, bridge, and smithy in the east of England and Scotland has been docketed in the German War Office.

Now, the assertion that the 'German Army has been trained for sudden transmarine descent', is simply not true. In fact, this special training is of a kind which, for geographical reasons, could only be imparted to a comparatively small portion of the German Army. Of the twenty-three Army Corps now composing the Imperial Host, only five have their districts adjacent to the sea (Baltic and German Ocean), and very rarely have even these riparian troops indulged in the operations imputed to them by Mr. Harrison. The largest-scale experiment of the kind was made in September, 1904, near Wohlenberg, in the Baltic, when a mixed force—of only about 4,000 men, 159 horses, and eight guns—was landed.

It so happened that, about the same time, Sir John French, with one of his Aldershot Divisions—say, 9,000 men—was engaged in a much more extensive operation of the same kind at Clacton, in Essex; but no German writer, in the shape of a counter-irritant to Mr. Harrison, ever thought of accusing us of thus practising for a sudden descent on Schleswig-Holstein. Ah, but then, '*quod licet Jovi, non licet bovi*', and the German is always the patient ox in English eyes. Why in the name of wonder should it have been thought strange of the Germans to practise some of their seaside troops in the art of debarkation, and thus correct the mistakes which had been committed when landing men in China and South-west Africa?

No, believe me, the Germans no more train their army for 'sudden transmarine descent' to the extent alleged by our Positivist philosopher than they practise the bush-fighting which would be required of them if ever they sought to invade a country like England with its labyrinth of roads, its natural field-fortifications of ditches, hedgerows and woods, and its absolute lack of areas—on the lines of invasion, at least—suitable for the tactics of cavalry. The Germans themselves would be the first to admit that the surface configuration of our country gives us military advantages equivalent to the possession of several Army Corps. Our late manoeuvres in Wilts and Berks—which I myself was there to see—resolved themselves into something very like the bush-fighting which fell to us in our advance on Coomassie; and I am not aware that the Germans—though, perhaps, Mr Harrison knows better—are also being trained for this peculiar kind of warfare which is not native to them in their own open, unenclosed country, across which you could almost move a Cavalry Division, on a regimental front, from Königsberg to Cologne.

'Well, we don't know anything about that,' bawls a thousand-throated chorus of alarmists, 'but what we do know is that the Germans mean to invade us—the proof being that they are now as busy as bees mapping out the country, and mopping up all our military secrets. Just see what they are doing!' Yes, and *how* they are doing it—that is what more particularly tickles me. For it is a curious circumstance that, while crediting the Germans with every kind of military virtue, we nevertheless deny them the merit of being masters in the art of espionage. They are made to do their spy work so clumsily that they are always being found out and pilloried in the Press. We are asked to believe that they hunt—not only in couples, but in trios, and walk abroad openly with sunshades, and cameras, and cycles, and note-books, and land-surveying apparatus, when, as I said before, they can obtain the best available maps for a few shillings. And the way they do their land-surveying, too, how German in its thoroughness and method—each inquisitor having a district all to himself, like a settler in Manitoba with a free grant of 160 acres to till and reap! But how, then, has this come to be known? The following anecdote will explain:

> Mr. M., of Southend-on-Sea, had a friend recently visiting in Germany. He was, on a certain occasion, in the company of German officers; knowing him to be an Englishman, he was asked what part of England he came from. He replied 'Essex.'

'What part of Essex?''Chelmsford'. The rejoinder was, 'Oh, Chelmsford; I know Chelmsford well, that is my district.'

Now this is a story which I have encountered in a hundred different forms, and it runs through all our espionage literature just as the myth of Bruce and the Spider—which, as a patriotic Scot, I am dreadfully sorry to have to part with—is to be found in the folk-lore of half-a-dozen other countries. 'Oh, yes, I know the place; that is in my "district!"' As if any German officer, with secret functions as an English topographer, could be such an utter fool as to give his game away like that!

Yet that is by no means the only kind of evidence for the prosecution which our alarmists import from Germany itself, and here is another tit-bit in point. I take it from an article which appeared in the *Pall Mall Gazette*, of 27th October last, headed 'With Eyes and Ears in Germany', by 'An Anglo-German'—whatever that may be:

> Some little while since I was visiting a relative in a bureau of the German War Department. While there, an opportunity came in my way, which I do not wish to describe in detail, of closely examining a map of the British Isles upon which certain parts of the coast line were annotated and charted with every appearance of laboured accuracy, including the Hinterland of each spot thus particularised. These points, which were fairly numerous, occurred wherever the configuration of a gently shelving shore facilitated the landing of troops. I may add that the document to which this above-mentioned chart was attached proved to be part of a German plan for the disembarkation of a large force in several detachments upon the shores of Great Britain.

Now, of this statement it can only be said that it bears internal evidence of being an impudent fabrication from beginning to end, and the only wonder is that any responsible English journal could have been got to print such ridiculous rubbish, and pay for it, too. To begin with, there can be very little of the German in this 'Anglo-German' who talks of a 'German War Department', which simply does not exist. Every German knows that, at Berlin, military affairs are divided between the Prussian Ministry of War, which controls the internal administration of the German Army that has no war-ministry of its own, and the Grand General Staff. The two bodies are located in different buildings, about a mile apart. If such a document as that asserted to have been seen by 'Anglo-German' really existed, it would be kept at the Grand General Staff, and safeguarded in such a way that no outsider could ever have the slightest chance of inspecting it, even if, like 'Anglo-German', he had 'a relative in the War Department'.

I myself know something about the character and ways of members of the General Staff at Berlin, and, believe me, they are by no means men of the stamp of fashionable ladies who drag out their latest dresses to show their afternoon visitors. No, none of them are inclined that way, even to Anglo-German relatives, if they happen to have any. Nor do they, as a rule, receive civilian visitors in their 'bureaux'. Besides, the document submitted to 'Anglo-German's' minute inspection was an impossible one—with an elaborate chart of our eastern sea-coast attached to it—a 'coast-line charted with every "appearance of laboured accuracy".' 'All Admiralty charts', writes a distinguished naval friend, in answer to an enquiry from me, 'may be bought from J. D. Potter, 145, Minories, E. They are very cheap.'

But there is another of our spy-alarmists—twin-brother in blatancy and balderdash to Mr. Maxse—who claims to know more about the secrets of the 'German War Department' than even the 'Anglo-German' who so cruelly victimized the *Pall Mall Gazette*. This is Mr. Arnold White, who thus wrote to the *Daily Telegraph* (21st August, 1908):

> The German danger is what astronomers and philosophers call a *novum*; it has no precedent in our experience. For the first time in modern history the greatest military Power anxiously avoids all conflict with other Continental Powers and concentrates herself upon England. Why are twelve high officers engaged in Berlin on the German General Staff in the study of England and the English?

The answer is that Mr. White simply does not know what he is talking about. For the truth is that the General Staff at Berlin *does not include a department for the special study of England*. It is studied in the same department as attends to the military affairs of France, Spain, Belgium, Holland, the United States of America, etc.; and there are only three or four officers who do the work—the highest in rank among them being a major, a very different kind of staff from Mr. White's 'twelve high officers'!

But what else can be expected of a man who is always giving 'reasons why Britain will shortly be attacked by Germany', and who has discovered that the jumping off place for this attack is to be Emden, of which the recently constructed quays, he says, are not intended for the service of the enormously increased shipping of the port due to the opening of the Ems-Dortmund Canal—that is a mere blind—but for the secret embarkation (the prelude to Mr Harrison's 'sudden transmarine descent') of the Kaiser's helmeted legions which shall shortly be launched upon our defenceless coasts to the blaring bugle-strains of 'Tommy, make room for your Uncle'; while the walk-over from Sedan to Paris shall be repeated from Clacton to the Corn Exchange—the massed bands of half-a-dozen Army Corps playing our conquerors along the Whitechapel Road to the jubilant air of 'Finis Britanniæ!'

It is no use referring those scaremongers to the War Office and to the negative replies which it has repeatedly returned about alleged acts of espionage, because the invariable rejoinder is that we have to do with a War Minister who simply doesn't know his business. One of those unconvincible alarmists is Mr. W. Le Queux, who has written several fiction-books about the Kaiser's hostile designs and multitudinous spies:

> As I write [he says] I have before me a pile of amazing documents which plainly show the feverish activity with which this advance guard of the enemy is working to secure for their employers the most detailed information. These documents have already been placed before the Minister of War, who returned them without comment.

And no wonder, because, of course, Mr. Haldane must be much better informed on the subject than Mr. Le Queux. This writer has set forth in a work of fiction, claiming to be based on actual facts, the exact nature of the German spy-organization in our midst—its *modus operandi*, salaries of its more than five thousand agents, and all the rest. But the trouble with Mr Le Queux is that he does not produce one single tittle of evidence in support of his allegations, and, so far as I know, he had been careful never to submit for the consideration of the public and the Press the 'amazing documents' which Mr. Haldane 'returned to him without remark'. I rather suspect that this astonishing spy-hunter had something to do with a series of articles on 'Espionage in England' which appeared in the *Standard* last summer, and thus began:

> Not very long ago it was the fashion in nearly all quarters to treat 'spy stories' with contempt and ridicule, either as the invention of sensation-mongers or the hallucination of hysterical 'old women of the male sex'. They cannot,

however, be so disposed of now. Properly authenticated accounts of specific acts of espionage have been produced in large numbers by responsible and even eminent persons, and questions on the subject are constantly being asked in Parliament, with the result that the attention of the public has been strongly aroused, and protestations of official ignorance or incredulity no longer serve to check a growing feeling of alarm and insecurity.

On the appearance of this I wrote to the editor of the *Standard*, inviting him and his contributor to favour their readers with chapter and verse—not for several, but only for *one* 'properly authenticated' act of German espionage in this country; but my letter was simply 'basketed', the most effectual of all means of silencing inquiry—for the time being—and stifling discussion in a matter where the interests of the nation and the credit of our Press are alike concerned.

'Well, then,' say the scare-mongers, 'but just look at this! Here is a human document for you; and if this won't carry conviction to your stubbornly sceptical mind, nothing ever will!' 'All right,' say I, 'let's have a look at it, by all means.' It turns out to be a letter addressed to the *Nation in Arms* (and reproduced in the *Standard*) by 'A Member of the National Service League':

> Sir,—The following incident, which took place a short time ago, may prove of interest to the readers of this journal.
>
> A gentleman with a thorough knowledge of the German language was having luncheon at a restaurant in London, and sitting at the next table to him was a foreigner, who, speaking in German in an undertone (but which, nevertheless, my friend was able to hear), addressed the waiter who was attending to him as follows:
>
> 'Where do you mobilise?'
>
> Answer: 'Sheerness.'
>
> My friend thought this somewhat strange and startling, so decided to try the same question himself, which he did the following day at another restaurant, and got the reply:
>
> 'Chatham.'
>
> I think the above is only another of many such indications of foreign organisation in these islands.

Now, even assuming that the 'gentleman with a thorough knowledge of the German language' was not afflicted with defective hearing, it is simply impossible—humanly, militarily, and otherwise—that the waiters in question could have answered as they were said to have done, and for this reason. Either their mobilization must have referred to a *Mobilmachung* of the German army in Germany itself, or to that portion of the German army which is supposed to be already in our own midst. If the former was meant, it would have been quite preposterous of the waiters to reply that their mobilization orders directed them to proceed either to 'Sheerness' or 'Chatham', since neither of these ports offers a point of departure for Germany at once the most direct and expeditious, which is certainly the route they would be expected to take.

'The men', explained 'another distinguished military officer', 'who answered, "Sheerness" and "Chatham" would no doubt be assembled at those places prior to their making their way to "Queenboro".' But why the dickens should they not have been told to go straight to Queenboro, or, better still, to Harwich, and take the first boat across? The truth is that, in the event of the German army being mobilized, the reservists living in England and elsewhere would only be asked to rejoin their regiments at once, it being left to themselves *how* to do it. Moltke never confused the minds of his subordinates by giving them detailed instructions. The general principle was good enough for him. His directions were always of a brief and comprehensive kind. 'Do this,' he would say, and they had got to do it—according to their lights.

Well, but then, there is the alternative assumption that the 'mobilization' might have referred to the mustering under arms of that formidable portion of the German army quartered in our midst under the guise of waiters, barbers, clerks and 'respectable tradesmen'. For the theory of the scare-mongers is that, at the very first blast of the war-trumpet which shall summon the Kaiser's multitudinous legions to cross the sea against us, the Germans living in this country will at once band themselves into spick-and-span battalions armed to the teeth, and thus catch us between two fires. At a given signal the German reservists amongst us would rush to their pre-appointed trysting-places at 'Sheerness', or 'Chatham', or even Tooting Bec, and then we should be done for!

But is there any sane man in the kingdom who believes in such a thing? I daresay Colonel A. Keene, DSO, secretary of the National Service League, claims to be gifted with at least an average degree of sanity and common sense; yet when interviewed on the subject of the 'mobilization' incidents,

There was [he said] a paragraph in Lord Roberts' great speech in the House of Lords last November which should have prepared the minds of the public for such a thing as that of which our correspondent writes. I refer to the words in which his lordship drew attention to the number of German soldiers in our midst.

And what were those words that fell from the lips of our foremost soldier, who had been talking of war between this country and Germany not only as 'possible', but also as 'probable'—which latter was a dictum altogether outside his lordship's competency as a fighting man, who is trained to be the instrument, but not a prophet or the mouthpiece of a policy?

> It is calculated, my lords, that there are 80,000 Germans in the United Kingdom, almost all of them trained soldiers. They work many of the hotels at some of the chief railway stations, and if a German force once got into this country it would have the advantage of help and reinforcement such as no other army on foreign soil has ever before enjoyed.

Yes, of course, in the view of Colonel A. Keene, DSO, this daring statement from our foremost soldier was well calculated to prepare the mind of the panicky public for the momentous revelation that a couple of German waiters had received orders to 'mobilize', i.e. muster and join their battalions in a certain contingency at Chatham and Sheerness; and the public mind was still more inclined to let itself be led away in the same direction when Sir John Barlow, in Parliament, asked Mr. Haldane whether he had any knowledge of the 66,000 German reservists in our midst, as well as of the arms and ammunition secretly stored away for their eventual use near Charing Cross—most probably in the Adelphi cellars!

The public were further informed by Major A. J. Reed, Perthshire secretary of the Primrose League—an interchangeable friend and ally of Mr. Le Queux—that the deadly work of those reservists would be all the more efficient when at last they rushed to arms in obedience to their mobilization orders, seeing that Messrs Le Queux and Reed had discovered the existence in this country of 6,500 paid German spies— male and female—1,500 of them in Scotland, and 5,000—very precise numbers, you see—in England. But worse was still to come, and it remained for Colonel Driscoll, of 'Driscoll's Scouts', to discover and proclaim aloud that 'living in our midst, under the protection of the British flag, were 350,000 "German soldiers"', a number more than half the entire peace-footing strength of the German army!

Well, now, let us see where we really stand as regards the number of German fighting-men in our midst; and for that purpose let me tabulate the figures, thus:

GERMANS IN ENGLAND

Major Reed's spies	6,500
Sir John Barlow's 'trained soldiers'	66,000
Lord Roberts' trained soldiers ('almost all of them')	80,000
Colonel Driscoll's trained soldiers	350,000

And now, if you please, let us turn to our own Registrar-General. The late Lord Salisbury's constant advice to his countrymen whenever, as so often happened, they worked themselves up into a state of panic-frenzy by the contemplation of purely imaginary dangers, was 'to consult a large-scale map'. So now, in turn, when these same panic-mongers are peopling England with phantom German armies, they might do equally well to exchange their works of fiction for solid Blue Books and other repertories of facts. I myself invested half-a-crown in the purchase of one of those Blue Books, being the General Report of the last Census of England and Wales, taken in 1901. And what did I find?

I found that the classified number of *all* foreigners in the kingdom was 247,758, and that of these only 49,133, or not much more than a half of Lord Roberts' 80,000 'trained soldiers', were Germans. It may be objected that these figures cannot be accurate. I can only say that I have taken them from the best available source, and if there be any other statistical authority of a more trustworthy kind on the same subject I should very much like to know what it is.

But now, for the purpose of argument, let us assume that, since 1901, the number of Germans in this country has risen from 49,000 to 55,000—a very liberal allowance, considering that since the previous Census the German element in our midst has not been increasing at the same rate as before—how many of these could be classified as 'trained solders'? At the very utmost I should say 10,000 or even 8,000, men, equivalent to something like a weak Aldershot Division of all arms. If you sub-classify the 55,000 Germans living amongst us into men, women and children, as well as into men who have served in the army but are now beyond the age of military service, and men who have never served with the colours at all, you will find that the number of trained Teutonic warriors now ministering to our comfort as 'respectable tradesmen', barbers, clerks, tailors, bakers, and what not, and available for imperilling the safety of this country by a sudden muster, or mobilization, on Tooting Common, would not have sufficed for annihilating the legions of Varus in the Teutoburger Wald.

One of our grossest illusions about Germany is to suppose that every one of her sons serves as a soldier. If that were so, the peace footing strength of the army would be infinitely greater than it is; but the strength of the German army is a fixed and constant figure like our own. The thing to remember is that every German capable of bearing arms is *liable* to do so, but it by no means follows that every German receives a military training. If, for example, in any one year, say, 150,000 recruits are wanted to take the place of time-expired men, and 200,000 young men are available, it is, of course, only the best of these that are taken, while the rest are relegated to certain lower classes of the reserve, which practically means their entire release from service with the colours.

It is my own experience that this is the category of men which mainly supplies us with our waiters and barbers, and contributes to the German colony in this country its largest contingent. I invariably ask my German barber or waiter, *Na, haben Sie gedient?*—'Well, have you served your time in the army?'—and in about four cases out of five—certainly three out of four—the answer is in the negative, with the addition of some such explanation as 'short sight', 'weak heart', 'insufficient breast-girth', 'flat feet', or other physical defect. It is another great mistake to suppose that many young Germans come over here to escape their military service. I should say that the number of those was exceedingly small. On the contrary, the bulk of the Germans in this country are men who have little or no military training at all, and the residue would make but a poor show, numerically, if 'mobilized' and massed at Sheerness, Chatham, or Tooting Bec.

So now let our alarmists clear their minds of all that silly nonsense about this aspect, at least, of the 'German peril', and thus cease to make themselves look so supremely ridiculous in the eyes of other nations. Those nations—and in particular the Germans—simply held their sides on hearing that another member of Parliament, Sir George Doughty—still more incredibly credulous than Sir John Barlow—gravely asked whether the Admiralty knew anything of two large German steamers which had been suddenly commandeered at Hamburg, filled up with soldiers, and sent across into the Humber and back again—just to show that the thing could be done without our getting wind of it beforehand! Of course, no incident of the kind had ever happened. But if the Germans had a hearty laugh over this, what was the extent of their contemptuous merriment on finding that the Yellow portion of our Press had taken to terrifying its funky readers with sensational tales of mysterious air-ships—or scare-ships, of the Zeppelin type—which had made their nocturnal appearance in various parts of England, more particularly the eastern counties—air-ships of which the inquisitive occupants could be distinctly heard talking in the guttural tones of the Fatherland, and even dropping down printed evidence of their *provenance!*

But who, then, was responsible for all this? The authors of the evil might be broadly divided into two kinds: those who were for ever crying 'Wolf!' for party purposes, and those whose interest it was to wolf the credulous public out of their pence. Most of the spy stories were simply invented in order to promote the agitation for a stronger fleet, an object as commendable in itself as the means employed for achieving it was contemptible; while, on the other hand, that portion of our Press which lives by sensation scrupled not to help in getting up these silly scares for its own selfish profit, than which nothing could be more unpatriotic and pernicious. Mr. Keir Hardie, for once, was not far wrong when he said that 'the threatened German invasion' was a deliberately manufactured scare 'concocted by the ghouls of both countries' who live by preying on 'the credulity of the public'; and it must sorrowfully be owned that these ghouls are much more numerous on this side of the water than on the other.

It may be argued that the spy and invasion fictions which have been pouring from the Press are beneath contempt from the literary point of view, and so they are. But, unfortunately, the degree of harm that can be done by the printed word is not dependent on its literary value. In these days of popular 'education' such sensational writers are readily believed by the masses who contribute to the formation of public opinion, which in turn tends to influence our rulers and our relations with other countries; and what these readers are wickedly taught to believe is that the Germans are arming and preparing to attack us by sea and land at the first available opportunity.

Thus the pernicious publications referred to, as well as the vamped-up and unscrupulous spy-sensations of our Yellow Press, constitute acts of criminal levity against the peace of two kindred nations—a poisoning of the wells of public truth—and that, too, at a time when each country is only too ready to believe the worst of the other. Such conduct is none the less a public crime for its being beyond the reach of the public prosecutor.

The Essence of Parliament

Charles Lowe must have known that Punch *had from time to time poked fun at the myth of the German spy. On 15 July 1908 gunfire descended on Colonel Lockwood, the man who 'was always heckling Mr Haldane about the dangerous activity of German spies'. The following short piece speaks for itself.*

Extracted from the Diary of Toby, M.P.

House of Commons, Monday, July 6
Colonel MARK LOCKWOOD, V.C., back on duty; his countenance has taken on a manlier bronze; his hat is tipped a little further back towards back of head, carnation in his button-hole nearer than ever to circumference of a sunflower. Excited some attention on entering the Lobby by carrying a telescope under his arm.

'What's that for?' WALTER LONG asked him. 'A new way of catching the SPEAKER's eye?'

Beneath the bronze a blush mantled MARK's ingenuous countenance.

'Beg your pardon,' he said, 'force of habit.'

Rushed off to locker, deposited spy-glass. Back in time to put a question which explained everything. For the past ten days, during which Lobby, House and Terrace have lamented his absence, MARK has been down in Epping Forest, stalking a couple of foreigners. By various strategic movements, such as climbing trees, crawling on all fours through the long grass (on one occasion hiding in an outhouse, the door of which the owner casually locked in passing, imprisoning the unsuspected Colonel for the space of five hours), he accumulated evidence revealing the true character of the self-styled tourists. They were, in brief, German spies, charged with missions of securing photographs of Epping Forest and water-colour sketches of the more picturesque views, with intent that the German Army, having sunk the Channel Fleet and gobbled up the Territorial Forces, should march by the nearest route on London.

This afternoon brought subject to notice of House in form of question addressed to SECRETARY OF STATE FOR WAR. With that hide-bound contempt which Ministers commonly show for information reaching them through any but official sources, NAPOLEON B. HALDANE made light of the affair. Told a little story relating to what he described as similar incident. Report made to War Office of three foreign officers taking observations in a rural district. Specially mentioned as conclusive evidence of guilty intent that they 'drank champagne and drove about in motors'. Investigation made, it turned out that they were totally innocent, even commonplace, visitors, wholly unconnected with military matters.

'This is the kind of thing', said N. B. H., casting a look of scorn in MARK's button-hole, 'that is constantly coming up.'

Thus is patriotism encouraged by the present so-called Government. After spending five hours in an out-house, breaking his watch-chain in forcing his way through inadequate outlet provided by a partly shuttered window, and carrying out the other strategic movements cited, for MARK to be put off by ill-timed badinage is not encouraging to further effort for the public weal.

Business Done—Eight Hours (Mines) Bill read a second time. Old Age Pensions Bill passed through final stage of Committee.

Tuesday

Like that other renowned warrior, General TROCHU, Captain KINCAID-SMITH has his 'plan'. It is more comprehensive even than the original one for the deliverance of beleaguered Paris. Having carefully considered the Territorial Army scheme, an eye trained in warfare perceives its weak points. As, many years later, the late Mr. BIGGAR, criticizing a Bill brought in by Mr. CHAPLIN relating to the breed of horses, observed, 'It's too narrer, Mr. SPEAKER, much too narrer.' It provides excellent machinery but lacks the force to work it. In brief, it does not make provision for raw material of an army—men, to wit.

This KINCAID-SMITH is prepared to do. Has drafted a scheme, elaborating plan of national military training, making it compulsory. This afternoon moves for leave to introduce his Bill. Avails himself of privilege of the Ten Minutes Rule to explain it clause by clause with reiterated formula. 'Clause 1 lays down—' he said. 'Clause 2 lays down—' and so on to the end, as if the Bill were a hen laying eggs for families.

House began to show signs of impatience at the quaint reiteration. KINCAID-SMITH took no notice of the restless movement, the increasing buzz of conversation, the murmur of 'Time! Time!'. He had, so to speak, a hen up his sleeve that would 'lay down' something sure to please Members, safe to secure a first reading of the Bill.

'Clause 11', he said, in due course, 'lays down that exemption from compulsory training shall be accorded to habitual drunkards, persons of weak intellect, and Members of both Houses of Parliament.'

A roar of cheers and laughter greeted this happy grouping. When it subsided, KINCAID-SMITH started off again. 'Clause 12 lays down—.' This brought up the SPEAKER with significant reminder that the allotted time had expired.

KINCAID-SMITH quite surprised. Was getting on so nicely. Process of laying down carried on with unvarying punctuality and dispatch. Though there might be no appeal from ruling of the Chair, he was not disposed to forego delivery of his peroration, carefully prepared after close study of JOHN BRIGHT's masterpieces.

In solemn voice, with impressive manner, he began to 'lay down' one of the longest sentences ever worked off in debate. Members, placated by the artful bribe of remission of compulsory training, listened in silence to the first furlong or so. As he went on, laying it down as if it were an Atlantic cable, the long unfamiliar cry of 'Vide! Vide!' broke forth, drowning orator's voice. This bad enough; mild compared with what followed on a division, when leave to introduce the Bill was refused by 250 votes against 34.

Les Fictions guerrières anglaises

In 1910 Charles Lowe had said quite rightly that the British merited the 'contemptuous merriment' of German readers, when they found that 'the Yellow portion of our Press had taken to terrifying its funky readers with sensational tales of mysterious air-ships—or scare-ships, of the Zeppelin type—which had made their nocturnal appearance in various parts of England, more particularly the eastern counties!'. The Germans, however, were not alone. In 1909 a French observer had already brought out a book, Les Fictions guerrières anglaises *('British War Fiction'), in which he sought to analyse and explain the extraordinary 'fear of invasion' that raged throughout the United Kingdom. By 1909, it seems, the British were in danger of losing their reputation for calm, phlegmatic behaviour for reasons almost beyond the comprehension of a French writer.*

A POWERFUL, LATENT ANXIETY

On the day when Blériot's aeroplane glided on white wings across the Channel and landed on the cliffs of Dover, there were tremendous cheers in honour of the brave aviator; and the British shook hands with him in the most friendly way. But from the very next day, in the midst of the unbroken chorus of praise that rose from the

British press to celebrate this new triumph of the French spirit, a note of anxiety was clearly discernible.

'It is frightening', the *Daily News* observed, 'to contemplate what the speed and the size of future aeroplanes may be, and to consider what effect they may have in war time!'

We must get to work—that was the advice of the *Daily Telegraph*: the words 'air power' will soon have just as important a meaning as the phrase 'naval power'. And the *Daily Chronicle* forecast: 'Soon fleets of aeroplanes will move through the skies in all weathers and rivalry between nations will take on new forms.'

And so, just because a daring expert had achieved an outstanding success, and just because a flying machine had flown more than 20 miles—which, as the *Standard* noted more reassuringly, had all been foreseen—the British began to have nightmares about an air invasion. This fear of invasion, which is endemic in Britain, arises from time to time; and the most recent outbreak, last Spring, was particularly severe. Indeed, if one were to believe certain alarmists, the greatest-ever threat to the security of Britain had come in the early months of the year 1909, with danger coming from all quarters— from the sea, from the air, and even from under the earth. And so it was that on 18 May a Member of Parliament by the name of Ashley put a question in the House of Commons, and asked the Secretary for War if he knew that many German merchant vessels carried small guns, and that their captains had their letters of commission, their naval uniforms, and their ensigns—all ready to be shown if need arose.

About the same time, farmers in Wales were frightened out of their wits by a mysterious airship that appeared in the night. Hot on their heels came many others who saw, or thought they had seen, this phantom balloon which—in the most suspicious way—only appeared at night. Soon after this, an English tourist wrote in all seriousness to a major London newspaper to say that, during his return journey from Hamburg, he had heard a regular, heavy noise that came from beneath the waves and sounded like a drilling machine. He wondered if the Germans were at work on the construction of a tunnel under the North Sea! Finally, on 29 June in the House of Lords, Lord Ellenborough declared that, on the occasion of the naval review, it seemed unwise to assemble such a large fleet in the Thames. A few torpedoes would be enough to blow them up. During this period, when Lord Weardale addressed a meeting of the Peace Society, he said with total truth: 'In fact, the invasion panic is so great that for every restaurant waiter the English see a

German soldier in disguise. They scan the sky in search of German balloons; and they dare not open their letters for fear of finding a German bomb.'

A large number of writers have exploited this permanent fear, which is the undoubted symptom of a powerful, latent anxiety in a people who seem so calm. They describe the dreaded invasion, usually in the gloomiest way. Most of them are patriots, and they write to show the British that their lack of interest in military matters is an invitation to disaster. Others write with a political aim in mind—to censure the party in power for their lack of foresight; and others write in a spirit of pure amateurism. These accounts of invasion make up a large bouquet, but only a few flowers will be selected for presentation in the following pages.

Selection is necessary, firstly, because all these tales are similar in their main features; and the repetition of comparable narratives would inevitably prove monotonous. And secondly, because boundaries in fiction are not precisely defined, you have to fix them for yourself in order to avoid, for example, having to include Wells's highly acclaimed *War of the Worlds* in the list of invasion stories. That, rightly speaking, is also an account of the invasion of Great Britain.

Despite these limitations, if the ideas on which the accounts examined in the *Fictions guerrières* are based should appear too fantastic, one has to realize that they are not half so fantastic as the crack-pot plans of invasion which were officially promulgated. One example: in 1804 Bonaparte received a document from an inventor. He offered to transport the French army to England in six-man submarines which he had invented. The proposal had the signature of Fulton; and when the First Consul had read it, he wrote to M. de Champigny: 'What a pity that Citizen Fulton's project was not presented to me earlier. It could have changed the entire complexion of things.'

The war stories concocted by these British authors do not all invariably end in humiliating invasions. There are some that keep to the offensive, and these end in victories. Amongst these, *Le Futur Waterloo* by Cairnes stands out from all the rest. Indeed, the engaging nature of that account of a successful war against France will, no doubt, justify the major place it has in these *Fictions guerrières*.[6]

Paris, 1 November 1909

Incidents of the Coming Invasion of England

Ten years into the new century the mythology of the war-to-come with Germany was complete. By 1910 all the elements in the tale of the 'Invasion of England' had made their special contributions to the consolidated version of secret preparations, spies and the Army in Waiting, sudden naval attacks, enemy landings, and the bombardment of London. The myth had evolved rapidly from the earliest notions about the hostile intentions of the enemy-to-be, which began to circulate after 1900, to the full-scale horror story in Le Queux's Invasion of 1910, *which first appeared in the* Daily Mail *in 1906. The counter-attack gathered momentum in 1908, when A. A. Milne took to mocking the high seriousness of Le Queux's tales of spies and invaders in a series of occasional squibs in* Punch. *On 26 May 1908, for instance, he had a hilarious account of 'The Secret Army Aeroplane' in which he warned readers in the Le Queux style (no difficulty there) that 'a dastardly attempt is about to be made to wrest the supremacy of the air from our grasp.' The preamble to the story mocks Le Queux and aims a shaft against Lord Northcliffe: 'Mr. William Le Queux wishes to deny indignantly that the following tale was written by him. On the contrary, he identifies himself completely with the proprietor of the* Daily Mail *in deprecating the publishing of spy stores.'*

The opposition went on to produce some remarkably derisive reactions to the propaganda stories. One notable counter-blast appeared in P. G. Wodehouse's comic inversion of the 'Invasion of England' story in The Swoop *in 1909; and in 1910 Heath Robinson had great fun with all the variants of the invasion myth in eleven full-page cartoons in* The Sketch.

The reactions of P. G. Wodehouse and Heath Robinson on the British side, like those of Carl Siwinna in his Vademecum für Phantasiestrategen *(pp. 296–313), show that many readers in Britain and Germany did not share in the enthusiasm that writers of future-war stories took for granted. There can be no doubt that there was a growing opposition to the frequent chauvinism of this fiction. Indeed, the editor of* The Sketch *was clearly confident that his middle-class readers would welcome an elaborate send-up of the invasion myth in all its parts, since he commissioned that most ingenious of artists, Heath Robinson, to make fun of German spies in Epping Forest and in the Greco-Roman galleries of the British Museum. His series of 11 cartoons began on 20 April 1910. In the caption to the first entry the editor gave an emphatic nod and a big wink to the readers: 'So many authors have described in detail the invasion of England by Germany that Mr Heath Robinson's patriotism has led him to make a thorough investigation of the subject with some remarkable results.' What now follows is a long forgotten but most important series of images that deserves a special place in the Hoover War Library and in the Imperial War Museum.*

I German spies in Epping Forest

The original caption expected readers to know the major elements in the 'Invasion of England' story, since Heath Robinson promised to display all he had found about 'German spies galore in Epping Forest, soldiers of the Kaiser ingeniously disguised in many ways and very much on the watch. His other revelations will be published week by week.'

II With the aid of an ingenious device, the Germans send English dispatches astray

After the discoveries reported last week, the editor writes, Heath Robinson 'discloses the ingenious turn-table sign-post designed to send English dispatches astray.'

III German officers endeavouring to enter an Englishman's home in disguise

Here Heath Robinson takes one of the principal myths of the 'Invasion of England' stories—the ceaseless activity of enemy agents—and reduces the projected menace to a farce of incompetent enemy soldiers. 'An Englishman's home' is a direct reference to Guy du Maurier's play of that name.

IV A masked raid on Yarmouth beach

Four weeks from the beginning of the cartoon series Heath Robinson had got into his stride. There was no lack of material for an artist eager to take the idea of secret German invaders a trifle further than the fantasies to be found in the original future-war stories. 'A masked raid on Yarmouth beach' is the then familiar notion of a sudden German foray carried to an absurd conclusion.

V German troops, disguised as British excursionists, crossing the North Sea

Careful examination of this cartoon (the boxes marked Lager *and* Schnitzel, *for example) will reveal the ingenious ways in which Heath Robinson chose to mock the primary ideas in the great invasion myth.*

VI German spies in the Græco-Roman galleries of the British Museum

Heath Robinson's acute sense of the grotesque takes control of the images in this cartoon—the dozing policeman, the goddess Minerva, and the physically challenged representation of a German Eros.

VII The hoisting of the hostage: silencing a German gun on the heights of Pontypridd

In the issue for 22 June 1910 the last five cartoons were devoted to the various stratagems and marvels of the British response to the German invaders. These followed page by page from the first, which showed this cunning scheme for hostage taking.

VIII Uh-land! Capturing Uhlans in the Westminster Bridge Road, with the kind
co-operation of the spiked helmets of the foe

IX Gather ye lilies while ye may: disguised Territorials in the German camp at the
Welsh Harp, Hendon

X Weight and do not see: Territorials eluding the vigilance of German sentries on the wastes of Wimbledon Common

XI 'Farewell, a long farewell to all our greatness': a German officer is removed from the
sphere of action on a detachable cliff-edge near Hove

*The series of illustrations for 'The Coming German Invasion of England'
ends with immense ingenuity and on a most appropriate note.*

Die Invasion Englands in englischer Beleuchtung

An early sign of German concern over the growth of British future-war stories was a well-informed and thoughtful article on British attitudes to 'the German invasion' (by a naval officer?) in the reputable Marine Rundschau *in November 1908.*

Invasion is a word that still fills the average Englishman of today with a more or less vague sense of horror. Is it a real possibility? Or is it just a nightmare story like *The Invasion of 1910*, read by hundreds of thousands in the *Daily Mail*, and like many similar literary productions of recent years that have presented the great British public with their long and biased accounts?

There can be no doubt that in Britain, at this very moment, they are all, once again, generally preoccupied with thoughts of an invasion—only by the German army, of course. In certain newspapers German espionage is a regular feature. Never before has this rabble-rousing propaganda against Germany had so widespread and so unsettling an effect on the country. The German fleet, less than one third as strong as the British, is supposed to clear the way across the North Sea for the unconquerable German army; and the building programme of the German fleet—today and tomorrow—has the sole objective of snatching world power from the island kingdom for ever. This idea surfaces again and again in the British Press and in personal contacts even with people who think seriously about politics. And this is in spite of the fact that there are constant assurances from Germany, in print, in written statements and in speeches, that an invasion of Great Britain by German troops is total fantasy; that an invasion would be contrary to the elementary principles that decide the commitment and the efficiency of military resources; and that it is eternally at odds with the unquestionable superiority of the British fleet. There is simply no believing our constantly repeated assurance that the German fleet has been created for one sole purpose: as a maritime defence force to guard the sea frontiers of the great German Reich, to ensure the safety of German coastal waters, and in addition to protect and to promote peaceful trade overseas.

Recently, however, some publications have appeared in a short space of time which, at least in the opinion of some knowledgeable judges, reveal a calmer approach. They seek a free and open discussion of our actual relationship; and we can only wish that their principal ideas will have the widest publicity in Britain. These appear in a series of articles ...

The author lists these articles (in the Morning Post *and in the* United
Services Magazine*); he goes on to summarize their main points, and at the
end he gives his conclusions. He begins by commenting on British views of
German intentions.*

The final judgment is left to the reader, who will find that in Britain
they can also think calmly and clearly even on so controversial a
topic as invasion. The sensible and informed considerations of these
knowledgeable writers lead to the conclusion that such an invasion
is unthinkable so long as the British fleet with all its far greater
strength continues to guard the island kingdom. These British views
are:

THE GERMAN POLITICAL OBJECTIVE

Whenever there is any talk about the possibility of an invasion, the
authorities always calm national apprehensions by pointing to the
overwhelming superiority of the British fleet. The force of that
pronouncement ends all further serious discussion. In like manner,
the War Office and the Admiralty say that everything is most confi-
dential and top secret, and that any mention of possible
counter-measures is nothing but surmise. However, this secretive-
ness is damaging in one area in which the entire country is so greatly
interested and for which they should all work closely together. On
the other hand, it is no longer a secret that an ever-increasing
number of German officers and agents travel through the country.
They make sketches of railways, bridges, telegraph communications,
munition dumps, and they note the number of available motor-cars,
horses, and so on.

Hence, it comes as no surprise that, given the constant encouragement from the Press over the years, the country should be
anxious about the political aims of the country which, in addition to
maintaining the most powerful army in the world, has at its disposal
a battle fleet that from year to year grows both in size and in power.
Germany is full of aggressive and ambitious plans for the future;
Germany is envious of Great Britain, of its trade and its empire. So,
it follows that there is the political possibility of a war with Britain
and of an invasion of the United Kingdom.

*The author goes through the main points in his selected texts, and he
concludes with his own view of the invasion.*

So much, then, for this summary of the opinions of some informed persons in Britain on invasion and the danger of invasion. As mentioned at the start, we will not embark on detailed comments about these ideas. Any reader with maritime experience will recognize the extraordinary difficulties which have been hinted at in a cursory manner; and he will subject them to the close scrutiny of his naval and navigational knowledge. Anyone who does not understand the naval and navigational difficulties should certainly not make public any opinion on invasion which will be read or heard by many. In a word, anyone who does not know the North Sea may not pass judgment on the necessary tactical and strategic conditions for landings or for the safety of a fleet in temporary command of the sea. It will, therefore, be clear what a myth the countless press statements about invasion have already created. They are for the most part the work of layfolk or—what is much worse—they are accounts deliberately falsified for layfolk.

If the opinions of British experts reproduced here could spread throughout the country with lasting effect, then the fear of Germany espionage and of a German invasion would diminish. Germany, which has a three-and-a-half times smaller fleet, has no thoughts of invading Britain—its soldiers are too good for that.

We end with a few comments which have recently appeared in print in Germany:

> Fortunately this question [that is, an offensive war against Britain] is not for us to decide at all. Since the appearance of Admiral Mahan's book (*The Influence of Sea Power in History*) it is more than ever certain that Britain could only be defeated by a power that seized permanent command of the British sea. That has to be a fleet that has not only reached the same size as the Royal Navy, but is also superior in big battleships. Boxed in between France and Russia, Germany has to maintain the greatest army in the world throughout the whole of the twentieth century. It is obviously beyond the capacity of the German economy to support at the same time a fleet which would outgrow that of the British. Sudden raids would be mere pinpricks against the marvellous isolation of the British people.

Vademecum für Phantasiestrategen

The sixty-one pages of Carl Siwinna's Vademecum fur Phantasiestrategen *('A Guide for Fantasy Strategists') (1908) provide additional and striking evidence of a general interest in, and concern for, the European debate about the future-war stories. The author assumes that his readers will be familiar with the warning projections of Beowulf, Hansa, Moriturus and the rest of the German armchair warriors; and he expects they will know the main points in the German version of William Le Queux's* Invasion of 1910. *His aptly named 'Guide for Fantasy Strategists' is the most remarkable of all the counter-blasts against the ideas and intentions of the many writers who turned out their tales of the* Zukunftskrieg *and of 'the Next Great War'.*

Carl Siwinna ignored all contemporary examples of the French Guerres de demain. *They were no more than variations on an old theme that had not changed since the War of 1870, whereas the political thinking behind the British and German stories had erupted into the new and increasingly aggressive fantasies of writers like William Le Queux and August Niemann. Siwinna works his way through the devices and absurd situations in this future-war fiction, laying about him with great energy and treading heavily on British and German toes.*

AN ACCOUNT OF THE NEXT WAR AS A CHRISTMAS PRESENT

One can compare oneself in activeness and resourcefulness with Herr Grünlich and yet one can be unlucky, which is, by the way, proof that Thomas Mann accurately portrayed Herr Grünlich and his fate simply because the man with the golden sideburns was likewise unlucky.[7]

If I do not compare myself and my situation with his, the thing that has happened to me is most annoying. The reason is both interesting and has its own particular charm. To put it briefly: the two kisses, exchanged between the German Kaiser and the King of England not so long ago on German soil, have wrecked great hopes. Indeed, they have led to a sudden burst of very different expectations. So, I had the idea of giving the German people an account of the Next War as a Christmas present. But all the publishers in Germany, whom I had approached with my original proposition, have been so depressed and despondent because of those kisses that, as recently as this Autumn, they have all been saying that they are virtually overwhelmed with manuscripts of every kind. Quite apart from that, it seems for the moment that no one in Germany is eager to hear about war. Our most important politicians are expecting the immediate publication of the *Entente Cordiale* which will unite all nations against militarism and will control the forces of reaction.

Naturally, people are happy to subordinate their own intentions and reservations to world events of this kind. Indeed, the prospect has made such an impression on me, that I would like to give my fellow citizens a truly brilliant display of altruism. Perhaps the situation could change again: there could be a cry for war, and in that way business expectations would be completely altered. In one move there would be once again a vast market for accounts of future world wars. So, I believe that it is a really useful public work, if I try to provide a guide for all who write about the future in order to give them the benefit of my observations and of my inner experiences. During the last year and a half a small selection of such war stories has been on offer. Now, it is well known that Goethe, without ever defending the right to plagiarize, often declared himself unequivocally in favour of using actual experiences and achievements. Even creative writers should not ignore this hint from the master. By that I do not wish to say that all writers—and I include authors of war stories—have so far refused such opportunities; for I hope to show that writers can use far better material, and perhaps far more unobtrusively than ever before. More about that later.

EXTERNAL AESTHETICS

Before an author even begins to consider the contents of the book he intends to write, he must always be clear about such important matters as: the title, the cover, and the name that he will use as the author.

To begin, as is only proper, with the last matter: the question of the author's name is most important. Whenever the book appears in a shop window, the first thing to catch the eye will be the author's name, or if the name cannot be made out at a distance, then people go in and ask. Here the first difficulty arises. Should the author have his name in large letters on the cover? This is the problem. If he does, then maybe the name will attract a purchaser, or it may leave a purchaser cold. Perhaps he thinks: What good can come out of Nazareth (or what sort of sense can the fellow write?) and then he goes on his way. But, if he can be enticed into the shop, then much has already been gained. He will hear nothing but good about the book and the author, and he will probably be embarrassed to leave without making a purchase. This problem can be avoided to a certain degree by a well-chosen cover illustration. (This thought has been a guiding principle with me.) When it comes to the reviewer's copy, the author's name is clearly far more important than the cover illustration, if it attracts the interest of the reviewers. These gentlemen are usually rather insensitive to pictures, but on the other hand an effective title can arouse their curiosity enough for them to look inside the book. It would, however, be in the best interests of publishers and readers to cut the pages of the review copies beforehand, otherwise the chances of the book being read will be seriously reduced. It may be interjected that this does not relate solely to the type of book we are discussing. That is true. None the less, it does apply to them as well; and if many of them come out together or one after the other in a short period of time, then it is unquestionably a matter of great importance.

But to return to the names of authors—there are various possibilities here. If the writer is known as an author, it can be very useful simply to have his own name on the book, but only if his name does not reveal the subject and the ending of the book. It was undoubtedly right that the author of the *Weltkrieg* did not choose a pseudonym and did not publish anonymously. That book came out about eighteen months ago and it marked the start of the blossom time of these war fantasies, the end of which unfortunately we seem to be witnessing. He was followed by the author of *1906: Der Zusammenbruch der alten Welt*. He called himself 'Seestern', and in that way shrouded himself in a subtle veil of secrecy. He was succeeded by: Hansa, Beowulf, Moriturus, and recently Nordlicht. From this last writer, the historian of time-to-come can see how not to do things.[8] Nordlicht reminds one too much of Seestern but he cannot rouse the same interest. The crafty Beowulf, on the other hand, added as the sub-title of his story the words, 'Vision eines Seefahrers', whilst at the same time ashamedly admitting that he belongs, or had indeed belonged, to the warlike band of sea-farers and so was at least able in the purely technical sense of the term to assume such rights.

Then, Hansa put his name in such big letters on the cover that he achieved the same objective. After that he had the idea (too late, however, to be a really good one) to write another pamphlet and put his own name and rank next to his pseudonym. In this way the two stories gained in respectability, and they must have given lay readers the confidence to believe they would truly learn how the German war of the future would evolve. Moriturus had the same idea: he even wrote on the cover that his book was objective, and he had a large naval battle-flag printed on it so that his competence could not be called into question. As if that were not enough, above and beneath the battle-flag he added a terse sub-title: *Mit deutschen Waffen über Paris nach London*. Thus, it was apparent enough that the readers would know for sure that the affair would end well and that they would not have any unpleasant or disturbing impressions. Now that means a great deal to many people.

These points should make future chroniclers of the *Zukunftskrieg* note above all that they must avoid at all costs any similarities in names and titles. Perhaps it would be profitable to revert to ancient and forgotten writings for ideas? For instance, how would it do to have: 'Videant Consules'; 'How did it happen?'; or, to choose something new, 'Die Prinzenschlacht' or 'Der Seefahrtsprinz'?

The German translation of *The Invasion of 1910* merits a specially laudatory mention. The author, William Le Queux, who had every right to fear that he was unknown in Germany, had entered under his name: 'Naval Battles by Admiral H. W. Wilson'. Naturally that immediately achieved its objective and some reviewers wrote in wonderment that it was quite extraordinary that a man like Admiral Wilson, commander of the British Channel Fleet, should find time in the midst of all his duties to set down his thoughts on the course of modern naval battles in Mr. Le Queux's book.[9] Of course, it was regrettable that the episode was not true, for unbelievable though it may appear, the Admiral is not the only one with the name of Wilson in England. On the contrary, according to detailed enquiries, it is said to be a common enough name. In any case one has to marvel at the self sacrifice of the naval writer, Wilson, that he allowed himself to be presented to German readers as the commander of the largest British fleet. Of course, we have no intention of holding this little lie against the author and the publisher; but it is quite another question whether it can serve us as a good example for the future. It would hardly do for internal use, since the names of our admirals could readily be found in the Navy Active List, and that would help to identify them. Besides it would hardly carry any weight in Britain and France. Maybe it would be possible in the German colonies—even there people have become sufficiently educated. It is common knowledge that Herr Paasche at home may be on his high horse and Germany at the same time may be wasting away with a disease they call bureaucracy.[10] However much one may admire the ingenuity of the *Invasion*, any future repetition is to be discouraged.

However, there is undeserved recognition for the cover illustration of this book. The author had undoubtedly been thinking of Ben Akiba and had coolly borrowed the image from the advertisement for the opening of the Simplon Tunnel. Two men, shown in blood-red colours, peer through a small port-hole over a rather small gun which is depressed towards the sea. On the horizon there is a ship going down in flames and a greenish-yellow stretch of water. The two men in red are clearly feeling very faint—bent double with the unmistakeable symptoms of sea-sickness, leaning far out so as not to spoil the proverbial spotlessness of the battleship. At such a time so high a level of self-command inspires admiration.

It is evident that the cover of the Le Queux book shows signs of enterprising plagiarism. Were the contents to correspond, that would not be of any consequence. Hansa, in his matter-of-fact manner, disdains such illustrations and simply resorts to exhortation, whilst the hapless Beowulf in his striving after 'realism' has adorned the cover of his book with a bird's eye view of Heligoland. That leaves the reader free to think what he likes, but the immediate impression will probably be one of astonishment at the triangular shape of the island, after it has become clear to him that it must be Heligoland. Then, the brain will get to work, and it will dawn on the reader that the island of Heligoland will have a major role in any Anglo-German naval war.

I liked Seestern best, since his cover illustration shows a battleship wreathed in gun-smoke, battle ensigns on all the masts and yard-arms, firing off like mad in all directions. From that one knows where one stands, and the only regret is that there are no real explosions going on. In contrast, Nordlicht displays a rather small gun-turret, and the would-be purchaser will probably say to himself that there is less fantasy and more explanation in the two cover illustrations. The question for the future is not exactly simple: we can no longer go on repeating ourselves. Probably many have already thought of a theme with which an unknown gentleman has already led the way forward in his book, *Völker Europas*: Death riding horseback and in the background a town in flames. Stop there! Maybe that is the source of a good idea: how would it be if an artist were to show some corpses or ghosts with evil faces floating on a greenish-yellow sea against black storm clouds or a red sky? Charon is no longer in fashion, and it is essential to avoid all classical topics. Perhaps it might also be possible to employ the Flying Dutchman in a modern form.

There is one motif which likewise has not yet been used: it would be no bad thing to introduce warlike but true-to-life portraits of well-known admirals and generals. One might envisage two stages. First, in order to represent the tension of the immediate pre-war period, it would be necessary to bring in the diplomats. The two sides, separated by a frontier line or a stream, look at each other in a cool yet courteous way, but no one can tell what dark thoughts lurk behind the mask. The second stage is all furious activity: men press electric buttons, the telegraph works incessantly. All their faces show total concentration and calm deliberation. However, engaged in serious but quiet conversation with junior functionaries who look trustingly up to him, the Reichs-Deputy Erzberger stands in the background.[11]

If one is not an artist, it is difficult to give any detailed advice on the extremely important problem of the cover illustration. In general, however, it will almost certainly be right not to use previous motifs any more. Modern styles should be the order of the day; and authors would also have to show that wars do not depend solely on the sword but maybe even more on economic resources. The take-up of loans can perhaps be pictured in an impressive way by using particularly striking physiognomies.

To come back once more to the question of authorship: If you are an expert, you have earned a high rank. So, don't hold back! Are you too tactful to reveal it on the dust-jacket? Then you can act like Hansa, who in his practical way records his commands and his service record in his two brochures, whilst hinting at his authority through the accompanying letter of the publishers and through discreet hints in the accompanying notes (supplied by the publishers). If you are not a service expert, but an established writer, then you can adopt some inspired military or naval pseudonym; or you can use your own name, but, you will then have to have a note, somewhere and somehow, to say that 'distinguished experts' have helped to write the story.

These are all matters of quite exceptional importance. You must consider them from every aspect, and discuss them beforehand from every angle with your publisher. The more purposeful and the more striking the cover, the less value—that is, work, effort, and factual expertise—needs to be added to the contents. Aspiring authors must keep this fact foremost in their minds, and some of them should make it their first consideration. It is not possible to require that everyone is an expert in the subject. In the hustle and bustle of modern life, how can anyone find the time to make a thorough study of the topics that are to be discussed? Only philistines and people with antiquated views can make such a demand. If anyone has the idea and the confidence to write a war fantasy, that person has *ipso facto* the inalienable right of the citizen to voice his opinion—a right that the German people have won in hard-fought battles. No one should dispute or denigrate this. But anyone who feels the compelling need should bear in mind that—between ourselves—the more of an ignoramus one is, the more important is the appearance of the book. As far as that goes, one should try anything, for every effort will be well rewarded and will produce a profit.

As I have indicated before, it is at times quite useful for a writer to reveal on the dust-jacket how he envisages what will happen. In general there are two types of reader you have to consider. The first group is undoubtedly the more numerous and is easy to please. In any *Zukunftskrieg* these are the ones who want to see Germany brought through a succession of mishaps and difficulties; and they would take it badly if they were not able to finish the book with the feeling that in the end everything 'will turn out for the best'. Others want an never-ending succession of German victories and only a few casualties. The title of the Moriturus book provides a good example of this, whilst the title of the anonymous *Völker Europas* states that in the course of the world war everything will lead imperceptibly to an end which all enlightened and liberal Germans see as worth fighting for. All authors up till now have been careful to avoid suggesting an unfortunate ending for the war in the title of their books. Now that would be wrong in all circumstances. Just as a reader is right not to be pleased with a novel that does end with a happy union, it goes without saying that in some way or other the author of a *Zukunftskrieg* has to produce a successful conclusion. Naturally, it is neither risky nor prejudicial if an author like Hansa reveals on the dust-jacket that Hamburg and Bremen do not have adequate defences, and that in the event of a war with Britain they would perhaps have a bad time.

Who would not willingly trust the reliable expert, and who is without doubts and does not expect to find unpleasant episodes in a war story? On the contrary, such specialization is most useful; but it should never be suggested that everything could go badly wrong. If that were to happen, you will be known from the start as a total pessimist, and with the superior smile of absolute confidence the reader would put your book unread to one side; or, what would be much worse, the critics would read it from the start with an uncontrollable urge to write it off at a stroke.

I would incline to the conviction that for the time being *Weltkrieg*

('World War') should not figure any more in the title of books. It might prove successful if contrariwise a writer were to begin—on the title-page, that is—with *Der deutsch-russische Krieg und seine Folgen* ('The Russo-German War and its Consequences') or *Die Selbstzerfleischung des Dreibundes* ('How the Triple Alliance Tore Itself to Pieces'). Do not be worried at having to look for new ideas. There is plenty of good material available. It is only a question of the title and some clever linking passages for which there are some extremely good examples in the political reviews of some daily newspapers. Indeed, the most recent war stories have made me think that no one has really hit upon Russia. That would be topical and I think that, if it could be managed, it would be appropriate to include a caustic reference to Russia in the title. That would certainly ensure the approbation of all free-thinking Germans. It would be easy to find a marvellous cover illustration for this. You could have, for example, something on the lines of a Fury, representing the European war and grinning horribly, as it crawls out of the gaping belly of Russian despotism.

THE CONTENTS

The narratives in these future wars differ from those in many other books: that is, the authors have to begin by making it fairly clear what their subject will be. Of course, I do not mean that in any factual sense. That is something completely different. However, the reader must soon discover where the story is going, and for my part I must know the way in which I intend to take the story. What that means I have already indicated, when I was discussing the matter of titles; and, once again, one should strongly advise against letting the war end in total disaster for Germany.

On this point the conduct of Mr. Le Queux is particularly instructive. He worked out two very different conclusions for his war story: one for his English readers, or as they say over there *for home consumption*, and the other for translations. That clever fellow had wisely foreseen that the British would take against him and his book, if he did not at least end with a British victory. Naturally, that is always easy to arrange. One side can win just as easily as the other; and there is not the least difficulty in transferring the causes of victory from one nation to another, nor in giving superiority to one or to the other. As for the consequences of such an action, which clashes with the original scheme of things, a writer has to be somewhat on guard and has to look fairly carefully through the narrative to see that in the earlier chapters he has not left clear indications of the inferiority or of the superiority of one side or another. In other respects these indications have a lot to be said for them: they prepare their readers for the catastrophe, but at the same time they keep them in suspense, since they think that other factors may still perhaps come into play. Finally, they see that their presentiments have not deceived them, and so they feel a sense of satisfaction in finding that they have been right. Incidentally, an author has always to work hard to give readers this feeling, and then he is behind 'his' book.

To return to Mr. Le Queux. In the English edition he allows the war to end with trifling losses, whereas in the German edition things go very badly for the British right from the very beginning.[12] Since Mr. Le Queux had no decided views of his own, as his distortion of generally known facts and relations shows clearly enough, these separate narratives were a clever idea. Many of his readers certainly wanted to know what he wrote in the other edition and for that reason they bought the other version. People are always wondering whether they will come to a happy or an unhappy ending. Hitherto all the German *Zukunftskriege* have had a good, and in any case always acceptable, ending. In most of them the British and the French had to pay immense sums of money, and in the end things went badly for them. That has apparently pleased their German readers; and I have no doubt that, if Germany were to be defeated, and robbed of Alsace-Lorraine and so on, they would have flung away the books in indignation and contempt.

And here a small complication arises, a difficulty not to be circumvented under any circumstance: if Britain as the enemy is not entirely eliminated, there remains the question of the Fleet. It has proved problematic even for all those who made it the point of origin in their stories and aspired to illustrate it in their descriptions. Most of all this concerns Seestern, whose book opens with the refusal to take part in a cruiser engagement. In his book he intends to show that the German parliament was to blame for allowing the strength of the German navy, for reasons of economy, to fall far below its proper level. So, the Germans have to be defeated at sea. From this supposition certain consequences followed, for Seestern saw instinctively that it would be awkward if the British took every possible advantage from their victory on the high seas. To prevent that he uses a method, but this we shall keep for later.

Earlier we referred to Niemann's *Weltkrieg* as the earliest future-war story; and in another connection this book may present a warning to future authors. It has dated rapidly and, in any case, it has been completely submerged in the subsequent flood of these stories. The main reason for this was probably Niemann's bad luck: he wrote shortly before the Russo-Japanese War and had an exceptionally high opinion of Russian military strength. Perhaps he went too far in displaying his ignorance of military and naval matters. On the other hand, his accounts of the *Hazardspiele* in India remain unforgettable, as does his love-story, to which we will refer later. Had the Russo-Japanese War not broken out, Niemann's stock would have fared better; but a gross error still remained: because India is too far away, it is impractical to locate the main action of the war there.

And then comes the question of the naval battles. Here, German readers want more; they want to see blood flow, or heads ripped off and battered limbs; they want the crack of exploding shells, and brains scattered in all directions. And throughout all this they wish to see the combatants display a steely calm, dark resolution, and bright enthusiasm. That is what they want to see, and they do not want it all wrapped up in just a couple of sentences. Then the Russo-Japanese War came soon after. Russia offended everyone, for they all had great respect for Russian military capabilities. It also affected the British, who largely affected a fear of a Russian threat to India; but it was no great trouble for them, so that nowadays they are just as much taken up with the Russian menace in Asia as ever they were before.

The overall point is: make a prudent choice of the time and place of the action in your stories so that in the near future the course of events will not make a complete liar of you. If you are just a little bit on the right side, then you have succeeded; but the risk is always present whenever a writer describes events of which he knows nothing, and then is later exposed as a false prophet. That must be avoided at all costs. Of course, it is certainly immaterial whether a year or even longer goes by, for a book does not last any longer; and then you will be able to show that, at the very time of writing, you were dealing with a very different set of circumstances. You would have got things exactly right, had the war then broken out, or you can say that you wrote your book shortly before the outbreak of the war.

If it is your intention to present your books as an urgent warning and a blazing admonition, then bear in mind: you will only reach a vast circle of readers if they have the impression that they are essentially all distinguished people, and that it will not cost them a fortune, neither in terms of effort nor of money, to achieve what you demand of them. Be unstinting in your praise, even if you think you are laying it on rather thickly. For those who are flattered, even unwillingly, praise can never seem enough; indeed it will seem hardly sufficient. The more a person is gratified, the more that person will be willing to admit to himself that you are right in everything else and he will not stop offering you his approval.

There is another general rule, against which several of our German authors have sinned. I can take it as common knowledge that the other future-war stories followed in relatively short succession quite soon after Seestern's book. Almost every one of them turned on their fore-runner and accused him of gross ignorance or at least of a complete lack of judgment. The thought, in itself surely not wholly without justification, makes one suspect that it usually stems from sincere conviction. One has to believe the authors that every one of them was entirely convinced he was presenting the true facts; and that every one of them knew for certain that he alone had full knowledge of all the relevant circumstances; and for this reason he was more able to foresee accurately the details of a war. Sincerity is always a dangerous thing, and likewise a sincere conviction is also dangerous.

Moreover, one must always consider whether or not there is another author in the production line. The latest arrival reckons he is undoubtedly right, and in this event the last, who is more right than all the others before him, is naturally a person of consequence. Unfortunately, only three small asterisks signalled this fact in the book *Völker Europas*. So, if you do not know that you will be the last, do not curse your predecessors too much. Try, rather, to ignore them or to treat them kindly; for that can only be to your advantage. It is quite another matter, however, if in fact you know far more than the rest, and you can demonstrate it in both a clear and a compelling way. But I would not advise you, for example, to pour scorn on your predecessor, just because he goes in for open warfare and you do not, or because you let the enemy press on to the Elbe and he reckons that that is impossible. You do not have any concrete evidence.

Matters are more favourable if, for example, you are an admiral and a valued collaborator. These are qualities that in German public opinion guarantee a certain infallibility. If you have not yet reached that eminence, then do not fail to list your various service appointments; and to add that you have far, far more experience and judgment to offer than the rest of the field. Hints of this kind rarely fail to have an effect. They are even more attractive than special notices, and in addition they have the added advantage that they make advertising unnecessary. In this respect one can only praise Hansa's way of proceeding. Soon after the publication of his war story he wrote a small book about the equipment of our fleet. In the preface he appeared under his real name with all the added authority of his lengthy record of service, and that showed that the Hansa of the war pamphlet was accurate in every detail. In his other arrangements, as already mentioned, he did not manage things in the best way, especially in the chronological order of his story; but I have no doubt that on the next occasion he will prove to be as accomplished as he will be successful. You will always do very well, if you let the word 'factual' shine through at times.

The author turns to consider the dangers of too much enthusiasm …

If you want to write an objective book, then do not go in for great displays of emotion. You can mention them briefly as something self-evident. Perhaps once or twice at the most you can let the emotions burst from a manly breast in all their elemental force, but no more than that. Everything else has to proceed swiftly and energetically in a cold and steely calm. As for the fiery passions beneath this surface appearance, these are revealed in the narrative and, as I have said, in those two outbursts of strong feelings.

It is quite understandable that a writer can go over the top when it comes to emotion; and the author of *Völker Europas* certainly hit the nail on the head when he stated that Seestern was quite wrong: that great emotional scenes would never happen in a *Zukunftskrieg*, rather one brief outburst. That is an original idea; but I would have found it more interesting to know who these German writers are who keep the emotions in check and where they let them rip. Perhaps an acoustic reproduction system might have much to recommend it here. Beowulf gives us an extremely gripping scene, when there is an outbreak of enthusiasm in the Officer Corps. It shows as much taste as knowledge of human nature that, just before a mission from which few will return, Beowulf has the commander of a torpedo-boat flotilla vow in exalted language—that he will not touch a drop of alcohol or of coffee until the beginning of the peace negotiations. The manliness of this decision certainly deserves the greatest respect; but unfortunately, the author himself impairs the effect of this striking scene, since he tacks on the fact that most of the officers would have made the same decision, though not all of them, however. Now that makes one take a hard look at their state of discipline. How do they manage to work together as a single unit?

And now that we are back to enthusiasm, we should take another

'William the Conqueror—a British dream. The fearful British look on the return of Halley's comet as a bad omen for the New Year. It appeared in 1066, the year when William the Conqueror landed in England'

look at Seestern's enthusiasm. He takes us to the square in front of the imperial palace in Berlin. Slowly, in a refined yet cumbersome manner, he opens the balcony door through which the Kaiser appears. This scene, I am convinced, has the most extraordinary effect on the majority of readers; but for the future the princes should be referred to once more. They are now close to adulthood; and it is really a great pity that not a single author has made use of this magnificent material. What one could do with such an opportunity! They could move their readers to tears, they could astonish them, or they could drive them wild with anger.

Later on Siwinna develops an ironic commentary on the general treatment of failure and success in the future-war stories ...

German diplomacy, as presented in these war stories, has always functioned with extraordinary success, speed, boldness and justice. Now, it might be worth considering, as well as being a welcome change, if authors did something to make German diplomacy less perfect. That would immediately lead to delightful complications. In particular, land warfare does not have to proceed so monotonously according to plan, as the practice has been so far. Instead of the unstoppable, victorious advance of the German army, it is far better to open with major mistakes. The blame for these can fall on the vacillations and shortsightedness of the Wilhelmstrasse. That would really reveal the furious rage and the indestructible power of the German people. Then, in the later chapters readers can await the progress of the land campaign with more or less equanimity. The armies will be sent into enemy territory, and in Germany people will think that perhaps the troops will not have it all their own way but they will do their job well.

I hear the questions: how can we do badly, since we probably have the edge over the French in terms of numbers, discipline, and the quality of our officers? On no account should you deny this: the story requires unfortunate circumstances such as the mistakes of the diplomats that lead to delays in mobilization; in addition there are civil disturbances, and finally the troublesome attitude of Austria and Russia. (You can always leave the Emperor of Austria to die, if you wish!) Even Denmark, in a state of incomprehensible blindness, thinks of the flesh-pots of South Jutland and adopts an unfriendly attitude.

It does not matter if this is in keeping with the predicted course of events. What is much more important is the major split that develops in the German armies as they are obliged to move towards widely spaced frontiers. There can be no question about it: for a time we have to have enemy soldiers on German soil. Although the author of *Völker Europas* recognized this point, he made no use of it. From the start he treats this invasion as a hopeless operation for the French. They rapidly find themselves in a most unfavourable strategic situation, and so the reader's attention flags; for the reader is never given any significant cause for alarm. But we must alarm and cast down our readers, if their spirits are to be raised later on. That way the terrible uprising of the German people comes as a greater relief. With such simple means you can obtain the result you want, because the normal course of events would imply an intensification of the action.

Mind you, all this relates to the drift of the story to which other considerations have to be subordinated. As an example of the consistent exploitation of this tendency, the British war stories are an almost perfect example. They have been written to make the British fearful of a German invasion with the political aim of promoting the enlargement of their army. Now, there can be little doubt amongst all impartial and unbiased people that, once a German army had landed in England, its victory would be secure. That, for most Britons, is far from self-evident. Indeed, they have always believed that their soldiers and their generals are the best in the world, and every British victory has accordingly been exaggerated. The first and only time that Napoleon and Wellington confronted each other, Napoleon was defeated and his army destroyed.

Now, in spite of this high opinion which the British have of themselves, Mr. Le Queux has devised some good stratagems in order to demonstrate to his fellow countrymen the possibility of defeat. First of all, there is the matter of espionage. Le Queux and other English writers know very well that many thousands of German spies are permanent residents in the country. Most of them work as waiters, but they do other jobs as well. Of course, they are always in touch with the German authorities and they are always ready to cut all the telegraph wires and disrupt the telephone installations in their area. And so, it is hardly surprising that one morning the unfortunate British suddenly find themselves facing a mighty German army on the sacred soil of Albion. Their fleet has naturally kept discreetly away from the action long enough for the German troops to come ashore: precise details are not given. That was basically a nonsense or a grotesque lie on the part of Mr. Le Queux; but for Le Queux and his colleagues it was their only way of arranging events to suit their stories; and so, with a few conciliatory phrases about the where-abouts of the British fleet, they get down to the business of the invasion.

German authors of future-war stories, thank heavens, have no need to employ such contrived devices, since it is obvious that the weakness of our fleet must lead to our inevitable defeat at sea. However, there is one first-rate idea of this same British writer to which attention should be drawn: the German invasion force has a dreadful and devilish weapon at its disposal—the petrol bomb. It has the advantage that it is very small, and so the resident German spies have no difficulty in carrying it about in the pockets of their coats or of their trousers. Just when no one is looking, they take the infernal device from their pocket and throw it at a house or some similar building; and then they move on in total calm as though nothing had happened. The house, the fortification, or whatever it is, imme-diately goes up in flames or it promptly collapses. Naturally, any decent nation has no defence against such methods of warfare, and so need not feel ashamed at defeat.

And now, Siwinna offers abundant ironic advice about the embellishment of the narratives ...

THE DIPLOMATIC MODES OF GETTING ROUND THINGS

Now that we are clear about theories and principles, it is time to start on the details. You have to decide whether you are going to describe no more than one episode in the war or you mean to relate the entire course of the war, together with the diplomatic and 'world political' background. Although there is much to recommend the latter form, it does require a considerable amount of work. Should you want to take that on, then my advice is: first, get yourself the works of Herr Gregor Samaroff, alias Meding, beforehand from a lending library.[13] From them you will learn the proprieties of diplo-matic dealings as well as a vast number of useful hints: how to conduct intrigues, and how to express oneself in the 'diplomatic' style. Your readers must unswervingly believe that you have the most intimate knowledge, but for obvious reasons you cannot reveal everything. The gentleman with the three stars allows foreign diplo-mats to conduct really pleasant conversations, even though they are rather long. In this, however, he commits an error that has been noted before. He does not introduce any German diplomats, although it is precisely these people we want to see; and we want to hear how cunningly and yet honourably, how ably and successfully, they go about their business. Of course, for the sake of contrast it is quite permissible, indeed desirable that a rash, arrogant fellow be amongst them.

But never forget that the Kaiser is the life and soul of the whole affair. The Germans are only too happy, and here I particularly include your readers, when the German Emperor appears as a universal genius the likes of whom has no comparison in history nor, indeed, in the realm of possibilities. At one and the same time he has to conduct diplomatic negotiations, compose his own telegraphic messages, direct every phase of the war on land and at sea, defeat the enemy within and bind them to himself with generosity and magnanimity; he has to conclude treaties and, what is equally important, he must receive the generals and representatives of defeated enemy states.

The characteristics of individual field-marshals and statesmen must, of course, be known to you. You have to know whether their services in war were as great as people expected of them in peace. This, naturally, can only happen in exceptional cases; for in general the names that cannot be found in the ranks of successful leaders are the ones we looked on with pride and hope in times of peace. You would meet with mixed emotions at the negotiating table if you were to drop a few bitter words into the conversation, just as you pleased.

You know it is a tradition for the commander-in-chief to remain alone on some hilltop or other during a battle—silent like a bronze statue. Now and then he has a smoke, but he never utters a word and at the most he only gives a brief nod. Perhaps it would be an innovation, and consequently advisable, to make at least one exception to this rule. As far as admirals are concerned, they belong by tradition in the forward armoured conning tower. So, if I were in your place, I would say: 'He could not bear to stay in the box-like cell and he felt unhappy that, unlike so many of his men, he enjoyed special protection. [That is not strictly true: in the last war the conning towers proved on many occasions to be death-traps; but this is of no importance.] He climbed up onto the wind-swept structure of the azimuth compass. From there he could see the dramatic scene in all its terrible beauty and could have a bird's eye view as he directed his squadrons. Shells, shrapnel and armour-piercing projectiles screamed round him in a whirring, ringing, sometimes an almost deadly uproar. In the very first moment, this solitary man by the compass had his cap ripped from his head, and his scant grey hairs tossed in the wind.' And that is more or less it. You could add: 'What a difference to the General on his horse surrounded by the usual glittering retinue.'

It goes without saying that the prime example of an admiral has to be Prince Henry of Prussia—but there must be no mention of thinning grey hair. Again, it would be no bad thing if his life were the price of a brilliant victory at sea, or if it served as a painful reminder of the ruinous consequences of a lost battle. I cannot repeat often enough how important and how profitable it is for the success of your descriptions to make the fullest use of princes. And here what makes it so much easier for you is the fact that they have all-too-human characteristics which are well-known to the masses.

The Swoop! or, How Clarence Saved England

The next entry in this chapter, and first in order of merriment, comes from the man who became the greatest comic writer in twentieth-century English literature, and the most inventive humorous writer since Charles Dickens. It was still early days for P. G. Wodehouse when he wrote The Swoop! or, How Clarence Saved England: A Tale of the Great Invasion, *but already this singular variant on the German invasion story reveals the promise of coming achievements. The narrative maintains its own logic of the absurd: the country 'was not merely beneath the heel of the invader. It was beneath the heels of nine invaders.' They had all arrived simultaneously on the August Bank Holiday; and, in contrast to the universal terror and panic in the invasion stories, bored indifference is the order of the day in the Wodehouse version. Like Carl Siwinna, Wodehouse expected the reader to be familiar with the stock situations in contemporary future-war fiction. The deadly earnestness of well-known episodes—the ritual bombardment of London, for instance—becomes the total farce of the things that do not go according to plan. In his first chapter, for example, Wodehouse sends up the opening scene in Guy du Maurier's* An Englishman's Home. *That patriotic drama was still playing to full houses when* The Swoop *was published in the May of 1909.*

AN ENGLISHBOY'S HOME

August the First, 19– –

Clarence Chugwater looked around him with a frown, and gritted his teeth.

'England—my England!' he moaned.

Clarence was a sturdy lad of some fourteen summers. He was neatly, but not gaudily, dressed in a flat-brimmed hat, a coloured handkerchief, a flannel shirt, a bunch of ribbons, a haversack, football shorts, brown boots, a whistle, and a hockey-stick. He was, in fact, one of General Baden-Powell's Boy Scouts.

Scan him closely. Do not dismiss him with a passing glance; for you are looking at the Boy of Destiny, at Clarence MacAndrew Chugwater, who saved England.

Today those features are familiar to all. Everyone has seen the Chugwater Column in Aldwych, the equestrian statue in Chugwater Road (formerly Piccadilly), and the picture-postcards in the stationers' windows. That bulging forehead, distended with useful information; that massive chin; those eyes, gleaming behind their spectacles; that *tout ensemble*; that *je ne sais quoi*.

In a word, Clarence!

He could do everything that the Boy Scout must learn to do. He could low like a bull. He could gurgle like a wood-pigeon. He could imitate the cry of the turnip in order to deceive rabbits. He could smile and whistle simultaneously in accordance with Rule 8 (and only those who have tried this know how difficult it is). He could spoor, fell trees, tell the character from the boot-sole, and fling the squaler. He did all these things well, but what he was really best at was flinging the squaler.

Clarence, on this sultry August afternoon, was tensely occupied tracking the family cat across the dining-room carpet by its footprints. Glancing up for a moment, he caught sight of the other members of the family.

'England, my England!' he moaned.

It was indeed a sight to extract tears of blood from any Boy Scout. The table had been moved back against the wall, and in the cleared space Mr. Chugwater, whose duty it was to have set an example to his children, was playing diabolo. Beside him, engrossed in cup-and-ball, was his wife. Reggie Chugwater, the eldest son, the heir, the hope of the house, was reading the cricket news in an early edition of the evening paper. Horace, his brother, was playing pop-in-taw with his sister Grace and Grace's fiancé, Ralph Peabody. Alice, the other Miss Chugwater, was mending a Badminton racquet.

Not a single member of that family was practising with the rifle, or drilling, or learning to make bandages.

Clarence groaned.

'If you can't play without snorting like that, my boy,' said Mr.

Chugwater, a little irritably, 'you must find some other game. You made me jump just as I was going to beat my record.'

'Talking of records,' said Reggie, 'Fry's on his way to his eighth successive century. If he goes on like this, Lancashire will win the championship!'

'I thought he was playing for Somerset,' said Horace.

'That was a fortnight ago. You ought to keep up to date in an important subject like cricket.'

Once more Clarence snorted bitterly.

'I'm sure you ought not to be down on the floor, Clarence,' said Mr. Chugwater anxiously. 'It is so draughty, and you have evidently got a nasty cold. *Must* you lie on the floor?'

'I am spooring,' said Clarence with simple dignity.

'But I'm sure you could spoor better sitting on a chair with a nice book.'

'*I* think the kid's sickening for something,' put in Horace critically. 'He's deuced roopy. What's up, Clarry?'

'I was thinking', said Clarence, 'of my country—of England.'

'What's the matter with England?'

'She's all right,' murmured Ralph Peabody.

'My fallen country!' sighed Clarence, a not unmanly tear bedewing the glasses of his spectacles. 'My fallen, stricken country!'

'That kid', said Reggie, laying down his paper, 'is talking right through his hat. My dear old son, are you aware that England has never been so strong all round as she is now? Do you *ever* read the papers? Don't you know that we've got the Ashes and the Golf Championship, and the Wibbley-wob Championship, and the Spiropole, Spillikins, Puff-Feather, and Animal Grab Championships? Has it come to your notice that our croquet pair beat America last Thursday by eight hoops? Did you happen to hear that we won the Hop-skip-and-jump at the last Olympic Games? You've been out in the woods, old sport.'

Clarence's heart was too full for words. He rose in silence, and quitted the room.

'Got the pip or something!' said Reggie. 'Rum kid! I say, Hirst's bowling well! Five for twenty-three so far!'

Clarence wandered moodily out of the house. The Chugwaters lived in a desirable villa residence, which Mr. Chugwater had built in Essex. It was a typical Englishman's Home. Its name was Nasturtium Villa.

As Clarence walked down the road, the excited voice of a newspaper-boy came to him. Presently the boy turned the corner,

Clarence Chugwater, Boy
Scout Extraordinary, sees
the bad news of a German
landing in England

shouting, 'Ker-lapse of Surrey! Sensational bowling at the Oval!'

He stopped on seeing Clarence.

'Paper, General?'

Clarence shook his head. Then he uttered a startled exclamation, for his eye had fallen on the poster. It ran as follows:

SURREY

DOING

BADLY

GERMAN ARMY LANDS IN ENGLAND

THE INVADERS

Clarence flung the boy a halfpenny, tore a paper from his grasp, and scanned it eagerly. There was nothing to interest him in the body of the journal, but he found what he was looking for in the stop-press space. 'Stop press news,' said the paper. 'Fry not out, 104. Surrey 147 for 8. A German army landed in Essex this afternoon. Loamshire Handicap: Spring Chicken, 1; Salome, 2; Yip-i-addy, 3. Seven ran.'

Essex! Then at any moment the foe might be at their doors; more, inside their doors. With a passionate cry, Clarence tore back to the house.

He entered the dining-room with the speed of a highly-trained marathon winner, just in time once more to prevent Mr. Chugwater lowering his record.

'The Germans!' shouted Clarence. 'We are invaded!'

This time Mr. Chugwater was really annoyed.

'If I have told you once about your detestable habit of shouting in the house, Clarence, I have told you a hundred times. If you cannot be a Boy Scout quietly, you must stop being one altogether. I had got up to six that time.'

'But, father—'

'Silence! You will go to bed this minute; and I shall consider the question whether you are to have any supper. It will depend largely on your behaviour between now and then. Go!'

'But, father—'

Clarence dropped the paper, shaken with emotion. Mr. Chugwater's sternness deepened visibly.

'Clarence! Must I speak again?'

He stooped and removed his right slipper.

Clarence withdrew.

Reggie picked up the paper.

'That kid', he announced judicially, 'is off his nut! Hullo! I told you so! Fry not out, 104. Good old Charles!'

'I say,' exclaimed Horace, who sat nearest the window, 'there are two rummy-looking chaps coming to the front door, wearing a sort of fancy dress!'

'It must be the Germans,' said Reggie. 'The paper says they landed here this afternoon. I expect—'

A thunderous knock rang through the house. The family looked at one another. Voices were heard in the hall, and next moment the door opened and the servant announced 'Mr. Prinsotto and Mr. Aydycong'.

'Or, rather,' said the first of the two newcomers, a tall, bearded, soldierly man, in perfect English, 'Prince Otto of Saxe-Pfennig and Captain the Graf von Poppenheim, his aide-de-camp.'

'Just so—just so!' said Mr. Chugwater, affably. 'Sit down, won't you?'

The visitors seated themselves. There was an awkward silence.

'Warm day!' said Mr. Chugwater.

'Very!' said the Prince, a little constrainedly.

'Perhaps a cup of tea? Have you come far?'

'Well—er—pretty far. That is to say, a certain distance. In fact, from Germany.'

'I spent my summer holiday last year at Dresden. Capital place!'

'Just so. The fact is, Mr.—er—'

'Chugwater. By the way—my wife, Mrs. Chugwater.'

The Prince bowed. So did his aide-de-camp.

'The fact is, Mr. Jugwater,' resumed the prince, 'we are not here on a holiday.'

'Quite so, quite so. Business before pleasure.'

The prince pulled at his moustache. So did his aide-de-camp, who seemed to be a man of but little initiative and conversational resource.

'We are invaders.'

'Not at all, not at all,' protested Mr. Chugwater.

'I must warn you that you will resist at your peril. You wear no uniform—'

'Wouldn't dream of such a thing. Except at the lodge, of course.'

'You will be sorely tempted, no doubt. Do not think that I do not appreciate your feelings. This is an Englishman's Home.'

Mr. Chugwater tapped him confidentially on the knee.

'And an uncommonly snug little place, too,' he said. 'Now, if you will forgive me for talking business, you, I gather, propose making some stay in this country.'

The prince laughed shortly. So did his aide-de-camp. 'Exactly,' continued Mr. Chugwater, 'exactly. Then you will want some *pied-à-terre*, if you follow me. I shall be delighted to let you this house on remarkably easy terms for as long as you please. Just come along into my study for a moment. We can talk it over quietly there. You see, dealing direct with me, you would escape the middleman's charges, and—'

Gently but firmly he edged the prince out of the room and down the passage.

The aide-de-camp continued to sit staring woodenly at the carpet. Reggie closed quietly in on him.

'Excuse me,' he said; 'talking shop and all that. But I'm an agent for the Come One Come All Accident and Life Assurance Office. You have heard of it probably? We can offer you really exceptional terms. You must not miss a chance of this sort. Now here's a prospectus—'

Horace sidled forward.

'I don't know if you happen to be a cyclist, Captain—er—Graf; but if you'd like a practically new motor-bike, only been used since last November, I can let you—'

There was a swish of skirts as Grace and Alice advanced on the visitor.

'I'm sure', said Grace winningly, 'that you're fond of the theatre, Captain Poppenheim. We are getting up a performance of "Ici on parle Français", in aid of the fund for Supplying Square Meals to Old-Age Pensioners. Such a deserving object, you know. Now, how many tickets will you take?'

'You can sell them to your friends, you know,' added Mrs. Chugwater.

The aide-de-camp gulped convulsively.

Ten minutes later two penniless men groped their way, dazed, to the garden gate.

'At last,' said Prince Otto brokenly, for it was he, 'at last I begin to realize the horrors of an invasion—for the invaders.'

And together the two men staggered on.

ENGLAND'S PERIL

When the papers arrived next morning, it was seen that the situation was even worse than had at first been suspected. Not only had the Germans effected a landing in Essex, but, in addition, no fewer than eight other hostile armies had, by some remarkable coincidence, hit on that identical moment for launching their long-prepared blow.

England was not merely beneath the heel of the invader. It was beneath the heels of nine invaders.

There was barely standing-room.

Full details were given in the Press. It seemed that while Germany was landing in Essex, a strong force of Russians, under the Grand Duke Vodkakoff, had occupied Yarmouth. Simultaneously the Mad Mullah had captured Portsmouth; while the Swiss Navy had bombarded Lyme Regis, and landed troops immediately to westward of the bathing-machines. At precisely the same moment China, at last awakened, had swooped down upon that picturesque little Welsh watering-place, Lllgxtpll, and, despite desperate resistance on the part of an excursion of Evanses and Joneses from Cardiff, had obtained a secure foothold. While these things were happening in Wales, the army of Monaco had descended on Auchtermuchty, on the Firth of Clyde.[14] Within two minutes of this disaster, by Greenwich time, a boisterous band of young Turks had seized Scarborough. And, at Brighton and Margate respectively, small but determined armies, the one of Moroccan brigands, under Raisuli, the other of dark-skinned warriors from the distant isle of Bollygolla, had made good their footing.

This was a very serious state of things.

Correspondents of the *Daily Mail* at the various points of attack had wired such particulars as they were able. The preliminary parley at Lllgxtpll between Prince Ping Pong Pang, the Chinese general, and Llewellyn Evans, the leader of the Cardiff excursionists, seems to have been impressive to a degree. The former had spoken throughout in pure Chinese, the latter replying in rich Welsh, and the general effect, wired the correspondent, was almost painfully exhilarating.

So sudden had been the attacks that in very few instances was there any real resistance. The nearest approach to it appears to have been seen at Margate.

At the time of the arrival of the black warriors which, like the other onslaughts, took place between one and two o'clock on the afternoon of August Bank Holiday, the sands were covered with happy revellers. When the war canoes approached the beach, the excursionists seem to have mistaken their occupants at first for a troupe of nigger minstrels on an unusually magnificent scale; and it was freely noised abroad in the crowd that they were being presented by Charles Frohmann, who was endeavouring to revive the ancient glories of the Christy Minstrels. Too soon, however, it was perceived that these were no harmless Moore and Burgesses. Suspicion was aroused by the absence of banjoes and tambourines; and when the foremost of the negroes dexterously scalped a small boy, suspicion became certainty.

In this crisis the trippers of Margate behaved well. The Mounted Infantry, on donkeys, headed by Uncle Bones, did much execution. The Ladies' Tormentor Brigade harassed the enemy's flank, and a hastily-formed band of sharp-shooters, armed with three-shies-a-penny balls and milky cocos., undoubtedly troubled the advance guard considerably. But superior force told. After half an hour's brisk fighting the excursionists fled, leaving the beach to the foe.

At Auchtermuchty and Portsmouth no obstacle, apparently, was offered to the invaders. At Brighton the enemy were permitted to land unharmed. Scarborough, taken utterly aback by the boyish vigour of the Young Turks, was an easy prey; and at Yarmouth, though the Grand Duke received a nasty slap in the face from a dexterously-thrown bloater, the resistance appears to have been equally futile.

By tea-time on August the first, nine strongly-equipped forces were firmly established on British soil.

THE GERMANS REACH LONDON

The Germans had got off smartly from the mark and were fully justifying the long odds laid upon them. That master-strategist, Prince Otto of Saxe-Pfennig, realizing that if he wished to reach the metropolis quickly he must not go by train, had resolved almost at once to walk. Though hampered considerably by crowds of rustics who gathered, gaping, at every point in the line of march, he had made good progress. The German troops had strict orders to reply to no questions, with the result that little time was lost in idle chatter, and in a couple of days it was seen that the army of the Fatherland was bound, barring accidents, to win comfortably.

The progress of the other forces was slower. The Chinese especially had undergone great privations, having lost their way near Llanfairpwlgwnngogoch and had been unable to understand the voluble directions given to them by the various shepherds they encountered. It was not for nearly a week that they contrived to reach Chester, where, catching a cheap excursion, they arrived in the metropolis, hungry and foot sore, four days after the last of their rivals had taken up their station.

The German advance halted on the wooded heights of Tottenham. Here a camp was pitched and trenches dug.

The march had shown how terrible invasion must of necessity be. With no wish to be ruthless, the troops of Prince Otto had done grievous damage. Cricket pitches had been trampled down, and in many cases even golf-greens dented by the iron heel of the invader, who rarely, if ever, replaced the divot. Everywhere they had left ruin and misery in their train.

With the other armies it was the same story. Through carefully preserved woods they had marched, frightening the birds and driving keepers into fits of nervous protestation. Fishing, owing to their tramping carelessly through the streams, was at a standstill. Croquet had been given up in despair.

Near Epping the Russians shot a fox.

The situation which faced Prince Otto was a delicate one. All his early training and education had implanted in him the fixed idea that, if he ever invaded England, he would do it either alone or with the sympathetic co-operation of allies. He had never faced the problem of what he should do if there were rivals in the field. Competition is wholesome, but only within bounds. He could not very well ask the other nations to withdraw. Nor did he feel inclined to withdraw himself.

'It all comes of this dashed Swoop of the Vulture business,' he grumbled, as he paced before his tent, ever and anon pausing to sweep the city below him with his glasses. 'I should like to find the fellow who started the idea! Making me look a fool! Still, it's just as bad for the others, thank goodness! Well, Poppenheim?'

Captain von Poppenheim approached and saluted.

'Please, sir, the men say, "May they bombard London?"'

'Bombard London!'

'Yes, sir; it's always done.'

Prince Otto pulled thoughtfully at his moustache. 'Bombard London! It seems—and yet—ah, well, they have few pleasures.'

He stood awhile in meditation. So did Captain von Poppenheim. He kicked a pebble. So did Captain von Poppenheim—only a smaller pebble. Discipline is very strict in the German army.

'Poppenheim.'

'Sir?'

'Any signs of our—er—competitors?'

'Yes, sir; the Russians are coming up on the left flank, sir. They'll be here in a few hours. Raisuli has been arrested at Purley for stealing chickens. The army of Bollygolla is about ten miles out. No news of the field yet, sir.'

The hapless Germans do not know that Clarence is about to save his country. The invading armies go from one disaster to another until in the last pages the remnants of the German forces are surrounded by the Boy Scouts. Clarence tells Prince Otto of Saxe-Pfennig that it is all over ...

'Resistance is useless,' said Clarence. 'The moment I have plotted and planned for has come. Your troops, worn out with fighting, mere shadows of themselves, have fallen an easy prey. An hour ago your camp was silently surrounded by patrols of Boy Scouts, armed with catapults and hockey-sticks. One rush and the battle was over. Your entire army, like yourself, are prisoners.'

NEPTUNE'S ALLY.

(*The First Lord of the Admiralty calls in a new element to redress the balance of the old.*)

Chapter Five
The Victors and the Vanquished

From 1900 onwards, as relationships between Great Britain and Imperial Germany went from bad to worse, the non-stop production of future-war stories rapidly created a composite myth of the conflict-to-come. Both sides were agreed that their 'Next Great War' would begin with a naval engagement or a sudden German landing. The authors then rang up the curtain of the future to reveal how, phase by phase, their nations would reap what they had sown. Victory went, with appropriate observations, to the more powerful navy. Either defeat was absolute—total destruction for the Hochseeflotte; surrender and conquest for the British—or there was the lesser evil and a less-than-happy ending when some foreign power intervened to save the Reich or the United Kingdom from total collapse.

Both sides obtained their desired today-and-tomorrow effect through close attention to details and to personalities in their chronicles of projected events. Eminent contemporaries—admirals, generals, ministers of state—acted out their assigned roles; warships on the navy lists of the two countries came over the horizon in their proper formations; and the general accuracy of the descriptions of town-and-country warfare showed that most of the authors had consulted the guide books and town plans. This careful historicizing was a primary narrative requirement. British and German propagandists had to establish the moral and political bases of their stories by showing, in the clearest way possible, that their future wars followed from, and were the immediate consequences of, the hostile actions and habitually intransigent attitudes of the other side. This preliminary confrontation with the Other allowed writers to present their narratives according to an established scenario selected from the book of contemporary expectations. In this way they were as free as their intentions allowed to show the best or the worst sides of their own nations.

Thus, William Le Queux ends his calamitous history of The Invasion of 1910 *by noting that the failure of the British armed forces 'merely reflected the moral tone of the nation, which took no interest in naval or military affairs, and then was enraged to find that, in the hour of trial, everything for a time went wrong'. In like manner, Paul Georg Münch began his triumphant tale of the conquest-to-come in* Hindenburgs Einmarsch in London *by looking forward from the Battle of Tannenberg in the August of 1914. In his mind's eye he could see the troop trains rolling westward for the attack on the United Kingdom. His vision ended with the defeat of the British and Hindenburg's occupation of London. 'The story of Britain's inviolabil-ity,' he wrote in his conclusion, 'that is a fairy tale! No, here are words of German reliance, as firm as a rock, which will lead through London to a world's peace, even quicker than we suspect.'*

There were unsuspected dangers in these fantasies of the feasible. The authors were coralled and confined within their own very different sets of expectations. Placed in a middle state, between the known present and the guessed-at future, they adjusted their narratives to the music of destiny. They defined themselves in their roles as dedicated citizens of the British Empire or of the German Reich by looking before and behind: scanning backward to the past achievements of their nations and pressing on ahead to find in the dark forward of time the well-deserved triumphs or the truly merited disasters that followed from the best, or the worst, of national policies.

The Boy Galloper

Some of these tales of the war-to-come found their models in the established behaviour patterns of past fiction. The narrative of The Boy Galloper, *for example, keeps close to the methods of that most prolific author of boys' adventure stories, George Alfred Henty. There is the stock middle-class hero: Jack Montmorency, seventeen years of age, a senior prefect, a member of the Cadet Corps, the son of a retired and gallant colonel. Our hero represents the Best of Young Britain: courageous, a good rider, eager to play his part in the defence of the nation. The author clearly thought Jack Montmorency spoke for his kind and for his country when he responds at once to a question about mobilization: 'It would be ripping,' said Jack. 'Especially against the Germans—I hate them so.'*

THE SITUATION IS VERY SERIOUS

Jack Montmorency and Leonard Smith were the only inmates of the Prefects' room. They were sitting in the back-window overlooking the quadrangle, discussing the small quantity of news which the morning's post had brought them. Jack Montmorency, a fair tall boy of seventeen, was reading to his friend, who was very interested, a portion of a letter he had that morning received from his father. Leonard Smith was Montmorency's junior by about six months, and was as short and sturdy as his friend was tall.

'Well, what do you think of that?' said Montmorency as he put down the letter.

'I think, as the Head said last night in his sermon, that the situation is very serious. I believe that it is far more serious than anybody out here in the country knows.'

'Well, you see the pater says that there is an officer in every newspaper office who, by order of the authorities, stops all the news being published. That in itself is serious enough. And then Mr. Clark told me only last night that he is going to issue orders this morning for the whole of the Cadet Corps to be served out with a real field-service kit. Wouldn't it be splendid if we were turned out to fight?', and Jack Montmorency jumped to his feet at the bare thought of such a contingency.

'I don't know whether it would be such a grand show,' answered his companion. 'It is all very well for you and me, commanding sections in a school cadet company, to play at soldiering in the summer, but it would be a very serious thing if we had really to turn out. Besides, how many boys can we put into the field? Only those who are about sixteen, and we should not have a complete section with them.'

'Oh, of course, I was not serious; but what is the use of having a commission when there is fighting going on and not being able to make use of that commission? But I expect we shall get some news to-day. Hullo! what's up! Look, there is quite a rush on the other side of the quad. What does it mean?'

Both the boys caught up their caps, and walked out into the corridor to ascertain the meaning of the sudden excitement in the quadrangle.

At the end of the corridor was the school notice-board, and as the two friends crossed the quadrangle they saw that something there was attracting an excited crowd. Pushing their way through the younger boys, they found the master of the week pasting a notice on the board. Both boys read the brief words which the announcement contained, and stood still, shocked at the few lines in black which had been flashed that morning from one end of the British Isles to the other to tell the nation that the most unexpected of all possible evils had befallen it.

The brief telegram ran as follows:

'A state of war exists between this country and Germany. The advance-guard of a German force landed in Sussex this morning.' That was all!

Boys though they were, one and all, from the tall senior Prefect to

the little fellows in knickerbockers, all realized the terrible significance of this announcement. Montmorency turned to his friend and
said:

'The pater was not far wrong. Let us go at once and see Mr. Clark.'

They went immediately to the room of the master who
commanded the school cadet company in which they were both
officers. He had just come from the common room when the boys
knocked at his door.

'Ah! I expected you,' he said as they entered the room. 'Terrible
news, isn't it?'

'Were you expecting it, sir?'

'No, I can't say I was expecting such news as this; but we knew
that the situation was very grave a month ago, as soon as we realized the completeness of the disaster to the Indian army in Persia.'

'But what does it mean to us, sir?' said the boys, almost in a breath.

'That I can hardly say. We know very little more than you do.'

'But shall we mobilize, sir?'

Even Mr. Clark could not forbear a smile at the enthusiasm which
their tone implied. 'That I cannot say. Would you like to?'

'It would be ripping,' said Jack. 'Especially against the Germans—
I hate them so.'

'Well, we shall see,' said the master; 'but until we get news, or
some orders or something more definite than we have at present,
there is little to be said or planned. I should like you two men to
overhaul your respective sections, and let me know which boys you
think, in an emergency, might be fit to take the field. How many are
there over sixteen?'

'I think I have nine, sir,' said Jack.

'How many have you, Smith?'

'I'm not sure, sir, but there may be eleven.'

'Yes; and we might get six or seven out of the other two sections.
There goes the bell! Everything is to go on as usual this morning.
You can come back at twelve, and then we will see if there are any
further developments.'

It was quite an easy thing for the fiat to go forth that the morning
work was to proceed as usual, but a very different matter to put the
order into effect. Both masters and boys were preoccupied with the
extraordinary information which had arrived that morning, and at
eleven o'clock the prefect of the week went round each form room
to give the information that the Headmaster required every boy in
the school to be in his place in the hall when the quarter-past eleven
bell went.

To some of the younger boys the situation presented little but the general excitement which they had caught from their elders; but the Upper school had realized a little of the terrible significance which the message implied. Consequently it was a silent, breathless crowd which awaited the Headmaster's arrival in the hall. All the masters filed in and took their usual places on the dais, and presently the Head entered from the bottom of the hall and walked up to the fireplace, which was the position from which he usually made a general announcement.

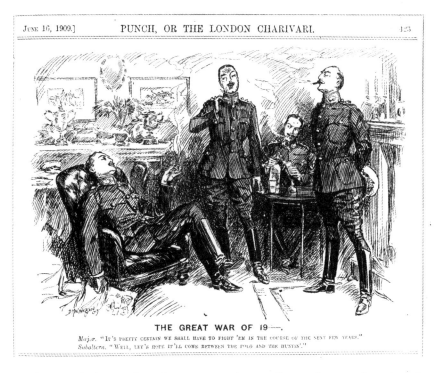

JUNE 16, 1909.]   PUNCH, OR THE LONDON CHARIVARI.   423

THE GREAT WAR OF 19—.

Major. "IT'S PRETTY CERTAIN WE SHALL HAVE TO FIGHT 'EM IN THE COURSE OF THE NEXT FEW YEARS."
Subaltern. "WELL, LET'S HOPE IT'LL COME BETWEEN THE POLO AND THE HUNTIN'."

In the Mess the hope is that 'The Great War of 19–' will 'come between the polo and the huntin'.'

'It is with the deepest regret that I have to confirm the information which was this morning posted on the notice-board. Now, there is no doubt that the recent disasters we have had in the Far East have plunged us into further complications on the Continent, and have resulted in the terrible information that has come upon us as a shock this morning. I have but few details to add, as, owing to the extraordinary situation which has existed during the last month, it has been impossible for political and military reasons to allow free publication in the press of the rapid march of events; but this much has been vouchsafed to me. Mr. Clark, who, as you know, commands our cadet company, has had a telegram from the general of the district instructing him to furnish a return of such members of the cadet company as he considers fit to undertake military duty at the base of operations. Therefore, while the rest of the school continues its studies as if nothing had occurred, the members of the cadet company will give up the whole of their time to military duties. I trust that the divine hand of Providence will so arrange that it may not be necessary for any members of our cadet company to leave the grounds of the school. If the situation should so develop as to demand the presence of our own cadets in the field, whether it be at the base or in the forefront of the battle, I know they will render such an account of themselves that we shall be proud to think that we have been responsible for their training. You may now go back to your studies, with the exception of the members of the Cadet Corps, who will fall in at the appointed place, and in future take their orders from Mr. Clark.'

As the Headmaster wound up his speech, some of the younger boys, not quite realizing the gravity of a situation that even required cadet companies to mobilize for national defence, essayed a cheer, but the Headmaster waved them to silence.

Within a quarter of an hour Jack and Leonard had 'fallen in' their respective sections in the quadrangle, feeling for the first time in their lives that they really were soldiers. As they waited for the commanding officer, the four section leaders grouped together and discussed the probability of the selected members from the ranks taking part in actual military operations.

'I wonder', said Jack, who from the fact that he was the senior prefect in the school generally took the lead in everything, 'if they are going to draw from the whole of the schools and furnish a battalion.'

'No,' said Johnny Sykes, who was credited with being the most subtle member of the school debating society; 'I don't think that they would be able to make us into a whole battalion. You see, all said and done, we are such youngsters. Now I should think that they would attach us to some regiment, in the same way that they attached the Volunteers in the South African War. We could then be some use; but by ourselves we should not have sufficient experience.'

Leonard was about to give his opinion when the commanding officer appeared. The youthful officers called their sections to attention as Mr. Clark, accompanied by the Headmaster, came on to the parade.

The first order was that every boy under sixteen should fall out. It was with a murmur of regret that those keen youths who could not boast sixteen summers took six paces to the rear of their more matured companions. It was found that there were only twenty-one in the ranks above sixteen, and these were at once formed into what was called, for want of a better phrase, 'the special service section', the command being given to Jack Montmorency as the senior subaltern. But the rest were informed that though they were beyond the present War Office order they were to remain in readiness in case further instructions were received, and were to devote the best part of the day to military instruction.

The parade was then dismissed, but those belonging to the special service section had orders to remain all day in uniform and to be prepared at any moment to pass the doctor, while Mr. Clark and the officers of the company arranged for the necessary equipment in case an order was received to proceed on duty.

It was a bitter blow to Leonard that there was no room for him as an officer in the special service section, and as soon as the parade was dismissed he went to Mr. Clark and volunteered to revert to the rank of sergeant if he might be allowed to take his place with the section, in the event of a call for service taking it away from the school. His disappointment was destined to be of short duration, because the parade had hardly been dismissed when the Headmaster summoned Jack Montmorency to his study. Thinking it was but some ordinary instruction with regard to the discipline of the school, Jack hastened to the Headmaster's room. The latter was standing by the fire.

'Montmorency,' he said, 'I have just received a telegram from your father. He says that he wishes you to go up to London at once, as he has secured you an appointment as ADC to one of the generals now taking the field to oppose this terrible invasion. You would like to go?'

The news came upon the boy like a thunderclap. For a moment he was so taken aback that he found it impossible to answer; and as the Headmaster saw the pleased excitement which the news had brought, he added, almost proudly, 'I can see, Montmorency, that you wish to go. Well, my boy, as it may mean a future career for you, I cannot stand in your way. I know that, whatever happens, you will be a credit to us, and will do your duty. Go to your house-master and get the necessary funds, and I wish you good-bye and good luck.'

Jack Montmorency was not really a very excitable boy; in fact his reputation in the school was quite the reverse. He was the coolest captain that the football XI could remember. So he quickly gathered his senses together and, thanking the Headmaster for what he had said, withdrew to make arrangements to leave at once for London. He met Leonard in the corridor, and clapping him on the back, said, 'Len, old boy, you will get the command of the service section, because I have been ordered to London to be ADC to some one unknown.'

Leonard's dark eyes opened wide with astonishment.

'Whatever do you mean, Jack?'

'I mean what I say, and that is that my governor has secured me an appointment on somebody's staff, and I am going at once to Clark to get the money to go to London. As you are next in seniority, you must command the company.'

Mr. Clark had already heard of the appointment, and although he said he was sorry to lose Jack, yet he congratulated him on the chance which had come to him. Jack suggested that he would not leave until the night train, but Mr. Clark advised him to go at once, saying, 'You will find that the whole of the train service is disconnected; everything is upside-down, and instead of two hours it may take you till midnight to get to London.' And so Jack Montmorency left the school, never to return to it as a boy.

Leonard Smith came to see him off at the station, and luckily Jack had not changed his uniform, for he found when he arrived at the station that all civilian traffic had been stopped until further orders. He was only able to catch a train which would take him as far as Woking.

'How you will get on from there', said the station master, 'it is impossible for me to say; but I fancy there will be plenty of trains running up and down between London and Aldershot, and you will probably get one at once.'

There were tears in Leonard's eyes as he shook his friend by the hand and then rode a little way on the footboard of the moving train as it carried him towards the great heart of the Empire. It is possible that Leonard was a tiny bit jealous of Jack's good fortune; but little did the boy dream, as he watched the train pass out of sight, of the circumstances in which he was next to see his friend.

It was four o'clock in the afternoon when Jack Montmorency arrived at Waterloo. The rush and tumble of ordinary traffic had given place to a military pandemonium. Although he had been in that labyrinth of a terminus during the holiday season, yet he had never seen it so crowded before. Never could he have imagined that so many troops could have been gathered together into a single station. A transformation seemed to have fallen over the whole of the city. The platforms were absolutely crowded with troops. Beyond the porters and policemen on duty there was no one in civilian attire at all. On the opposite platform from which he had alighted were three battalions from the Guards Brigade. The centre way was blocked with a battery of Royal Horse Artillery and the two horse batteries of the Honourable Artillery Company; while on the platforms beyond, as far as Jack could see, were three or four more battalions of infantry with their arms piled, waiting for the trains to carry them away.

Four officers were standing at the exit through which Jack wished to pass. They were talking rapidly, and took no notice of the tall slip of a subaltern in grey who saluted them punctiliously. Jack would have liked to ask them for news, but they rather awed him, so he turned to a good-natured-looking sergeant of the Coldstream Guards who was standing on the curb-stone just outside the station.

'Can you tell me if anything has happened?'

The great six-foot guardsman jumped to attention so quickly that he almost startled the boy.

'I don't think that anybody knows anything for certain, sir; but we have heard as how they have landed near the mouth of the Humber as well.'

Jack passed on, and looked about the yard for the customary cabs. To his astonishment neither cabs nor buses were in the precincts of the station, only a considerable number of police, and just as he got clear of the station the Royal Fusiliers, headed by their band, came marching into the yard. Beyond the line of police was a large crowd of people. It was evident that the station was being kept clear of civilians, but it seemed that the whole of London was in the streets. As the Royal Fusiliers passed the station gates the silence was broken, and a great volume of shouting broke the air. It was evident that London was working under the influence of intense national feeling, and as Jack elbowed his way through the crowd he could not help being struck by the large number of old men and women of which it was composed. It took him perhaps twenty minutes to work his way to the outskirts of that crowd: everybody was asking his neighbour for information; no one seemed able to give any. In one place a man in a frock coat and top hat had climbed upon a railing and was endeavouring to make some sort of speech. Jack was unable to hear what he said, but the crowd howled at him, and presently a sturdy bricklayer bore down upon the tub-thumper and pulled him over, crumpling his hat down upon his head. At last Jack was clear of the crowd, and presently was able to find a cab, one of the few that seemed to be out that evening.

'Where to, sir?' said the cabby.

'To Gloucester Terrace, Bayswater.'

'Can't do that under ten bob, sir.'

'Why not?' said Jack; 'the fare is only two shillings.'

'You forget, sir, that they will nab my horse to-morrow, and that I shall then be out of work.'

It was no time for arguing, so the boy jumped in.

'All right, if you take me fast I will give you ten shillings.'

It was a memorable drive, for at every turn there was evidence of the subdued excitement which had taken hold upon the people, now that the enemy was at their gates. A third of the male population was in uniform: for the most part, as Jack saw, these were volunteers. Crowds were collecting at every corner, and news sheets were being sold as fast as the printing press could turn them over to the vendors. Various little processions and crowds were moving along the wider thoroughfares, breaking into snatches of patriotic song. He constantly passed detachments of troops, and at the very sight of a uniform men, women, and children burst into hysterical cheering. Another vast concourse of people stood collected round Wellington's statue at Hyde Park Corner. It was so dense that the cabby shouted through the trap, 'It will be impossible to go this way, sir. I shall have to drive you through the Park, and turn down a side-street.'

Hyde Park itself presented a wonderful sight, for in a few hours it seemed to have grown into a vast military bivouac, and was as crowded with troops and people as if the King were about to review some enormous force.

In the midst of this excitement Jack at last arrived at his home. He paid the cabby his fare and dashed up the steps. His sister Gwendoline opened the door for him. She was a tall fair girl, perhaps a year older than Jack, and her first remark as she kissed him was, 'Oh! isn't it terrible, Jack! And to think that mother and the girls are at Eastbourne, and can't get back here.'

'They will be all right,' said Jack, cheerily; 'but where is the pater? I must see him at once.'

'He is in the library.'

'Well, pater, here I am. It has been a great struggle to get here.'

Jack's father rose and took his son's hands.

'I am glad to see you, my boy; but it is a terrible business. I am too old to come back to the service now, unless they have to fall back on the "cripples". But the first man I met in the club this morning was Bethune of the 16th Lancers, and he told me that he had been given the command of a London Yeomanry brigade, and said if I could get you up at once he would take you as his galloper. I asked him to give me a quarter of an hour to think it over, and in that quarter of an hour I made up my mind that it would possibly be the best start in life I could give you, and I accepted for you.'

'How splendid, dad!'

'Well, my boy,' said his father, putting his hand on Jack's shoulder, 'I trust I have done the right thing. You are going with a first-rate man, and as a galloper you need not incur so many risks as some others.'

'But when am I to join him?'

'I think you had better go at once, because everything is now moving in such frenzied haste that he may be off to the front tonight—how awful to think that the front should be in our own country!'

'But where shall I find him?'

'I think I will come down with you. He has opened an office in Victoria Street.'

It was quite impossible to find a conveyance, and there was nothing left for father and son but to make their way across the Park on foot. Avoiding the block at Hyde Park Corner, they eventually, just as it was striking eight o'clock, arrived at the door of the mansion on which a hurriedly scrawled placard had been posted to say that it was 'the temporary headquarters of the 6th Yeomanry Brigade'.

Colonel Montmorency took his son up to the third floor, and asked a sergeant, who appeared to be on duty there, to take in his card to the brigadier. The sergeant returned in a minute, and said for the time being the general was engaged, but if Colonel Montmorency would be good enough to wait in the next room he would see him as soon as his present business was finished.

The sergeant then showed them into a small sitting room, which at the moment was full of officers. Chairs there were none, but a young subaltern in khaki who had a corner of a settee at once rose and offered his seat to Jack's father. There were at least nine officers in the room, eight of whom were discussing the situation with great vehemence over a parcel of maps which had just been brought in by an orderly. The ninth was talking rapidly at the telephone. Jack observed them all closely, and tried to recognize from their uniforms the regiments to which they belonged. The majority were in khaki, but nearly all had some distinguishing marks upon their tunics. Three or four had purple collars and cuffs, while one or two possessed scarlet facings. Jack was on the point of asking his father what these distinctions in uniform might mean when the sergeant again appeared at the door and said, 'Will Colonel Montmorency come in and see the general?'

They were shown into a bigger room, at the end of which stood two officers in uniform studying, with the aid of a candle, a great map of the south of England, which was hanging from the wall. The elder of the two, a tall, good-looking man, turned round and welcomed Jack's father. The first thing that Jack noticed was that the tall officer had only one arm; his right arm was gone, and its place taken by a leather-covered stump. He was a fine, soldierly-built man, and Jack could not help noticing that, while everybody else in the building wore an anxious, and in many cases a despondent look, the brigadier seemed in no way to be concerned, and received his visitors with a genial smile.

'Hullo, Monty! So you've brought the nipper along?' and then turning to Jack, he placed his left hand encouragingly upon his shoulder. 'So you're coming along to gallop for me, are you? If you carry your messages as smartly as your sister rides to hounds, you'll make a first-class galloper. Have you a horse?'

Here Colonel Montmorency interposed. 'Yes,' he said; 'I am letting him have the horse his sister usually hunts, and he can bring it over to-morrow.'

'To-morrow, my dear fellow,' said the brigadier. 'If he does, he'll have to ride all the way down to the South Downs. I am leaving about three this morning myself, and Kenna here is bringing the brigade on before daylight, as soon as he can get them into the trucks. Do you know Kenna? Let me introduce you.'

Colonel Kenna, the same man who won the Victoria Cross for gallantry at the battle of Omdurman, came forward and shook hands with both Colonel Montmorency and his son. A short, fair, handsome man, with a bright smile, he saluted Jack warmly with the significant remark, 'You have cut in for stirring times.'

'Yes,' said the brigadier; 'Kenna is my staff officer, and between us we have got to try conclusions with the beer-swillers before twenty-four hours are out.'

'What is the latest news?' asked Colonel Montmorency.

'The latest that I have,' answered the brigadier, 'is that I am to detrain my Yeoboys at Lewes as soon after daybreak to-morrow as possible.'

'But what is the news about the enemy?' persevered Colonel Montmorency.

'They don't seem to have any very certain information so far,' said the brigadier. 'At least, my divisional general hasn't sent much on to me; but as far as I can gather, old man Kaiser is trying to play William the Conqueror at eleven stone four, and has effected a landing somewhere between Hastings and Pevensey. Any way, first blood has been drawn, and cyclist scouts have run up against their outposts.'

'Well, I had better take the boy and fit him up with his horse, and send him back to you, had I not?'

'I think, Monty, that the best thing you can do is to leave him here; I shall have plenty for him to do. Send a man round with his horse and riding kit. And now, old fellow, good-bye—I'm full of work.'

Colonel Montmorency was on the point of making another observation when he cut himself short, and turning round to his son, said, 'Good-bye, Jack. The general is right; it is best that I should leave you here. I have only one word of advice to you—wherever you are, and whatever may be in store for you, play the man. And if you are satisfied that you have played the man, everything will come right. Good-bye, my boy; put your trust in God and yourself, and I know that you will be a credit to us.'

The brigadier and his staff officer had turned away to restudy their map, and tears stood in the old colonel's eyes as he bent forward and kissed his son on the forehead, and then hurriedly left the room.

As soon as the door had closed behind him, the brigadier turned to his ADC and said kindly, 'Well, young fellow, when did you last have food?'

'I have not had anything since midday to-day, sir.'

'Then it is high time that you had something, and a good fat meal to boot. You come along with me, and we'll go across and see what the Grosvenor *table d'hôte* can do for us.'

As soon as the brigadier opened the door which separated him from his anteroom, the group of officers already mentioned rose to their feet and crowded round him. The brigadier addressed them generally:

'Gentlemen, you will get your instructions from Colonel Kenna, and I trust that within twenty-four hours you will be chasing Uhlans into the sea. We have got orders for Lewes, and will form part of

General Baden-Powell's cavalry division. Good night; we shall meet again in the morning.'

The dining saloon of the hotel was crowded with officers, who had come with the object of getting a decent meal before entraining at Victoria. With some difficulty Jack and the brigadier were able to secure places. As they at last sat down, a couple of officers at the next table called across to the brigadier and asked him his destination. He told them, and then asked if they had received any news of fighting.

'Nothing so far, beyond an exchange of shots between cyclists and their cavalry out-posts,' came the answer. 'But some one was in here just now who said that the weather had somewhat delayed the landing. He said he had got this direct from Sir Ian Hamilton.'

'Well,' said the brigadier, as he turned to his dinner, 'weather or no weather, they have got a footing, and that footing is worth everything to them.'

In The Boy Galloper *danger had come like random lightning from the clear sky of future fiction. In the real world of 1904 the British and the French had buried past differences in order to become the allies of tomorrow in terms of the* Entente. *Then, on 31 March 1905, the Germans tried to drive a wedge between France and Great Britain, when the Kaiser came in person to Tangier and announced that Germany had 'great and growing interests in Morocco'. The British response to that veiled threat was a redistribution of the navy into three fleets—Mediterranean, Atlantic, and Channel—and in 1906 the laying down of the Dreadnought, a class which made all other battleships obsolete. In 1907 there came another fateful event—the Anglo-Russian Convention, which created the Triple* Entente *between Britain, France and Russia.*

These were bumper years for the future-war stories: Carl Bleibtreu found a connection between the Moroccan crisis of 1905 and the war he described in Die 'Offensiv-Invasion' gegen England. *In* The Death Trap *R. W. Cole called in the Japanese navy to save the United Kingdom; and in* The Message *the narrative goes from one calamity to another to show how 'the greatest, wealthiest Power in civilization was brought to its knees in the incredibly short space of one week, by the sudden but scientifically devised onslaught of a single ambitious nation, ruled by a monarch whose lack of scruples was more than balanced by his strength of purpose'.*

The Message

The author of The Message *chose another favoured mode of instruction—the panoramic view of future events. This allowed him to present the enemies of the nation—'The Destroyers'—as a collection of anti-militarists, socialists, and radicals who had no interest in the defence of their country. They represented the weaknesses and follies of the British people, as the author saw them in 1907. His narrator is a know-all journalist, at the centre of news, and ever ready with a comment on events. Here he describes the first rumours of a German invasion and a peace demonstration in London. He hears a newsboy 'crying a "special" edition of some paper', and he goes out to buy a copy ...*

THE NATIONAL DEFENCE CRANKS

I found in it no particular justification for any special issue, and, as a fact, the probability is the appearance of this edition was merely a device to increase circulation, suggested mainly by the fact that the ordinary issue had been delayed by the East Anglian telegraphic breakdown. Regarding this, I found the following item of editorial commentary:

> As is explained elsewhere, a serious breakdown of telegraphic communication has occurred between London and Harwich, Ipswich, and East Anglia generally, as a result of which our readers are robbed of special despatches regarding last night's conclusion of the East Anglian Pageant. It is thought that the breakdown is due to some electrical disturbance of the atmosphere resulting in a fusion of wires.
>
> But as an example of the ridiculous lengths to which the national defence cranks will go in their hatching of alarmist reports, a rumour was actually spread in Fleet Street at an early hour this morning that this commonplace accident to the telegraph wires was caused by an invading German army. This ridiculous *canard* is reminiscent of some of the foolish scares which frightened our forefathers a little more than a century ago, when the Corsican terrorized Europe. But our rumour-mongers are too far out of date for this age. It is unfortunate that the advocates of militarism should receive parliamentary support of any kind. The Opposition is weakly and insignificant enough in all conscience, without courting

further unpopularity by flouting British public feeling in this way, and encouraging the cranks among its following to bring ridicule upon the country.

The absurd *canard* to which we have referred is maliciously ill-timed. It will doubtless be reported on the Continent, and may injure us there. But we trust our friends in Germany will do us the justice of recognizing at once that this is merely the work of an irresponsible and totally unrepresentative clique, and in no sort a reflection of any aspect of public feeling in this country. We are able to state with certainty that last Tuesday's regrettable incident in the Mediterranean has been satisfactorily and definitely closed. Admiral Blennerhaustein displayed characteristic German courtesy and generosity in his frank acceptance of the apology sent to him from Whitehall; and the report that our Channel Fleet had entered the Straits of Gibraltar is incorrect. A portion of the Channel Fleet had been cruising off the coast of the Peninsula, and is now on its way back to home waters. Our relations with His Imperial Majesty's Government in Berlin were never more harmonious, and such a *canard* as this morning's rumour of invasion is only worthy of mention for the sake of a demonstration of its complete absurdity. If, as was stated, the author of this puerile invention is a Navy League supporter, who reached London in a motor-car from Harwich soon after daylight this morning, our advice to him is to devote the rest of the day to sleeping off the effects of an injudicious evening in East Anglia.

Failing the East Anglian pageant, the paper's 'first feature', I noticed, consisted of a lot of generously headed particulars regarding the big Disarmament Demonstration to be held in Hyde Park that afternoon. It seemed that this was to be a really big thing, and I decided to attend in the interests of *The Mass*. The President of the Local Government Board and three well-known members on the Government side of the House were to speak. The Demonstration had been organized by the National Peace Association for Disarmament and Social Reform, of which the Prime Minister had lately been elected President. Delegates, both German and English, of the Anglo-German Union had promised to deliver addresses. Among other well-known bodies who were sending representatives I saw mention of the Anti-Imperial and Free Tariff Society, the Independent England Guild, the Home Rule Association, the Free

Trade League, and various Republican and Socialist bodies. The paper said some amusement was anticipated from a suggested counter-demonstration proposed by a few Navy League enthusiasts; but that the police would take good care that no serious interruptions were allowed.

The Enemy are halted at a barricade in Tottenham Court Road. The advert for *An Englishman's Home* on the bus reinforces the message of national defence in Guy du Maurier's play

As the Demonstration was fixed for three o'clock in the afternoon, I decided to go up the river by steamboat to Kew after my late breakfast. It was a gloriously fine morning, and on the river I began to feel a little more cheerful.

He goes on up river, passes under Hammersmith Bridge, and finds a place under a tree in Kew Gardens. The newspaper sellers again attract his attention …

The newsboys were putting a good deal of feeling into their crying of special editions when I reached the streets again; but I was not inclined to waste further pence upon the *Sunday News'* moralizings over the evolution of *canards*. I took a mess of some adulterated pottage at a foreign restaurant in Notting Hill, as I had no wish to return to Bloomsbury before the Demonstration. The waiter—either a Swiss or a German—asked me:

'Vad you sink, sare, of ze news from ze country?'

I asked him what it was, and he handed me a fresh copy of the *Sunday News*, headed: 'Special Edition. Noon'.

But the only new matter in this issue was a short announcement, headed in poster type, as follows:

EAST ANGLIA'S ISOLATION

RAILWAY COMMUNICATIONS STOPPED

STRANGE SUPPORT OF INVASION CANARD

IS THIS A TORY HOAX?

(SPECIAL)

The preposterous rumour of a German invasion of England is receiving mysterious support. We hear from a reliable source that some Imperialist and Navy League cranks have organized a gigantic hoax by way of opposition to the Disarmament Demonstration. If the curious breakdown of communication with the east coast does prove to be the work of political fanatics, we think, and hope, that these gentry may shortly be convinced, in a manner they are never likely to forget, that, even in this land of liberty, the crank is not allowed to inter-fere with the transaction of public business.

No trains have reached Liverpool Street from the north-east this morning, and communication cannot be established beyond Chelmsford. Whatever the cause of this singular breakdown may be, our readers will soon know it, for, in order finally to dispel any hint of credence which may be attached in some quarters to the absurd invasion report, we have already dispatched two representatives in two powerful motor-cars, north-eastward from Brentwood, with instructions to return to that point and telegraph full particulars directly they can discover the cause of the stoppage of communication.

Further special editions will be issued when news is received from East Anglia.

'Yes,' I said to the waiter; 'it's a curious affair.'

'You believe him, sare—zat Shermany do it?'

'Eh? No; certainly not. Do you?'

'Me? Oh, sare, I don't know nozzing. Vaire shstrong, sare, ze Sherman Armay.'

The fellow's face annoyed me in some way. It, and his grins and gesticulations, had a sinister seeming. My trade brought me into contact with so many low-class aliens. I told myself I was getting insular and prejudiced, and resumed my meal with more thought for myself and my tendencies and affairs than for the East Anglian business. I have wondered since what the waiter thought about while I ate; whether he thought of England, Germany, and of myself, as representing the British citizen. But, to be sure, for aught I know, his thoughts may have been ordered for him from Berlin.

The Demonstration drew an enormous concourse of people to Hyde Park. The weather being perfect, a number of people made an outing of the occasion, and one saw whole groups of people who clearly came from beyond Whitechapel, the Borough, Shepherd's Bush, and Islington. As had been anticipated, a few well-dressed people endeavoured to run a counter-demonstration under a Navy League banner; but their following was absurdly small, and the crowd gave them nothing but ridicule and contempt.

The President of the Local Government Board received a tremendous ovation. For some minutes after his first appearance that enormous crowd sang, 'He's a jolly good fellow!' with great enthusiasm. Then, when this member of the Government at last succeeded in getting as far as: 'Mr. Chairman, ladies and gentlemen', some one started the song with the chorus containing the words: 'They'll never go for England, because England's got the dibs.' This spread like a line of fire in dry grass, and in a moment the vast crowd was rocking to the jingling rhythm of the song, the summer air quivering to the volume of its thousand-throated voice.

The President of the Local Government Board had been rather suspected of tuft-hunting recently, and his appearance in the stump orator's role, and in the cause of disarmament, was wonderfully popular. In his long career as Labour agitator, Socialist, and Radical, he had learned to know the popular pulse remarkably well; and now he responded cleverly to the call of the moment. His vein was that of the heavy, broad bludgeoning sarcasm which tickles a crowd, and his theme was not the wickedness, but the stupidity and futility of all 'jingoism', 'spread-eagleism', 'tall talk', and 'gold-lace buncombe'.

'I am told my honourable friends of the opposition', he said, with an ironical bow in the direction of the now folded Navy League banner, 'have played some kind of a practical joke in the eastern counties today. Well, children will be children; but I am afraid there will have to be spankings if half that I hear is true. They have tried to frighten you into abandoning this Demonstration with a pretended invasion of England. Well, my friends, it does not look to me as though their invasion had affected this Demonstration very seriously. I seem to fancy I see quite a number of people gathered together here.' (It is estimated that over 60,000 people were trying to hear his words.) 'But all I have to say on this invasion question is just this: If our friends from Germany have invaded East Anglia, let us be grateful for their enterprise, and, as a nation of shopkeepers should, let us make as much as we can out of 'em. But don't let us forget our hospitality. If our neighbours have dropped in in a friendly way, why let's be sure we've something hot for supper. Perhaps a few sausages wouldn't be taken amiss.' (The laughter and applause was so continuous here that for some moments nothing further could be heard.) 'No, my friends, this invasion hoax should now be placed finally upon the retired list. It has been on active service now since the year 1800, and I really think it's time our spread-eagle friends gave us a change. Let me for one moment address you in my official capacity, as your servant and a member of the Government. This England of ours is about as much in danger of being invaded as I am of becoming a millionaire.'

There was, of course, no hoax: the Germans had landed. The story goes on to describe the British failure to resist the invading forces, and in the last two chapters the author shows how those opponents of conscription, 'The Destroyers', have been responsible for the national disaster ...

THE TRAGIC WEEK

It is no part of my intention to make any attempt to limp after the historians of the Invasion. The Official History, the half dozen of standard military treatises, and the well-known works of Low, Forster, Gordon, and others, have allowed few details of the Invasion to escape unrecorded. But I confess it has always seemed to me that these writers gave less attention to the immediate aftermath of the Invasion than that curious period demanded. Yet here was surely a case in which effect was of vastly more importance than cause, and aftermath than crisis. But perhaps I take that view because I am no historian.

To the non-expert mind, the most bewildering and extraordinary feature of that disastrous time was the amazing speed with which crisis succeeded crisis, and events, each of themselves epoch-making in character, crashed one upon another throughout the progress toward Black Saturday. We know now that much of this fury of haste which was so bewildering at the time, which certainly has no parallel in history, was due to the perfection of Germany's long-laid plans. Major-General Farquarson, in his *Military History of the Invasion*, says:

> It may be doubted whether in all the history of warfare anything so scientifically perfect as the preparations for this attack can be found. It is safe to say that every inch of General von Füchter's progress was mapped out in Berlin long months before it came to astound and horrify England. The maps and plans in the possession of the German staff were masterpieces of cartographical science and art. The German Army knew almost to a bale of hay what provender lay between London and the coast, and where it was stored; and certainly their knowledge of East Anglia far exceeded that of our own authorities. The world has never seen a quicker blow struck; it has seldom seen a blow so crushingly severe; it has not often seen one so aggressively unjustifiable. And, be it noted, that down to the last halter, and the least fragment of detail, the German Army was provided with every conceivable aid to success—*in duplicate.*
>
> Never in any enterprise known to history was less left to chance. The German War Office left nothing at all to chance, not even its conception—a certainty really—of Britain's amazing unreadiness. And the German Army took no risks. A soldier's business, whether he be private or Field Marshal, is, after all, to obey orders. It would be both foolish and unjust to blame General von Füchter. But the fact remains that no victorious army ever risked less by generosity than the invading German Army. Its tactics were undoubtedly ruthless; they were the tactics necessitated by the orders of the Chief of the Army. They were more severe, more crushing, than any that have ever been adopted even by a punitive expedition under British colours. They were successful. For that they were intended. Swiftness and thoroughness were of the essence of the contract.
>
> With regard to their humanity or morality I am not here concerned. But it should always be remembered by critics that British apathy and neglect made British soil a standing temptation to the invader. The invasion was entirely unprovoked, so far as direct provocation goes. But who shall say it was

entirely undeserved, or even unforeseen, by advisors whom the nation chose to ignore? This much is certain: Black Saturday and the tragic events leading up to it were made possible, not so much by the skill and forethought of the enemy, which were notable, as by a state of affairs in England which made that day one of shame and humiliation, as well as a day of national mourning. No just recorder may hope to escape that fact.

In London, the gravest aspect of that tragic week was the condition of the populace. It is supposed that over two million people flocked into the capital during the first three days. And the prices of the necessities of life were higher in London than anywhere else in the country. The Government measures for relief were ill-considered and hopelessly inadequate. But, in justice to 'The Destroyers', it must be remembered that leading authorities have said that adequate measures were impossible, from sheer lack of material. During one day—I think it was Wednesday—huge armies of the hungry unemployed—nine-tenths of our wage earners were unemployed—were set to work upon entrenchments in the north of London. But there was no sort of organization, and most of the men streamed back into the town that night, unpaid, unfed, and sullenly resentful.

Then, like cannon-shots, came the reports of the fall of York, Bradford, Leeds, Halifax, Hull, and Huddersfield, and the apparently wanton demolition of Norwich Cathedral. The sinking of the Dreadnought near the Nore was known in London within the hour. Among the half-equipped regulars who were hurried up from the south-west, I saw dozens of men intercepted in the streets by the hungry crowds, and hustled into leaving their fellows.

Then came Friday's awful 'Surrender Riot' at Westminster, a magnificent account of which gives Martin's big work its distinctive value. I had left Constance Grey's flat only half an hour before the riot began, and when I reached Trafalgar Square there was no space between that and the Abbey in which a stone could have been dropped without falling upon a man or a woman. There were women in that maddened throng, and some of them, crying hoarsely in one breath for surrender and for bread, were suckling babies.

No Englishman who witnessed it could ever forget that sight. The Prime Minister's announcement that the surrender should be made came too late. The panic and hunger-maddened incendiaries had

'I saw Buckingham Palace attacked—Scots Guards did their best—short of
ammunition—shot down like pigs'

been at work. Smoke was rising already from Downing Street and
the back of the Treasury. Then came the carnage. One can well
believe that not a single unnecessary bullet was fired. Not to believe
that would be to saddle those in authority with a less than human
baseness. But the question history puts is: Who was primarily to
blame for the circumstances which led up to the tragic necessity of
the firing order?

Posterity has unanimously laid the blame upon the
Administration of that day, and assuredly the task of whitewashing
'The Destroyers' would be no light or pleasant one. But, again, we
must remind ourselves that the essence of the British Constitution
has granted to us always, for a century past at least, as good a
Government as we have deserved. 'The Destroyers' may have
brought shame and humiliation upon England. Unquestionably,
measures and acts of theirs produced those effects. But who and
what produced 'The Destroyers' as a Government? The only possible answer to that is, in the first place, the British public; in the
second place, the British people's selfish apathy and neglect, where
national duty and responsibility were concerned, and blindly selfish
absorption, in the matter of its own individual interests and pleasures.

One hundred and thirty-two men, women, and children killed,

and three hundred and twenty-eight wounded; the Treasury buildings and the official residence of the Prime Minister gutted; that was the casualty list of the 'Surrender Riot' at Westminster. But the figures do not convey a tithe of the horror, the unforgettable shame and horror, of the people's attack upon the Empire's sanctuary. The essence of the tragedy lay in their demand for immediate and unconditional surrender; the misery of it lay in 'The Destroyers" weak, delayed, terrified response, followed almost immediately by the order to those in charge of the firing parties—an order flung hysterically at last, the very articulation of panic.

No one is likely to question Martin's assertion that Friday's tragedy at Westminster must be regarded—'not alone as the immediate cause of Black Saturday's national humiliation, but also as the crucial phase, the pivot upon which the development of the whole disastrous week turned'. But the Westminster Riot at least had the saving feature of unpremeditation. It was, upon the one side, the outcry of a wholly undisciplined, hungry, and panic-smitten public; and, upon the other side, the irresponsible, more than half-hysterical, action of a group of terrified and incompetent politicians. These men had been swept into great positions, which they were totally unfitted to fill, by a tidal wave of reactionary public feeling, and of the blind selfishness of a decadence born of long freedom from any form of national discipline; of liberties too easily won and but half understood; of superficial education as to rights, and abysmal ignorance as to duties.

But, while fully admitting the soundness of Martin's verdict, for my part I feel that my experiences during that week left me with memories not perhaps more shocking, but certainly more humiliating and disgraceful to England, than the picture burnt into my mind by the Westminster Riot. I will mention two of these.

By Wednesday a large proportion of the rich residents of Western London had left the capital to take its chances, while they sought the security of country homes, more particularly in the south-western counties. Such thoroughfares as Piccadilly, Regent Street, and Bond Street were no longer occupied by well-dressed people with plenty of money to spend. Their usual patrons were for the most part absent; but, particularly at night, they were none the less very freely used—more crowded, indeed, than ever before. The really poor, the desperately hungry people, had no concern whatever with the wrecking of the famous German restaurants and beer-halls. They were not among the Regent Street and Piccadilly promenaders.

The Londoners who filled these streets at night—the people who sacked the Leicester Square hotel and took part in the famous orgy which Blackburn describes as 'unequalled in England since the days of the Plague, or in Europe since the French Revolution'; these people were not at all in quest of food. They were engaged upon a mad pursuit of pleasure and debauchery and drink. 'Eat, drink, and be vicious; but above all, drink and be vicious; for this is the end of England!' That was their watchword.

I have no wish to repeat Blackburn's terrible stories of rapine and bestiality, of the frenzy of intoxication, and the blind savagery of these Saturnalia. In their dreadful nakedness they stand for ever in the pages of his great book, a sinister blur, a fiery warning, writ large across the scroll of English history. I only wish to say that scenes I actually saw with my own eyes (in trying to check the horror of one episode I lost two fingers and much blood) prove beyond all question to me that, even in its most lurid and revolting passages, Blackburn's account is a mere record of fact, and not at all, as some apologists have sought to show, an exaggerated or over-heated version of these lamentable events.

In the last chapter, 'the Field Marshal in command of the British forces' is undoubtedly meant to be the military hero of the day, Field Marshal Lord Roberts (1832–1914). He resigned his post as commander-in-chief of the army in 1905, and as head of the National Service League devoted himself to urging the nation to introduce military training for all. There is yet another lesson for the nation in the chivalrous action of the German commander, when 'the man of iron saluted the heart-broken Chief of the shattered British Army' on the day the sun finally set on the British Empire.

BLACK SATURDAY

In the afternoon of Black Saturday, General von Füchter, the Commander-in-Chief of the German Army in England, took up his quarters, with his staff, in the residence of the German Ambassador to the Court of St. James in Carlton House Terrace, and, so men said, enjoyed the first sleep he had had for a week ...

The enemy's line of communications stretched now from the Wash to London, and between Brentwood and London there were more Germans than English. I believe the actual number of troops which entered London behind General von Füchter was under forty-eight thousand; but to the northward, north-east, and north-west the huge force which really invested the capital was spread in careful formation, and amply provided with heavy artillery, then trained upon central London from all such points as the Hampstead heights.

Although a formal note of surrender had been conveyed to General von Füchter at Romford, *after* the annihilation of our entrenched troops, occasional shots were fired upon the enemy as they entered London. Indeed, in the Whitechapel Road, one of the general's aides-de-camp, riding within a few yards of his chief, was killed by a shot from the upper windows of a provision shop. But the German reprisals were sharp. It is said that 57 lives paid the penalty for the shooting of that aide-de-camp. Several streets of houses in north-east London were burned.

By this time the Lord Mayor of London had been notified that serious results would accrue if any further opposition were offered to the German acceptance of London's surrender; and proclamations to that effect were posted everywhere. But the great bulk of London's inhabitants were completely cowed by hunger and terror. Practically, it may be said that, throughout, the only resistance offered to the Army of the invaders was that which ended so tragically in the trenches beyond Epping and Romford, with the equally tragical defence of Colchester, and some of the northern towns captured by the eighth German Army Corps.

In London the people's demand from the first had been for unconditional surrender. It was this demand which had culminated in the Westminster Riot. The populace was so entirely undisciplined, so completely lacking in the sort of training which makes for self-restraint, that, even if the Government had been possessed of an efficient striking force for defensive purposes, the public would not have permitted its proper utilization. The roar of German artillery during Friday night and Saturday morning, with the news of the awful massacre in the northern entrenchments, had combined to extinguish the last vestige of desire for resistance which remained in London.

Almost all the people with money had left the capital. Those remaining—the poor, the refugees from northward, irresponsibles, people without a stake of any kind—these desired but the one thing: food and safety. The German Commander-in-Chief was wise. He knew that, if time had been allowed, resistance would have been organized, even though the British regular Army had, by continuous reductions in the name of 'economy', practically ceased to exist as a striking force. And therefore time was the one thing he had been most determined to deny England.

The air war of the future: 'Wireless information may be communicated to the bombarding fleet; and bombs may be dropped with effect where the ships' guns would be powerless'

It is said that fatigue killed more German soldiers than fell to British bullets; and the fact may well be believed when we consider the herculean task General von Füchter had accomplished in one week. His plan of campaign was to strike his hardest, and to keep on striking his hardest, without pause, till he had the British Government on its knees before him; till he had the British public—maddened by sudden fear, and the panic which blows of this sort must bring to a people with no defensive organization, and no disciplinary training—cowed and crying for quarter.

The German Commander has been called inhuman, a monster, a creature without bowels. All that is really of small importance. He was a soldier who carried out orders. His orders were ruthless orders. The instrument he used was a very perfect one. He carried out his orders with the utmost precision and thoroughness; and his method was the surest, quickest, and, perhaps, the only way of taking possession of England.

At noon precisely, the Lord Mayor of London was brought before the German Commander-in-Chief in the audience chamber of the Mansion House, and formally placed under arrest. A triple cordon of sentries and two machine-gun parties were placed in charge of the Bank of England, and quarters were allotted for two German regiments in the immediate vicinity. Two machine-guns were brought into position in front of the Stock Exchange, and all avenues leading from the heart of the City were occupied by mixed details of cavalry and infantry, each party having one machine-gun.

My acquaintance, Wardle, of the *Sunday News* was in the audience chamber of the Mansion House at this time, and he says that he never saw a man look more exhausted than General von Füchter, who, according to report, had not had an hour's sleep during the week. But though the General's cheeks were sunken, his chin unshaven, and his eyes blood-red, his demeanour was that of an iron man—stern, brusque, taciturn, erect, and singularly immobile.

Food was served to this man of blood and iron in the Mansion House, while the Lord Mayor's secretary proceeded to Whitehall, with word to the effect that the Commander-in-Chief of the German forces in England awaited the sword and formal surrender of the British Commander, before proceeding to take up quarters in which he would deal with peace negotiations.

Forster's great work, *The Surrender*, gives the finest description we have of the scene that followed. The Field Marshal in command of the British forces had that morning been sent for by a Cabinet Council then being held in the Prime Minister's room at the House of Commons. With nine members of his staff, the white-haired Field Marshal rode slowly into the city, in full uniform. His instructions were for unconditional surrender, and a request for the immediate consideration of the details of peace negotiations.

The Field Marshal had once been the most popular idol of the British people, whom he had served nobly in a hundred fights. Of late years he himself had been as completely disregarded as the grave warnings, the earnest appeals, which he had bravely continued to urge upon a neglectful people. The very Government which now dispatched him upon the hardest task of his whole career, the tendering of his sword to his country's enemy, had for long treated him with cold disfavour. The general public, in its anti-national madness, had sneered at this great little man, their one-time hero, as a jingo crank.

(As an instance of the lengths to which the public madness went in this matter, the curious will find in the British Museum copies of at least one farcical work of fiction written and published with considerable success, as burlesques of that very invasion which had now occurred, of the possibility of which this loyal servant in particular had so earnestly and so unavailingly warned his countrymen.)

Now, the blow he had so often foreshadowed had fallen; the capital of the British Empire was actually in the possession of an enemy; and the British leader knew himself for a Commander without an Army.

He had long since given his only son to the cause of Britain's defence. The whole of his own strenuous life had been devoted to the same cause. His declining years had known no ease by reason of his unceasing and thankless strivings to awaken his fellow-countrymen to a sense of their military responsibilities. Now he felt that the end of all things had come for him, in the carrying out of an order which snapped his life's work in two, and flung it down at the feet of England's almost unopposed conqueror.

The understanding Englishman has forgiven General von Füchter much, by virtue of his treatment of the noble old soldier, who with tear-blinded eyes and twitching lips tendered him the surrender of the almost non-existent British Army. No man ever heard a speech from General Füchter, but the remark with which he returned our Field Marshal's sword to him will never be forgotten in England. He said, in rather laboured English, with a stiff, low bow:

'Keep it, my lord. If your countrymen had not forgotten how to recognize a great soldier, I could never have demanded it of you.'

And the man of iron saluted the heart-broken Chief of the shattered British Army.

We prefer not to believe the report that this, the German Commander's one act of gentleness and magnanimity in England, was subsequently paid for by the loss of a certain Imperial decoration. But, if the story was true, then the decoration it concerned was well lost.

It was a grim, war-stained procession that followed General von Füchter when, between two and three o'clock, he rode with his staff by way of Ludgate Hill and the Strand to Carlton House Terrace. But the cavalry rode with drawn sabres, the infantry marched with fixed bayonets, and, though weariness showed in every line of the men's faces, there was as yet no sign of relaxed tension.

Throughout that evening and night the baggage wagons rumbled through London, without cessation, to the two main western encampments in Hyde Park. The whole of Pall Mall and Park Lane were occupied by German officers that night, few of the usual occupants of the clubs in the one thoroughfare, or the residences in the other, being then in London.

By four o'clock General von Füchter's terms were in the hands of the Government which had now completed its earning of the title of 'The Destroyers'. The Chief Commissioner of Police and the principal municipal authorities of greater London had all been examined during the day at the House of Commons, and were unanimous in their verdict that any delay in the arrangement of peace and the resumption of trade, ashore and afloat, could mean only revolution. Whole streets of shops had been sacked and looted already by hungry mobs, who gave no thought to the invasion or to any other matter than the question of food supply. A great, lowering crowd of hungry men and women occupied Westminster Bridge and the southern embankment (no German soldiers had been seen south of the Thames) waiting for the news of the promised conclusion of peace terms.

There is not wanting evidence that certain members of the Government had already bitterly repented of their suicidal retrenchment and anti-defensive attitude in the past. But repentance had come too late. The Government stood between a hungry, terrified populace demanding peace and food, and a mighty and victorious army whose commander, acting upon the orders of his Government, offered peace at a terrible price, or the absolute destruction of London. For General von Füchter's brief memorandum of terms alluded threateningly to the fact that his heavy artillery was so placed that he could blow the House of Commons into the river in an hour.

At six o'clock the German terms were accepted, a provisional declaration of peace was signed, and public proclamations to that effect, embodying references to the deadly perils which would be incurred by those taking part in any kind of street disorder, were issued to the public. As to the nature of the German terms, it must be admitted that they were as pitiless as the German tactics throughout the invasion, and as surely designed to accomplish their end and object. Berlin had not forgotten the wonderful recuperative powers which enabled France to rise so swiftly from out of the ashes of 1870. Britain was to be far more effectually crippled.

The money indemnity demanded by General von Füchter was the

largest ever known: one thousand million pounds sterling. But it must be remembered that the enemy already held the Bank of England. One hundred millions, or securities representing that amount, were to be handed over within twenty-four hours. The remaining nine hundred millions were to be paid in nine annual instalments of one hundred millions each, the first of which must be paid within three months. Until the last payment was made, German troops were to occupy Glasgow, Cardiff, Portsmouth, Devonport, Chatham, Yarmouth, Harwich, Hull, and Newcastle. The Transvaal was to be ceded to the Boers under a German Protectorate. Britain was to withdraw all pretensions regarding Egypt and Morocco, and to cede to Germany Gibraltar, Malta, Ceylon, and British West Africa.

It is not necessary for me to quote the few further details of the most exacting demands a victor ever made upon a defeated enemy. There can be no doubt that, in the disastrous circumstances they had been so largely instrumental in bringing about, 'The Destroyers' had no choice, no alternative from their acceptance of these crushing terms.

And thus it was that—not at the end of a long and hard-fought war, as the result of vast misfortunes or overwhelming valour on the enemy's side, but simply as the result of the condition of utter and lamentable defencelessness into which a truckling Government and an undisciplined, blindly selfish people had allowed England to lapse—the greatest, wealthiest Power in civilization was brought to its knees in the incredibly short space of one week, by the sudden but scientifically devised onslaught of a single ambitious nation, ruled by a monarch whose lack of scruples was more than balanced by his strength of purpose.

In the last paragraph of The Message *the author goes into the ritual mode so characteristic of this prophetic fiction. His message for the nation is short and sharp: the blame for the projected disaster lies with 'a truckling Government and an undisciplined, blindly selfish people'. The lesson for all is painfully self-evident: although an island people may have a powerful navy, in times of danger when a great continental power threatens the security of the nation, every man has to be a soldier.*

So, these tales of German hordes on British soil went on from one variant to another in their life-or-death accounts of the coming struggle. One device, much favoured in its day, was the malign activity of 'the Enemy in our Midst'. This was a true nightmare—the realization of total impotence and the fear of the Other—that came from an eagerness to believe in the immense efficiency and ruthless will of the Kaiser and his dark invaders. So, the perceived threat from without was internalized within the frequently repeated episode of 'The Army in Waiting'. Without warning, in the midst of peace, German troops suddenly pour out of their hiding places to seize strong points, destroy telephone lines, and occupy London. This form of para-noia—a consequence of thinking too much about the future—matches every fear with its own proper nightmare. It has worked its prodigious effects from the earliest days of science fiction, notably in the dawning fear of an unreg-ulated science in Mary Shelley's Frankenstein *and in the later fear of an inhuman yet perfected weaponry in Wells's* War of the Worlds. *That fantasy of the alien invader foreshadowed and preceded the British anticipa-tions of the war-to-come with Germany. The Martians made their journey through space in order to break out from the circumscribed conditions of their planet; and the Germans were expected to make their dash across the North Sea to secure a greater* Lebensraum *and so seize 'the dominion of the globe' from the British, as August Niemann forecast in* Der Weltkrieg— Deutsche Traüme *in 1904.*

When England Slept

A dominant lament runs throughout these British tales of the German invas-ion—a requiem for a nation that has been fore-warned but is not yet fore-armed. In 1903 Erskine Childers revealed the secret preparations for invasion in The Riddle of the Sands. *By 1906 London had been bombarded, occupied and looted by German troops in Le Queux's* Invasion of 1910. *Why were the Germans so successful? One answer appears in the chapter, 'How It Was Done', where the author of* When England Slept *(1909) describes how the Londoners wake up to find that the Germans have seized London. The first news comes from a police inspector who later recorded how, having received reports of troops on the move through central London about three o'clock in the morning, he 'started out himself to see what he could find out ...'*

...it was then about half-past four by Big Ben as he came out of the Westminster end of the Embankment, and the next thing his eyes rested upon was a dense column of infantry soldiers pouring over Westminster Bridge. He began, by then, to have some suspicions of what was occurring, aroused by the fact of the non-return of the men he had sent out on the motor-bicycles, and, therefore, hid himself in a doorway.

'The soldiers', as he explained to me, 'were marching in columns of half-companies, which took up pretty nearly the whole breadth of Westminster Bridge, and they came on one solid mass of men under three mounted officers.' He calculated that they numbered between two and three thousand; they made very little noise as they marched, and he came to the conclusion that their boots were covered with felt.

'They had scarcely passed, crossing the square towards Birdcage Walk, when another column crept up along the Embankment nearly as strong; they marched noiselessly as the others had done, in absolute silence, with their rifles at the slope. These also passed up towards Birdcage Walk, and were followed almost immediately by two batteries of field-guns, four guns in each.'

By this time the inspector was pretty well amazed; he could not get near enough to the columns to see the soldiers' faces clearly, but he was perfectly certain that they were not British troops from the way they marched, although they were clothed in khaki, which he was, however, quite able to see was slop-made.

He lost no time in returning to Scotland Yard, and there he was met on the doorstep by a German officer, who informed him that he was under arrest. It was perfectly useless to resist; half a company of German infantry were drawn up in the courtyard with fixed bayonets.

The narrative shifts to a London club, where the members assemble to hear the latest news read from a copy of the Liverpool Courier *which reveals 'How It Was Done':*

STUPENDOUS COUP BY THE GERMANS

LONDON SEIZED IN ONE NIGHT

WITHOUT DECLARATION OF WAR

Appalling though the intelligence will undoubtedly be to our readers, yet it is, nevertheless, a fact beyond question that the six million odd inhabitants of London, who went to bed with a feeling of perfect security on Saturday night, awoke on Sunday morning to find the capital of the British Empire occupied by a great German Army!

Even now the means by which this great coup—perhaps the greatest known in history—was accomplished can only be guessed at. Several well-known London journalists, and others connected with the Press, have fortunately succeeded in evading the chain of German vedettes and outposts which attempt to cut off London from the provinces, and, fortunately, as might be expected, only partially succeed.

It would appear that the first intimation conveyed to the sleeping population that something was wrong arose from the sound of firing heard in almost all parts of the Metropolis soon after five o'clock on Sunday morning: this brought many from their beds into the streets on a voyage of discovery towards the centre of the West End, from which the firing principally proceeded.

To those who had turned out, and to the inhabitants of the immediate districts, a perfectly incomprehensible state of affairs was disclosed in the following centres:

Wellington Barracks, in which were stationed two battalions of the Guards, were besieged by some thousands of foreign troops, who proved to be Germans, and who eventually brought a battery of artillery to bear upon the Household troops, who resolutely refused to surrender. We regret to state that nearly two-thirds of these gallant men were killed or seriously wounded before the Germans, in enormous numbers and preceded by a storm of shells and hand-grenades, succeeded in rushing the barracks and making prisoners of the very small unwounded remainder of the two battalions.

It is an extraordinary fact that the two battalions, the 1st Scots Guards and 3rd Grenadiers, fought practically under the command of their non-commissioned officers, all the commissioned officers, excepting the adjutants and quarter-masters, living out of barracks.

Chelsea Barracks and the 3rd Coldstreams were rushed by an overwhelming force of Germans before daylight, many of the men being bayoneted in their beds. The Horse Guards (Blue), who turned out within a few minutes, were almost annihilated by a hellish magazine-fire from the hordes of German infantry whom they most gallantly charged twice before Chelsea Barracks.

The battery of Horse Artillery stationed at St. John's Wood was captured after a gallant resistance, and when the latest news left London on Sunday evening, the 2nd battalion of the Grenadiers was still holding out at the Tower of London, though from the heavy fire directed against it, it was expected to fall every hour. The 1st Life Guards at Albany Barracks,

Regent's Park, in obedience to superior orders, succeeded in breaking through the Germans and making for Aldershot, where they arrived about mid-day on Sunday, having sustained over fifty casualties.

Such is a brief record of some of the principal catastrophes which befell London early on Sunday morning; but, as will be seen, by no means all, nor, indeed, the most important. The first question asked will, of course, be:

'Where did the Germans come from in such enormous numbers? How did two hundred thousand men—that is their estimated strength—succeed in one night in making themselves masters of the capital of the world?'

That question can only be answered at present in part, or, to be correct, in fragments, pieced in with surmise; in other words, by our putting together in one narration the various reports which have reached us; and among these, certain events seem to be beyond contradiction and to stand by themselves.

First, there cannot be a vestige of a doubt that for some weeks past large bodies of German soldiers in civilian dress have been dribbling into the United Kingdom through every available port. So cleverly has the scheme been put together, that it is doubtful whether these men even knew what they were brought here for, many having been engaged by private German and other foreign firms who were evidently 'in the know'.

But to these must be added a great number of tourists, men who had been encouraged by their government to visit England for various reasons, and who, of course, were all trained reservists. Every one of these visitors, and, indeed, every German reservist in the United Kingdom, must have been well known and marked, and his address tabulated for instant use.

It is also a fact well established that a great number of Germans of the better class—first and second-class passengers —also entered various ports of the United Kingdom during the last month, and distributed themselves, some in London, but principally in the pleasure resorts of England, Scotland, and Wales. These were in groups of twos and threes—never more than three together—thus they escaped observation, and generally gave themselves out to be either Russians, Swiss, or French. In any case, the two or three thousand distributed up and down England, Scotland and Wales, and even perhaps in Ireland too, created no remark.

In some way at present unknown, on Saturday last, the guiding spirit of this great movement gave the signal; there cannot be a shred of doubt that on that day every German reservist in the United Kingdom received notice to concentrate in London, and that, too, by the last train entering the Metropolis on that night. Thus far the facts are pretty plain reading. The next phase in the story is less clear—that is, from the arrival of the last trains at the London termini, not counting the mails which come in at all hours—until the information furnished by the police which dates from three o'clock on Sunday morning.

It is perfectly certain that during those hours a great army of Germans, with its full complement of officers and sub-officers, a mighty organization was either hid somewhere in London, or, what is more probable, its components, as the night was very fine, were walking about the streets in plain clothes! The first overt act which laid bare the workings of this great plot was recorded by a police-constable at Pentonville. At a quarter-past three he reported at the police station that the local Territorial infantry battalion, the 11th London, was assembling and preparing to turn out. He stated that the drill hall was lighted up, and that the men were rapidly equipping and arming themselves.

The Inspector on duty at first attached little importance to the matter, thinking the Territorials had been marching out; but at the request of the constable, who was convinced that all was not right, rang up Scotland Yard and reported the circumstance. This was the last communication that Scotland Yard received from Pentonville police-station. Within a few minutes it was rung up by nine police-stations in various parts of London, who all reported that Territorials were assembling at the neighbouring drill halls. Thoroughly puzzled, the heads of the police rang up the districts for further information, only to find that all communication was cut off. The reason for this is easily explained; taking the state of affairs at Pentonville station as a fair example of the rest, this is what occurred:

The Inspector had scarcely put the receiver of the telephone back on its hook, when the heavy tramp of men was heard passing the police-station; this proved to be a strong battalion of infantry. A section of it halted before the police-station and fixed bayonets; an officer in a strange khaki uniform, not of the British pattern, then entered the station with two men and informed the police officers in good English that they were all prisoners!

The state of affairs was so astounding that the Inspector states that he was almost speechless with astonishment to find himself 'detained' in his own police-station. His first impulse was to ring up Scotland Yard and report the circumstance; but at his first move towards the telephone he was covered by the rifle of one of the men who accompanied the German officer. These men were evidently clothed in the khaki uniform of British Territorials, and, as a matter of fact, one of the police officers read the letters on the men's shoulders: '11th London'. The uniforms were obviously misfits and rather ludicrous in appearance, but the men were under the most perfect discipline.

The German officer formally took possession of the police-station in the name of the German Emperor, while the Inspector and constables stood around as in a dream. He then explained to them that if they were willing to give their parole not to take up arms against the German Emperor, they would be released and allowed to carry on their duty as usual in the preservation of order, but subservient to the German military law, which, he further explained, over-rode all. If they decided not to give their parole, then they would be immediately imprisoned; but in the event of their giving their parole and breaking it, they would, he impressed upon them, be immediately shot should they be captured again. Two of the constables flatly refused to promise not to serve against the Germans, and were marched off to join a squad of similar non-jurors without. The Inspector, after reflection, gave his parole, and advised the constables to do the same in the interests of order. This was evidently the wisest course he could have pursued under the circumstances.

The most astounding thing to the Inspector was that the German officer who made the police-station his headquarters seemed perfectly acquainted with the whole neighbourhood. He produced voluminous typed lists and despatched portions of the waiting body of soldiers in various directions: the first for a motor-car at such-and-such an address; horses at this, that, and the other street. Two of these, having been equipped with spare saddles and bridles from the police-station—under protest—were hastily marched away for the use of the officers commanding. The remainder of the horses were used, some to furnish mounted patrols, and others, the heaviest, drafted off under the care of evidently competent men to a neighbouring district, where it turned out they were required to horse guns.

Within half an hour the German officer had everything in working order, including a requisition of the neighbouring tradesmen's stocks, the proprietors themselves being unceremoniously aroused from their beds to furnish them. Within three-quarters of an hour of his first entry, the German officer's servant was making coffee in the Inspector's coffee-pot, and with the aid of the police-station kettle, to the amazement of a few constables who lived near, and who, coming in to see what was 'up', were promptly made prisoners, and 'paroled' where they would accept it.

The proceedings at Pentonville were a fair type of what took place in every district of London at that hour which possessed a local Territorial corps, whether of horse, foot, artillery, or engineers. In each case the whole of the material—field guns, howitzers, rifles, bayonets, a vast quantity of ammunition and transport, and the khaki uniforms of the men—were appropriated for the use of the soldiers of His Imperial Majesty the German Emperor.

It is clear that for a long time past these Territorial headquarters and the districts around them have been the subject of most patient and exhaustive inquiry on the part of the German spies. These spies, no doubt harmless-looking clerks and workmen, have found means to obtain minute information, probably through too confiding members of the Territorial units, who have introduced them, perhaps boastfully, as friendly visitors into their headquarters to observe the 'perfect systems' of their respective regiments. Be that as it may, the information has been obtained somehow, for the German preparations have gone on without a hitch. The fact of the arms being returned at this time of the year to the headquarters, after the summer drills, to be overhauled and browned, has been a very determining factor evidently in the German calculations; otherwise the invaders might have found empty racks at the armouries, and the rifles and bayonets in the hands of their rightful owners; as it is, they have calculated matters to a nicety, and the German commanding officers of these centres are acquainted with the productive resources of the neighbourhood down to the last pound of candles in the grocers' shops.

By 1906 it had become apparent that, although British and German writers agreed about the possibility of war between their two countries, there were marked differences between the conduct of the Zukunftskrieg *and the shape of 'the Next Great War'. For instance, the Germans never produced anything to compare with the British tales of the nation under enemy occupation, since the arguments of their propagandists could only put the case for a great navy. German writers had every reason for believing that on land the greatest army in Europe could take on all comers in any future war. With British writers, however, the ever-repeated question was: What would happen when that great army arrived on British soil?*

Ever since the appearance of Chesney's Battle of Dorking *in 1871 the routine answer had been: a crushing defeat, the payment of a crippling indemnity, the elimination of the Royal Navy, and the end of the Empire. British authors sought to show that an invasion would be little more than annual manoeuvres for the Germans—their cavalry trooping through well-known areas of the British countryside, their artillery putting down a creeping barrage across London. The propaganda required that British readers should suffer all the agonies of outrageous misfortune— smashed homes, starving citizens, and firing squads for the heroic defenders.*

The North Sea Bubble

Up to 1906 these writers had told their stories as they had happened; then Ernest Oldmeadow changed the point of view in The North Sea Bubble *by cutting out the preliminaries and coming directly to the consequences. After all the action canvases—the landings and the rapid advances—there comes the painful observation of a still life under enemy rule. The invasion has long since finished. The United Kingdom is part of the Reich, and a German* Statthalter *rules in London. This is life as it will be under the jackboot: a time for penance and for pondering those moral failings that led to the great collapse. Ernest Oldmeadow reveals the worst of all possible worlds in his opening paragraphs.*

THE GERMAN CONQUEST OF GREAT BRITAIN

By the middle of December 1910, the German conquest of Great Britain was practically complete. The execution of the Mayor of Birmingham and the deportation to Heligoland of all politicians tainted with Imperialist opinions had not been without effect. Even Warwickshire and Kent lay sullenly quiet at last under the heel of martial law.

So far, Ireland had been left alone. Europe rightly guessed that motives of high politics rather than military considerations accounted for German inaction on the western shores of St George's Channel. It was the secret intention of the Imperial Chancellor to give Ireland a liberal measure of Home Rule and to restore the Parliament on College Green, reserving to Berlin little more than the control of Ireland's armed forces and foreign relations. The sane and well-informed testimony of Knubsen (who, as Norwegian Minister at Berlin, had access to the truth at its fountainhead) is conclusive on this point. He writes:

> The Imperial Chancellor was determined not to repeat the blunder of 1871. Stricken to the dust and bleeding at every pore, it seemed in that year, both to herself and to the world, that France must be powerless for a generation, or at least until the German Empire had obtained so long a lead that France could never hope to overtake her. Yet, in a few years, the indemnity was paid, and the Republic could count on armies incomparably superior to the ill-fated legions which had followed Louis Napoleon 'à Berlin', only to find their graves at Sedan.
>
> Among the devices whereby the Chancellor intended to frustrate the regeneration of England as a first-class power was the granting of autonomy to Ireland under German suzerainty. At one stroke he would thus rid himself of Ireland's perilous domestic politics during the years of occupation, and, at the same time, he would plant a perpetual menace on England's western flank. With Belgium and Holland practically in German hands, England would lie like a filbert in a pair of nut-crackers.*

Additional light is shed upon the workings of the Chancellor's mind by the more sprightly but generally accurate *Memoirs* of the Countess

* Eric Knubsen, *Three Years in Berlin*, Eng. trans., 1914, pp. 313–14.

de Coutigny. She says, under the date Dec. 20, 1910:

> It turns out that the Imperial Chancellor is an angel after all.
> From what von Piflitz tells me, the Fatherland is only taking
> liberty away from England to pass it on to Ireland. All pure
> philanthropy and love of freedom, of course. Nevertheless
> virtue is to be rewarded in two ways. First, all this handsome-
> ness to Ireland will please the American-Irish so much that it
> will counteract the growing pro-British movement in the
> United States. Second, after so much good-will to the faithful
> Isle of Saints, the Vatican can hardly go on sulking.
>
> The Chancellor is prepared to justify himself by the prece-
> dent of Cuba and the Philippines. And he is quite ready with
> an answer for anybody who may choose to throw Poland in
> his teeth. It seems that discontented Islands, being self-
> contained, are not in the same category with discontented
> Peoples just over a land-frontier.*

Finally, we have the dark saying, inscrutable to those who first
heard it, of that bitter oracle Sir Terence Joyce, who declared to the
Commons during its panic-stricken session at Bristol:

> The government is fulfilling at least one of its pledges. The
> government is giving Ireland Home Rule.

No suspicion, however, of these designs entered the heads of the
beaten English during the black days of December 1910. Almost
without exception, they believed that the enemy's inaction in
Ireland was due partly to the need of rest for the troops, and chiefly
to the well-known desire of the Irish to be done with British rule. In
other words, the German invasion of Ireland would be a dress-
parade, and there was plenty of time for the invaders to make
themselves look presentable for the occasion.

As if to make up for the dejection of the conquered, the
conquerors everywhere prepared to keep Christmas on an imposing
scale. The postal system having been fully restored, even the
remotest outposts of the army of occupation received every day
from their friends and relatives in Germany parcels containing all
things needful for a thoroughly German Christmas on British soil.
So as to rub down the sharp edges of defeat, a few of the higher officers endeavoured to persuade their men to repay these home
kindnesses by buying and sending to Germany plum-puddings,

---

* *The Coutigny Memoirs*. Eng. trans., vol. ii, pp. 28–29.

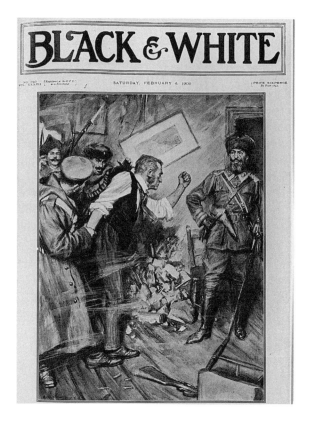

A dramatic statement
on the need for
conscription: the
moment of truth in
Guy du Maurier's *An
Englishman's Home*

mince-pies, crackers, and other British products. In this way the officers hoped to increase work and wages among the native
population. But Hans and Franz preferred to keep their cash in their
pockets, and contented themselves with sending off picture post-
cards (printed in Germany) representing the beauty-spots and
historic buildings of England, Scotland, and Wales.

With characteristic sagacity, the Imperial Commissioner
earmarked £30,000,000 of the gold found in the vaults of the Bank
of England for prompt disbursement in the cities which had suffered
most grievously during the war. These millions were disseminated as
wages in return for services which kept the recipients fully
employed. The damaged railways and public works were repaired,
and scores of thousands of men were engaged improving the roads
in East Anglia. For those who could not work with their hands,
innumerable little duties were found or devised.

Under gentle pressure from the censors, the newspapers began to
enliven their dismal pages with paragraphs and articles describing

the imminent revels. The following samples will give a fair idea of the bulk:

From the *Morning Marconigram*, Dec. 19, 1910:

> It is an ill-wind that blows nobody good: and the unhappy events of the year about to close are no exception to the rule. Season after season, the growers of Christmas trees, and the makers of the tiny toys and gaudy candles with which the boughs are decked, have bewailed a steadily dwindling trade. Owing, however, to the presence among us of so many visitors from the land where the Christmas-tree first struck root, quite a boom has begun in young firs and spruces, while 1910 promises to be a record year in glass humming-birds, mouth organs, and toy baa-lambs.

From the *Daily Mail* of the same date:

> With a delicacy which the London public will not be slow to appreciate, General Wurstheim has given orders that the arrangements for the colossal Weihnachtsfest of the German General Staff at Olympia shall be carried out as unobtrusively as possible. 'It is a soldier's business to cut down his enemy,' the General is reported to have said to a tactless subaltern, 'but not to rub salt into his wounds.' Nevertheless, it has transpired that the preparations already made are of unprecedented magnitude. Half a million sausages of eighty-three different kinds have been hanging since Sunday morning from half a million nails, and a hundred thousand barrels of lager beer will be placed in position by noon to-morrow. As for the sauerkraut, pfefferkuchen and Bismarck herrings, they are declared to be beyond the dreams of appetite.

From the *Daily News*, Dec. 21, 1910:

> Across this saddest of all sad Yuletides there has fallen this morning a ray of sunshine. Field-Marshal von Senf has issued orders to all officers commanding throughout the country, whereby the hanging of persons convicted under martial law will be suspended during this season of peace and good-will. From Christmas Eve until New Year's Day, such offenders, instead of being hanged, will be shot.

So Christmas drew on. In passing, it is worth noting that, despite the small area of England, its density of population, and the supposed omnipresence of the invader's garrisons, there were still hundreds of villages and country towns where Christmas, though chastened and subdued, was honoured in the old English fashion by men and women and children who had not yet heard the bursting of a German shell or seen a German uniform. In the snowy lanes of these favoured spots even the waits went their ways unchallenged, and there is no more touching lay in all the writings of Barretson, the curate-poet, than his lines called, 'Waits in War-time'. But there was a dark side even to this little picture. At Thirsk, at Wellington in Shropshire,* at Kendal, at Merthyr Tydvil, and at Birchington-on-Sea, parties of carol-singers were shot down in the snow by patrols who misinterpreted such nocturnal forgatherings; while four men and two women lost their lives in Yorkshire during an ill-timed attempt to sing 'Christians, awake! salute the Happy Morn'.

Despite the stringent regulations concerning public assemblies, permission was given in many places for the traditional singing of 'The Messiah'. It was, however, made a binding condition that the name of Handel on the placards should be correctly spelt Haendel.

Christmas Day dawned dully. And it did not cheer either German or Englishman to learn from the morning papers that the steamship *Prinz Eitel,* conveying the two hundred banished Members of Parliament from Hamburg to Heligoland, had encountered a fog and was two days overdue.

When William Came

The contrast between the British and German styles in future-war fiction appears most strikingly in the elegiac prose of When William Came *(1913) by 'Saki'. There can be no doubt that his tale of the German occupation of the United Kingdom derives from a literary tradition distinct from, and indeed alien to, the sober and earnest accounts of the* Zukunftskrieg. *The 'Saki' story connects with modern times. Published one year before the outbreak of the First World War and joined in spirit with the nostalgic yearning for a lost paradise that is central to the later fiction of Evelyn Waugh, it reveals a peculiarly English interest in the transformation by some catastrophic change of the familiar—landscape, society, the entire known order. The world chronometer comes to an instant stop. The narrative tracks*

---

* With his never-failing inaccuracy, Slobbings, in *The Germans in England*, vol. iii, p. 91, writes 'Wellington in Somerset'.

across the bad lands of the coming chaos to reveal the last human beings in Mary Shelley's The Last Man *(1816), or the barbarian world of Richard Jefferies's* After London *(1885), or the pastoral communities of W. H. Hudson's* A Crystal Age *(1887). After the colossal destruction wrought by the Martian fighting machines in Wells's* War of the Worlds *(1898), after the terror and the panic, early on the fifteenth day of waiting the time-frame freezes and the narrator comes out of hiding into an empty, desolate and silent world. 'For a time,' he reports, 'I believed that mankind had been swept out of existence, and that I stood there alone, the last man left alive.'*

In like manner, the narrator in When William Came *returns from a long absence in Russia to find his country under German occupation. Disgusted by the time-servers and opportunists in the London of the Hohenzollerns, Yeovil leaves for the country home of an old friend, Eleanor, Dowager Lady Greymarten. She had 'for more than half a century been the ruling spirit at Torywood ... in the wider field of national and Imperial service she had worked and schemed and fought with an energy and a far-sightedness that came probably from the blend of caution and restlessness in her Scottish blood.'*

The train journey from London is the beginning of a voyage to another, better world of established hierarchies and old values, of loyalty and patriotism. On the way, Yeovil discovers the moral failings that had led to the defeat of his country.

SURELY A COUNTRY WORTH FIGHTING FOR

The train bearing Yeovil on his visit to Tared slid and rattled westward through the hazy dreamland of an English summer landscape. Seen from the train windows, the stark bare ugliness of the metalled line was forgotten, and the eye rested only on the green solitude that unfolded itself as the miles went slipping by. Tall grasses and meadow-weeds stood in deep shocks, field after field, between the leafy boundaries of hedge or coppice, thrusting themselves higher and higher till they touched the low sweeping branches of the trees that here and there overshadowed them. Broad streams, bordered with a heavy fringe of reed and sedge, went winding away into a green distance where woodland and meadowland seemed indefinitely prolonged; narrow streamlets, lost to view in the growth that fostered them, disclosed their presence merely by the water-weed that showed in a riband of rank verdure threading the mellower green of the fields. On the stream banks moorhens walked with jerky confident steps, in the easy boldness of those who had a couple of other elements at their disposal in an emergency; more timorous partridges raced away from the apparition of the train, looking all leg and neck, like little forest elves fleeing from the human encounter. And in the distance, over the tree line, a heron or two flapped with slow measured wing-beats and an air of being bent on an immeasurably longer journey than the train that hurtled so frantically along the rails. Now and then the meadowland changed itself suddenly into orchard, with close-growing trees already showing the measure of their coming harvest, and then straw-yard and farm buildings would slide into view; heavy dairy cattle, roan, and skewbald and dappled, stood near the gates, drowsily resentful of insect stings, and bunched-up companies of ducks halted in seeming irresolution between the charms of the horse-pond and the alluring neighbourhood of the farm kitchen. Away by the banks of some rushing mill-stream, in a setting of copse and cornfield, a village might be guessed at, just a hint of red roof, grey wreathed chimney and old church tower as seen from the windows of the passing train, and over it all brooded a happy settled-calm, like the dreaming murmur of a trout-stream and the far-away cawing of rooks.

It was a land where it seemed as if it must be always summer and generally afternoon, a land where bees hummed among the wild thyme and in the flower-beds of cottage gardens, where the harvest-mice rustled amid the corn and nettles, and the mill-race flowed cool and silent through water-weeds and dark tunnelled sluices, and made soft droning music with the wooden mill-wheel. And the music carried with it the wording of old undying rhymes, and sang of the jolly, uncaring, uncared-for miller, of the farmer who went riding upon his grey mare, of the mouse who lived beneath the merry mill-pin, of the sweet music on yonder green hill and the dancers all in yellow—the songs and fancies of a lingering olden time, when men took life as children take a long summer day, and went to bed at last with a simple trust in something they could not have explained.

Yeovil watched the passing landscape with the intent hungry eyes of a man who revisits a scene that holds high place in his affections. His imagination raced even quicker than the train, following winding roads and twisting valleys into unseen distances, picturing farms and hamlets, hills and hollows, clattering inn yards and sleepy woodlands.

'A beautiful country,' said his only fellow-traveller, who was also gazing at the fleeting landscape; 'surely a country worth fighting for.'

He spoke in fairly correct English, but he was unmistakably a foreigner; one could have allotted him with some certainty to the Eastern half of Europe.

'A beautiful country, as you say,' replied Yeovil; then he added the question, 'Are you German?'

'No, Hungarian', said the other; 'and you, you are English?' he asked.

'I have been much in England, but I am from Russia,' said Yeovil, purposely misleading his companion on the subject of his nationality in order to induce him to talk with greater freedom on a delicate topic. While living among foreigners in a foreign land he had shrunk from hearing his country's disaster discussed, or even alluded to; now he was anxious to learn what unprejudiced foreigners thought of the catastrophe and the causes which had led up to it.

'It is a strange spectacle, a wonder, is it not so?' resumed the other, 'a great nation such as this was, one of the greatest nations in modern times, or of any time, carrying its flag and its language into all parts of the world, and now, after one short campaign, it is—'

And he shrugged his shoulders many times and made clucking noises at the roof of his voice, like a hen calling to a brood of roving chickens.

'They grew soft,' he resumed; 'great world-commerce brings great luxury, and luxury brings softness. They had everything to warn them, things happening in their own time and before their eyes, and they would not be warned. They had seen, in one generation, the rise of the military and naval power of the Japanese, a brown-skinned race living in some island rice-fields in a tropical sea, a people one thought of in connection with paper fans and flowers and pretty tea-gardens, who suddenly marched and sailed into the world's gaze as a Great Power; they had seen, too, the rise of the Bulgars, a poor herd of *zaptieh*-ridden peasants, with a few students scattered in exile in Bukarest and Odessa, who shot up in one generation to be an armed and aggressive nation with history in its hands. The English saw these things happening around them, and with a war-cloud growing blacker and bigger and always more threatening on their own threshold they sat down to grow soft and peaceful. They grew soft and accommodating in all things; in religion—'

'In religion?' said Yeovil.

'In religion, yes,' said his companion emphatically; 'they had come to look on the Christ as a sort of amiable elder Brother, whose letters from abroad were worth reading. Then, when they had emptied all the divine mystery and wonder out of their faith naturally they grew tired of it, oh, but dreadfully tired of it. I know many

English of the country parts, and always they tell me they go to church once in each week to set the good example to the servants. They were tired of their faith, but they were not virile enough to become real Pagans; their dancing fauns were good young men who tripped Morris dances and ate health foods and believed in a sort of Socialism which made for the greatest dullness of the greatest number. You will find plenty of them still if you go into what remains of social London.'

Yeovil gave a grunt of acquiescence.

'They grew soft in their political ideas,' continued the unsparing critic; 'for the old insular belief that all foreigners were devils and rogues they substituted another belief, equally grounded on insular lack of knowledge, that most foreigners were amiable, good fellows, who only needed to be talked to and patted on the back to become your friends and benefactors. They began to believe that a foreign Minister would relinquish long-cherished schemes of national policy and hostile expansion if he came over on a holiday and was asked down to country houses and shown the tennis court and the rock-garden and the younger children.

'Listen. I once heard it solemnly stated at an after-dinner debate in some literary club that a certain very prominent German states-man had a daughter at school in England, and that future friendly relations between the two countries were improved in prospect, if not assured, by that circumstance. You think I am laughing; I am recording a fact, and the men present were politicians and statesmen as well as literary dilettanti. It was an insular lack of insight that worked the mischief, or some of the mischief. We, in Hungary, we live too much cheek by jowl with our racial neighbours to have many illusions about them. Austrians, Roumanians, Serbs, Italians, Czechs, we know what they think of us, and we know what to think of them; we know what we want in the world, and we know what they want; that knowledge does not send us flying at each other's throats, but it does keep us from growing soft. Ah, the British lion was in a hurry to inaugurate the Millennium and to lie down grace-fully with the lamb. He made two mistakes, only two, but they were very bad ones; the Millennium hadn't arrived, and it was not a lamb that he was lying down with.'

'You do not like the English, I gather,' said Yeovil, as the Hungarian went off into a short burst of satirical laughter.

'I have always liked them,' he answered, 'but now I am angry with them for being soft. Here is my station,' he added, as the train slowed down, and he commenced to gather his belongings together.

'I am angry with them', he continued, as a final word on the subject, 'because I *hate* the Germans.'

He raised his hat punctiliously in a parting salute and stepped out on to the platform. His place was taken by a large, loose-limbed man, with florid face and big staring eyes, and an immense array of fishing basket, rod, fly-cases, and so forth. He was of the type that one could instinctively locate as a loud-voiced, self-constituted authority on whatever topic might happen to be discussed in the bars of small hotels.

'Are you English?' he asked, after a preliminary stare at Yeovil.

This time Yeovil did not trouble to disguise his nationality; he nodded curtly to his questioner.

'Glad of that,' said the fisherman; 'I don't like travelling with Germans.'

'Unfortunately,' said Yeovil, 'we have to travel with them, as partners in the same State concern, and not by any means the predominant partner either.'

'Oh, that will soon right itself,' said the other with loud assertiveness, 'that will right itself damn soon.'

'Nothing in politics rights itself,' said Yeovil; 'things have to be righted, which is a different matter.'

'What d'y' mean?' said the fisherman, who did not like to have his assertions taken up and shaken into shape.

'We have given a clever and domineering people a chance to plant themselves down as masters in our land; I don't imagine that they are going to give us an easy chance to push them out. To do that we shall have to be a little cleverer than they are, a little harder, a little fiercer, and a good deal more self-sacrificing than we have been in my lifetime or in yours.'

'We'll be that, right enough,' said the fisherman; 'we mean business this time. The last war wasn't a war, it was a snap. We weren't prepared and they were. That won't happen again, bless you. I know what I'm talking about. I go up and down the country, and I hear what people are saying.'

Yeovil privately doubted if he ever heard anything but his own opinions.

'It stands to reason', continued the fisherman, 'that a highly civilized race like ours, with the record that we've had for leading the whole world, is not going to be held under for long by a lot of damned sausage-eating Germans. Don't you believe it! I know what I'm talking about. I've travelled about the world a bit.'

Yeovil shrewdly suspected that the world travels amounted to nothing more than a trip to the United States and perhaps the Channel Islands, with, possibly, a week or fortnight in Paris.

'It isn't the past we've got to think of, it's the future,' said Yeovil. 'Other maritime Powers had pasts to look back on; Spain and Holland, for instance. The past didn't help them when they let their sea-sovereignty slip from them. That is a matter of history and not very distant history either.'

'Ah, that's where you make a mistake,' said the other; 'our sea-sovereignty hasn't slipped from us, and won't do, neither. There's the British Empire beyond the seas; Canada, Australia, New Zealand, East Africa.'

An aeroplane comes in low and fast to destroy an enemy vessel

He rolled the names round his tongue with obvious relish.

'If it was a list of first-class battleships, and armoured cruisers and destroyers and airships that you were reeling off, there would be some comfort and hope in the situation,' said Yeovil; 'the loyalty of the colonies is a splendid thing, but it is only pathetically splendid because it can do so little to recover for us what we've lost. Against the Zeppelin air fleet, and the Dreadnought sea-squadrons and the new Gelberhaus cruisers, the last word in maritime mobility, of what avail is loyal devotion plus half-a-dozen warships, one keel to ten, scattered over one or two ocean coasts?'

'Ah, but they'll build,' said the fisherman confidently; 'they'll build. They're only waiting to enlarge their dockland accommodation and get the right class of artificers and engineers and working men together. The money will be forthcoming somehow, and they'll start in and build.'

'And do you suppose', asked Yeovil in slow, bitter contempt, 'that the victorious nation is going to sit and watch and wait till the defeated foe has created a new war fleet, big enough to drive it from the seas? Do you suppose it is going to watch keel added to keel, gun to gun, airship to airship, till its preponderance has been wiped out or even threatened? That sort of thing is done once in a generation, not twice. Who is going to protect Australia or New Zealand while they enlarge their dockyards and hangars and build their dreadnoughts and their airships?'

'Here's my station and I'm not sorry,' said the fisherman, gathering his tackle together and rising to depart; 'I've listened to you long enough. You and me wouldn't agree, not if we was to talk all day. Fact is, I'm an out-and-out patriot and you're only a half-hearted one. That's what you are, half-hearted.'

And with that parting shot he left the carriage and lounged heavily down the platform, a patriot who had never handled a rifle or mounted a horse or pulled an oar, but who had never flinched from demolishing his country's enemies with his tongue.

'England has never had any lack of patriots of that type,' thought Yeovil sadly; 'so many patriots and so little patriotism.'

That evocation of the English countryside in When William Came *was not the private love affair of a writer. It was rooted deep in the national literature, manifest in Chaucer and working in the most effective and formative way with Shakespeare. He married the sense of nationhood with the separateness of 'this precious stone set in a silver sea'. In his history plays,* Henry V *for example, he implanted the notion of heroic action beyond the seas:*

> *Suppose within the girdle of these walls*
> *Are now confin'd two mighty monarchies,*
> *Whose high upreared and abutting fronts*
> *The perilous narrow ocean parts asunder.*

That was the beginning of a traditional literary association between an imperilled island—'Now all the youth of England are on fire'—and the dangerous outer world. That connection has worked with great effect during times of heightened national feelings. During the long years of the Napoleonic Wars, for instance, the confrontation between liberty and tyranny was a frequent theme and a most powerful stimulus for Wordsworth. Throughout the forty-six entries in his 'Poems Dedicated to National Independence and Liberty', he celebrated the historic bond between what had been and what would be—freedom, the sea, the heroic past, and the English language. These came together, for instance, in Sonnet XVI:

> *It is not to be thought of that the Flood*
> *Of British freedom, which, to the open sea*
> *Of the world's praise, from dark antiquity*
> *Hath flowed, 'with pomp of waters unwithstood,'*
> *Roused though it be full often to a mood*
> *Which spurns the check of salutary bands,*
> *That this most famous Stream in bogs and sands*
> *Should perish; and to evil and to good*
> *Be lost for ever. In our halls is hung*
> *Armoury of the invincible Knights of old:*
> *We must be free or die, who speak the tongue*
> *That Shakespeare spoke: the faith and morals hold*
> *Which Milton held.—In every thing we are sprung*
> *Of Earth's first blood, have titles manifold.*

This poetic perception of a special destiny continued throughout the nineteenth century. Alfred, Lord Tennyson, felt called upon to write poems that celebrated military courage—'The Charge of the Light Brigade'—or to applaud the inauguration of the Volunteer Movement—'Riflemen, riflemen, riflemen form!'—or to protest against any reduction in the strength of the Royal Navy—'The Fleet of England is her all in all'. The prose and poetry of Rudyard Kipling offered comparable meditations on the sea, military achievement, the glorious past and imperial duties. Even Konrad Korzeniowski caught the benign infection, and as Joseph Conrad he placed the return of the Narcissus *in the context of the national history. The vessel hastens home up the Channel, 'like a great tired bird speeding to its nest'. As the coast appears ever closer, Conrad salutes the island that lay there to port, 'like a mighty ship bestarred with vigilant lights ...*[1]

> *A great ship! For ages had the ocean battered in vain her enduring sides; she was there when the world was vaster and darker, when the*

sea was great and mysterious, and ready to surrender the prize of fame to audacious men. A ship mother of fleets and nations! The great flag-ship of the race; stronger than the storms! and anchored in the open sea.

The Cliffs

Given so constant and powerful a tradition, it is not surprising that the conflict-to-come with Germany should find versifiers ready with their lays of the future. Alfred Noyes, for instance, has recorded that about 1902 a sense of approaching catastrophe made him realize that the Royal Navy 'was a defensive, not an offensive, weapon, and the weakening of it might be an invitation to aggression. It was with this conviction that I wrote "A Phantom Fleet", in which the great sailors of the past were depicted as coming to England's aid.'[2] Similar thoughts inspired Charles Doughty, then in the tenth year of work on his long epic poem, The Dawn in Britain. *When that appeared in 1906, this extraordinary traveller and writer, the author of the classic* Arabia Deserta *(1888), turned his attention to the German peril; and, in his singular way, wrote* The Cliffs *(1909) and* The Clouds *(1912)—the only long verse dramas about the invasion-to-come that have appeared in European literature. As a poet, he had set himself the aim of restoring the English language to the tradition of Chaucer and Spenser, ignoring all later changes and developments in syntax and vocabulary. His dedication to what he considered 'English undefiled' will be immediately apparent in the passages from* The Cliffs, *where two Persanians—that is, German invaders—talk about their nation and their vision of the future. One scene opens with the descent of an aerostat. The Baron and the Ingenieur discuss preparations for the landing of the enemy troops ...*

THE ENGLANDERS KEEP NO WATCH

ING. Yet can it be, the Englanders keep no watch,
Save in few towers and lightships on their Coast?
Like to rich city, without gates and walls,
Or garrison; midst strong, treacherous enemies!
BAR. They are too slow of heart and Island-bred.
Confusion born is in the English blood
As clouds in Britain's skies: besides they deem
It their prerogative to excel, with small

Endeavour: they live thus in blind illusions,
And evil counseled; seeing their Parliament men
Do, each side honestly, wellnigh anything
So they may votes win. Who set over them,
Their penny-wise fool-hardy mandarins,
Will make believe, (for votes too!) they, by shifts,
Spare hundred thousand marks; though for that sot
Few pounds saved; like the churl, who would not paint
His house till its nigh falling, certain is,
They must tomorrow panic-million spend;
Not nine, but ten times ninety-fold that they saved;
To their undoing, and grossly them misspend.
Meanwhile their State's in danger to be lost.
Blinded by Providence, that it seems loves us!
Their Admiralty, in the last year, have disbanded
Their last reserve the Coastguard: now they could not
Supply the waste of war, in one sea-fleet.
Were aught to go at first against our warships,
We've hundred thousand, to repair our loss;
Men, which have passed their sea-time in war-service.
You'll find no docks, on all East England's Coast;
Whereas they might refit one battered Dreadnought!
Whence those should fall an easy prey to us,
In second fight: thus holds our *Generalstaff!*
ING. Yet, have they not the greatest merchant navy?
BAR. Ships, but all too few seamen of their own:
Nor are their untrained merchant sea-folk apt,
To serve in warships: and so those sunk up
Are all in swinish vices of the ports,
They're quite unfit to render stedfast service.
Their merchants sooner wage now foreign shipfolk,
As of more temperate living and more trust.
Nay, and even, in English waters, foreign pilots
They'll hire to guide their ships.
ING. That's *wondersworth!*
But hold they not a sovereignty of seas?
BAR. Not in the opinion of our *Generalstaff*
English warships, like merchant vessels ride,
By night-time careless, on seas open water;
Their stems, sterns, steering-gear without defence,
Gainst sudden offence of enemy submarines.
Those cannot see you, and they cannot shoot;

Their guns bear not so low. To fight by night,
Their gunners be untaught. We in one night might
Sink, by surprise, the strength of Britain's war-fleets.
ING. Is their marine artillery of none account?
BAR. When last time these contended on high seas,
Three British frigates did not once the frigate,
To each opposed, a ship of equal force,
Hit with great shot; and those were Nelson's ships,
Nine only years after Trafalgar's fight!
They six times fought, and five times had the worse:
'Tis so recorded in our Service books.
I might tell you the names of all twelve frigates,
Offhand; the artillery is mine arm.
ING. How is
Decayed so great sea-faring Nation thus?
BAR. They're governed now, by loose-brained demagogues:
The dusty feet rule England, not the head.
All carries now the irrational Parliament vote,
Of a brain-addled crooked populace.
Part their sheeplike conditions be in fault.
Each will-with-the-wisp, that hovers from their mist,
Through fens, through briars, over strange steeps and floods,
This soul-blind people follow like a flock.

Doughty goes on to give his version of the contemporary end-of-Empire story:

ING. Can this proud Island Nation, once so stout,
Make only slight resistance to our arms?
Too long have these faint Englanders cried, *Chuck-Chuck*!
Over vast cock-pit of the World; that live
By our longsufferance, like the very Turk.
ING. Some dream they'll indemonitately fight;
Dispute the fate of England, inch by inch.
BAR. Even that would hardly avail them: force untaught
Is easily broken. Jews, that frenziedly fought.
Coveting, as heaven's riches, wounds and death,
Saved not Jerusalem. Impious Romans laughed,
Ate pork and beat them! Shall not likewise pass
Britain, found not World-worthy; and by us
Her Empire be destroyed. I have myself,
Among them lived, Hanse Consul, certain years;
And have felt thus their pulse. After six days;
When our highseas fleet shall have sunk their fleets,

And shall our mines have sealed their entry-ports;
When their home shires our army corps possess;
Will clamour Englands abject multitude,
(Since all with them is less than daily food,
Nor reck such, who them rule, so they eat bread!)
To king and parliament, for wage and bread:
And willy-nilly, them compel make peace;
Such then, as we, their conquerors, will concede:
That's annexation or indemnity.
ING. What?
BAR. Ten hundred millions; all the wealth of England,
That's ours by conquest: we'll them bleed to death.
Being heirs then of her merchandise: which was what
They had besides; (for Britain in herself
Is, without rich mens substance, a poor Land!)
Persania shall be great indeed henceforth.

Later on Doughty rehearses the general view that Germany will go to war to gain colonies ...

                                    ...their best Providence,
Have been these cliffs and wild wave-rows, till now;
Waves that have we tonight overflown and passed.
Our folk grows daily, and lacks now Colonies:
Wherefore must vast Australien soon be ours;
In Europe must the Netherlands fall to us.
(That shall enhance to heaven, our Naval Force!)
With all her overseas great Dependencies.
South Africa shall be ours too. Of late years,
Our Rulers it have coveted; with the there-
To joining, settlements of old effete States.
The Nile Lands then; and when Time is more ripe,
By right derived from Charlemagne to us;
We'll challenge France, North Italy, Sicily and Spain;
Ja, and Barbary, that's so wide, from East to West;
By virtue of these old conquests of our arms,
Shall all these be Persania, in the new maps.
    As for this Isle, it plainly appertains,
To our Imperial Crown, by antique right.
Came not her *Sachsen* out of our *Alt-Sachsen*?
Persania *Irredenta* yet rèmains;
The *Eastriche* then and Baltic Provinces.

There are moreover certain doubtful States,
Ungarn, three Scandinavias, and the rest.
In fine, shall all be ours to Moskow gates.
    We hoped for Turkey; there's great warlike stuff
In Turkey, more than fifty myriad soldiers;
Little Asien's a sweet sugarplum in that cake:
And Mesopotamien too might go with us,
Beyond lies Persien, and great Indiens Gulf.
    Besides, we would they'd join our Triple League:
But Turkey's *hareem*-cry of her *beaux-yeux*.
We've barely gotten her goodwill, till now.
Yet having that, it is a Key of State.
    Be, as may be; it costs no more to us
Than promises; and that's only paper-breath.
To us all's one, Muslem or Galilean;
So there's but profit or *Welt-politik* in it.
And by their gates our road to Delhi lies.

The Battle of the North Sea

The mirror image of the weak-kneed, pacific British citizen in Doughty's drama was the nightmare figure of the German invader—disciplined, efficient, accustomed to military service, exceptionally well-armed, and ever ready for instant action. This bogey-man was a favoured means of demonstrating how tomorrow's enemy was all that the British were not. As the political commentators and foreign correspondents were constantly pointing out, German propagandists had drawn up their own Tagesordnung for the future. For many, the order of battle had appeared as early as 1887 in Das Volk in Waffen *by Baron Colmar von der Goltz. Loyalty to the Emperor, passionate love for the Fatherland, self-denial, cheerful sacrifice, no shrinking from hard trials—this constant striving would keep the great engine of state in perfect working order, ready for the day when 'the German army, which must be and shall ever remain the German nation in arms, [would] enter upon the coming conflict with full assurance of ultimate victory.'[3] Others believed there was abundant evidence of German intentions in General Friedrich von Bernhardi's* Deutschland und der nächste Krieg *(1912), especially in the more notorious passages that parcelled out the world—reshaped to suit German ambitions.*

    What did these Germans want from the future? World power and world empire—that was the charge from the British side. For proof there was the historical view of German destiny that ran through the writings of that able,

partisan and gifted historian, Heinrich von Treitschke. In his various publi-
cations, especially in his History of Germany in the Nineteenth
Century, *he wrote as an enemy of Great Britain and he did more than any*
other writer to arouse anti-British feeling in Germany during the last decade
of the nineteenth century. His problem—the German problem—was that the
British had an empire and the Germans did not. The message Treitschke
found written into the future was: the establishment of a German overseas
empire:[4]

> *The kind of colonization which maintains the neutrality of the*
> *country of origin is a matter of immense importance for the future of*
> *the world. On it depends the extent to which each people will take its*
> *share in the domination of the world by the white race ... Hence we*
> *must not lapse into that state of stagnation which comes of a purely*
> *continental policy, and the issue of our next successful war must be the*
> *acquisition of a colony.*

The future-invasion story was one British answer to belligerent statements
of this kind. For most of the prophets, the German danger was so evident that
they clearly felt they had nothing to explain: their stories could begin on D-
Day with a short statement, like the brief telegram in The Boy Galloper*: 'A*
state of war exists between this country and Germany. The advance-guard of
a German force landed in Sussex this morning.' It was a rare participator in
the great debate about the future who felt it necessary to set out the reasons
for the expected conflict. In the first chapter of The Battle of the North Sea
(1912), *Rear-Admiral Wilmot set down the facts as he saw them. They were,*
for their time, a reasonable statement of the differences between the two
countries.

Twenty years ago the idea of war between Great Britain and
Germany seemed impossible. Indeed our whole concern then was to
guard against a possible struggle with France and Russia, countries
which might legitimately have felt aggrieved against us. We had
fought against both, and not been worsted; supported Turkey
against one, and, having opposed the construction of the Suez Canal
when de Lesseps sought our help, we gradually became predominant in Egypt. With Germany, on the other hand, we were allied by
memories of mutual help against aggression.

When Blücher came to England after Waterloo, he received an
ovation only equalled by that to Wellington. In case of a powerful
combination against us, might not we again expect support from
such a quarter? After the events of 1870, what more natural than to
provide a Fleet worthy of a united Germany? Though that issue was

decided on land, the humiliation remained of having seen a hostile squadron off their coast, without ability to meet it, or afford protection to a commerce at sea already of considerable bulk and value. We had fostered her small Navy from its earliest days. A British frigate exchanged for two small steamers trained Prussian seamen over fifty years ago. We welcomed, therefore, the construction and acquisition of battleships by our former ally.

What a change in twenty years! England, France, and Russia, no longer viewing each other with scarcely veiled hostility, now on the best of terms, all sources of difference between them removed; while the old friend is the enemy of today. How had this come to pass? No portion of our Empire had been wrested at any time from Germany. We sympathized with but gave no help to France in 1870. Denmark received no assistance from us in her struggle with Prussia and Austria in 1864. Heligoland passed from British to German rule in a peaceful exchange. Where the cause, then, for hostility? That it existed became very apparent during our war in South Africa. British residents in and visitors to Germany at that time had unpleasant experiences of this feeling. But for our command of the sea, it would not, probably, have found expression only in abuse. Then commercial rivalry arose as it had three hundred years before with England and Holland. The Dutch were then the waggoners of all seas, and had the best places in the sun. Germany now aspired to some of the good things. With a growing population and commerce, she sought expansion over sea, and found all suitable sites occupied, chiefly by Great Britain. In nearly every trading and important port, the Union Jack or Red Ensign was conspicuous. The sum of individual jealousy becomes national envy.

Finally the old question of rivalry in power kindled the smouldering fire which culminated in a blaze. Originally based, no doubt, on capability to meet any Continental Navy, the advance of the German Fleet after 1900 seemed destined for a greater object, and to constitute a menace to that sea supremacy essential to the existence of the British Empire. We might put the case to her in this way: You can only be overcome on land. No Fleet will avail if your soldiers are defeated. Therefore we are not concerned if you consider it necessary to provide an Army of five or even ten millions of men. We, on the other hand, would lose everything if overcome at sea, and therefore must have such an overwhelmingly superior Navy that its defeat could only be accomplished by an almost impossible combination against us. This line of argument is not accepted, and the answer given over fifty years ago by a French Admiral, when a similar question between France and England had cropped up, would probably apply today. Writing to Captain Mends—a friend made during the Russian War—General Jurien de la Gravière in 1860 says:

> At heart the French and English wish on nearly all questions the same things. The great subject of disagreement is the increase which each nation is making in her Navy. You wish to be incontestably masters of the sea, and to fear neither us nor any maritime coalition. We do not object to this pretension up to a certain point. We do not wish, however, that your security should be such that you should imagine yourself able to treat us in any way you like. Suppose, for instance, your naval supremacy enabled you to come without much effort and blockade our commercial ports, ravage our coasts, insult our naval ports. Do you not think we should have as much reason as yourselves to be as discontented and anxious as you are when menaced with an *impossible* invasion? How then are we to avoid such a danger if not by increasing our Navy?
>
> Under these circumstances agreement as to a limitation of armaments is impossible, because neither party will accept a preliminary standard on which negotiations can proceed. Napoleon III put the matter in a nutshell. When vexed by representations from Lord Palmerston that he was building ships too fast, he said to our Ambassador, 'Let each build what he considers the right number,' and he added that we were entitled to have many more ships than France, as they were our principal protection.

The German explanations of the 'War with Britain' varied. The most belligerent appeared in August Niemann's Der Weltkrieg—Deutsche Träume *in 1904, where the author promised his readers 'a new division of the possessions of the earth as the final aim and object of this gigantic universal war'. The most prophetic of all the German future-war stories was the plea for peace and international understanding that runs through* 1906: Der Zusammenbruch der alten Welt ('The Collapse of the Old World') (1906). *Friedrich Grautoff attacked all those —politicians, patriots, and the Press on both sides of the North Sea—who stirred up hatred between their two countries: '... who had thought that a passage of arms between Britain and Germany would clear the air, like a thunderstorm, and that either side would be able, today or tomorrow, or whenever they pleased, as soon as the tension was relieved, to call a halt'.*

'Sink, Burn, Destroy': Der Schlag gegen Deutschland

Many Germans, readers and writers, found a reason for war in the commercial rivalry between the Reich and the British Empire. Strike first, they argued, before the British copenhagen our fleet. This proposition began to circulate in Germany about the time of the Navy Bill of 25 January 1900, when the German Navy League organized meetings of its 286 local societies throughout the country. In the spring of 1900 'an army of lecturers, taken from the élite of official, intellectual, and social Germany, delivered 30,000 lectures to several million people ... ':

> *Generals, admirals,* Regierungspräsidenten, *and the most distinguished university professors vied with one another in demonstrating to the public that the rapacity of the Anglo-Saxon nations was a danger to Germany, that Great Britain intended to attack Germany's trade, that the danger could only be provided against by a fleet strong enough to overawe this country, and that it would be best for Germany if Great Britain's naval supremacy was destroyed.[5]*

These ideas were the theme of 'Sink, burn, destroy': Der Schlag gegen Deutschland. *This anonymous tale of 1905 is the equal and opposite of the British invasion stories.*

It must be ten to twelve years ago since the British admiral Tryon, who later went down with his flag-ship *Victoria*, stated that the words *'sink, burn, destroy'* composed the basic proposition in any future war. In a naval war everything that belonged to the enemy, private property or state property, had to be ruthlessly destroyed.

In our fast-moving times that declaration was soon forgotten, and no one thought any more about the situation in which those words could be realized. Everyone knew, it is true, that Germany's vigorous competition in world markets would awaken the envy and jealousy of Britain, the country that considered it had the monopoly of world trade. Few had any suspicion, however, that Britain would one day seize the opportunity to attack Germany and thereby destroy the German fleet, the guardian of its trade. If prudent persons, from time to time, told the public that they should be wary of the British and should keep their powder dry, well-known appeasers gave them scornful answers and told the world that was all a matter of cowardice and the chattering of ale-house politicians. It was these selfsame appeasers who, just before the outbreak of the Russo-Japanese War, did their best with a flood of denials to make our German Michael think that a war between Japan and Russia was not to be expected in the foreseeable future. Well, quite soon these gentlemen will have their eyes thoroughly opened.

The sparkling festival of the Kiel Week was quickly over. The top people with their steamships and yachts were on the homeward voyage; and with them went the foreign spies who used the occasion to inspect at their leisure the coastal defences and other naval installations. For the German warships in home waters there then began days of hard work—formation sailing and gunnery practice—which was not always to the liking of the participants, since it imposed increased demands on the crews and at the same time required them to do without many things. Kiel harbour, usually bustling with warships of every class, was empty. The ships came back again at the end of July for a few days to have a rest and to take on supplies; and then they made ready for the major manoeuvres which set the entire fleet off on operations. This period of exacting activity passed off without incident; and on this occasion there was nothing to report in the annual tally of vessels damaged by groundings or by collisions. The reason was that the commanders of the line-ships had been through a close review, and those not equal to their posts had been previously removed from their commands. The fleet breathed more easily, when at last the flagship made the signal 'Manoeuvres Completed', and at the same time gave orders for the return to base.

It happened on 20 September 19–, when the battle ships, the cruisers and the torpedo boats of the main fleet were on their way from Danzig to assemble in Kiel harbour at the end of the autumn manoeuvres in order to begin discharging their time-expired crews and changing some of their officers. After the demanding manoeuvres and the inspections, a beneficent calm had descended on the ships. All had the pleasant feeling that they were entering on a few months of lighter and less demanding service. Those ratings due for discharge were taken to the railway station with bands playing, and they sped on their way in long special trains to the most distant parts of Germany. Then something happened that in a moment changed the entire situation.

On 25 September, on a fresh and sunny autumn day, a telegram came early in the morning for the canal management and for the Station Commander: 'Steamer in the canal; sunk close to Levensauer Bridge; canal closed until further notice.' It was a calamity! The ships from the North Sea Station, which were in the act of going through the Kaiser-Wilhelm Canal to Wilhelmshaven, had once more to take on coal in order to get ready for the journey round Skagen. No one had counted on this unpleasant extra. The accident had not been foreseen even in the general instructions of the fleet commander; for it stated there that: 'The ships of the North Sea Station should go in good time to Wilhelmshaven, so that the discharge of the reservists can take place there shortly before 30 September.'

The Director of the Kaiser-Wilhelm Canal, Counsellor Löwe, known in Volksmunde as the Canal Lion, got to the site of the accident in the fastest way possible in order to discuss with his colleagues the best steps to be taken for clearing the canal. The Naval Commissioner for the Kaiser-Wilhelm Canal, Rear-Admiral St—, arrived in his steam pinnace and the head of the Baltic Naval Station, His Royal Highness Prince Henry of Prussia, came to the place to help by word and deed. Divers reported that the steamer, which was loaded with Swedish granite, had sunk because the sea-cock had been destroyed and water had flooded unchecked into the hold. The entire crew of the steamer had got safely ashore; but when the usual proceedings began to establish the causes of the accident, it appeared that the captain, the first officer and the ship's engineer had vanished. Enquiries showed that they had travelled north through Flensburg, and had presumably got to Denmark. This took the canal management and the naval authorities aback, and the suspicion slowly arose that the accident, as it seemed to be, had been done with the intention of putting the canal out of action....

And more bad news follows the next day, when it was discovered that ...

At Kiel early in the morning on 26 September two large steamers had been sunk, during the night, close to the lighthouse at the entrance to the canal. Only small vessels could get through; for bigger vessels and for warships of deep draught, however, it was closed. According to the report of the lighthouse-keeper, the steamers had arrived during the night between two and three o'clock; they had opened their sea-cocks in the middle of the shipping channel by the lighthouse; then they anchored and shortly afterwards they had gone under. The vessels appeared to be full of water, for as far as could be seen by moonlight their rails barely appeared above the surface. Nothing could be discovered about the whereabouts of the crews of the two steamers; but later on it was established that they had got away to the Danish island of Langeland by means of steam pinnaces. This unexpected turn of events left the naval authorities in the greatest confusion. Telegrams flashed from

Kiel to Berlin and from there back to Kiel. Everyone suspected that there was something going on; but doubts only vanished on the morning of 26 September, when news came from Wilhelmshaven that a squadron of British men-of-war had arrived off the River Jade and were about to sail up the river to Wilhelmshaven. It suddenly broke on all that Britain was about to begin the long matured plan of launching an attack on Germany.

Immense anger seized Germany when this event became known and news came that the British embassy in Berlin had announced the declaration of war. The unbelievable had happened. Britain had simply taken them by surprise. People felt they were living in a political steam-bath: that our cousins across the North Sea were daily making ever greater efforts to ensure that their almost two-hundred-year-old command of the sea would continue into the future. It was known that extraordinary activity had been going on in the British ports; no one had any idea of the great historical drama that was to unfold in the next few days—a drama in which the cold, calculating, almost inhumanly ruthless character of the British would appear in its true light. Russia, the natural enemy of Britain, was out for the count, exhausted after the unfortunate war with Japan, so that for some years she could not bestir herself abroad. Indeed, Russia could not consider any military action that would thwart Britain. So, the opportunities for a British attack on German were exceptionally favourable, especially after the conclusion of the *Entente Cordiale* with France, which promised that in case of war Britain would at least maintain a benevolent neutrality. Political defeat in Morocco, the removal of Britain from the Yangste area, the German attitude during the Boer War, the Kruger Telegram, the German navy—these had combined to raise the political tension to boiling point and they had given the British chauvinists the means of lighting the torch of war.

Early on the morning of 26 September, when the coastguard station at Schillig informed the Station Command in Wilhelmshaven of the arrival of a squadron of eight battleships—*Prince of Wales, Queen, London, Bulwark, Venerable, Formidable, Irresistible, Implacable*—of the four cruisers—*Duke of Edinburgh, Black Prince, Devonshire, Roxburgh*—together with six destroyers, it was still not known if these ships had come with hostile intentions. So, the Station Command prudently signalled an alert to naval personnel, raised the general alarm, and ordered the manning of the coastal forts. The British ships, which had already seized the Bremen pilots from the pilot vessels cruising in the North Sea, steamed with tide up the River Jade, in line ahead—the cruisers in the van with the destroyers guarding the big ships—until they reached the new harbour entrance to Wilhelmshaven. They then came about, ran up their flags, and on a signal they fired simultaneously on the forts.

The effect of the 30.5 centimetre shells was indescribable. Pieces of masonry, mixed with earth and clods, flew through the air. The shells made vast holes in the walls; and the explosives took their toll of the fortress garrisons who hesitated no longer to open regular, well-aimed gunfire on the ships. Unfortunately only some of the guns in Fort Heppen were able to join in the action, since the angle of fire did not allow all of them to engage. The flagship *Prince of Wales* received two direct hits from the 28 centimetre guns, which destroyed the conning tower and the after funnel. In addition the commander, two officers and some 30 ratings were killed. The *Queen* was badly holed on the water-line, and the other ships soon suffered considerable damage. The complete destruction of the superstructure on the *Irresistible* and severe damage to the rudder of the *Formidable* caused these vessels to be towed from the line of battle towards the sea. In spite of that, the British ships went on shooting and after two hours of enfilading fire they silenced Fort Heppen and the neighbouring flank battery. By that time the forts were a heap of ruins. Some of the heavy guns had been flung from their mountings; some of them had been hit by shells and put out of action. The whole area was an unbelievable chaos of shrapnel fragments, collapsed masonry, and mounds of earth.

Naval engagements follow with heavy German losses. The British fleet sails up the Elbe to Hamburg and secures the payment of 30 million marks from the terrified inhabitants. Hundreds of German vessels are seized in the British blockade, making fortunes for the British naval commanders 'just as it was in Nelson's time'. Trade is at a standstill; and unemployment on the increase, as 'the totally helpless Germans faced an enemy they could not defeat, and on whose mercy they depended ...

In this calamitous situation help came unexpectedly from the United States. President Roosevelt intervened with Great Britain, not so much out of concern for the German Empire itself, but far more for the reason that American trade had suffered enormous damage because of the consequent breakdown in relations with Europe. Roosevelt made proposals to the International Court of Arbitration in the Hague for the ending of the war; and after long resistance the British gave their consent.

For Germany the consequences of the war were incalculable. The major shipping lines suffered most of all thanks to the loss of many vessels; the cessation of trade deprived them of profit for years to come, and their shares lost all value. In like manner the great import houses of the Hansa towns had suffered comparable losses, so that they faced ruin. It was not much better for the factories in the major industrial centres that had to discharge large numbers of workers. There was an immense drop in the intake of custom duties and of commercial taxes, so that it was no longer possible to meet the normal expenditure of the Reich without large loans. It was not possible to impose new taxes on the population: indeed, such a measure would hardly have obtained a majority in the Reichstag. The nation could take it for granted that Germany would need at least thirty years to recover from the effects of the war, and all the time Great Britain would go on as before—flying the flag of world power.

The Germans in Hampton Court

These German writers were, like their British counterparts, as rigorous in their choice of possible futures as the propaganda required. Episode by episode, their stories clicked through the time-frames of the worst, or the best, of all conceivable histories. As August Niemann demonstrated in his Der Weltkrieg—Deutsche Traüme *(1904) the best part of a popular future-war story would be the contemplation of a British defeat at the end of the story and the final realization of national ambitions with the inauguration of a greater Reich ...*

The long rows of windows in Hampton Court Palace were still a blaze of light, notwithstanding the lateness of the hour. The double post of the royal Uhlans before the entrance was still busy, for the unceasing arrival and departure of officers of rank of the three allied nations demanded military honours. Immediately after the naval engagement at Flushing, so disastrous to the British, a large French army and some regiments of the Russian Imperial Guard had landed at Hastings and were now quartered at Aldershot, on the best of terms with the French and the German troops who had marched from Scotland. The Prince-Admiral's headquarters had been removed to Hampton Court, whose silent, venerable, and famous palace became suddenly the centre of stirring military and diplomatic life.

Any further serious military operations were hardly considered, for the supposition that the landing of large hostile armies would practically mean the end of the campaign had proved correct.

In the resistance which bodies of British troops had attempted to offer to the French advance on London, the volunteers had clearly shown their bravery and patriotic devotion; but they had been unable to check the victorious course of their better-led opponents. Accordingly, an armistice had been concluded for the purpose of considering the terms of peace offered by Britain, even before the German troops advancing from Scotland had the opportunity of taking part in the land operations.

The conclusion of peace, eagerly desired by all the civilized nations of the world, might be considered assured, although, no doubt, its final ratification would be preceded by long and difficult negotiations. The idea, mooted by the German Imperial Chancellor, of summoning a general congress at the Hague, at which not only the belligerents but all other countries should be represented, had met with general approval, since all the states were interested in the reorganization of the relations of the Powers. But the settlement of the preliminaries of peace was necessarily the business of the belligerents, and it was for this purpose that the German Imperial Chancellor, Freiherr von Grubenhagen, the French Foreign Minister, M. Delcassé, and the Russian Secretary of State, M. de Witte, accompanied by Count Lamsdorff and a full staff of officials and diplomatic assistants, had met at Hampton Court Palace.

The preliminary negotiations between these statesmen and the British plenipotentiaries, Mr. Balfour, Prime Minister and First Lord of the Treasury, and the Marquis of Londonderry, Lord President of the Privy Council, were carried on with restless eagerness. But the strictest silence in regard to their results up to the present was observed by all who had taken part in them.

The conduct of the Prince-Admiral was an obvious proof that the military leaders were not inactive, in spite of the commencement of peace negotiations. Although he took no part in the diplomatic proceedings and simply occupied himself with military affairs, not only every minute of the day, but a good part of the night, was spent by him in work and discussions with his staff officers, with the chief officers of the land forces, and with the chief commanders of the allied Franco-Russian army. Everyone was full of admiration for the Prince's never-failing vigour and indefatigable power of work; his tall, slender, Teutonic form, and fair-bearded face, with the quiet, clear sailor's eyes, never failed to impress all who came in contact with him. Only his imperial brother, who held in his hand all the threads of political action, could rival the Prince in the traditional Hohenzollern capacity for work at this important time.

It was close on midnight when, after a long and lively consultation, the French general, Jeannerod, left the Prince's study. No sooner had the door closed behind him than the adjutant on duty, with an evident expression of astonishment in the sound of his voice, announced: 'His Excellency the Imperial Chancellor, Freiherr von Grubenhagen.'

The Prince advanced to the middle of the room to meet his visitor and shook him heartily by the hand.

'I thank Your Excellency for granting me an interview with you to-day, although it is so late and you are overwhelmed with work. I had a special reason for wishing to confer with you, which you will understand when I tell you that all kinds of rumours have reached me as to exaggerated demands on the part of our allies. My previous attitude will have shown you that I have no intention of interfering in diplomatic negotiations, or even exercising my influence in one direction or another. I feel that I am here not as a statesman, but simply as a soldier; and for that very reason I think you can speak the more openly to me. I have been told that the complete annihilation of Britain is intended as indispensable to the conditions of peace.'

The Chancellor, whose manly, determined face showed no signs of exhaustion, notwithstanding his almost superhuman labours, looked frankly at the Prince and shook his head.

'Your Royal Highness has been incorrectly informed. Neither we nor our allies have the intention of annihilating Britain. Certainly we are all fully agreed that this fearful war must not be waged in vain, and that the reward must correspond with the greatness of the sacrifice at which it has been purchased.'

'And to whom is the reward to fall?'

'To all the nations, Your Royal Highness. It would have been a sin to kindle this universal conflagration had it not been taken for granted that its refining flames would prepare the ground for the happiness and peace of the world. For centuries Great Britain has misused her power to increase her own wealth at the cost of others. Unscrupulously she grabbed everything she could lay hands on, and, injuring at every step important and vital interests of other nations, she challenged that resistance which has now shattered her position as a power in the world. The happiness of the peoples can only be restored by a peace assured for years, and only a just division of the dominion of the earth can guarantee the peace of the world.

Therefore Britain must necessarily surrender an essential part of her possessions over sea. Russia wants the way free to the Indian Ocean, for only if she has a sufficient number of harbours open all the year round will the enormous riches of her soil cease to be a lifeless possession. And France—'

'Let us keep to Russia first, Your Excellency. Has the Russian Government already formulated its demands?'

'These demands are the essential outcome of the military situation; they culminate in the cession of British India to Russia.[6] Whatever else our Eastern neighbour may strive to gain is intended to ensure the peace of Europe more than her own aggrandizement. The standing danger which threatens the peace of Europe from the stormy corner of the old world, the Balkan Peninsula, must be finally removed. A fundamental agreement has been arrived at between the Powers concerned that the Russian and Austrian spheres of influence in the Balkans are to be defined in such a manner that a definite arrangement of affairs in the Balkan States will be the result. There is talk of an independent Kingdom of Macedonia, under the rule of an Austrian archduke. The equivalent to be given to the Russian Empire as a set-off to this increase of the power of Austria will have to be finally settled at the conference at the Hague. But in any case the dangers which threaten the peace of Europe from Bulgaria, Servia, and Montenegro will be effectually obviated for the future.'

'But are you not afraid that the Sultan will resist such an agreement, by which Turkey is essentially the sufferer?'

'The Sultan will have to yield to the force of circumstances. We must not forget, Your Royal Highness, that Turkey has hitherto retained her European possessions more from the lack of unanimity among the great Powers than any consecrated rights of the Porte. The unceasing troubles in Macedonia have shown that the Sultan has neither the power nor the intention to give the Balkan countries under his rule a government corresponding to the demands of modern civilization. If the Porte loses the support it has hitherto received from Britain, the Sultan is at the same time deprived of all possibility of serious resistance.'

'And what is arranged about Egypt?'

'Egypt is the prize of victory for France; but only what she can justly claim on the ground of a glorious history will be restored to her. The sovereignty of the Sultan, which is a mere formality, will remain. But Britain's present position in Egypt—certainly with a definite limitation—will henceforth fall to France.'

'And what is the limitation?'

'It will be administered not by France alone, but by an international commission, appointed by all the Powers, under the presidency of France, in the place of the present British administration. The first condition is that Britain must cede all her financial claims and her Suez Canal shares to the allied Powers. These financial sacrifices will at the same time be part of the war indemnity which Britain will have to pay.'

'Does France raise no further claims?'

'France is the more satisfied with the results of this war, since an annexation of Belgium to the French Republic is very probable. Germany, however, claims the harbour of Antwerp, which we have occupied since the beginning of the war.'

'If I am correctly informed, was it not suggested that Aden should fall to France or be neutralized?'

'The idea was certainly mooted, but the allied Powers have decided to leave Aden to Britain. On the other hand, Britain will have to pledge herself to raise no obstacles which would render the construction and working of the Bagdad railway illusory. The harbour of Koweit on the Persian Gulf, the south-eastern terminus of this railway, must remain the uncontested possession of Turkey.'

'And Gibraltar? It raised a storm of indignation in Britain, when the report suddenly spread that the cession of this fortress would be demanded.'

'And yet the British Government will have to submit, for the surrender of Gibraltar is an indispensable condition on the part of the allies.'

'It is impossible to raze this natural fortress.'

'It would suffice if the British garrison were withdrawn, and all the fortifications dismantled. Gibraltar will cease to exist as a fortress, and will be restored to Spain on definite conditions. However, as it is not the intention of the allies completely to destroy British influence in the Levant, Malta will continue to form part of the British Empire. Thus Britain retains in the Mediterranean the most important *point d'appui* for her fleet.'

'It will not be easy to get the British Government to accept these conditions. But you have not yet spoken of the demands of Germany—Antwerp does not touch Britain's interests directly.'

'The policy of the German Government will culminate in ensuring settled commercial and political relations with Britain and her colonies and the rounding off of our own colonial possessions. We therefore demand Walfish Bay for German South-West Africa, the only good harbour, which, at the present time, being British, is closed to our young South African Colony. Besides this, we must insist upon the East African districts, which we gave up in exchange for Heligoland, being restored to us. This serious mistake in German policy must be rectified; for the abandonment of the Protectorate of Zanzibar to Britain was a blow, which not only paralyzed the zeal of our best colonial friends, but also depreciated the value of our East African Colonies.'

'If I understand you correctly, Your Excellency, your policy is directed towards setting Germany's colonial efforts on a firmer basis.'

'I certainly regard this as one of the most important demands of our time. We must recover what the policy of the last centuries has lost by neglect. At the same time that Your Royal Highness's great ancestor waged war for seven years for a mere strip of land—for tiny Silesia—the far-seeing policy of Britain succeeded, at a smaller sacrifice, in getting possession of enormous tracts of territory far larger in their whole extent than the entire continent of Europe.'

'But for centuries Britain has been a naval power, and obliged to direct her efforts to the acquisition of colonies over sea.'

'And what was there to prevent Prussia, centuries ago, from becoming a naval power that should command respect? It was our misfortune that the mighty ideas and far-seeing plans of the great Elector were frustrated by the inadequate means at his disposal. Had his successors continued what he had begun, Great Britain's power would never have been able to reach such a height. We should have secured in time, in previous centuries, our due share of the parts of the world outside Europe.'

The Prince looked thoughtfully before him. After a brief silence the Imperial Chancellor continued:

'Your Royal Highness may have heard that the Netherlands are firmly resolved, in the interest of self-preservation, to be incorporated with the German Empire as a federal state, like Bavaria, Saxony, Wurtemburg, Baden, and the other German states, after the Franco-German War. The rich and extensive Dutch colonies would then also become German colonies; that is to say, they would enter into the political union of the other German colonies while remaining under the administration of Holland. Our intention of repairing the wrong done by Britain to the Boers has made a very good impression on the Dutch population. The Boer states will enter into the same relation to us in which they stood to Britain before the Boer War, and their independence will be restored to them.'

'Meaning self-government with the recognition of German supremacy. Certainly, they are kinsmen of the Dutch. But, my dear Baron, will not the German people be alarmed at the consequences of an extension of our possessions over sea? Larger colonial possessions necessitate a larger fleet. Think of the struggle which the allied Governments had to carry through Parliament even a modest increase in the German fleet!'

'I am not so much afraid of this difficulty, for the German people have learnt the value of the fleet. We have got beyond the tentative stage, and have paid enough for our experience. We must hold fast what we possess and recover what we have lost during the last decades through the unfortunately unbusiness-like spirit of our foreign policy. Then the German people will have renewed confidence in our colonial policy.'

'But how will you raise the sums necessary to make our fleet strong and powerful?'

'Our negotiations with the friendly Governments of France and Russia are a proof that in these states, just as in the German people, there is a desire for a diminution of the land army; there is an equally strong feeling in Italy and Austria. The people would break down under the burden if the expenses for the army were increased. If we diminish our land army we shall have the means to increase our naval forces. Now, after a victorious war, the moment has come when the whole Continent can reduce its enormous standing armies to a footing commensurate with the financial capacities of its people. The external enemy is conquered; we must not think of conjuring up the internal enemy by laying excessive burdens on all classes.'

'You spoke just now of the unbusiness-like spirit of our foreign policy. How is this reproach to be understood?'

'Quite literally, Your Royal Highness! The bargain which gave up Zanzibar to get Heligoland would never have been possible if our diplomacy had shown the same far-sightedness and intelligence as the British in economic questions, which I can only designate by the honourable title of a "business-like spirit". This business-like spirit is the mainspring of industry and agriculture, of trade and handicrafts, as of all industrial life generally, and it is necessary that this business-like spirit should also be recognized in our ministries as the necessary condition for the qualification to judge of the economic interests of the people. In this respect our statesmen and officials and our industrial classes can learn more from our vanquished enemy than in anything else. Britain owes her greatness to being "a nation of shopkeepers", while our economic development and our external influence has been hindered more than anything else by the contempt with which the industrial classes have been treated amongst us up to the most recent times. In Britain the merchant has always stood higher in the social scale than the officer and official. Amongst us he is looked upon almost as a second-class citizen compared with the other two. What in Britain is valued as only a means to an end is regarded by us as an end in itself. The spirit of that rigid bureaucracy, of which Prince Bismarck has already complained, is still unfortunately with few exceptions the prevailing spirit in our Empire, from the highest to the lowest circles; the lack of appreciation of the importance of economic life is the cause of the low esteem in which the industrial classes are held. The sound business-like spirit, which pervades all British state life, cuts the ground from under the feet of Social Democracy in Britain, while with us it is gaining ground year by year. I am convinced that our German people have no need to fear Social Democracy, for in reforming social cancers those who govern are of more importance than those who are governed.'

'There may be much that is true in what you say, Herr Chancellor. But the extension of our colonial possessions will, first and foremost, benefit trade, and the merchant will naturally become of greater importance with us. There is already talk of great plantation societies to be started with enormous capital.'

'It is just against the formation of these societies that I intend to exert my whole influence, Your Royal Highness. We could commit no more fatal error than to allow the state-privileged speculation in landed property, which has produced such unwholesome fruits in the old civilized states, to exist in our colonies. Real property must be no object of speculation; it must remain the property of the state. Agriculture belongs to the classes who at the present time suffer most from economic depression. Nothing but an increase of the protective duties can preserve the agricultural population from the threatening danger of economic ruin. Increase of protective duty will bring with it increased profit, combined with a further increase in the value of land, which is also an article of traffic. Then the increase of land values will at the same time create an increase of the rents to be obtained from landed property, and for this reason I cannot help fearing that, in spite of an increase of protective duties, agriculture will have to suffer in the next generation from the further increase in the value of land and the higher rents that will be the result.

'In our colonies we must not fall into the same error that has produced the socialist question in modern civilized states. The earth belongs to those creatures who live on it and by it in accordance with a higher law than human imperfection has framed. Therefore the soil of our earth must be no object of traffic. Its growth is inseparable from that of the body of the state. I dare not hope that it will be allotted to me or my contemporaries to solve this question, yet I shall never tire of using all my influence to prevent at least a false agrarian policy in our young colonies. Injustice dies from its results, for injustice breeds its own avenger. Mankind committed a fatal wrong in permitting the land that supported him to become an object of speculation. This noxious seed brings noxious fruits to light. It must be the highest task of all governments to carry out land reform—the great problem that decides the destiny of a world—by all possible legislative measures. Now that, in all human probability, peace is assured, now that external dangers no longer threaten the existence of our Empire, there is nothing to exonerate us from the serious and sacred obligation to commence the greatest and most powerful work of reform that humanity can undertake. Then our path will lead us—from the conquest of nations to self-conquests.'

At this moment the door of the room opened, and a royal messenger, introduced by the adjutant on duty, handed the Prince a letter decorated with the imperial crown and the initial of the imperial name.

The first glimmer of dawn entered the open window, and through the tops of the venerable trees of Hampton Court Park was heard a mysterious rustling and whispering, as if they were talking of the wonderful changes of fortune, of which they had been the mute witnesses since the remote days of their youth.

The blue eyes of the Hohenzollern Prince were shining proudly, while they scanned the imperial missive. For a few moments a deep silence prevailed. Then the Prince turned to the Imperial Chancellor:

'It will be a great day for us, Your Excellency! His Majesty the Emperor will enter London at the head of the allied armies. Peace is assured. God grant that it may be the last war which we shall have to wage for the future happiness of the German nation!'

100 Jahre deutsche Zukunft

Some German writers found the key to the future of the Reich in the events of their own time. In December 1912 one prophet, Max Heinrichka, looked back to the beginning of the Balkan Wars in the October of that year, when

Bulgaria, Serbia, and Greece moved against the Ottoman Empire, then in its last days. The rapid victories of the Bulgarians and the Serbs gave him the notion of looking backwards from the year 2021 to the foundation of the Reich in 1871. He found reasons for hope in the contemporary expectation of an early and successful conclusion to the local conflict in the Balkans. What Bulgaria, Serbia, and Greece were about to do to the remnants of the Turkish Empire in Europe, he thought, the Germans would do to the European states in their predestined rearrangement of world affairs. In his account, 100 Jahre deutsche Zukunft *('Future Germany One Hundred Years On'), he has a whole chapter on the final war with Britain.*

THE ORIGINS OF A FUTURE WAR BETWEEN GERMANY AND BRITAIN

Germany had begun building a major canal which was to connect the Rhine in the Cologne area with the German section of the North Sea. As soon as the canal project began to take a definite form, a movement emerged in Holland which revealed the economic hardships such a canal would bring to the Dutch shipping industry. Two parties emerged: the first did not dispute the German right to divert Dutch ships into German waters. They proposed, therefore, that they should seek to establish a closer relationship with Germany, so that the hardships caused by the canal link could be greatly reduced. The second party disputed the German right to divert the traffic on the Rhine from its natural course; and they saw the German canal project as a hostile act against Holland. This group supported an alliance between Holland and Great Britain, a country which was purported to be exceptionally anti-German. Britain would have entered into such an alliance only too gladly, as it could then use Holland as a gateway for a future invasion of Germany. The Dutch government did not appear to be swayed by either party; but another matter came up that required a decision from them.

As a result of its glorious past, the tiny country of Holland still possessed its East Indian colonies. The Government had recently run into difficulties in these countries, and these had led to a rebellion amongst the inhabitants. In addition to this there was a dispute with China—about the treatment of Chinese coolies in the Dutch East Indies—which was becoming quite serious despite the pacific attitude of the Dutch Government. China, which had become an economically powerful force in recent years, on this occasion seemed bent on turning a relatively insignificant dispute into a power struggle, and in this it undoubtedly had the support of Japan.

Perhaps China and Japan hoped that a war would enable them to obtain the Dutch colonies in the East Indies for themselves. But Britain too had her sights set on the Dutch colonies, and so was at work to seize them at a later date. Moreover, it seemed that Britain was busy behind the scenes, fuelling the fiery dispute between China and Holland.

The Dutch government was obviously fully aware of the threat to their colonial possessions, since they decided on an alliance not with Britain, as the latter had expected, but with Germany. It may have been that they saw that the British were more concerned with securing the Dutch colonies than with supporting their Dutch allies. Again, it may have been that an alliance with Germany brought them many more advantages. In fact, Germany could offer her neighbour greater benefits in real terms than anything the island kingdom could give.

As a result of her alliance with Germany, Holland could expect an improvement in the Rhine shipping industry, despite the Cologne–North Sea canal. Unlike that man-made canal, the natural waterway had greater advantages, since the Rhine–North Sea canal could only gain a commanding importance through the political and economic separation of Germany and Holland. However, the canal remained important enough—both in strategic location and commercial advantage—to justify its construction. The Dutch–German alliance would bring benefits to the main centres of trade in Holland. Amsterdam and Rotterdam would profit greatly, should the alliance result in the abolition of economic barriers, as the Dutch could then enjoy the unimpeded expansion of their trade into the vast hinterland. Indeed, Hamburg also gained substantially from this, since it secured a vital political and economic footing within the German empire through the expansion of its trade, and in consequence it was able to develop trade links in unexpected ways. As a next-door neighbour of Germany, Holland found a better military protector in the Reich than in Britain, which was separated from Holland by the sea. Secure military protection is imperative for the unhindered pursuit of peaceful trade.

The Dutch–German alliance was primarily considered a purely protective alliance; it would be strengthened economically by the political and communal results of trade. When the conclusion of this alliance became known, there were immediate and favourable results for Holland, since China and Japan at once showed themselves to be more conciliatory. There was, however, great disappointment in Britain: after many years of effort they felt them-

selves deceived by the Dutch, and they expressed this disappointment openly. Never before had foreign affairs been debated so
vociferously in the Houses of Commons as in the period after the
signing of this alliance. British anger was directed in particular
against Germany, which was portrayed as the destroyer of world
peace. The British maintained that the alliance had disrupted the
European balance of power: the map of western Europe, the British
'back-door', had changed for the worst in respect of the island
kingdom.

Although the treaty was no more than a protective alliance
between Germany and Holland, there was little doubt that an even
closer political alliance would develop between the two countries.
There were demands in the House of Commons that the British
government should refuse to recognize the alliance, and that the lost
balance of power, in which Britain as a European superpower was
particularly interested, should be restored.

For a long time, the British government seemed unsure about its
response to the signing of the Dutch–German alliance. Finally, they
sent a note to Holland, which stated at great length that the alliance
between Holland and Germany was contrary to the interests of
Britain and other major European powers (namely France and
Russia) and that this alliance created a completely new political situation. It was therefore deemed necessary for the Dutch to distance
themselves from the agreed terms of the alliance until such time as
the major European powers came to an agreement on how, and
under what conditions, such a change might be acceptable to them.

When the Dutch gave an evasive reply, with the full support of the
German government, the British sent them an ultimatum: if Holland
did not declare within three days that it would withdraw from the
alliance with Germany, until the question was settled by a conference of the European superpowers, then Britain would see this as a
reason for declaring war on Holland. Could Germany, as an ally of
Holland, allow this to happen? Could Germany allow herself to be
backed into a corner indirectly by Britain over a matter of national
interest, such as the choice of allies? Never! If Germany did not wish
to become the laughing stock of the world, the British ultimatum
had to lead to a German declaration of war on Britain. Admittedly,
this had the effect of weakening the agreement between Germany
and Japan. This obliged the Japanese, in the event of a British attack
on Germany, to blockade the eastern exits of the Panama canal, and
so prevent aid from the United States reaching Britain.

Even in this matter, however, little would have changed, had

Holland quietly bided her time and waited on a British declaration
of war. Naturally, Germany would have given full military support
to her Dutch ally, although this would not have justified a British
invasion of Germany, as Holland did not actually belong to
Germany, but was only an ally. As it was, however, there was no
other choice for Berlin than to declare war on Britain immediately,
whatever the consequences. Germany could not abandon her ally in
time of need, nor could she tolerate the British in their role as
guardians of the European balance of power, and thereby the over-
lords of Germany. Germany's prestige throughout the world
demanded the painful step of a declaration of war.

All Germans were united in confronting the situation, in seeing
the injustice evident in British actions, and in supporting their
government and the commanders of their armed forces. Though the
thunder of cannons from afar already resounded in German ears,
despite the unfavourable circumstances, Germany went to war. All
Germans were agreed that it had to be! For the honour of Germany!
For a friend and ally of Germany!

THE ANGLO-GERMAN WAR AND THE TERMS OF PEACE

Everyone expected that the war then beginning would become a
European war, and that it would prove decisive both in solving the
West European problem and in clarifying the situation in Central
and Eastern Europe. From Day One almost every state in Europe
began to rearm, since the German declaration of war led to a widespread feeling of uncertainty about the way in which the war
might affect any of them. The major powers were already
involved. Split into two camps as they were, they had to act
according to the commitments in their various treaties and they
had to respond to appeals for help according to their established
obligations. The smaller powers rearmed as well, since they wanted
to safeguard their neutrality or they meant to invade certain areas.
The Italians, who were not committed by treaty to either party in
any war between Britain and Germany, declared at first that they
wished to remain neutral. As the German and British fleets assembled in readiness for action, and as the first naval engagements
began in distant waters, the armies of France, Austro-Hungary, and
Russia began to move. The mass of them did cross over their own
borders, but seemed at first intent on waiting in order to discover
the outcome of the first battles at sea. In any battle for the

command of the sea, it was thought that the first encounters were of primary importance.

Russia had positioned the main body of her troops on the Austrian border, a move which the French would see as a signal for them to cross the German border. The French, however, held back and showed no immediate desire to invade Germany. The main body of the German army was concentrated on the French border and there were forces on the Russian frontier—all of them ready for battle, should the enemy at any time wish to move forward. Yet there was no inclination on the German side to begin an offensive. There were major troop concentrations along the shores of North Germany; and in the south there were troops on the Austrian borders, who could rapidly be dispatched as reinforcements to the east or the west, or they could be sent to help the Austrians.

From an economic point of view, the first consequences of the war were most apparent outwith Europe—in the United States. A panic on the stock exchange caused the value of American shares to plummet to a new low, more than halving their original value, and many great enterprises collapsed like houses of cards. There was practically no ready money to be had, although the American government supplied the banks with large amounts. In the main American ports, all available ships were feverishly loaded with grain and provisions in order to ship them to Britain. German shipping was almost paralyzed, for no matter where any German vessel appeared, it could expect to be captured by the countless number of British cruisers. The enemy fleets began operations: a large British fleet, divided into several squadrons, cruised the waters off the shores of Holland and Germany on the look-out for German vessels. However, a section of the German fleet had managed to reach British shores by a round-about course. With the help of airships and guided by air-pilots, they had landed German troops in an unguarded coastal area. Although there were not large numbers of these troops, nevertheless they were able to cause considerable damage. Thanks to adroit manoeuvring, they were able to inflict substantial casualties on the British troops; and, considering the numbers of the British, these were far greater than they could have expected.

The first naval battle, which took place not far from the island of Heligoland, did not go well for the Germans. It ended, however, without any great losses, since the German fleet was able to take refuge in coastal waters, where the more numerous British ships did not venture to follow for fear of sea-mines. Meanwhile, thanks to

numerous successful flights across the English Channel and unobserved landings in England, a German air-group was able to bring
over more infantry. With constant air support they were able to
carry on their destruction of enemy installations, and they managed
to intercept some important dispatches about naval movements.
Mines laid by the Germans seriously damaged an entire British naval
squadron and left them useless for action. In a great naval battle off
the Dutch coast the British navy, supported by French ships,
suffered a defeat; and, although a subsequent victory off the British
coast over a German squadron was some consolation, there were
heavy losses in ships. Thus both sides went on experiencing good
luck and bad luck for many weeks without either side knocking out
the other.

Fortunately, France was too preoccupied with the situation in the
Mediterranean, and was so much more concerned with the protection of her own coastline that she was unable to give her British ally
any decisive naval support.

In the meantime the war on land had begun. Eventually, the
French could no longer contain their impatience and crossed into
Germany. No sooner had they set foot on German soil than they
were thrown out from Germany and defeated in their own territory.
The Russians had invaded Austria and, although they had suffered
great losses at first, they had pressed further into Austrian territory
with the help of the Serbs and the Montenegrins who were operating on the other flank. Still the Russians stationed on the German
border, much to the annoyance of the French, had not yet invaded
Germany, and so the Germans were able to send some of their
reserves to the aid of Austria. These troops raised the morale of the
Austrians, which had sunk considerably, and so it was possible to
push back the Russians, Serbs and Montenegrins so that they were
no longer on German and Austro-Hungarian territory. Finally, a
surprise manoeuvre enabled the Germans to take Britain.

A division of German troops had slipped across to Britain, travelling in various transport ships which passed for American food ships.
As good fortune would have it, they were able to sail in the shipping
line maintained by the Americans. These ships, together with their
cargo of German soldiers, then sailed into the British port, armed to
the teeth, and to the stupefaction of all, they stormed ashore and
seized the harbour. Many more German landings followed in Britain
with the help of these troops and of the German and Dutch warships
that lay hidden out at sea. This united German force went from one
victory to another. They captured a huge arsenal, and with the aid

of further German troops, who had successfully landed on British soil despite the greatest difficulties, they secured their hold on the country. In the end Britain had to surrender to Germany.

A German 'Dream of the Future' from the cover illustration for A. Niemann, *Der Weltkrieg*, 1904

   Thus, the outstanding services of the German navy and the German land forces had given them a victory over Britain, a victory that opened the way for the German domination of the world.

   The German victory over the British, together with the military successes that Germany had also gained in the land war on the continent, was the decisive factor in bringing hostilities to an end. The terms of peace were ratified in the Hague, where the World Peace Tribunal is in constant session. The British were presented with a harsh peace treaty: they had to pay Germany, Austria and Holland 12 billion marks in reparations; Canada was surrendered to

Germany; and, in addition, Britain had to agree to the stationing—on her own soil and at her own cost—of two German army corps for ten years.

The outcome of this war was exceptionally important for Germany. Above all, the West European problem—the question of naval power—had been decisively resolved. With the defeat of her British rival, Germany ruled the waves; and yet, in fixing the peace conditions, Germany had shown no desire to prevent nor to hamper British foreign trade in the future. Only in so far as British power had been weakened did Britain have to accommodate herself unprotestingly for decades to Germany's quest for world commerce and world domination. As a result of a full decade of a visible military presence in Britain, Germany established a far-reaching influence in all the maritime and military affairs of the island kingdom during this period and was therefore able, contrary to the legitimate self-interest of Britain, to obstruct British rearmament and the building of capital ships. Furthermore, Germany could also anticipate that, during the ten years of military occupation, the British would have become so used to German military superiority that perhaps, at the end of the decade, the time would be right for an alliance with Germany. Every German believed that Germany did not want her British cousins to live in constant subjugation for the duration of the allotted time, but rather believed that their nation's only concern was for Britain to accept German naval power as equal to her own. Indeed, it was Germany's ultimate hope to win her over as an ally of equal status. As a result of centuries of naval supremacy, however, Britain had become too used to her position to tolerate another naval power of equal standing, which wanted to share world dominion with her; and it was this intolerance which had led to the war with Germany. Now that that war was over, and decisions had been made that were not in Britain's favour, it was only a matter of eventually accepting the inevitable and of validating Germany's position as the first naval power and—alongside Britain—the supreme world power.

If this had happened, both major powers would have been able—without mistrust or suspicion—to maintain their war fleets at the level necessary to assure them world superiority. Indeed, they could have protected and supported each other in their maintenance of power, so that neither would have had to keep their fleets at the highest level possible as had previously been necessary. The outcome of the war was to provide the foundations for this change.

But also on the Continent Germany had reaped the benefits of the

German–British war. First, the war had shown that the German–Russian conflict, which was a result of the triple alliance between Russia, France and Britain, did not amount to anything at all in real terms. Neither Germany nor Russia had set foot over each others' borders. As a result, neither empire had the slightest intention of seizing territories from the other. France had demonstrated that the old idea of *révanche*, which had been the cause of conflict in 1871, was still alive and well, and was directed against Germany wherever and whenever the opportunity arose. As for Austro-Hungary, the war proved that the explosive force of the Pan-Slav movement, which had been extremely active since the Treaty of London in 1913, was even stronger, as was the centrifugal principle of the Austro-Hungarian empire. Without German intervention, Austro-Hungary would have collapsed in the war.

The war brought three matters to light: the absence of hostility between the leading Pan-Slav empires (Germany and Russia), even more the ever-continuing hostility between France and Germany, and the serious weakening of the centralizing power of the Austro-Hungarian state. These had made the war worthwhile, at least from a German point of view. Germany could now implement her foreign policy properly in order to solve the Central European (Pan-Germanic) problem decisively and to avoid any political complications with the Slav states which would, in turn, become significant in dealing with the East European (Pan-Slav) problem. Slav Bulgaria, just like pro-German Romania, had played a waiting game during the war, even though both states had prepared themselves for war. Germany, therefore, had to endeavour to seek the friendliest relations with Russia and Bulgaria, the two principal Slav states, as well as with Romania. The German attitude towards Serbia and Montenegro depended on the outcome of the forthcoming dissolution of the Austro-Hungarian Empire.

One year after Max Heinrichka had arranged the future to give the Germans all they wanted, the crisis of July 1914 burst upon Europe. Did Heinrichka recall his forecast about 'the forthcoming dissolution of the Austro-Hungarian empire', as one ultimatum followed another and the armies mobilized in keeping with long-established plans? As the Europeans prepared for the war they had long expected, the British invasion stories and the German Zukunftskriege *went into a terminal decline.*

The prophesying, however, did not end with the outbreak of the First World War. In the last months of 1914, when Oswald Spengler was completing the first version of his future history of the doom-to-come, The Decline of the West, *he still expected that there would be an invasion of England. The war would evolve in keeping with German ambitions. On 25 November he wrote to a friend:*[7]

> We shall win and in such a way that the great sacrifices will be richly compensated. The possession of Belgium alone, which will certainly remain German, is an enormous gain: 8,000,000 inhabitants, a harbour on the Channel, a gigantic industry, and a very old civilization. Also we shall get what we need, an African Colonial Empire. The invasion of England is technically possible and is included in the plans of the General Staff. I assume that it will take place at the beginning of November.

Another still hopeful, but not so confident letter followed on 18 December:[8]

> Whether we shall succeed in reaching London in this war (for the British a Zama), I am not quite sure. I know there is a plan to carry this out. If it is now not practicable, a second war against England will bring the victory history demands.

Hindenburgs Einmarsch in London

Another German writer was then completing the last of the old-style tales of the coming victory. Paul Georg Münch looked ahead from the great German victory at Tannenberg, and he foresaw written into the future: a successful landing on the Channel coast, the rapid defeat of the British forces, and Hindenburg's triumphant entry into London …

Beside herself, Albion saw how the Russian legions which had once, with the primeval force of the Flood, broken into East Prussia and Galicia, fell to pieces under the merciless pursuit of Hindenburg's inferior numbers; how the war-mongers of the Quadruple Alliance, the men after the pattern of Grey, from Nikolai Nikolaiewitch to the divine Gabriele, one after the other sank into the darkness of the world's history.

Would this uncanny Hindenburg, after settling Russia, take a holiday for recuperation, or lead his armies to the West? Might Hindenburg be the stormer before the gates of London? Such ideas shook people's nerves on the other side of the Channel.

The Germans land, break out from the beachheads, and advance in a vast unstoppable flood on London. The last pages of Paul Georg Münch's story record the German triumph:

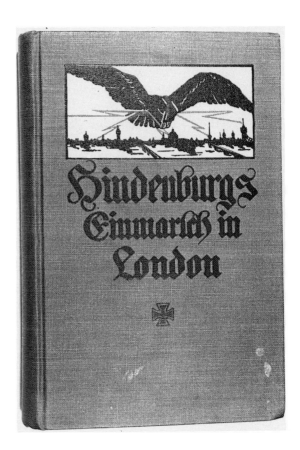

The last of the German invasion stories appeared in 1915, with the message that Hindenburg would lead his troops into London

In the evening Hindenburg orders the great bell of Big Ben, the tower clock of Saint Stephen's, to be rung. Then all the army bands assemble for the great tattoo on foreign soil!

Never had the sound of the trumpets penetrated so deeply in a soldier's heart! Many a comrade who lies buried in the clay trenches of Arras and Ypres, or in the white sand of Galicia, had dreamt at the hour of his death of this entry into London and this tattoo, and death has called him away from the world's theatre before the last and most pleasing act: such thoughts go to the depth of one's heart!

The London mob gaping round the German troops witness something unheard of. The poor simpletons who have been led by the nose by their mischievous Press hear the anthem 'Now Praise ye

God' roaring through Hyde Park, and they ask each other, 'Do the Huns believe in God?'

Hindenburg will tonight start his homeward journey to the Continent, but before leaving he addresses to his gallant men a few short words to take with them on the path of life:

> Soldiers! It has been a hard fight, but you have carried your flags from victory to victory, and have shown to the world that none can set the German frontier ablaze without his own house being burnt down. When you return to Germany shortly, go to church and thank God. And tell your children the great things you have witnessed in these days, and write all this with a firm stylet on your family tablets, so that in the future, if in the course of the next centuries a war-like feeling arise again in Europe, your children's children shall say, to your honour and to the confusion of our enemies: 'One of my forefathers once bivouacked before Buckingham Palace after helping to subdue a whole world of enemies.' Good night comrades!

As the great German war-hero, whose ruthless, hard 'must' on the battlefields extracted from the last man the last atom of strength, now rides once more through the ranks of his battalions, many eyes fill with tears.

Now, friends, fall out!

ABOUT NOON ON THE DAY OF CAPITULATION, MAY
25, 1921, A DETACHMENT OF GERMAN SOLDIERS
MARCHED QUIETLY UP BROADWAY, TURNED INTO
WALL STREET, AND STOPPED OUTSIDE THE BANKING
HOUSE OF J. P. MORGAN & COMPANY.

German soldiers march through Wall Street. A scene from the terror-to-come for
Americans in Cleveland Moffett, *The Conquest of America*, 1916

Epilogue
Meanwhile, Across the Atlantic

America Fallen

Ten months after the outbreak of the First World War, it seemed to some Americans that a German victory in Europe could lead to the establishment of a great world power across the Atlantic. Suppose that superpower were to assemble a great navy and sail westwards to the United States. What then? This was the Chesney syndrome of 1871 transferred to Manhattan. One response to that nightmare came from the greatest American publisher of the time, George Haven Putnam: the United States had to increase its armed forces. His introduction to America Fallen, *an invasion-of-America story, held up Chesney's* Battle of Dorking *as an admirable model and as a means of looking at the future of the United States.*

INTRODUCTION

Nearly half a century ago Sir George Chesney brought into print a bit of prophetic history entitled *The Battle of Dorking*. There was, even as far back as the late sixties, increasing apprehension with certain groups of Englishmen in regard to the designs of their big neighbour across the North Sea. At that time Germany had practically no fleet, or at least no fleet which Englishmen needed to take into account. But military leaders like Sir George Chesney, who certainly could not be accused of hysterical imagination, pictured to themselves that it might be possible, nevertheless, to transport into England, during some temporary absence of the Channel Fleet, a scientifically organized army strong enough to overcome any forces which could be brought together from the small posts of Regulars and from the Militia. *The Battle of Dorking* is the work of a man who was a great staff officer and an accomplished student of military history. The author possessed also dramatic power and literary skill, and his prophetic story has been compared to the famous account given by De Foe of the plague in London.

The Battle of Dorking sold by the thousands, and the influence that it exerted upon the thinking power of patriotic Englishmen was sufficient to bring into existence the Volunteer Force, a force the purpose of which was the defence of England. The methods under which the patriotism of English citizens has since been utilized for defensive organization have changed somewhat in the later decades, but the Territorials who are now sturdily defending the Empire in the trenches of Northern France may be considered as the direct result of the forcible arraignment by Chesney of the policy of leaving England undefended.

The author of *America Fallen* is a leading member of the New York Bar, who has made a careful study of the possibilities of defence for his country and has given special attention to the needs of the American Navy; and he has presented in *America Fallen* a similar bit of prophetic history. Mr Walker makes no claim to being an authority on strategy or military science; but he has taken an active part in the organization of the National Security League, the purpose of which is an intelligent and effective development of the resources of the United States for national defence, and he himself is the Chairman of the League's Committee on the Navy.

America Fallen is a very cleverly presented bit of possible history, and the book makes an appeal for the realization on the part of American citizens of the risk of invasion, which is very similar to the appeal made in *The Battle of Dorking*.

A volume was published in Berlin a few years before the present war under the title of *Operations on the Sea*, by Freiherr von Edelsheim, at that time a colonel on the General Staff of the Prussian Army. The first portion of the book is devoted to a carefully studied scheme for the invasion of England, while the second part is devoted to the details of a plan for the capture of two or three of the most important coast cities of the United States. The Prussian colonel presents calculations, based upon the transport service available in the year in which he wrote, to show that Germany would have no difficulty in sending across the North Atlantic, from the ports of the Elbe, the Weser, and the Ems, in weekly shipments, three successive armies of 250,000 men each.

He points out that, however strong the fortifications might be of Boston, of New York, and of the mouth of the Potomac, a properly equipped force would have no difficulty in landing troops at some point on the coast from which the defences could be taken in the rear. There is, says von Edelsheim, 'no American army, and there would, of course, be nothing to prevent the occupation of these cities and the retention of them as long as might prove convenient'.

He has the further impression that the Republic would be so cowed by the capture of its capital and of its chief Atlantic ports that resistance would crumble. Germany, after securing full indemnities from the millionaires of the eastern cities, would impose its own conditions and its own policy upon the United States.

It is, of course, certain that the Republic would decline to crumble simply because New York, Boston, and Washington had been occupied. Chicago, which feels itself perfectly capable of running the Republic without any aid from the Atlantic sea-coast, would have something to say about that, and so would Denver and San Francisco. There is, however, no reason why Americans should accept the risk of any such disastrous invasion. The Germans would, of course, sooner or later be expelled, but the cost of bringing about the expulsion would be heavy.

It is the contention of the Security League, whose membership since the sinking of the *Lusitania* has increased by leaps and bounds, that the expenditure for 'national insurance' would be a small matter as compared with the waste of an invasion, even though such invasion might secure but temporary success. The Security League is demanding the development of the Navy on plans repeatedly submitted by the scientists of the Naval Board. It is demanding further the development of the Army, first by the addition to the present force of regulars, bringing it up to not less than 150,000 or 125,000 men; and, secondly, by the constitution of a strong reserve force of men who, having received training, would be available for call at need.

The introduction ends with a call for 'intelligent measures for national defence' that would have very been very familiar to European readers:

Mr Walker's volume emphasizes in dramatic form the importance of the work of the Security League, and it can but have a powerful influence in arousing the public opinion of Americans in regard to the present need of intelligent measures for national defence. The League holds that the nation should provide not one cent for aggression, but as many millions as may be necessary for defence. The independence, the honour, and the prestige of the American Republic must be preserved, and its citizens must see to it that their country is maintained in a position to fulfil its obligations as a world-Power.

Geo. Haven Putnam
Veteran Member, Committee on the Army
National Security League
New York, June 1915

THE BOMBARDMENT OF NEW YORK

From his point of vantage, over 700 feet in mid-air, Kennedy, the attendant on the observation platform of the tower of the Woolworth Building, might have swept his eye over the grandest panoramic view of a great city that it has ever been granted to mortal eye to look upon. But on that particular day, April 2, and at that particular hour, 9 a.m., he gazed neither east, north, nor west. His face was to the south, and his eye riveted upon a group of dark-grey ships that stretched in two parallel lines across the main ship channel of the Upper Bay, somewhat to the north of Robbin's Reef—the German Dreadnoughts!

He had read in the papers of the night before about that absurd demand for five billion dollars, and from the papers, also, he knew that the city had made a counter-proposal of one billion. The morning extras had told him that no reply had come from the German Admiral, 'who, doubtless, was awaiting instructions from Berlin'. He picked up a pair of field-glasses (an investment of his which had long ago paid for itself, and was now a steady source of income in tips from country visitors to the tower) and sought out the flagship. Yes, there she was at the head of the first line, with the Admiral's flag flying at the—but what was that flash, keen as the flash of a mirror in the sun! Could it be that—and there came a crash, louder than that of any thunderbolt from heaven, and he was clutching wildly at the railing, as the whole mass of the tower shuddered, and then swayed for a few seconds like a reed shaken by the wind.

Driven by the instinct of flight, he rushed around the platform to the north side, and, looking down, saw that the buildings were obscured by a cloud of bricks, dust, and broken terra-cotta, which fell with a prolonged roar, like a fall of Cyclopean hail, upon the roofs and pavement far below. Another crash! Again the tower staggered under the blow!

He jumped for the elevator. Yes, it was intact. A few floors down it stopped. He managed to undo the door, crawled out, and ran down the stairway. Three flights below he stood dumbfounded. The stairs ended in space, and through a gaping hole, where the hollow-tile flooring had been blasted entirely away, he saw that the whole of two stories, with their floors, outer walls, and inside partitions, had been blown clear into space, leaving the skeleton of the building—columns, floor beams, and braces—stripped as clean of its brick and terra-cotta walls as it was when the erecting gang had swung it into place, a few years before.

The stairs were gone; the elevator shafts also. There was nothing for him but to return. If he could not go down, he would go up. Odd to relate, fear was giving place to curiosity. He heard the roar of the 12-inch shells, as they hurtled past the tower to fall upon the doomed city, and the observation platform would enable him to watch the stupendous spectacle of its destruction.

He gained the platform just in time to see two shells, in quick succession, pass through the top stories of the towering Equitable Life Building, and blast two gaping holes in the south wall.

The next mark was the beautiful tower that crowned the Municipal Building. The percussion fuses were functioning with deadly precision; nothing wrong with *these* German shells. Just one hit—and the walls and columns of the tower had been tumbled in a confused mass upon the roof of the main building and into the street below, leaving the twisted steel skeleton stripped as bare as the trees in midwinter.

And now it dawned upon Kennedy that the Germans were shooting up the city upon a predetermined plan, picking out the principal buildings and putting a couple of shots into the upper stories of each. In rapid succession the Singer Tower, the City Investing Building, the Adams Express, and the new Western Union Building were struck; and always the gaping holes were blown out hundreds of feet in mid-air, where the ruin was visible to the surging mass of people that swarmed out, like bees from a hive, into the streets below.

And then the din of the alternating boom of guns and crash of bursting shells ceased as suddenly as it began. Kennedy turned his glasses on the fleet and saw a couple of hydro-aeroplanes lifted by cranes from the deck of an auxiliary ship and placed on the water. They rose as they advanced on the city, over which they flew at an altitude of 1,500 feet. One of them swung off at the Battery and began to fly in a circular path. The other passed on until it reached the Fifty-ninth Street power station of the Subway, above which it began to describe a path of the figure eight. Kennedy turned his glasses upon the fleet. One of the guns in No. 1 turret of the flagship was being slowly elevated until it pointed well into the sky. There was a flash—a long, droning hum—and thirty seconds later he saw the shell burst against a building north of the power station. From the hydro-aeroplane above there was dropped a puff of white smoke. Another flash and this time the shell burst somewhat to the south of the station. There followed two more puffs of smoke from the 'plane. A few minutes later every 12-inch gun on the ship rose to the range and flashed forth its 860-pound shell loaded with deadly explosive. Kennedy heard the salvo go roaring by miles up in the air, and, lo! the walls of the great power station seemed to fall asunder and a huge cloud of smoke and dust rose high in the heavens.

The power station was utterly wrecked, and every train in the Subway from the Bronx to Brooklyn stopped with its terror-stricken passengers in a darkness which could be felt!

Then the aviator sailed north-east and began his fateful manoeuvres above the Seventy-sixth Street power station of the Elevated Railways. The same routine followed: two or three ranging shots; the dropping of smoke signals, which were relayed by the 'plane at the Battery to the ship; and, finally, the salvo. In a few minutes every train on the Elevated was out of commission.

North the aviator now sped, until he was hovering like a remorseless fate above the Ninety-first Street power station, which runs the street-railway system of Manhattan. The relay hydro-aeroplane moved up to First Street. In ten minutes' time a salvo had found its mark, and Manhattan was absolutely bereft of all means of transportation.

*   *   *   *

That hive of busy workers known as 'the down-town district' received its quota of the morning 'rush' earlier than usual on April 2. The optimistic tone assumed by the New York Press was reflected among the citizens, who were satisfied that there would be at least a period of negotiations preceding any bombardment, the result of which, it was not doubted, would be a compromise. It was curiosity which filled up the business offices half an hour earlier than usual— and curiosity it was that carried the employees by thousands to the roofs for a look at the Kaiser's Dreadnoughts.

But when that first 12-inch shell flashed from the flagship, and went roaring overhead across the skies to burst in the Woolworth Tower, curiosity gave place to fear and fear to panic. From the roof to the floors below the fleeing crowd of clerks and stenographers ran, shouting that the Germans were bombarding the city. Every office floor disgorged its occupants, and a growing crowd rushed for the elevators and filled the stairways. Out of the entrance of every building there surged a human flood, and the waters of this inundation met and swirled in the side streets and turned in increasing volume to Broadway—seeking a means of quick escape by the Subway. In a few minutes the streets were filled from building line to building line with a frantic mob, so tightly jammed that all movement ceased. Then, as shell after shell burst far above, huge masses of masonry came hurtling down upon that hapless mob, killing and wounding the unfortunates where they stood, held fast. And still the terror-stricken pushed their way, with that fatal accumulation of pressure which marks a fleeing mob, out of every office-building entrance, the emerging mass acting with the cumulative effect of a hydraulic ram upon the already compacted mass in the streets. Under that fatal pressure the weak went down, ribs were crushed in, breathing was no longer possible. By the hundred, the people died where they fell.

And up from the streets of the city there rose the prolonged wail of the dying, answered from above by the savage roar of the flying shells, and the swish and clatter of the ever-falling masonry.

There was a slight relief at each Subway entrance, into which the waters of that stricken human flood twisted and gurgled like water through a sink. And further relief was given on the outskirts of the mob, where such of the police as had not been engulfed, attacking from the side streets, unloosened the fringe of the horror by reminding the terror-stricken that the Elevated and the ferries afforded other avenues of escape.

And then, as the great power stations fell beneath the salvos of the bombardment, and every wheel in New York's vast system of transportation ceased to turn, fear redoubled and frantic horror began again to crush the life out of that hope-abandoned mob.

And just at this very hour, as though the anguish were not complete, the lawless element in the city broke loose in every quarter in a wild orgy of pillage and arson. From many a resort of crime and infamy, the gun-man, the safe-cracker, and all the brood that hides from law and order streamed forth to gather in the spoil. The police, aye the whole ten thousand of them, swept off their feet by the wild terror of Manhattan's millions, were unable to co-operate for effective work. Crime had found its millennium. Into the jewellery stores, into the houses of the rich on Fifth Avenue and the West Side, a mob, armed and stopping at no crime of violence, broke its way, gathering into grip and handbag, or thrusting into pocket at each grasp, the ransom of a prince!

The terror of the bombardment swept through the densely populated tenement-house district like the rush of a prairie fire, and at
once there arose in a babel of many tongues the universal cry, 'To
the bridges; to the bridges!' And to the bridges they swept, men,
women, and children, Jew, Italian, Greek, and Russian, bearded
rabbi and toddling child, in a wild stampede to put the river between
themselves and the bursting shells. Eastward to the bridges they
surged, half a million strong; the mob becoming denser as it
converged on the various approaches.

Overwhelmed by that human flood, vehicular traffic stopped.
Roadways and footways, subway tracks and trolley tracks, all were
submerged. The Manhattan Bridge, among others, in spite of its
width of 120 feet, was packed from rail to rail with the fleeing host,
and when the crush was at its worst the inevitable happened.
Somewhere a fugitive slipped, a foot passing between the railway
ties of the tracks—someone stayed to help—more stumbled and fell.
The crowd behind, infuriated by the delay, made a rush, throwing
down others in the van. Soon, there was a mass of struggling,
cursing humanity wedged tight from rail to rail. The crushing out of
life that was being enacted on lower Broadway was being repeated
150 feet above the East River.

The crowd stopped its convulsive struggle. Except for the down-
trodden and dying, silence fell on that multitude, and, awestruck,
they gazed skyward at the harbinger of death and waited for his
messengers.

Then they came. A roar as of an express train on the Elevated, and
with a blast of air that swept down upon the victims, a 12-inch shell
passed over the centre of the span.

But before signalling to correct the range, the aviator planed down
so as to obtain a closer view of the bridge. With amazement he saw
that it was swarming from end to end with a helpless mass of
humanity. The purpose of the bombardment was to damage—not
destroy; and he realized that if the shells of the *Koenig* should cut the
bridge cables, 50,000 souls would be hurled to their death in the
river below!

Hastily he rose and signalled to the *Koenig* to cease fire.

*The Germans are everywhere victorious: they destroy the US fleet, seize
Washington, and occupy the principal Eastern sea ports. The author follows
Chesney in applying the utmost rigour to the situation of the nation. The
final paragraphs describe in painful detail the last days of a defeated people.
The Chief of Staff tells the President that:*

The enemy is in undisputed possession of the richest, most valuable, and most densely populated section of the United States ... Being in command of the sea and possessing ample transport, he is free to land on our shores as many troops as he may desire.

The last words from the author are spoken by the Chief of Staff. He says, in effect, that the end has come for the United States. Let the nation accept the peace terms, harsh though they may be, he tells the President. Let them pay the war indemnity of 10 billion dollars—or else. After so many tales of the war-to-come from British and German writers, the last word has to come from an American author:

I would suggest that the Government pay this indemnity, and write it off on the National Ledger as the cost of being taught the great national duty of military preparedness.

Notes

Introduction

1. For an account of the origins of these stories see I. F. Clarke, *Voices Prophesying War* (Oxford: Oxford University Press, 1992); and for a selection of short stories see (a) I. F. Clarke, *The Tale of the Next Great War 1871–1914* (Liverpool: Liverpool University Press, 1995); and (b) H. Franke, *Der politisch-militärische Zukunftsroman in Deutschland, 1904–1914* (Frankfurt: Peter Lang, 1985).

2. Erskine Childers, *The Riddle of the Sands* (London: Nelson, 1910) p. *v*.

3. August Niemann, *Der Weltkrieg—Deutsche Traüme* (Leipzig: F. W. Vobach, 1904). The extract comes from the English translation, *The Coming Conquest of England*, trans. J. H. Freese (London: Routledge, 1904), pp. *v–vi*.

4. Edith Olivier, *Without Knowing Mr Walkeley* (London: Faber & Faber, 1938), p. 198. Robert Graves had comparable expectations: 'I was at Harlech when war was declared; I decided to enlist a day or two later. In the first place, though only a very short war was expected—two or three months at the very outside—I thought it might last just long enough to delay my going to Oxford in October, which I dreaded.' *Goodbye to All That* (London: Cape, 1929), p. 99.

5. Alfred Russel Wallace, *The Wonderful Century* (London: Swan Sonnenschein, 1901), p. 37.

6. C. De W. Willcox, 'Changes in Military Science', in *The 19th Century: A Review of Progress* (London and New York: G. P. Putnam, 1901), pp. 492–94.

7. H. G. Wells, *Anticipations of the Reaction of Mechanical and Scientific Progress upon Human Life and Thought* (London: Chapman & Hall, 1902), pp. 204–05.

8. Sir Basil Liddell Hart, *History of the First World War* (1930) (London: Papermac, 1992), p. 28.

9. Karl Eisenhart, *Die Abrechnung mit England* (Munich: Lehmann, 1900), p. 3.

10. *The Times*, 9 April 1904.

11. von R., 'Die Invasion Englands in englischer Beleuchtung', *Marine Rundschau*, November 1908, p. 1246.

12. *Annual Register*, Part II, p. 104, 1906.

13. Hilaire Belloc, 'In the Case of War', *The London Magazine*, 28 (19), May 1912, pp. 279–90.

14. Eisenhart, op. cit., pp. 3–4.

15. General Friedrich Adam Julius von Bernhardi, *Germany and the Next War*, trans. Allen H. Powles (London: Edward Arnold, 1912), p. 102. The original was *Deutschland and der nächste Krieg* (Stuttgart: J. G. Cotta, 1912)

16. Robert Blatchford, *Germany and England*, (London: Associated Newspapers, 1909), p. 7. The articles first appeared in the *Daily Mail*, 13–23 December 1909.

17. D. C. Boulger, 'British Distrust of Germany', *The Nineteenth Century*, 59 (347), January 1906, pp. 4–5. See also O. Eltzbacher, 'The Anti-British Movement in Germany', *The Nineteenth Century* 52 (306), August 1902, pp. 190–200. Eltzbacher writes (p. 196): 'German-Anglophobia of the present day is an unceasing violent agitation, and a constant preaching of the gospel that a war with Great Britain is imminent and unavoidable ... The intellectual circles have taken up the cry that in view of Germany's increasing population she absolutely requires colonies in a temperate zone, that Great Britain is decaying, that the Anglo-Saxon races and the Anglo-Saxon Governments are rotten to the core, that Anglo-Saxon nations brutally and wantonly attack weaker nations for lust of gain, and that, driven by jealousy, they may one day attack and destroy German export trade, German shipping, and German prosperity.'

18. J. L. Bashford, 'Great Britain and Germany', *The Nineteenth Century*, 56 (334), December 1904, pp. 873–81.

19. Karl Blind, 'Germany and War Scares in England', *The Nineteenth Century*, 58 (345), November 1905, pp. 698–99.

20. *Annual Register*, Part II, p. 104, 1909. When, by chance, Thomas Hardy saw *An Englishman's Home*, he thought 'it ought to have been suppressed as provocative, since it gave Germany, even if pacific in intention beforehand, a reason, or excuse, for directing her mind on a war with England': Florence Emily Hardy, *The Later Years of Thomas Hardy* (London: Macmillan, 1930), p. 162. A contemporary commented on the extraordinary popularity of the play: 'The entrances at Wyndham's Theatre are besieged for hours before every performance. And after each of the three acts the audiences applaud and cheer with an unanimity and vehemence without parallel in the history of the British stage.' Quoted by Daphne du Maurier in *Gerald: A Portrait* (New York: Giant Cardinal Editions, 1963), p. 96.

21. Quoted in Frances Donaldson, *P. G. Wodehouse* (London: Futura, 1983), p. 2.

22. P. J. Wodehouse, *The Swoop! or, How Clarence Saved England* (London: Alston Rivers, 1909), p. 59.

23. Quoted in Selina Hastings, *Evelyn Waugh: An Autobiography* (London: Minerva, 1995), pp. 32–33.

24. Max Heinrichka, *100 Jahre deutsche Zukunft* (Leipzig: Vogel & Vogel, 1913), pp. 34–35.

25. Anonymous (Paul Georg Münch), *Hindenburgs Einmarsch in London: Von einem deutschen Dichter* (Leipzig: Grethlein, 1915), pp. 62–63.

Chapter One

The Great War of 189–

1. The editor of *Black and White* had chosen wisely: Vice-Admiral Philip
Colomb (1831–1899), known as 'Column and a Half' from his habit of
writing long letters on many matters to *The Times*, had made major contributions to the new steam navy. He wrote at length on naval tactics and
naval history; and the use of 'Colomb's Flashing Signals' became standard
practice with the Royal Navy. See Chapter 2 Notes (p. 428) for a possible
connection with Erskine Childers's *Riddle of the Sands*. Charles Lowe
(1848–1931) was a distinguished foreign correspondent of *The Times* in
Berlin. He returned to London in 1891, and continued diplomatic reporting. David Christie Murray (1847–1907) was the special correspondent of
The Times during the Russo-Turkish War. Frederick Villiers (1852–1922) had
a considerable reputation as one of the best war artists, mostly for the
Graphic. The other artists were well known in their time. There is a good
account of the war artists in Pat Hodgson, *The War Illustrators* (London:
Osprey, 1977).

2. The editor's introduction is taken from the first part of the serial, *The
Great War of 1892*, which opened in *Black and White* on 2 January 1891 and
ended on 21 May. The rest of the extracts come from the subsequent,
revised publication: Rear-Admiral P. Colomb and others, *The Great War of
189–: A Forecast* (London: William Heinemann, 1893). This reproduced most
of the outstanding illustrations of the serial. The German translation, *Der
grosse Krieg von 189–*, with an introduction by General von Bülow, had run
through five editions by 1894.

The extracts are taken from:
'Attempted Assassination of Prince Ferdinand', pp. 1–5; 8–11.
'We are Now at War', pp. 18–22.
'Russian Movement upon the Austrian Frontier', pp. 26–30.
'Warlike Excitement in Paris', pp. 44–49.
'Public Feeling in England', pp. 66–71.
'Night Attack by the Russians', pp. 78–85.
'The Battle of Sardinia', pp. 165–69.
'The Battle of Machault', pp. 184–91.
'Great Victory of the French', pp. 268–75.
The major figures in the book come straight from contemporary history.
First, the Prince Ferdinand of the narrative was Maximilian Karl Leopold
Ferdinand (1861–1948), youngest son of Prince Augustus of Saxe-Coburg
and Gotha; he was elected Prince of Bulgaria on 7 July 1887, but Russia
refused to acknowledge the election for several years. The mention of
Russia agents (p. 37) puts the projected assassination well within the range
of probabilities for that time. Assassination was another name for politics in

the Balkans, especially with the Macedonian revolutionary committees. They attacked Stambulov in the streets of Sofia (15 July 1895) and he died three days later.

Second, the history of the Balkans has many pages for Stefan Stambulov (1854–1895). He began his long, violent political career at the age of 20 by organizing insurrections in Bulgaria. On the abdication of Prince Alexander on 21 August 1886, he stood out against the Russians and secured the election of Prince Ferdinand. Appointed prime minister in the new government, he sought to secure the recognition of Prince Ferdinand.

Third, Kaiser Wilhelm II here makes the first of many appearances in future-war fiction. He is the new ruler of Germany, and has not yet become the arch-enemy of Great Britain as he was to be portrayed in the invasion stories after 1900.

3. Count Georg Leo von Caprivi (1831–1899) was a German soldier and statesman. In the War of 1870 he served as chief of staff to the X Army Corps. Bismarck, who considered Caprivi a possible successor, appointed him to high office in March 1890—chancellor, Prussian minister president, and foreign minister. He negotiated the Anglo-German Agreement on spheres of influence in Africa with Great Britain in July 1890. Count Alfred von Schlieffen (1833–1913) was a distinguished German soldier, best known as the originator of the 'Schlieffen Plan' which called for a great turning movement on the right flank, pivoting on Metz, and moving forward on the line Dunkirk–Verdun. The narative is up to date: Schlieffen was appointed chief of staff to the army in 1891, and Caprivi became chancellor in 1890.

4. Jean de Reszke (1850–1925) was a Polish operatic singer who came to fame and a world audience (London, New York, Paris) in the 1880s. He was best known for his tenor parts in Wagnerian opera.

5. Arthur James Balfour (1848–1930), philosopher and politician, was appointed chief secretary for Ireland in the Salisbury administration in 1887, and then in 1891 first lord of the Treasury and leader of the House of Commons. He succeeded his uncle, Lord Salisbury, as prime minister in 1902. Sir William George Harcourt (1827–1904) was a major parliamentary figure in his day. Appointed secretary of state on the Liberal return to office in 1880, he does not deserve the unflattering role he is given in the story.

6. Count Joseph Vladimirovich Gourko (1828–1901) would have been a trifle old for Balkan campaigning in 1892—perhaps Charles Lowe intended a contrast between old-style warfare and 'the most recent innovations in the field warfare of the Germans': barbed wire and electric lights. General Gourko distinguished himself in the Russo-Turkish War of 1877, when he commanded the advanced guard; he crossed the Danube and secured the principal Balkan passes. His subsequent investment of the Turkish troops at Plevna was the beginning of the end for Mohammed Ali.

7. Another strange coincidence: Admiral Sir George Tryon (1832–1893) was appointed to command the Mediterranean Fleet in August 1891, when

Colomb and associates must have been at work on their story; and on 22 June 1893, two years after the serialization of the *Great War of 189–*, he was responsible for a major naval disaster. When the fleet was cruising in two columns off the coast of Syria, Tryon signalled for the ships to invert their course and turn inward in succession. This most dangerous manoeuvre ended with a collision between the two leading ships: the *Camperdown* rammed and sank Tryon's flagship, *Victoria*, which sank with all hands. This was taken as a confirmation of the value of the ram as a means of naval warfare.

The Final War

Louis Tracy (1868–1928) had a varied and successful career: first as a reporter for the *Northern Echo* in Darlington, then in editorial posts with newspapers including *The Times*. Early in the 1890s he worked on the *Sun*, which had its office opposite the Harmsworth office in Tudor Street. Tracy advised Harmsworth of the sale of the *Evening News and Post*. He became editor of the renamed *Evening News* for a short time; soon after he sold his shares in that paper, and then discovered not long afterwards that, had he kept them, he would have made a fortune. He took to fiction, and wrote some thirty novels.

The major contemporary figures are: (1) Count Georg Leo von Caprivi, who makes a second appearance here (See n. 3); (2) Albert August Hanotaux (1853–1944), French historian and statesman, who made his way through the diplomatic service, from counsellor at Constantinople in 1885 to foreign minister in 1894, and worked to secure better relations with Russia; (3) Count Joseph Vladimirovich Gourko (see n. 6).

The extracts are taken from the first edition: Louis Tracy, *The Final War* (London: Pearson, 1896): 'The Ball at the Embassy': pp. 1–3; 'A Council of the Powers': pp. 9–13.

The Spies of the Wight

Francis Edward Grainger was a prolific writer, the author of some two dozen stories of adventures and romance. All of them were published under his pseudonym of Headon Hill.

The extract is taken from Headon Hill (Francis Edward Grainger), *The Spies of the Wight* (London: C. A. Pearson, 1899): 'A Secret Mission' pp. 7–19.

Die Abrechnung mit England

8. Anon., 'Anti-English Sentiment in Germany', *Blackwood's Magazine*, 169, April 1901, pp. 585–96.

The extracts are taken from: Dr. Karl Eisenhart, *Die Abrechnung mit England* (Munich, J. F. Lehmann, 1900), pp. 32–45 and pp. 68–72.

9. The author here attacks the then new European peace movement. Frau Selenka was a German associate of Baronness Bertha von Suttner (1843–1914), an Austrian writer, born in Prague, daughter of the Austrian field marshal, Count Franz Kinsky. In 1876 she married the novelist Freiherr von Suttner. She was a major figure in the European peace movement before 1914, having founded the Austrian Peace Society in 1891, and started the monthly journal of the peace movement, *Die Waffen Nieder,* at Dresden in 1892. In 1905 she was awarded a Nobel Prize for her peace work.

10. The introduction of 'the Sturdees', like the mention of Kautz and Coghlan, has its origin in German displeasure at the actions of certain naval officers. Sir Frederick Sturdee (1859–1925), who destroyed Admiral von Spee's squadron in the Battle of the Falklands on 7 December 1914, was in command of the British forces on Samoa at the time of some tension between Americans and Germans about areas of influence. (The Samoan Islands were jointly administered by the Americans, British, and Germans.) The trouble had begun in 1888, with intertribal warfare between rival candidates for the kingship. The Germans supported Tamasese; Malietoa had the support of the Americans and the British. He was deported by the Germans, whereupon the British and Americans supported his successor, Mataafa. All three nations sent landing parties ashore, and in the various encounters with the Samoans some fifty German sailors and marines were killed. A conference of the three powers in Berlin reached an agreement: Malietoa was restored to the kingship, and a joint protectorate established over Samoa. After the death of Malietoa in 1898, civil war broke out again. Sturdee was promoted in recognition of his tactful handling of a delicate international situation. The American forces were under the command of Captain (later Rear-admiral) Albert Kautz, who received a naval commendation for his conduct.

The name of Coghlan, however, belongs to another place and a different grudge. Captain J. B. Coghlan (1844–1908) had rendered conspicuous service in the Battle of Manila Bay in 1898, and after the defeat of the Spanish fleet he was the senior officer charged with maintaining the blockade established by Admiral Dewey. A German force of five vessels arrived in the Bay. They ignored the laws of blockade; their officers visited the Spanish positions in Manila; and they landed men to take possession of the quarantine station at Mariveles harbour. Admiral Dewey, rightly considering these actions a breach of maritime law by a neutral power, despatched Coghlan in USN *Raleigh* to prevent any further German action. This action led to protests from Admiral von Diedrichs, who sought the support of the senior British naval officer, Captain Chichester. Chichester received the German admiral on board his ship, the books of international law spread out on his table. An account of the incident appears in Archibald Hurd, *An Incident of War* (London: Joseph Causton, 1918).

11. The author evidently had no time for the contemporary international peace movement. The first international peace conference, promoted by the Russian tsar, Nicholas II, was attended by delegates from twenty-six countries and continued from 18 May to 29 July 1899. Although the objections of the German delegates led to the abandonment of the discussions on the subject of excessive armaments, there were important conventions on the settlement of international disputes, on land warfare, and on the application of the Geneva Convention to maritime warfare.

12. The imaginary peace terms represent the dream package of the German Colonial Society and the *Flottenverein*; they give Germany a commanding naval base in the Mediterranean and desirable colonies in Africa and the South Seas.

Chapter Two

1. Archibald S. Hurd, 'The Kaiser's Fleet', *The Nineteenth Century*, 52, July 1902, p. 42.

The Invaders

The extracts are taken from Louis Tracy, *The Invaders* (London: Pearson, 1901): 'The Ides of March', pp. 9–11, pp. 55–61.

The Enemy in our Midst

The extract is taken from Walter Wood, *The Enemy in our Midst* (London: J. Long, 1906): 'The Plan of War', pp. 36–46.

The Riddle of the Sands

Robert Erskine Childers (1870–1922), son of Robert Caesar Childers, the noted Pali scholar, and an Irish mother, was a clerk in the House of Commons from 1895 to 1910. He volunteered for the artillery in the Boer War and was commended for outstanding service in the First World War. He became an ardent supporter of the movement for an Irish state and, in the tragic way of Irish history, was shot by a firing squad from the other side. One clue to the genesis of the *The Riddle of the Sands* could be in the friendship between Childers and Robert Colomb, whose uncle was Vice-Admiral Philip Colomb, compiler of *The Great War of 189–*. There is a full account of Childers and the writing of his story in the excellent account by Maldwin Drummond, *The Riddle* (London, Nautical Books, 1985).

The *Riddle* is the solitary survivor from the 'German Invasion' stories. It has been in print for most of the twentieth century; and in 1997 it appeared in the 'Popular Fiction' series of Oxford University Press.

The extract is taken from Erskine Childers, *The Riddle of the Sands* (London: Heinemann, 1903): 'The Luck of the Stowaway', pp. 344–60.

A New Trafalgar

The story is a celebration of the new warship, the destroyer: a British invention which first came into service in 1893.

The extract is taken from A. C. Curtis, *A New Trafalgar* (London: Smith & Elder, 1902), pp. 36–51.

Little is known about Albert Curtis, a minor writer.

2. Archibald S. Hurd, 'The Kaiser's Fleet', *The Nineteenth Century*, 19 (305), July 1902, pp. 31–42. Other articles were: Ogniben, 'Great Britain and Germany', *Contemporary Review*, 81 (434), February 1902, pp. 153–72; O. Eltzbacher, 'The Anti-British Movement in Germany', *The Nineteenth Century*, 19 (306), August 1902, pp. 190–200.

3. The author is quite right when he writes that 'the march of invention has been rapid in naval affairs'. The *Collingwood* had been 'struck from the fighting division of the Navy', according to T. A. Brassey, *The Naval Annual* (Portsmouth: Griffin & Co., 1906). Others, like the *Howe, Camperdown*, and *Benbow*, had been completed in the 1880s.

The Invasion of 1910

William Tufnell Le Queux (1864–1927) was born in France of a French father and an English mother. He came to London as a young man and quickly established himself as the prolific author of sensational stories—romance, espionage, future wars and the occult. He produced over 130 books.

The serial version of *The Invasion of 1910* opened in the *Daily Mail* on 20 March 1906 and continued daily until the last instalment on 4 July. The April numbers appeared under the heading of 'The Siege of London' and the last three instalments under 'The Revenge'.

The extracts come from William Le Queux, *The Invasion of 1910* (London: Eveleigh Nash, 1906): 'State of Siege Declared', pp. 125–30; 'The Bombardment of London', pp. 326–35.

When the Eagle Flies Seaward

4. R. B. Haldane, *Richard Burdon Haldane: An Autobiography* (London Hodder & Stoughton, 1929), p. 187.

The extracts come from Patrick Vaux and Lionel Yexley, *When the Eagle Flies Seaward* (London: Hurst & Blackett, 1907): 'State of Siege Declared', pp. 36–51. The authors were minor writers.

The Death Trap

5. Michael Balfour, *The Kaiser and His Times* (London: The Cresset Press, 1964), p. 157.

6. Ibid., pp. 226–27.

The extracts are from R. W. Cole, *The Death Trap* (London: Greening, 1907), pp. 1–13.

The Child's Guide to Knowledge

7. Anonymous, 'The Child's Guide to Knowledge', in Aldeburgh Lodge Magazine, Spring 1909, pp. 188–89. I am much indebted to Chris Gilmore who brought this short catechism to my attention. He tells me that Aldeburgh Lodge (now Orwell Park School) was a preparatory school; and he surmises that the contribution 'was presumably the work of a master'. It undoubtedly came from someone who knew the German language well enough to parody the word-order and make fun of the characteristic liking for compound words.

Chapter Three

The Coming Conquest of England

August Niemann (1839–1919) was a one-time officer in the Hanoverian Army (1857–66), and then a private tutor. He wrote more than 40 books: accounts of major battles, histories of campaigns, and many romances.

The extracts are taken from August Niemann, *The Coming Conquest of England*, translated by J.H. Freese (London: George Routledge, 1906), 'Author's Preface', pp. *v–vii*; 'The Council of State', pp. 1–15; and 'The Landing in Scotland', pp. 348–55. The original was *Der Weltkrieg—Deutsche Träume* (Leipzig: F. W. Vobach, 1904).

1. The Treaty of Shimonoseki concluded the Chino-Japanese War of 1894–95. Russia, supported by her ally France, with the co-operation of Germany, prevented Japan from obtaining the Liaotung peninsula.

2. The affair of the Kruger Telegram began on 3 January 1896, when the German emperor sent his congratulations to the president of the Transvaal Republic on the capture of Jameson and his raiders. The message read: 'I would like to express my sincere congratulations that you and your peoples have succeeded, without having to invoke the help of friendly powers, in restoring peace with your own resources in face of armed bands which have broken into your country as disturbers of the peace and have been able to preserve the independence of your country against attacks from outside.' This calculated act of state—interference in the affairs of another nation—

incensed the British public, since the popular expectation assumed that nothing could affect the friendly relations between the two countries. The telegram proved to a major factor in convincing the British that Germany had started on a hostile course.

3. The Tsar was the ill-fated Nicholas (1894–1917).

4. Count Serge Julievich Witte (1849–1915) was a man of great energy and of high administrative ability: he played a major part in developing the railway system in Russia. In 1892 he became minister of ways of communication, and then minister of finance in 1893. Here, Witte, demoted from finance minister in 1903, appears in his new role as president of the committee of ministers. In August 1905 he was appointed principal negotiator for the peace discussions with the Japanese.

5. The Russo-Japanese War began on 8 February 1904 and ended 23 August 1905. The mention of 'the first despatch of the Viceroy Alexieff' on p. 184 suggests that Niemann was writing during an early stage in the war, when Admiral Evgeni Alexeiev was directing Russian operations from Port Arthur, and there were still expectations that the Russians would defeat the Japanese.

6. The principal characters are from life. General Alexei Kuropatkin, however, should have been far away in Manchuria in command of the Russian army.

7. The Fashoda Incident of 1898, an episode in the end-play for African colonies, brought the United Kingdom and France close to war. Although the British government had warned the French in 1895 that any advance into the Nile valley 'would be an unfriendly act', the French went ahead with their expedition. Captain Marchand and his small detachment of Senegalese troops spent close on two years in marching 2,800 miles. They reached Fashoda south of Omdurman on 18 September 1898. The British commander and Sirdar of the Egyptian army, Sir Herbert Kitchener, handled the matter with tact and courtesy. Eventually the Anglo-French Convention of 21 March 1899 put an end to the friction between the two governments: it was agreed that the British would not move westward along the watershed between the Nile and the Congo, and the French would not move eastward.

8. Pobedonostev, Chief Procurator of the Holy Synod, gives a good display of his ferocious xenophobic, anti-western views.

Armageddon 190–

'Seestern' was the pseudonym of Ferdinand Grautoff (1871–1935). He was for many years the editor of the *Leipziger Neuesten Nachrichten*; he also wrote books on naval history.

The extracts are taken from Seestern (F. H. Grautoff), *Armageddon 190–*, translated by G. Herring (London: Kegan, Paul, 1907): 'The Most Terrific War in History', pp. 1–3; 'The Incident of Samoa', pp. 4–35; 'The

Bombardment of Cuxhaven', pp. 97–117. The original was *1906–Der Zusammenbruch der alten Welt* (Leipzig: Dieterich, 1906). In Germany the book had a sale of 100,000 copies in the first year; and the identity of 'Seestern' was ascribed to the Emperor, to senior naval officers, and sometimes to journalists. The introduction to the English edition opens with kind words for the author: 'It is refreshing to read this anonymous book, which, with its general accuracy of detail, has been unmistakably "made in Germany", after the numerous sketches of future European wars with which we have been favoured by British writers. In the latter we have our shortcomings and unreadiness consistently brought forward in the laudable desire to call attention to defects, and to our fundamental disregard of the necessity for making adequate preparations for war in piping times of peace' (p. xi).

9. See Chapter 1, note 10, for an account of the situation on Samoa.

10. The translator's note reads: 'The *Iltis* is the German parallel to the British *Birkenhead*. The *Iltis* went down on July 23rd, 1896, off Cape Schantung, only eleven men being saved. While waiting for death, the men sang the "Song of the Flag", which is to the Germans much what "Rule Britannia" is to us.'

11. 'Die alte Liebe' was an old pier at the mouth of the Elbe close to the entrance lighthouse—once an ideal place for watching the great ocean liners on their way to or from Hamburg.

Die 'Offensiv-Invasion' gegen England

Carl, sometimes Karl, Bleibtreu (1859–1928) was the son of the well-known battle-painter, Georg Bleibtreu. For most of his life he was a journalist or editor. From 1879 onwards he turned out a vast number of books. These included critical and historical works on English literature and several very successful histories of past wars.

The extract comes from Karl Bleibtreu, *Die 'Offensiv-Invasion' gegen England* (Berlin: Schall & Rentel, 1907), pp. 3–9.

12. *Annual Register*, 1906, p. 136.

13. This must refer to the visit of the German Burgomasters to London in 1907.

14. Lord Charles Beresford (1846–1919) was one of the most distinguished naval commanders of his time. In March 1905 he was promoted to admiral and appointed commander-in-chief (Mediterranean). In 1907 he was transferred to command the new Channel Fleet, and in 1909, when the Channel Fleet was abolished, he retired from the Royal Navy.

15. Sir Arthur Wilson (1842–1921) was the best fleet commander of the pre-1914 period. He developed a new fleet formation which became standard practice for the Navy: ships to advance in columns and deploy into

single line in order to engage the enemy. The German fleet formed in single line and altered direction to engage. This was a tactical weakness, which told against the German High Seas Fleet (6.15 p.m., 31 May 1916, the Battle of Jutland) when Jellicoe signalled the British battle fleet to deploy on the port or easterly column. This masterly decision gave the British naval forces an overwhelming advantage as the battle cruisers, cruisers, and destroyers took up their pre-arranged positions. At 6.35 p.m., when Vice-Admiral Scheer realized that the entire British battle fleet was bearing down on the High Seas Fleet, he ordered an immediate 'emergency retirement'. Admiral Wilson is here confused with H. W. Wilson and he appears later, falsely accused, in Karl Siwinna's discussion of future-war fiction in Chapter 4 (see n. 9, p. 436).

Berlin–Bagdad

Rudolf Emil Martin (1876–1916) was a civil servant (Imperial Statistical Office), a frequent contributor to political and social journals, and the author of popular books on aircraft.

The extract comes from the abridged translation, 'The Age of the Air-ship: Facts and Fantasies', in 'The Book of the Month', *Review of Reviews*, 35, pp. 427–33. The original was Rudolf Martin, *Berlin-Bagdad: Das deutsche Weltreich im Zeitalter der Luftschifffahrt, 1910–1931* (Stuttgart and Leipzig: Deutsche Verlags-Anstalt, 1907).

16. H. G. Wells, *The War in the Air* (London: George Bell, 1908), p. 107. The story first appeared in the January number of the *Pall Mall Magazine*, 1908, and continued until December.

Chapter 4

The Real Le Queux

1. William Le Queux, 'How I write my Sensational Novels', in *Pearson's Weekly*, no. 862, 24 January 1907, p. 1.

The extracts come from N. St Barbe Slade, *The Real Le Queux* (London: Nicholson & Watson, 1938): 'The Kaiser's Spy Bureau', pp. 181–83; 'The Invasion of 1910', pp. 190–97.

2. The eminent persons cited in the account were all major figures in their time. (1) Lord Haldane (1856–1918) was a distinguished philosopher and a Liberal member of Parliament. Appointed secretary for war in the Campbell-Bannerman cabinet of 1905, he carried through a series of most important army reforms. Later he held conversations with France to discuss Anglo-French cooperation in terms of the *Entente* of 1904. He was the prin-

cipal agent of the Cabinet in the search for an understanding with Germany that would avert the risk of war. (2) Field-Marshal Earl Roberts of Kandahar (1832–1914) appears in many tales of the war-to-come. He served with distinction (seven times mentioned in despatches and awarded the Victoria Cross) in many Indian campaigns. Later appointed commander-in-chief in South Africa, he brought the Boer War to a successful conclusion. He retired from active service in 1905 and devoted himself, as head of the National Service League, to presenting the case for universal military service. (3) Prince Louis of Battenberg (1854–1921) was born at Gratz, the eldest son of Prince Alexander of Hesse. He became a British subject in 1868 and that same year entered the Royal Navy. He was assistant director of naval intelligence in 1900; was promoted rear-admiral in 1904, and, after commanding the Atlantic and Home fleets, was appointed first sea lord. In 1917 he relinquished all German titles, assumed the surname of Mountbatten, and was granted a peerage as 1st Marquess of Milford Haven. (4) Herbert Wrigley Wilson (1866–1940) was a writer of great influence: a friend of Lord Charles Beresford, an assistant editor and leader writer for the *Daily Mail* and a frequent contributor to the *National Review* edited by Leopold Maxse. His life was dedicated to the sea power of the United Kingdom. He was well-known in Germany as a skilful propagandist.

3. See the note on p. 436 on Carl Siwinna for a full account of the German translation of the *Invasion of 1910*.

Bouquets for Fleet Street

Bernard Falk (1882–1960) had a varied and distinguished career in journalism. He was the editor of several newspapers and a well-known writer on literary and art subjects.

The extract comes from Bernard Falk, *Bouquets for Fleet Street* (London: Hutchinson, 1951), pp. 64–65.

Before the Lights Went Out

Esmé Wingfield-Stratford (1882–1971) was an able and interesting writer, the author of a long succession of historical studies on naval, military, and Victorian subjects.

The extract comes from Esmé Wingfield-Stratford, *Before the Lights Went Out* (London: Hodder & Stoughton, 1945), pp. 209–11.

About German Spies

Charles Lowe, 'About German Spies', *Contemporary Review*, January 1910, 97 (529), pp. 42–56.

4. Leopold James Maxse (1864–1932), son of Rear-admiral Frederick August Maxse, was one of the most able editors of the pre-1914 period. He suffered a severe illness early in life which left him unfit for a career at the bar, and his father bought him the *National Review* in 1893 as a means of giving him an occupation. Under his editorial direction, the *National Review* become a most influential source of expert opinion—politics, international affairs, and the growth of the German navy. Clemenceau was a friend of the Maxse family, and all of them were decidedly francophile.

5. See 'The Essence of Parliament', pp. 276–78, for the *Punch* view of Colonel Lockwood.

The Essence of Parliament

Amelius Mark Lockwood (1847–1928) joined the British Army in 1864; he later resigned to become Conservative MP for Epping in 1892. He appeared frequently at Question Time in the House of Commons to ask about German spies and the state of the Army. He served to general satisfaction as Chairman of the Kitchen Committee—a popular figure, known to all as 'Uncle Mark'.

Les Fictions guerrières anglaises

'A Powerful, Latent Anxiety', dated Paris 1 November 1909, is the preface to Louis C. (Capperon), *Les Fictions guerrières anglaises* (Paris: Bertrand, 1910).

6. *Le Futur Waterloo* was the French translation of Captain Cairnes, *The Coming Waterloo* (London: Constable, 1901)—one of the last of the anti-French war stories.

Incidents of the Coming Invasion of England

William Heath Robinson (1872–1944) was a much admired artist, cartoonist and book illustrator. His reputation began to grow with his illustrated editions of *Don Quixote* (1897) and of the *Arabian Nights* (1899). He began to exploit what proved to be his most celebrated mode—humorous drawings—with the cartoons he made for *The Sketch* in 1910. By the 1920s 'Heath Robinson' had become a recognized term for intricate drawings of elaborate and absurd mechanical devices that mocked technological inventiveness with their most evident capacity to use a Nasmyth 50-ton steam hammer for cracking a hazelnut.

The cartoons began in *The Sketch* on 20 April 1910. They appeared one per week to the sixth, 'German Spies in the Græco-Roman Galleries of the British Museum' on 1 June 1910. The last five cartoons appeared in sequence in the issue for 22 June 1910, pp. 346–50.

Die Invasion Englands in englischer Beleuchtung

von. R., 'Die Invasion Englands in englischer Beleuchtung' ('British Views on the Invasion of England'), *Marine-Rundschau*, November 1908, pp. 1246–47; 1247–58.

Vademecum für Phantasiestrategen

Carl Siwinna was a successful writer and publisher. In 1905 he established his own publishing firm, Phönix Verlag, and began publishing a series of pocket books which offered practical advice on trade, commercial affairs, taxation, etc. During the First World War he brought out a series of handbooks on military matters. His *Kommandobuch* for infantry provided advice for 'young officers, reserve officers, officer-cadets, and one-year volunteers'. It was a best seller.

The extracts are taken from Carl Siwinna, *Vademecum für Phantasiestrategen* ('Guide for Fantasy Strategists') (Kattowitz and Leipzig: Phönix Verlag, 1908): 'The Next War as a Christmas Present', pp. 2–4; 'External Aesthetics', pp. 4–12; 'The Contents', pp. 12–28; 'The Role of Eminent Persons', pp. 34–36.

7. Bendix Grünlich was a solid businessman in Thomas Mann's *Buddenbrooks* (1901) and a symbol of unfulfilled ambition. He married Toni Buddenbrook and was later declared bankrupt.

8. The authors and their books are: Beowulf (pseud.), *Der deutsch–englische Krieg: Vision eines Seefahrers* (Berlin: H. Walther, 1906); Hansa (Hoepner, Kapt. a D.), *Hamburg und Bremen in Gefahr!* (Altona: J. Harder, 1906); Moriturus (pseud.), *Mit deutschen Waffen über Paris nach London* (Hanau: Clauss & Feddersen, 1906); for Seestern (F. H. Grautoff), *1906: Der Zusammenbruch der alten Welt* (see extract above, pp. 202–24).

9. See pp. 256–57 for the report by Le Queux's biographer on what happened to the German translation. Siwinna seems to have believed that Le Queux was originally responsible for the note, 'Die Seeschlachtkapitel von Admiral H. W. Wilson' ('Naval Battles by Admiral H. W. Wilson') on the title-page of the *The Invasion of 1910*. What appeared in the English edition was 'Naval *Chapters* by H. W. Wilson'—a very different matter. The falsifier was the German translator, Traugott Tamm, and not Le Queux, as Siwinna assumed. Tamm removed many passages from the English original: he cut out almost all of 'Book III: The Revenge'; and, presumably with the blessing of the publishers, he gave the Germans a final victory they did not gain in the original. In fact, although German readers did not know this, the British regained their command of the sea and destroyed the German Fleet; a massacre of the Germans in London followed and the German forces capitulated. It is, however, conceivable that Traugott Tamm did not know there were two naval persons called Wilson. There was Le Queux's associ-

ate, who wrote the naval chapter for him—Herbert Wrigley Wilson (1866–1940), an assistant editor and leader writer for the *Daily Mail*, a well-known writer on naval affairs, and a frequent contributor to Maxse's *National Review*; and there was Admiral Sir Arthur Wilson (1842–1921), generally considered the best fleet commander of his day, who had nothing to do with Le Queux.

10. Siwinna takes an occasional swipe at do-gooders. Evidently he did not approve of Hermann Paasche, a close friend of, and collaborator with, Carl René, who established the Franco-German Reconciliation Committee in 1908.

11. Reichs-Deputy Matthias Erzberger (1875–1921) was a member of the Zentrum Party. He played a major role in founding trade unions.

12. Siwinna could not have read the original story. Le Queux concludes: 'The British Empire emerged from the conflict ... internally so weakened that only the most resolute reforms accomplished by the ablest and boldest statesmen could have restored it to its old position' (p. 548).

13. Samaroff was a writer of popular romances under many pseudonyms.

The Swoop! or, How Clarence Saved England

The extracts are from P. G. Wodehouse, *The Swoop! or, How Clarence Saved England: A Tale of the Great Invasion* (London: Alston Rivers, 1909): 'An Englishboy's Home', pp. 9–15; 'The Invaders', pp. 16–20; 'England's Peril'; pp. 21–26; 'The Germans Reach London', pp. 33–36.

14. There is a cheerful abandon in the way Wodehouse has the invading forces landing at well-known coastal resorts—Scarborough, Brighton, Margate. Was he having a wee Sassenach joke when he wrote that 'the army of Monaco decended on Auchtermuchty, on the Firth of Clyde'? Auchtermuchty is some eight miles inland, south of the Firth of Tay. The Firth of Clyde is 80 miles away on the other side of Scotland.

Chapter Five

The Boy Galloper

The extract comes from Anonymous (L. James), *The Boy Galloper* (Edinburgh: W. Blackwood, 1903): Chapter 1, 'War', pp. 1–26.

The Message

The extracts are taken from A. J. Dawson, *The Message* (London: Grant

Richards, 1907): 'The National Defence Cranks', pp. 131–33 and 136–40; 'The Tragic Week', pp. 184–91 and 'Black Saturday', pp. 195–203.

When England Slept

The extract comes from Captain H. Curties, *When England Slept* (London: Everett, 1909), Chapter 10, 'How it Was Done' pp. 131–44.

The North Sea Bubble

The extract is from Ernest Oldmeadow, *The North Sea Bubble* (London: Grant Richards, 1906), Chapter 1, pp. 3–11.

When William Came

Saki (H. H. Munro) was born in Akyab, Burma, 18 December 1870, and was killed in action during the assault on Beaumont Hamel, 14 November 1916. His last words were shouted: 'Put out that bloody cigarette!' He had considerable experience as a foreign correspondent for the *Morning Post* (Balkan War of 1902–03: Warsaw; St Petersburg; Paris 1904–06). He was one of the more original writers of his time with a gift for witty, ingenious, and satirical stories.

'Saki' (H. H. Munro), *When William Came: A Story of London under the Hohenzollerns* (London: John Lane, 1913). The extract is taken from the 1929 reprint (John Lane), Chapter XII, pp. 148–59.

The Cliffs

Charles Montagu Doughty (1843–1926) was one of the great Victorian travellers. After graduating in natural science from Cambridge in 1865, he took off for foreign parts to pursue his interests in geology and archaeology. He wandered for some ten years from Norway to Italy, Spain, North Africa, and Greece. In November 1876 he set out from Damascus with pilgrims for Mecca. After many adventures with wandering Bedouin, he finally reached Jidda in 1878. The account of his journey, *Travels in Arabia Deserta* (1888), presented new and important information about the geology and ethnology of the area. It was even more remarkable for the style: a resurrection of what he believed to be the purest English prose— a return to the directness of English achieved by avoiding anything that had to do with the grammar and vocabulary used after Shakespeare and Spenser.

1. Joseph Conrad, *The Nigger of the Narcissus*, 1897 (London: Penguin Books, 1963), p. 135.